TIM PARKS

Mimi's Ghost

VINTAGE BOOKS
London

Published by Vintage 2014

2 4 6 8 10 9 7 5 3 1

Copyright © Tim Parks 1995

Tim Parks has asserted his right under the Copyright,
Designs and Patents Act 1988 to be identified as the author
of this work

First published in Great Britain in 1995 by
Martin Secker & Warburg Limited

Vintage
Random House, 20 Vauxhall Bridge Road,
London SW1V 2SA

www.vintage-books.co.uk

Addresses for companies within
The Random House Group Limited can be found at:
www.randomhouse.co.uk/offices.htm

The Random House Group Limited Reg. No. 954009

A CIP catalogue record for this book
is available from the British Library

ISBN 9780099572602

The Random House Group Limited supports the Forest Stewardship
Council® (FSC®), the leading international forest-certification
organisation. Our books carrying the FSC label are printed on
FSC®-certified paper. FSC is the only forest-certification scheme
supported by the leading environmental organisations, including
Greenpeace. Our paper procurement policy can be found at
www.randomhouse.co.uk/environment

Typeset in Iowan Old Style BT by
Palimpsest Book Production Ltd, Falkirk, Stirlingshire

Printed and bound in Great Britain by Clays Ltd, St Ives plc

'The realms of thought, philosophy and the spirit break up and shatter against the unnameable, myself.'

Max Stirner, *The Unique and his Property*

PART ONE

CHAPTER ONE

MORRIS RAN SOFT FINGERTIPS along the silk finish of coffee-coloured tiles designed by Valentino. It was almost the only room in the flat he felt unreservedly happy about. The polished walnut fittings were particularly attractive, he thought, holding here a fleshy beige soap dish, there the thick white towels that made such a change from the skin-scraping variety he had grown up with. What's more, the babble of radios, televisions and raised voices from the other households in the condominium rarely penetrated this sanctum – some trick of modern construction methods, some unplanned relief. So that here one could shave in peace, admire the clean line of one's jaw, the perfect complexion of two cheeks exactly poised between youth and maturity, the neat cut of still-thick hair above clear blue eyes . . . and dream of a life in which one had made different decisions.

For Paola had been a mistake of course.

Having straightened his tie beneath the freshly pink chin, this successful property owner walked around his sunken bath to a window tastefully double-glazed in a frame of orange pine. Enjoying the simple movements, the feel of the brushed steel handle, the still-new smell of resiny wood and paint, he pulled open the window, and unlatched the shutter. But there was rust on the black varnished metalwork here; that was something he would have to talk to the builder about. Morris scratched with manicured nails at a series of blisterings. Sometimes it seemed you had hardly settled down to enjoy some luxury detail of the place before you were finding a fault, a blemish, some niggling little thing that made you feel you couldn't settle down and relax. Morris examined. Clearly the builder had been accepting junk from cheap suppliers and banking on the fact that the purchaser couldn't possibly notice everything in the couple of quick inspections he'd be granted before being told that if he didn't pay up (in cash!) then someone else was more than willing to. No, he had been taken for a ride there. Taken for a ride by a provincial, tax-evading shark. And the thing about being taken for a ride of course was to face up to it, admit it, take it square on the chin. Never, never tell yourself things were all right when they weren't.

Things were definitely not all right with Paola.

Pushing back the shutter revealed an oppressively grey winter dawn, hatching out the uninspired silhouette of the next 'luxury' condo the same builder was now throwing up on an area of land that only six months ago he had promised would be forever part of their beautiful cross-country view. Morris shivered in the cold air but forced himself to look, to savour this little defeat, so eloquent of his failure to really grasp the Italian character. For it was not enough to have got hold of a fortune, one would have to learn how to defend it. It occurred to him how smug that man must feel every time their cars crossed along the avenue, how confident of Morris's humiliation!

Still, it was fitting weather for the Day of the Dead: icy, a touch of fog. Good. There would be the dressing up, which he always enjoyed, the family gathering, the procession of cars to the cemetery, the flowers, the poignancy of seeing Massimina's photograph by the family tomb. Morris liked these traditions. He liked the way they framed your experience and gave it rhythm. Certainly Father had never visited the rose tree where Mother's ashes were deposited. Next time he went home he must make a point of getting out there to show the man what civilisation and respect were all about.

Having closed the window, Morris again stopped and gazed in the mirror: the Armani cardigan, the Versace tie, the shirt by Gianfranco Ferre – there could be no denying the elegance of all this. Just that now one had it, one realised it wasn't enough. One wanted more. One wanted art and culture and dignity and one wanted to live with people who appreciated such values and cultivated them. Which was why his marriage had been such a tragic, such a stupid mistake. If there was time this afternoon he would visit Forbes . . .

'Paola!' Morris stepped out into the corridor. 'Paola, it's past eight-thirty!' There was no reply. He looked into the bedroom. His wife was luxuriously sprawled under the goosedown quilt. Expensively permed chestnut hair bubbled over pink pillows. But there wasn't that girlishness, the radiant innocence and ingenuousness her sister Massimina had had. What's more, Massimina, in the brief halcyon month of their elopement, had always been up and about at a decent hour.

He sat down at the bedside and stared at the creature he had so hastily joined his life to. At some point or other he was going to have to impose himself. Otherwise one would find oneself just another weak husband providing the wherewithal for a simpering woman to waste her time exactly as she wished. Eventually, without opening her eyes, Paola enquired: 'How come you're not off to work this morning, Mo?'

He disliked being called Mo.

'*Sono i morti*,' he said. 'The Dead.'

'*Giusto*. Why did you get up then? We don't have to be at the cem till elevenish. Come back to bed and play.'

Morris said stiffly: 'There are the flowers to collect for Massimina. Anyway I thought you had your big exam tomorrow.'

'Oh, what a bore! Come to bed, Mo, come on, do what you did last night. I can't wait.' She groaned and made a rude gesture.

Trying to put kindness and encouragement into his voice, he said: 'Every hour counts the day before an exam, you'll regret it tomorrow.'

The young woman sat up sharply in a night-dress of such creamily thin silk her nipples beneath seemed Cadbury's chocolate buttons Mother had tucked in his Christmas stocking twenty years before. She had smaller breasts than Massimina, but more pert and, he was aware, fashionable. Pouting, she reached across the bed, found a pack of Rothmans and lit up with a lighter, apparently of brushed silver. Along with the discothèques, the punkishly showy clothes in the poorest taste and the moronic if locally well-placed circle of friends, this smoking of hers was another habit which Morris now realised was out of line with the vision of a better life that had always been his inspiration.

Anyway, his father had smoked Rothmans.

'Well?'

'Oh, I don't think I'm going to do it.'

He opened his mouth to object. Was she going to throw away the possibility of a career, he protested, just for fear of the very last exam?

'Well, you know, Mo, I was thinking, what do I really want with a degree in architecture in the end? Do you see what I mean?' She cocked her head to one side. 'The fact is we've already got money. Another couple of months and Mamma will be joining Mimi under the old angel anyway. You get to run the company and it's plain sailing.'

The angel was a reference to the somewhat pompous monument that topped the family tomb.

Wincing at the crudity of this, Morris observed that quite apart from the money, which was always a plus, a career in architecture would offer her a path to self-realisation.

'Oh, Morris, you're such a bore!' She laughed out loud, her husky, patronising laugh, and as she did so he reflected that it wasn't so much the fact that she smoked that bothered him, but the way she did it: with the brash confidence, he thought, the particularly unpleasant arrogance of stylish young women in films. Was this why his father had been so appreciative during their visit to England? He hoped he himself would never be guilty of radiating intimidation in this way.

'I told you before,' she continued, 'the only reason I went to university in the first place was to get out of that stuffy house and as far away as possible from Mamma and that reek of mothballs and polished furniture. And the only reason I did architecture was because they don't have it at Verona, so I had to go to Padua four days a week and there was the chance of having some fun. Now come on, take those silly clothes off and get back in the sack.'

Again Morris suffered from the crudity of all this, though he had heard a lot worse of late. When they made love, for example, which he still rather enjoyed, and surprised himself by being so good at (though there was always that feeling of repulsion afterwards that would send him hurrying to the shower) – yes, when they made love she would come out with the most amazing stream of obscenities, things he had never imagined anybody could want to say to anybody. He protested: 'But, Paola, my love' – he enjoyed hearing himself say 'my love' – 'you always seemed so happy at home; I mean, when I visited that first time and you and Antonella were complaining about how badly Massimina was doing at school.'

Paola positively pealed with laughter. 'What an act!' she giggled. 'What an act it always was! Poor Mimi was so hopeless. I knew she'd end up badly.'

But this was too painful. He said abruptly in the intimate gloom of their bedroom: 'So you're giving up your career?'

She puffed. 'I never had one, darling. Just passed all my exams copying everybody else. You know how it is here. I could never understand why Mimi didn't do the same.'

Then Morris startled himself by saying with genuine tenderness: 'OK, but then let's have a child. I've always wanted a little boy.'

But again she positively shook with laughter. '*Nemmeno per sogno*, Morris! That can wait at least five or six years.'

'So what are you going to do in the meanwhile? I mean, we've never really talked about this.'

'Have a good time.' She blew out a smoke ring and cocked her head to one side in a sly smile. Certainly she was not the picture of demure bereavement that had first drawn him to her and put the whole idea into his head the day of Mimi's funeral. And she added: 'I feel I'm only just starting to live.'

'While I slave at the company?'

'I thought that was what you wanted. You nearly jumped for joy when Mamma had her stroke.'

He stared at her.

'And now, if you are not going to do the honours, I think I'll take a shower.'

She stood up and, coming round the bed, tweaked his nose. 'Silly old Mo,' she laughed, again speaking pidgin

English, and walked out with some deliberately exaggerated arse wiggling in tiny tight white pants.

Morris shut his eyes.

A few minutes later he was outside the smart and decidedly expensive condominium. The air was biting. Under the grey fog, frost rimed every surface. A stately row of cypresses loomed rigid and white. The laurel hedge by the gate was draped with icy cobwebs. Morris was the kind of person who noticed and appreciated such things.

Wearing a tastefully grey wool coat and lilac cashmere scarf, he drove into town in a small white Mercedes. If he had had his way of course, he would have bought a place right in the ancient centre and not bothered with a car at all. But Paola had wanted to be quite sure she wouldn't have to put up with unexpected visits from her mother, who was endlessly bothering sister Antonella and brother-in-law Bobo; she had thus felt that one of these chic new condominiums out in the country the other side of town from Mamma would be more to her liking. Morris, still in a state of foolish euphoria at being accepted, at least legally, into the family, had been at his most accommodating.

Given Mamma's sudden deterioration these last couple of months, this decision had probably been a mistake, Morris now realised. Especially since no one knew quite how the company was to be divided up on her departure. Had he and Paola been living that bit nearer they would have been in a better position to show respect for her, their compassion and maturity. Certainly Antonella and Bobo were being most assiduous. Morris felt he should have foreseen all this and not been so ready to let Paola have her way. But he was new to marriage, had embarked on it with the best intentions, and anyway it was easy to be wise after the event. One thing Morris was learning these days was not to be too hard on himself.

Driving fast, he picked up the car phone and called Forbes. The man's cultured, gravelly voice enquired: *'Pronto?'* in an accent that was more or less a declaration of British superiority. Morris, so proud of his own achievements in sounding Italian, becoming Italian, truly being Italian, was nevertheless fascinated by this older man's refusal to adapt in any way, by the ostentatious manner in which he appreciated Italy and Italian art as a foreign connoisseur, an outsider. He didn't seem to share or even understand Morris's need for camouflage at all.

Morris announced himself and apologised if perhaps he had wakened the older man.

'Ah, Morris, I would forgive you more than that.' There was immediately a fruity generosity in his pensioner's voice.

'It's just I was thinking of going down to Florence at the weekend. Do you want to come? There's a picture I'd like to look at. In the Uffizi.'

'Splendid idea.'

'What I was thinking was, if I took you with me you could explain everything. I hope you don't consider that presumptuous of me. I'm a bit weak on some of that early Renaissance stuff.'

'Only too glad to help, no problem.'

'And on the way maybe we could talk about that little piece of business you suggested.'

'If you think there's any hope of raising the capital,' Forbes said humbly. 'I'm afraid that with my limited means . . .'

'Something might be arranged,' hinted a Morris who had married into a wealthy family and didn't need to hide the fact. Or at least not from Forbes. On the contrary, it was nice to think he had this asset that encouraged a man like Forbes to give him some of his time. The only danger was he might have exaggerated.

'I'll be over to pick you up Saturday morning, around nine,' he said.

'Er, do you mind making it nine-thirty, Morris? I'm not an early bird.'

'Not at all.'

They both rang off. But then it was so much fun, talking on a designer phone in a fast car, so much the perfect symbol of his well-deserved success, that, as quite often these days, this handsome blond Englishman continued to chat away, even after the line had gone dead.

'*Pronto?*' he enquired coolly. 'Massimina, can you hear me? Bit of a bad connection, I'm afraid. Can you hear me? It is the Day of the Dead, you know.'

He imagined he heard her saying yes in her intimate, breathless, girlish voice. Or rather *sì*. '*Sì, Morri, sì.*'

The fog suddenly thickened on the road into town and was swirling all round the car now.

'You know I've seen a painting of you? Yes. No, I knew you wouldn't believe me.' He spoke very casually into the elegant white receiver, cruising in overdrive into zero visibility. Somehow it seemed important to take these risks, as if every time one escaped one had bought some good fortune for oneself. 'I was reading one of my art-history books and there you were. Yes, it was Fra Lippi's *La Vergine incoronata*. I mean, it must be you. It's so exactly the same. And it made me think, you know, Mimi, seeing as he'd painted you five hundred years before you were born, that perhaps you were still alive now, that perhaps in a way you *were* the Virgin, reincarnated again and again, for one *incoronazione* after another . . .'

Heavens, this was oddball stuff, Morris thought. He hadn't known he was going to come out with this sort of sick drivel at all. On the other hand, one of the things that most gratified him, that most convinced him he must be something of an artist deep down, was the way he never ceased to surprise himself. He wasn't getting old and stale at all. On the contrary, his train of thought was ever richer.

The fog pressed down on the car, seemed to clutch and catch at it as it flew past.

'. . . So that I couldn't really have killed you at all, could I, Mimi?'

Suddenly finding a pink blur of tail lights only feet ahead, Morris braked hard and geared down violently. But it wasn't enough. To avoid a collision, he swung left to overtake into absolute grey blindness. Immediately headlights appeared. The local bus skidded towards him. Morris squeezed round a 126 to a chorus of klaxons.

He picked up the receiver from the passenger seat where it had fallen. '. . . And I just thought, Mimi, I thought, if you could give me some sign, or something, you know, that you're alive and well, it would mean so much to me. Any sign. So long as I really know it's you. And that you've forgiven me.'

Morris frowned. For, of course, the worst part of recognising her in that Madonna by the Renaissance painter had been remembering how the post-mortem had shown she was pregnant. Mimi was pregnant and he had killed his own child, their love-child, a saviour perhaps. This horrible fact could still occasionally rise to the surface of Morris's consciousness, bringing with it a sense of nausea and profound unease. Though again, this was actually rather gratifying in a way, since otherwise one might have been concerned that one had no sensibility at all. Experience suggested it was a common enough failing.

'Will you do that for me, Mimi? Give me a sign? I don't care what form it takes, just that it be clear.'

Again he imagined her saying: '*Sì, Morri, sì,*' in that most accommodating voice she had had. Certainly Massimina could never have been accused of having addressed him as Mo or having invited him to jump into the sack and give her a poke. Sex had been something special with her, something holy. Mimi, had he had the good fortune to marry her, would never have been so selfish as not to want to have children. Then all at once an idea had him laughing. What a funny old bloke I am, he thought. Get Paola pregnant despite herself is what I should do. Give her a purpose in life. Before she becomes a mere fashionable parasite. She'll thank me for it in the end. Wasn't that the purpose of marriage, as declared in the wedding service?

Amidst these and other thoughts, some of them only half-conscious perhaps, Morris suddenly changed his mind. Acting on one of those intuitions he had learnt to trust over the years, he chose not to go straight to the florist's to pick up the huge wreath he had ordered, but turned right, up the Valpantena, on the fast road into the hills where the family had its winery.

He came out of the fog shortly above Quinto and drove very fast on this holiday morning as far as Grezzana. In grey winter light the valley was rather ugly, with its ribbon development of light industry and second-rate housing projects, many of which had a disturbingly English flavour to them. Certainly it wasn't the Italy his spirit had yearned for when he had decided to marry into one of their rich families. He had talked this over at length with Forbes: the race was obviously degenerating. They still produced and loved beautiful things, and this was very important for Morris, who could imagine few other reasons for being alive; but they didn't seem to care if they made their country ugly in the doing of it, and they appeared to think of beauty more as a consumer product than something of spiritual value, a question of owning a particular shirt and tie, a particular style in furnishing. Many of them had no idea at all of their own historical art and heritage.

It was a shame, Morris thought, a real shame, and he turned off the road along a gravel track that after a couple of turns brought him to the three long, low, breeze-block constructions that made up the vinification, bottling and storage facilities of Trevisan Wines.

He fiddled in his glove compartment for the right remote control and a long, low gate began to rattle and whine. The new dog barked wildly, as it always would at Morris, as dogs always had with him since as early as he could remember. He must talk to Bobo about it, try to get through to him that it was completely pointless keeping such a beast, since if somebody did want to break in they would surely have no difficulty shooting the thing. No one was around to hear a gunshot in these low-key industrial areas outside working hours. You had to think of such things.

Unless Bobo had been meaning to prevent precisely visits of this variety, Morris wondered. His own. But that was paranoia. He was a member of the family now. And once you were family, you were family.

He pulled up and turned off the engine. The big Dobermann or whatever it was (for Morris had not the slightest interest in animals) snarled and leapt around the car. Uncannily, it seemed to be aware of the door he would have to get out of. Oh, for Christ's sake! This was a problem he hadn't considered at all. But far too silly to make him change his mind, surely.

He started up again and drove through shale and puddles to the door of the office located in a kind of annexe at the end of the long building that housed the bottling plant. He managed to negotiate the car into a position only six inches or so from the door, and while the dog was squeezing, panting and yelping to get into the narrow space, Morris buzzed down the window, slipped his key into the lock and turned it twice. He then drove away, heading around the building at little more than walking pace, thus luring the stupid animal into a following trot through parked trucks and stacks of bottles. Then, turning the last corner, he accelerated hard to arrive back at the door with just the few seconds' grace he needed to be out of the car and into the building. He slammed the door behind him. The dog was furious. Likewise Morris. And he decided on the spot he would poison the thing.

CHAPTER TWO

THERE ARE THREE MAJOR wine-producing areas around Verona: the Valpolicella to the north and west; Soave twenty kilometres to the east; and, between them, the Valpantena, stretching north from the eastern suburbs of the city. The first two need no advertising anywhere in the world. Indeed Morris even remembered his father picking up the occasional 'Suave' to impress one of his tarts after Mother's death, while Morris himself had drunk many a glass of 'Valpolicelly' at artsy-fartsy Cambridge parties without having the slightest idea where the place really was. Had the Trevisans, then, had their vineyards in either of these two areas, there would have been no obstacles to the grandiose plans of expansion Morris liked to conjure (the principle being, surely, that if one deigned to do something, and above all something commercial, then one should do it in grand style).

But the Valpantena . . . the Valpantena was decidedly second rate. It was difficult to get DOC certification. The soil was too clayey. The alcohol rating was low. The wine had no body and less flavour. Worse still, it simply had a name for being plonk. With the result that sales were falling sharply as the population moved up-market in the wake of snobbery and brand-name advertising, while the dour hard-drinking peasantry succumbed to cirrhosis and the miserliness (since Thatcher) of those European subsidies aimed at keeping them on the land and inside the thousands of smoky rural dives where Valpantena was drunk over interminable games of *briscola*.

What, Morris often dreamed, if it had been one of the Bolla family's girls had run off with him, and not Massimina Trevisan? He could then have become the respected export manager of a major company with a vast international distribution network. He could have been responsible for sponsoring small cultural ventures, workshop theatres, local exhibitions of Etruscan art, sober books of artistic photography. Or again, what if he had taught English in more exclusive circles in Milan (as why the hell shouldn't he with his educational background)? Then only the sky would have been the limit: the Berlusconis, the Agnellis, the Rizzolis, quite unimaginable wealth and *signorilità* . . . Given that he had pulled it off with the suspicious and decidedly refractory Trevisans, was it so unfeasible that he could have done the same with the more generous industrial nobility? Could still do it perhaps, if only he put his mind to it.

But there lay Morris's snag. Morris didn't, except in emergencies, put his mind to practical things. And sometimes not even then. He allowed himself to be drawn into aesthetic considerations, existential dialogues. His brain was incredibly fertile territory, but it seemed that what had been planted there was exotic and ornamental, rather than practical. He prided himself on flying off at tangents, on making acute observations, but he could never plan anything more than a day or two ahead. (Would he ever have started the Massimina business had he had the faintest inkling of how it must end? Surely not. That had been an appalling discovery of the very last hour.) He was like a novelist who could never remember what his plot was supposed to be, or more appropriately, a miserable opportunist, picking up crumbs wherever they fell.

Hadn't it been the same with his marriage? The situation had presented itself; it was Paola had made the offer, just as two years ago it had been Massimina approached him, rather than he her. And Morris had been unable to hold off and play for higher stakes, unable to see that he was made for better things.

Of course, there had been certain alleviating circumstances on the second occasion: the euphoria arising from his having survived a major police investigation had doubtless played its part. In the happy-go-lucky mood he'd been in, the surprise invitation to accompany sister Paola to England had had a smack of destiny about it. Riding high, he had accepted, plus of course there had been that prurience, that perverse poignancy of remaining, socially and emotionally, so close to the scene of the crime. Ostensibly Paola had been going on an extended holiday to help her get over the family bereavement, and this again was the kind of pathos that attracted Morris, rich as it appeared to be with noble emotion and dignity. In the event, however, it all too soon emerged that the real reason for her English trip was her need to avoid her friends until such time as she could get over the snub of having been dropped by her long-time dentist fiancé.

Be that as it may, when they had arrived at the airport and were sitting in a taxi (the very first taxi of Morris's life as it happened), her cosy suggestion that he stay in the expensive Notting Hill flat which family friends had provided for her had been nothing if not explicit. Still excited, understandably, by his newly acquired wealth (certificates for 800 million lire's worth of Eurobonds in his suitcase), lulled by the excellent Barolo they had drunk with their snack on the plane, and by no means averse to pursuing the sexual experiments which had so pleasantly if poignantly brightened up his abduction of Mimi, Morris did not even look for reasons for not agreeing. He was riding the crest of a wave. He could do nothing wrong. And it had been particularly good fun, one London afternoon to invite his dumb, proletarian, carping father over to the Pembroke Villas address and flaunt an ambience of Persian rugs and Mary Quant curtains that even the pigheaded Mr Duckworth must have recognised (in money terms if nothing else) was a definite step up.

Shrewd herself, Paola had quickly developed a fatal attraction for Morris's own particular brand of shrewdness, his curiously polite stiffness and reservation, which she found a 'terrific turn-on' (and imagined was exquisitely English and fashionable, not realising, as Morris himself was all too painfully aware, that on the whole Anglo-Saxons were an uncouth and violent lot). For three, four, five months they had thus lodged together, enjoying a sex life as ambitious as it was exquisitely free from sentimental complications. Paola had learned not a word of English and spent a great deal of money. Unlike dear Mimi, it turned out that she shared, more than shared, Morris's interest in expensive food and drink, with the result that Morris had made the mistake, for the first and hopefully the last time in his life, of succumbing to an almost constant state of inebriation, something that had doubtless blurred his awareness of other, less attractive sides to her personality.

Returning to Italy together in the spring of the following year, it had been to find that as a result of an unplanned pregnancy elder sister Antonella was being hurried into marrying the ugly heir to a battery chicken empire, Bobo Posenato, or Pollo (chicken) Bobo, as Paola disparagingly called him (one of the few things Morris genuinely liked about Paola was her ability to be wittily disparaging). All kinds of extravagant arrangements were under way. Mamma Trevisan was over the moon with the expediency of this marriage, which obviously far outweighed the tawdry circumstances that had precipitated it. Very large sums of money were being spent. A beautiful apartment had been bought, designer wedding clothes were even now being made. The Due Torri, Verona's most expensive hotel, had been booked for the reception.

With all this extravagance and festivity, sharp Paola had not unnaturally felt herself being upstaged by her blander, rather goosy elder sister. For his part, Morris, having vaguely wondered in London if he mightn't set himself up as the man of the family, had felt his previous antagonism for Bobo reinforced if not doubled or trebled. Hadn't this arrogant boy with his nosiness and enquiries been responsible after all for the rejection of Morris's initial attempt to court Massimina in a traditional fashion, and thus, in the long run, for forcing Morris to become a criminal? And surely it wasn't right that a taciturn, acned young man with no imagination and less manners should be so extraordinarily well set up in terms of wealth and power? It was the kind of naked injustice that fed Morris's insatiable appetite for resentment. Of course, he did have some wealth himself now, enough to buy – what? – two or even three apartments perhaps (why hadn't he asked for more when he'd had the knife by the handle?), but absolutely nothing like the *miliardi* available to Pollo Bobo and his ilk; and to make matters worse, Morris, at that time, still had to be painstakingly careful that nobody noticed him spending this money, whose existence he would never be able to explain. Like a fool, he must continue to play the pauper, the poor mouse of the family, even when he wasn't. It was infuriating. Because you weren't rich until you had your hands on the means of producing wealth – Marx had been right about that. With just a few hundred million (lire!) in Eurobonds you were barely hedging against inflation. So that when one evening Paola had very coolly remarked how upset the others would be if she and Morris got in on the act by making it a double marriage, he had immediately said yes, wouldn't they? Plus, if they didn't watch out, Paola had further observed, there was every danger that Pollo Bobo, still kept out of his own family business by Father and elder brother, would worm his way into Trevisan Wines and even further into Mamma's good graces, no doubt with the intention of annexing the company to his own family empire. Whereas if they married immediately, Mamma would have to give Morris a position of some, and hopefully equal, importance.

Of course in retrospect Morris saw now what a sad, sordid poverty-stricken kind of opportunism it had been which had made him agree to this: surrendering his privacy to a creature he barely knew out of the sack or in various states of intoxication (because she was keen on marijuana too), committing his very considerable brain power to the promotion of a few plonky vineyards, and above all entering (for there seemed no alternative if he was to make a go of the Trevisan clan) into a partnership with a gawky, spoilt, chinless young man who was as unworthy of Morris's opposition as he was of his collaboration.

But one was who one was in the end. Wasn't this what Morris had been trying to tell his father in spool after spool of dictaphone tape these past five years and more? One was who one was. Character was destiny. This was the kind of thing that Morris Duckworth did (still afraid of ending up on the street despite that 800 million). And if he had recently stopped trying to explain himself to Dad after a cupboard full of cassettes stretching over six or seven years, wasn't it precisely because he had at last realised that by that very same token – character, destiny – his father could and would never understand anything Morris tried to tell him? The uncouch old goat was an uncouth old goat. How could you expect him to be otherwise? Morris was Morris, and thus he would remain, locked into his own skull, his own inadequacy, to the bitter end: an under-achieving, desperate, somehow panto-mime Morris. Wisdom meant accepting this.

Though sometimes he felt quite different about life. Sometimes he felt there was nothing could stop him. Or at least that he might as well enjoy himself.

Events had moved with soap-opera rapidity. The apartment had been bought (with his money, in his name – leaving less than 400 million – but he would never be held to ransom by his wife). Morris had attended a catechism course for adults and turned Catholic (inter-estingly enough it was here that he first came up against those Third World sufferers whose fate so often occupied his mind these days). A summer date had been set for the wedding. All had appeared to be going well. But then, despite this considerable effort on Morris's part to conform with local mores, Paola, with typical instability, had at the very last moment changed her mind and decided she wanted to be married in the register office so romantically, albeit ominously, located on the supposed site of Juliet's tomb. This was, and was intended as, a deliberate snub to her mother, a punishment for her being so syrupily ingratiating with the Posenato clan and so offhand if not actually cold with Morris.

In the event it turned out to be a brilliant idea. Not only was Mamma furious (for the Posenato family would be upset by the idea of down-market, register-office in-laws), but Morris was actually able to gain ground with the old lady, and even with the fiercely pious (despite her pregnancy) Antonella, by presenting himself as the wise and reserved Englishman ostensibly struggling to have capricious young Italian Paola see reason. Indeed, the ruse worked so marvellously that, come the great day, Mamma's frustration at being crossed like this had been too much for her and she was struck down by a thrombosis precisely as Morris turned from signing the papers to smile at the small gathering of Paola's friends (including, rather disturbingly, the dentist).

Mamma collapsed and was rushed off to *rianimazione*. Hearing the news during a last-minute dress-pinning session for her own ceremony later in the afternoon, Antonella had tripped on her train while hurrying down the stairs and, after much panic, ambulance-calling and toing and froing at the hospital, was found to have lost her child. When Morris had tried (and he had cancelled his honeymoon flight to the Azores, for God's sake) to express his quite sincere condolences to Bobo, the unpleasant young Veronese had scowled at him as if it must somehow be his fault. But there was no limit, Morris sometimes thought, to people's desire to find a scapegoat. Nobly he decided not to bear a grudge against the boy. Perhaps in time and against all the odds they would learn to like each other.

After three months' intensive treatment, Mamma had still not regained the use of the left side of her body. Without having any specific instructions, Bobo simply stepped in and took over Trevisan Wines, inviting Morris, after a couple of violent arguments with Paola, to open a small commercial office for the company in town. And of course what Morris should have said was no. He was not cut out for trade and commerce. Fundamentally, he had a delicate, aesthete's personality, and no desire at all to engage in the hurly-burly of commercial life. He should have been a photographer, a fashion designer, a theatre critic. Yet the opportunist in him wouldn't pass it up. Perhaps because in another department of his mind he had always wanted to be who he wasn't, always wanted to please macho Dad as much as darling Mum. And then because he wanted to be Italian of course, a real member of a real Italian family, and because he felt strangely drawn to the surly Bobo. Either he would make the boy like him, or make him pay for not doing so. In any event, he was given an office two metres by two in the centre of town and invited to find new buyers for a company he knew nothing about. That was six months ago.

Morris slammed the door on the barking dog outside. He was in a small grey office which nothing could redeem – certainly not the cheap gun-metal desks, nor the fifties filing cabinets, nor the squat computer, the smeared windows with their sad view of two large trucks tucked between dirty trees, the shelves with their manuals on vinification and piles of brochures on Trevisan Wines (published in 1973 and far from being exhausted). One of the first things Morris had done on joining the company had been to flick through the English translation of this brochure, which told the unsuspecting buyer that: 'Born of moronic soils and famous stock of vineyard plants, this nectar of the pre-Alps cannot not satisfy the updated gusto for palette harmony and a fragrance that entices.' His suggestion that the piece be rewritten had been met with scepticism. The company had only a handful of foreign clients and none of them was English. It wasn't worth the printing costs. So that there the brochures still sat in dusty piles, unused and unusable. Indeed, the only new thing around was a down-market pornographic calendar, free gift of the Fratelli Ruffoli bottle-producing company, where the said company's product was presented in intimate proximity to what most men presumably thought of as the great focuses of pleasure. A small plastic crucifix hung opposite the calendar over the door that led through to the bottling plant proper. Morris found both decorations equally distasteful.

Reckoning he had about half an hour, he switched on the computer on the production manager's desk and one after the other slipped in the disks he found in the top drawer. Unfortunately he had no experience of computers, nor any desire to gain any; thus when finally he found the file, *Salari e stipendi, 1990,* he was unable to access it. It was too infuriating, especially since this was precisely the kind of information that should have been freely available to a member of the family. Another file on another disk promised to tell him about *Fornitori – uvalvini,* but again he couldn't get at it. Still, there was something odd there just in that title, 'Suppliers – grapes/wines'. Morris stared at the unpleasantly glowing green letters, the irritating wink of the cursor that seemed to mesmerise thought rather than encourage it. Suppliers?

'*Ciao,*' said a voice.

Morris swung round on the rotating chair. The pale young man stood in the doorway.

'*Ciao,*' Morris said warmly. '*Benvenuto.* How are you?'

'It's a holiday,' Pollo Bobo said. 'And this is not your office.'

'Just doing a little homework,' Morris said. 'It's difficult selling a company when you don't know enough about it. I got wind of a big order this week and I wanted to know if you could meet it.'

'Ask me,' Bobo said. He came and sat on the edge of the desk, reached over and switched off the computer. Morris was surprised to see that the boy was tense, if not actually trembling. This somehow made Morris feel more friendly.

'I didn't want to appear stupid,' he said. 'You know, always having to run to ask you. You've got enough on your plate.' Then briefly he said what he had said before: how impressed he was by Bobo's grasp of the business, and how growing up in a business family had no doubt helped him a great deal, whereas Morris was still very much learning the ropes.

Bobo appeared to relax a little. 'How much was the order for?'

'Four thousand cases,' Morris told him coolly. 'Doorways, an English chainstore.'

'Four thousand. We can't possibly do that.'

'I know,' Morris agreed, 'but what if we buy out?'

'We have a policy of never buying out.'

Morris gave his colleague a sunny, just faintly inquisitive stare, allowing the boy a full thirty seconds to change his tack.

'Ah,' he sighed. But then overcome by a sudden desire to be friendly, to gain confidence by giving it (why shouldn't they be friends – were they so unalike in the end?), he rather ingenuously (but there were these moments when he liked to think of himself as ingenuous, innocently generous) began to explain his plan. Listen, he said, did Bobo realise how full the city was of illegal immigrants? Of labour of the cheapest possible kind? Yes? And far from being uncultured or anything like that they were all, and especially the Senegalese, quite well behaved, probably from the upper middle classes in their own country, honest, hard-working, not unintelligent. Now if Trevisan Wines were to take on some of these people on the most casual, under-the-table basis to bottle and package the sort of plonk they could buy out almost anywhere – God knows the country was swimming in wine no one wanted to drink – then Morris was pretty sure he could place most of it on the British market, where frankly they wouldn't know the difference between the rubbish they had been drinking to date and the rubbish they would be drinking from now on, if Bobo saw what he meant. And if things went wrong, well, they wouldn't have any serious overheads, the immigrants would melt away as rapidly as they had materialised.

About halfway through this spiel Morris realised that Pollo Bobo thought he was joking. Or lying. There was an expression on his waxy boy's face in which incredulity and suspicion were mixed in more or less equal proportions.

Morris asked: 'But you have seen them on the streets?'

'*Certo*. Bothering me to buy cigarette lighters and pirated cassettes and the like.'

'I just felt I wanted to help them,' Morris said candidly. Then with a brutally deliberate allusion to their first meeting, when Mimi had brought Morris to the Trevisans' house as a prospective *fidanzato*, he added: 'I mean, I've been an outsider myself. I know what it's like to have people always suspecting you.'

He looked this rich sibling straight in the fishy eyes. A look, as Bobo obviously registered, of naked challenge.

CHAPTER THREE

SIGNORA TREVISAN WAS IN her wheelchair, with that unpleasant tic she had developed at the corner of the mouth. Morris thus faced the problem of choosing between pushing her chair and carrying the very large wreath of flowers he had bought. But would they imagine Paola had bought the flowers? Morris knew there was no limit to people's inattention. Sometimes it was useful and sometimes it wasn't.

Fog had melted into rain and the cemetery car park was overcrowded. Antonella was fussing hopelessly with the chair's brake release; she couldn't get the thing to move. Bobo had apparently mislaid the remote control to his Audi 100 in one of his tailored pockets. Morris stepped forward, seeing the solution. 'May I?' he offered, and handed the wreath to Signora Trevisan. 'I thought perhaps you might like to put this on Mimi's grave.' Then, without waiting to decide whether the twisted mouth meant a grimace or a smile, he bent down to release the brake. After all, if the stiff-necked woman had welcomed him into the family in the first place, Mimi would never have met the end she had, there would never have been any register-office marriage, because Mimi would have settled for nothing less than the Duomo, so there would have been no stroke and no corpse to visit. Or rather, they could have walked together, arm in fashionable arm, to lay a couple of token chrysanths beside old Signor Trevisan, dead these fifteen years and more.

There was quite a crowd flowing through the gate, past the gloomily hooded statues, the confidently engraved RESUR-RECTURIS on the arch above. Impeccably dressed mourners strutted slowly beneath sober umbrellas, their voices suitably low, greeting friends, muttering sensible clichés. Inside, the porticoes offered a precise geometry of well-swept colour. The grave niches up on the walls were festooned with flowers and there was the pleasant click of expensive patent leather echoing on flags of provincial stone.

Immediately Morris felt a sense of quiet satisfaction. The ritual formality of it all was so exhilarating, so right. Where would you find such an exquisitely poised communion of the living and the dead in grimy, pragmatic old England, such a sensual mix of extravagant furs and wine-warm marble, a whole population turning out to tip their hats to the industrious ancestry that had generated all this wealth and then so decorously departed? Son-in-law Morris was desperately delicate, easing Signora Trevisan's chair down travertine steps to where the more pompous family tombs offered a competitive range of alabaster Madonnas, guardian angels and stony Crucifixions. Suddenly he felt so pleased with himself, he turned to smile intimately at Pollo Bobo, and thoroughly enjoyed the boy's discomfort, the ripple of incomprehension passing over his mask of sobriety. Did he think Morris was homosexual or what?

Pious Antonella picked up the smile and returned it, though coloured now by a sort of sad propriety, the consolations of religion playing unmistakably across her goosy cheeks. Could she be pregnant again? An heir to the Trevisan fortune? That would be most unfortunate. Sharing an umbrella with him, Paola was feeling down her fur on the left side to check that it wasn't getting wet. Ten million lire's worth, of course, and one had to be careful, but there were moments when a proper sense of occasion was even more important. Morris nudged his wife sharply as he swung the wheelchair into a small avenue of crushed white stones.

NON FORTUNA, SED LABOR, the letters were six inches high, gold-edged in a slab of white carrara, and the angel above had not come cheap either. *Labor* no doubt there must have been. All the same, Vittorio Trevisan had apparently been unable to work his way around a doubtless deserved cirrhosis. Now his photo stared bleakly from an oval blimp screwed into the marble, a respectable square-jawed man in a collar and tie that must have been too tight. Obviously the family had plumped for black and white to hide the broken veins. Morris smiled at his own ingenuity. *NON CALAMITAS, SED VINUM* would have been more appropriate. And putting the brake on Signora Trevisan, he stepped out from under Paola's umbrella, took the red handkerchief from his jacket pocket and carefully wiped the beads of rain from the image of his defunct father-in-law. If even this didn't win a nod of acknowledgement from the old witch, then quite simply he could rest his case. They had got no more than they deserved.

But Morris knew that the real reason his heart was racing was because of Massimina round the other side. The only woman who had ever loved him, whom he had ever loved. And life had forced him to . . . but he must not think about it. He must not and would not dwell on the past, weep over spilt milk. Yet what could one do with spilt milk if not weep over it?

For a moment then he was almost afraid of seeing her photograph. Why hadn't this occurred to him? This confrontation. And in company. Would something flicker across his face? Some expression of self-betrayal. Or would he burst into tears? Really he ought to have come here ages ago on his own to get the measure of the thing, see which picture they had chosen. But at the same time he relished his anxiety. Tomorrow, at the Uffizi, he could contemplate her transformation into art. Today he would have to suffer the immediacy of a photograph. So be it.

Signora Trevisan's tic had speeded up at the sight of her dead husband. The corner of her mouth twitched obscenely as she tried to say something. In the portico beyond, two old women were exchanging insults over the use of the step-ladder for placing flowers in the higher burial niches. Apparently Paola wasn't the only one with a poor sense of occasion. Antonella stepped forward and began to arrange a spray of flowers in the vase by the photo of her father. Crouching down, her small pale hands worked quickly, picking stalks from cellophane wrapping. Back behind Signora Trevisan again, Morris watched, trying to still his beating heart. He forced himself to observe what a perfect image of devotion it was: the curved back of the young woman in white seal fur against the rain-wet tomb behind, the quick hands fiddling amongst the flowers. The fingers had that same pudginess tapering to delicate pink that Massimina's had had. Perhaps Morris had been too hard on Antonella. Perhaps her gestures were not naked hypocrisy, but carried some genuine cultural resonance, the nobility of her race. An intelligent person was always willing to revise an opinion, *n'est-ce-pas*? In his ear, Paola whispered: '*Cristo santo*, Mo, push Mamma round the other side, dump the wreath and let's get out of here. It gives me the creeps.'

The wheels crunched on the stones. The rain stiffened. It was the first time they had all come to visit her. Last year he and Paola had still been in London for *i morti*. And the curious thing was that Morris was thinking more about Mimi now than he had then. Or in all the months in between. Far more. As if his real mourning had only just begun. Only now had he begun to want to see her grave. Only now was he ready to face the truth: that he had loved Massimina and lost her; that he had let life slip through his fingers, or rather, tossed it violently away. Sometimes the girl was so intensely present to the inner senses, he would have to bite his tongue and clench his fists. And Morris had an inkling that this new and precarious state of mind could only be presageful. Certainly he felt incredibly nervous and excited now. What kind of photo would they have chosen? What effect would it have on him? Out of the corner of his eye he caught sight of Bobo checking his watch.

They waited for an old man wobbling by with a stick, then Morris negotiated the chair round the other side. But he deliberately didn't look down at where the photograph would be. Instead he lifted his eyes to the angel above. A trite saccharoid rendering of feathers and flesh, as if the sculptor hadn't really been able to imagine how they might go together. He heard Antonella say: 'Perhaps she was too good for this world.' A heavy sigh. 'She was always so innocent.' Bobo grunted some sort of appropriate male agreement. '*Povera Mimi*,' Paola said mechanically. Signora Trevisan, to her great credit, was crying softly.

They stood in the rain, making this public gesture of paying respect, other people walking slowly past. Morris let his eye move down to the inscription, THE LORD GIVETH AND THE LORD TAKETH AWAY. He rather liked this. Paola sometimes accused him of being critical about everything, whereas nothing could have been wider of the mark. The Lord giveth and the Lord taketh away. There was no question of feeling guilty when one reflected on a simple truth like that: appearance, disappearance.

A noise of crinkling cellophane made him aware that Signora Trevisan was fiddling with the wreath on her lap, trying to lean forward on her chair. Still without looking at the photo, Morris walked round the chair, took the wreath from her hands, stepped over the little rail that served to keep passers-by at a respectful distance, and crouched down by the tomb.

He thus saw Massimina from only inches away, in intimacy, his own face safely invisible to the others. It was the first time he had looked her in the eye since the day he had brought down the paperweight on her precious skull.

The family had chosen the same photo they'd used in the papers after her disappearance: the intensely black hair, the radiant breadcrumbs-in-cream complexion, great hazel eyes, a winning smile. Immediately he sensed all the old complicity flooding back. They were lovers and the rest of the family disapproved. The bond was still there. Caught by a tidal wave of emotion, Morris suddenly appreciated what a truly tragic figure he was. He had to fight back the tears. If only she would give him some sign of forgiveness!

'I blame myself sometimes,' he heard Bobo saying solemnly behind him. 'I should have realised something of the kind might happen.'

'*Caro,*' Antonella said. 'Don't torment yourself. Who would have thought?'

Morris laid the wreath delicately so that the petals were almost brushing her cheeks. He was just straightening to get back on his feet when the dead girl winked.

He froze. But there was no mistaking it. It was just the wink she would give him when she was a student in his class and their eyes met. The only student ever to wink at him. Or again when they were in Sardinia and she would say: 'Come and make love, Morree, *per favore.*'

And she did it again. From out of the solemn oval of the photo, screwed into the marble below which her precious body must already have rotted in its coffin, she winked.

'*O Dio santo!*' a female voice shrieked behind him.

So they had seen! Morris whirled round, his body filling with a sudden dangerous heat. The flush prickled up in his face. His buttocks were tight. He was ready to defend himself. Turning, his eyes met the atrocious stare of Signora Trevisan, head twisted unnaturally to one side, an audible wheezing in her throat.

'*Un dottore!*' Antonella cried, '*Bobo, un dottore!*'

But neither the grim-faced factory-chicken heir, nor the elegant Paola beside him so much as moved. It was thus left to English in-law Morris Duckworth to run off along the porticoes screaming and shouting for the help that perhaps everybody hoped would come too late.

CHAPTER FOUR

MORRIS WAS TRYING TO explain to Forbes about the immigrants. The older man was sunk into the white leather of the passenger seat, his eyes half closed against the winter glare of the autostrada. First at catechism, where they came to ingratiate themselves with the local priest in the hope of getting into some of the accommodation the Church controlled. Then in the queue at the office that dealt with health insurance for foreigners. On both occasions Morris had been appalled by the way the blacks were treated, and had said as much to the officials involved. It was the complacent arrogance of these people that so upset him. The way acquired position and relative wealth were flaunted as superiority pure and simple. Much the same as with this fellow Pollo Bobo he had to work with: all birth and presumption, not a shred of merit. Except it wasn't just that. How could he explain himself? It was the way you couldn't feel such people had ever really suffered, or even had the quality required to suffer. Sometimes you felt they hardly deserved to live. If they were to disappear tomorrow the world would be a better place. Whereas there was a quiet nobility about the Ghanaians and Senegalese he'd talked to. They put up with so much and never complained. They had that sort of sublime resignation you saw in food queues in Ethiopia, or in a Giotto Crucifixion. It was quite beautiful.

'I feel I'd quite like to help them somehow,' Morris finished simply.

Forbes didn't so much as stir. He was wearing his customary grey suit, white shirt, flowery tie. His face, upturned, looked the kind of surface one dusted rather than shaved. Deep wrinkles where dirt must collect. His hair was a silky, perhaps perfumed, silver.

'I've always felt, if I came into some money I should use it to help people.'

As he spoke, Morris enjoyed hearing his mother's voice echo in his own, her endless involvement in local church charities, despised by his father of course, though it had given the pig the freedom he needed for his philandering, while she was out helping the handicapped or collecting for the blind. And Massimina had been involved with the *Giovani cattolici*, taking clothes to the poor and so on. Yes, Massimina had been a busy, well-meaning, humble-shall-inherit-the-earth girl. Massimina would not have been lying in bed smoking Rothmans when she was supposed to be doing her final university exam. Morris suddenly felt furious. Though not a tremor came through in his voice.

'I mean, I always give them a few thousand lire when they clean my windscreen at the traffic lights and things like that. But I feel it's not enough. A few thousand lire isn't going to solve anything, is it?'

Nor a few million, he privately thought. What it took was a job, a steady source of wealth. And his wife was coolly throwing up a position as an architect with all the opportunities that entailed. He hadn't realised how angry he was.

'So I was wondering,' he went on evenly, 'if perhaps we couldn't somehow work these poor people in with your little project.'

Forbes finally opened his eyes, shifted in his seat.

'I beg your pardon, Morris, I, er . . .'

But quite on impulse Morris had picked up the phone

from the dashboard. He pressed a single button and the instrument dialled from memory.

'Sorry, be with you in a moment,' he told Forbes, then was immediately afraid he might have irritated the man, whose superior culture he needed, something to still his whirring mind. These lapses of concentration were disturbing.

The phone trilled. They were approaching the intersection for Florence and Rome, travelling at 130 kilometres per hour, right on the speed limit. A law-abiding Morris kept his left hand lightly on the wheel, his right gripping the Valentino receiver. Came a very laid-back 'Pronto', and clearly she was eating something.

'It's me,' Morris said. Then using a formula he never had before, he added: 'Your husband.'

'Oh, is anything the matter?'

He left the briefest pause. Then his voice was dutiful. 'I was wondering about Mamma.'

'I haven't heard anything yet this morning.'

'Are you going to visit?'

'There hardly seems to be any point if one can only look in through the glass.'

'No.'

As he was overtaking some slow-moving Fiat or other in the central lane, a Saab came racing up behind him, way over the limit and flashing his headlights aggressively. Morris immediately adjusted his speed down to that of the car he had been passing.

'So you may as well go and do the exam, cara. What time is it? Two o'clock?'

The car behind began to honk. Morris gave his brake the lightest tap. He was enjoying the division of consciousness involved in doing two things at once. Or rather three, since in the back of his mind he was still wondering how best to present his grand idea to Forbes.

'*Mo, per l'amore di Dio*, I can hardly go and do my exam when my mother might die at any moment. How could I ever concentrate?'

Well, the same way she had been concentrating on the morning TV Morris could hear in the background. One of those local channels that sold fur coats, lingerie, lucky charms and mountain bikes, twenty-four hours a day.

The honking was continuous now as Morris played with brake and accelerator pedal. Doubtless the idiot would be gesticulating. Then the first sign for the intersection was racing towards them.

'Well, as you wish, *cara*.' He had long since learnt that you couldn't actually force people to do what was best for them.

But unexpectedly his wife said: 'Are you upset, Mo?' in such a sweet voice it almost took his mind off the road.

Forced to think, he answered: 'You know I only want the best for you, *cara*, that's all.'

He stabbed his foot on the brake and, as the furious Saab all but exploded in the rear mirror, steered fiercely right to slip between the Fiat in the central lane and a van behind, then across the slow lane between two trucks carrying livestock, and so off onto the tightly curving slip-road. A deeply pained look crossed Forbes's face, but Morris sensed an inkling of admiration too. And he hadn't actually broken the law, had he? Just taught a hog a lesson. At the same time he managed to register the confiding voice in his ear saying: 'Fact is, Mo, I feel I should be around because I wouldn't like anything odd to happen with the will, or for Mamma to wake up and make a new one. If you get me? There was a look on Bobo's face yesterday that I didn't like at all.'

Morris hadn't actually thought of that. He steadied the car and kept his eye on the signs. You imagined you were wise to everything, you had seen it all, then some mere girl turned out to be light-years ahead, and you realised you were only a poor amateur, an ever-ingenuous Morris. You had no chance of keeping up with all the sick perversions other people were capable of. Getting an old woman to change her will on the very point of death indeed!

'I'll call you later,' he said brusquely.

But she didn't want him to hang up. Her voice changed again, became husky and soft. 'Are you alone, Mo?'

'Of course. Who would I be with?'

'Mmm.'

There was a brief silence. Forbes had sunk down in his seat again, a faint smile on his aristocratic face.

'Will you do something for me?' The voice was vulgarly seductive. Ashamed, Morris jammed the receiver to his ear.

'What?'

'I'm feeling very . . . mmm,' Paola said. 'Here all on my own. You know how I get.'

Morris knew.

'I mean, if someone very sweet told me to unzip my pants and do something that they like doing too, I think I might just have to obey.'

Morris closed his eyes for a moment, then remembered to blink them open as they came racing out onto the other autostrada, Florence-bound. His body had filled with an exciting prickly heat. At the same time there was that strong feeling of distaste. If he didn't watch out he'd be nothing more than a sex toy to her.

'If you stopped for a while, little Mo could obey orders too. What are car phones for after all?'

Morris said: 'I was supposed to see a client at ten-thirty and I'm already late.'

'Come on, Mo, *sii dolce!*'

'*Veramente*, I can't.'

'*Antipatico!*' she whispered fiercely. 'Spoil-sport, I'll make you pay for that later.'

It was unclear whether this was meant as a promise or a threat.

'Paola?' he said. Was he slightly in awe of her?

'*Dio*, will I make you pay!' She hung up.

Morris clicked back the receiver, put both hands firmly on the wheel. You phoned your wife of six months standing to try to get her to take a responsible attitude towards her life and career, and what did she do? First she pleaded the excuse of a dying mother, a predatory brother-in-law, and then she tried for mutual masturbation over the car phone. There were times when dismay was the only proper response. Morris drove on for quite some while in bitter silence.

The car rode up into the browns and dull greens of the Apennines, a rollercoaster landscape of olives and cypresses, bare vines reduced to fields of gnarled crucifixions against the stone-speckled soil. Morris tried to concentrate on the aesthetic pleasure of taking every curve at exactly the right speed while always leaving the same distance between wheel and white line. Forbes, meanwhile, seemed in no hurry to return to their previous conversation, despite the delicate point at which they had left it. And Morris appreciated that. Forbes was the kind of intelligent man who would be sensitive to his temporary discomposure. Morris had done the right thing in escaping from the feckless crowd of younger expats who had tormented and humiliated him in his earlier days in Verona, the ex-hippies and would-be artists, their coercive mateyness and empty dreams (not to mention the rather unnerving fact that community leader Yankee Stan had actually seen him that day at Roma Termini with Massimina: there was a danger!). No, the wisdom of an earlier generation was so much more gratifying. Indeed it occurred to Morris that if he had met Forbes earlier on perhaps, when he first arrived in Italy, yes, if he had frequented someone like Forbes, rather than the Stans of this world, then there would have been no need for the extraordinary aberration of two summers ago. Or, better still, if he had had Forbes as a father, if . . .

'Siste viator!'

They had just passed a sign for a service station. Interrupting Morris's promising train of thought, the older man's voice pronouncing one of his endless Latin tags had a gravelly, emphatically upper-class texture.

'Sorry?' Morris said. He had decided never again to pretend to understand something when he didn't. Only people with an abject self-image did that kind of thing.

'The spirit is willing but the flesh is weak,' Forbes explained with a deprecating smile. 'Stop.'

It was the second time in only an hour's driving.

Morris pulled in at the service station and watched as Forbes's tall, spindly figure shambled over to the *servizi*. Inevitably, as he watched the flapping grey suit in the cold winter light, the word 'Gents' sprang to mind. Morris felt calm and happy again. In the end he had good friends, exciting projects. His psyche was not irremediably damaged. All would work out.

He was just lifting the phone to ask dear Mimi whether she mightn't confirm yesterday's sign with something more concrete today, some indication that she approved of his plan, when a movement beside the car startled him.

'Vu cumpra'?'

A squat Moroccan was grinning through the window Morris had unwisely buzzed down. The man's bad breath came through despite freezing air and diesel fumes.

'Vu cumpra'? Wanna buy? Very good video camera. *Molto economico*.'

Morris stared at him.

41

'*Economico, molto* cheap, *molto buono.*'

'*Davvero?*' His mind moved rapidly. Paola had talked about doing some videotaping, and it wasn't the man's fault if society had reduced him to this illicit trade and parlous state of personal cleanliness. There had been a time when Morris rather feared he was headed that way himself.

A long scar snaked down from the bloodshot corner of the Moroccan's left eye.

'*Quanto?*' the Englishman asked.

'Two hundred.'

'A hundred and fifty,' Morris said, since of course this was what was expected. They didn't want charity.

'Two hundred.'

'I said a hundred and fifty.' He was rather enjoying this. Forbes appeared, and so would see the aplomb with which Morris carried it off.

'A hundred and eighty.' The Moroccan's leathery smile was forced. But Morris was used to forced smiles.

'A hundred and fifty and it's a deal,' he said.

The Moroccan scowled. As he must. Forbes climbed stiffly into the car, one dusty eyebrow raised. '*Caveat emptor*, m'boy,' he said wryly. But Morris felt he was on a winning streak. 'I said a hundred and fifty, not a lira more.'

Already he had half a vague idea of videotaping Massimina's winking eye on the tomb photograph. Might she eventually be sanctified if one could prove something like that?

Reluctantly, the Moroccan gave in. 'OK. You have the money ready. You stop by that white van.' He pointed to a decrepit VW beyond the petrol pumps, where a small boy was apparently filling a flat tyre from the air stream. Morris duly drove over, wallet in hand. Then a few moments later, on the road again, box with video on the back seat, he was enjoying such a high that he went and explained his whole plan to Forbes in just a few well-chosen sentences. His main aims being, he insisted, first to help out his friend, Forbes, and second, not to let this Pollo Bobo merely exploit the poor immigrant folk in his bid to increase production. If one had to be an industrialist, Morris said, he would like to think of himself as being in the benevolent Cobden tradition, rather than a Gradgrind.

Forbes was clearly surprised. If not floored. It wasn't exactly what he had had in mind, he said. He fiddled in his jacket pocket for pipe and tobacco, a look of prim concern on his face. 'What I was planning to do, as you know, was to bring over public-school children from England, teach them a little Italian and art history in pleasant surroundings, and give them an opportunity to see the country firsthand. As a means of earning my daily bread, of course. I wasn't intending to, er, set up a hostel for Ghanaians and Senegalese on shift work.'

Morris hated smoking in the car, but let it pass. He was mature enough to appreciate that everybody had their shortcomings. For two or three minutes he drove steadily, letting his idea sink in, waiting for any further objections to surface. Then, with a businesslike frankness he was consciously cultivating these days, he set about persuading Forbes as to which side his bread was buttered.

'The point is you'll need a fair slice of capital to set up this school, correct?'

'*Res angusta domi,*' agreed the old man.

'I beg your pardon?'

'I was merely accepting your premise.'

Well, Morris of course had access to that capital through the Trevisan family. Say, four or five hundred thousand a month to rent an old farmhouse somewhere, plus a few million to make it functional. The problem being, he explained, that the selfish Trevisans would never make an investment like that just for Forbes. There would have to be something in it for them. Immediately if possible. Hence the idea of using the place to house the immigrants for shiftwork in bottling and packing. In fact it was rather fortunate that Forbes had spoken to him just when Pollo Bobo had got this bee in his bonnet about stepping up production and using the machines at night. Then if Forbes could teach them, the immigrants, a little Italian and art history into the bargain, for which he would of course be paid, he would not only be carrying out an act of charity, but they would also be willing to accept lower wages. 'Maybe the local government would even give us a grant or something. Everybody would be happy.' And since bottling was seasonal, as soon as the immigrants were gone, Forbes would have the building ready and could get over the kind of people he wanted, the public-school children. It was a way of setting up. Within a couple of years he'd have exactly the kind of institution he wanted: a gentlemanly live-in school of culture. 'Hopefully with a couple of scholarship places for people from my own kind of background,' Morris added complacently. He did have this genuine feeling of needing to repay a debt.

Forbes was silent. They were descending the far side of the Apennines now, picking up the first signs for Florence.

'The only trouble, as I see it,' Morris admitted, 'is that they'll all be boys. You know? They don't seem to have any of their women with them as yet.'

'Ah.' Forbes paused, brow knitted over a packed pipe. He sighed heavily, then spoke with that generosity Morris had come to associate with true class: 'I suppose if it really is the only way, I shall have to let you twist my arm.'

CHAPTER FIVE

MOTHER HAD BEEN INTERESTED in art. Father was a piss artist. Morris was aware of a Lawrentian banality in this analysis, this antithesis. But if things were banal it was presumably because they did indeed happen a lot. As caricature also had its unmistakable authenticity. So, his case had been no different from thousands of others. But what could you expect? Indeed it was precisely that lack of uniqueness, the sheer number of those united by a common cultural poverty, that gave his childhood its poignancy. Though by the same token, the anonymity of that starting line must render his later distinctions all the more remarkable.

Mother had been interested in art. She had encouraged him to read, draw, play the violin. Drawing he had never been any good at (his instinct was for the succession of events in time, not the deployment of objects in space), and then Father had trampled all over his jumble-sale violin when the boy's practising had coincided – but it was hardly an improbable coincidence – with a particularly dire hangover. But nobody had been able to stop Morris reading. Indeed there were times when it seemed he had read every book Acton library had to offer, from *Aachen: Her history* to Stefan Zweig's not unformative *The Tide of Fortune* (Jewishness was something Morris had often found himself deeply attracted to). Father told him that only idlers and wankers read all the time, because reading was the only 'activity' which allowed you to keep your hands in your pockets. Morris had been aware of a certain crude veracity in Father's observations. There was the rub.

But he would not talk to his father about it any more. No, no and no! There would be no more self-justificatory hours with the dictaphone. Absolutely not. No more post-cards with boastful allusions. After that brief summer with Massimina he need prove his manhood no more.

Due to the difficult circumstances at home, Morris had done his reading in the library's reference room amongst diligent schoolboy Sikhs and the unemployed rustling their *Suns* and *Mirrors*. Happy, happy days. Knowledge of the visual arts, on the other hand, had mainly been limited to visits to provincial museums when climatic conditions on their unfailingly coastal holidays finally made the beach too grim a prospect even for Father's pioneering spirit. Or rather, Father would roll his towel round still-damp swimming trunks and announce that they were off for their dip anyway, come hell or high water, and Mother would at last rebel and weep, gesturing at the bowing poplars round the caravan site, the racing clouds, the drizzle spotting their view of the communal toilets. Courageously, she called attention to Morris's cough, his weak chest. So while Father eventually agreed to sit out the long wait till opening time in one of the seafront amusement parlours, she would take the boy to the local art gallery, or, better still, on a country bus ride to the nearest stately home where a cap-in-hand aristocracy had just begun allowing the likes of Morris to savour their wealth the better to be able to keep it for themselves.

Above all he remembered the steady eyes of powdered faces in high white neck ruffs, and the kind of gothic, angst-torn romantic landscapes that only the well-off could afford to contemplate with equanimity. Yet the ten-year-old Morris loved it. He loved the smell of polished parquet, the flower-patterned chaises longues, the tall windows with their sash-tied velvet curtains looking out on manicured slopes cradling dainty fish-ponds. He loved the hush and echo of spacious interiors whose designers had always put abundance before necessity. And he knew he had been born into the wrong class.

And quite probably into the wrong race too. For after Mother's death, when West London became so alien he was all but forced to spend his weekends at the Victoria and Albert, the National Gallery, the British Museum or the Tate, a restless, adolescent Morris had slowly begun to appreciate that the sort of elegance he felt most attracted to, even akin to, did not originate in the glorious military and meteorological past of his native land: the Wellingtonian battle scenes, Constable skies, Turner seas. But in Italy.

It was an undistinguished triptych by Cespo di Garofano that finally brought the idea to the surface of his consciousness. There were Santa Cecilia, the Madonna, and San Valeriano. They stood so straight, yet at the same time with such ease and enjoyment. They were dressed so well, but not with that strait-laced English constriction of ruffs and bodices, as if correct presentation were some kind of social curse. No, these people took pleasure in their clothes, the soft swathes of red and blue, the glittering brooches, elegant sandals. And what senuousness about lips and eyes! The Madonna no less than the others. Sensuousness expressed through formality. Formality growing out of sensuousness. So that Morris saw for the very first time how the rude pleasures of his father and the piety of his dear dead mother need not always be at odds.

Also, despite the darker hair colour, San Valeriano bore a definite resemblance to himself.

Hence, when events conspired – and there really could be no other word for it – to get him thrown out of Cambridge, it had seemed only natural for Morris to head for Italy.

'Do you ever look for people you know in paintings?' he enquired of Forbes now, as they drove round Piazza della Libertà a second time. As always in this chaotic country, parking was proving impossible. There were cars on the pavement, cars on the central reservation, cars double parked even at the bus-stops. But Morris did not wish to break the law. Surely there must be a car park somewhere. He was perfectly willing to pay.

'How do you mean?' Forbes enquired.

'People you know, who are dear to you, do you ever look for them in paintings?'

'You mean for portraits which resemble them?' Forbes specified.

'Yes.' For the sake of the conversation Morris chose to accept this loss of meaning, niggling though it was.

'Not really my line in art history.'

'I know. I appreciate that. But out of curiosity. You've never found a face in a picture? Your wife, for example.'

'No.' Forbes was emphatic now. 'Neither found nor looked for.'

Morris was silent, his eye searching the car-cluttered twentieth-century pavements beneath the majestic elegance of Renaissance palazzi. Forbes was watching him from small green eyes. Then the phone trilled.

Morris was so engrossed in the rich pleasures of thought and the tribulations of parking he almost made the mistake of picking it up. But no, he had told her he would be seeing a client at ten-thirty and it was only ten to eleven. He wasn't such a greenhorn as to make a slip like that.

Forbes watched. After exactly ten trills and another turn round another piazza the phone stopped.

'You know, you are a curious chap, Morris,' Forbes told him.

Morris turned and flashed him his most brilliant smile from beneath the blond thatch. He could almost feel the blueness of his own eyes, he felt so flattered, and in a gesture of anarchical flamboyance he stopped the car on a pedestrian crossing right outside Palazzo dei Signori.

The gallery was certainly a great improvement on the street. Yet curiously a reflection of it too, Morris thought, performing one of those sudden penetrative turns of mind that always pleased him. There were the same colours, but frozen here in the dull pink of the marble, the cream of frothy travertine. There was the same sensuality of the men and women in the piazza, but stilled into perpetual contemplation by brush and chisel, a sort of shadowy distillation of the intense and too often vulgar world outside, a cool simulacrum, purged of urgency and appetence. He decided he would extend this visit as long as was reasonably possible. Massimina was on the third floor in Room VIII, but she could wait. Morris had always been a great believer in the deferment of pleasure.

After a brief trip to the loo, Forbes took him by the elbow and began to guide him through the Vasariano corridor, then the Hermaphrodite's Room. The man was so knowledgeable, so intelligent. He invited Morris to touch the smooth thighs of an Apollo, to feel the volume, the muscle-bound fullness of the stone. This was the kind of thing he wanted to teach his young students, he said, when the school was finally set up. To appreciate the pleasure of art, rather than just being in awe of it. Children should be invited to copy and then to create. It was really the only way to learn the *gratia placendi*.

Which meant? How Morris loved that Latin! His hand ran down the stone across a perfect knee that might have been his own but for the lack of reflex.

'The delight of pleasing.' Forbes's voice was plummier than ever.

'*Attenzione, signore!*' The attendant appeared from nowhere. A firm hand pulled at Morris's elbow. '*Non si tocca*, not to touch. Or out! Is very bad! *Capito?*'

Morris whirled round. Why did authority always make him so nervous? That sense of being caught doing something he shouldn't. Immediately he was ready to run. And at exactly the same moment he remembered he was supposed to have sent a fax to Doorways stores to confirm their order. The trip was ruined, the mood he had been so carefully nurturing gone.

'Philistine mentality masquerading as protector of the arts,' Forbes commented with a sad shake of the head as the attendant returned to his seat. 'Surely he could see we weren't doing any harm.' In a rare moment of self-revelation, he added: 'One of the reasons I left England actually.'

But Morris was too shaken to pick up on this. All he wanted to do now was to see Massimina and get out of here. All at once the tapestried walls and frescoed ceilings and all the glories of Renaissance art and harmony had become no more than a dangerously enclosed space. He waited until about halfway through the Tuscan School before telling Forbes that he had the most awful stomachache and would have to leave. If they could just take a look at that Filippo Lippi first.

In Room VIII they had to hang on for a few minutes while a noisy crowd of poorly dressed East Europeans stood in front of her. A guide spoke incomprehensibly. But even looking through the gaggle of grizzled, unkempt, blockish heads Morris could see that it was definitely Massimina, right down to the fleshy nose and milky cheeks. At once an extraordinary excitement flooded downwards through his body. 'As of a man returning to his lover.' He mouthed the words with silent lips, then found Forbes was looking at him with growing concern.

'You seem terribly tense, old boy.'

'I just can't see why these bloody Polacks have to hog my picture for so long.'

'All in good time,' Forbes smiled. 'Relax. Even the plebs must have their day.' Then he asked politely: 'This is, er, one of those resemblances to someone you know? Or a purely aesthetic interest?'

There was such a lump in Morris's throat he couldn't reply.

'Ah,' Forbes remarked, his face a mask of philosophy.

The Poles, if they were Poles, moved away now and Morris stepped quickly right up to the canvas. Very simply, a blue-and-red-robed Virgin was being crowned by two delightfully fleshy cherubs. The face looked downward. And there was exactly that demure, somehow seductive (seductive because demure) cocking of the head, dipping of the chin, which was one of Massimina's characteristic expressions. Quite unmistakable. And even, incredibly, unless it was just a fleck of dirt on the canvas, the tiny mole she had under her left ear. Which he had kissed with such tenderness once. Since nothing aroused his tenderness so much as vulnerability, blemishes.

But above all there were her eyes. Those great liquid brown eyes were looking straight at him. The sense of her presence was so much more intense than in the tiny photograph at the cemetery. Simply, this *was* Mimi.

'Famous for the vividness of his colours and the sensuous epidermis of his figures,' Forbes was informing him, 'though clearly rather limited in scope and ambition when set alongside his master, Masaccio, or immediate successors, like da Vinci and Michelangelo.'

Morris just couldn't get over that tilt of the chin, the way the hair framed the face exactly as Mimi's had, at least until the day he had made her get it permed to avoid recognition.

'Old girlfriend?' Forbes enquired with gentle amusement. 'Mother, aunt, cousin?'

'My one and only love,' Morris croaked, at once thoroughly anguished and at the same time sensing the quality of this melodrama. Other people wouldn't be able to suffer like this.

'*La donna è mobile*,' Forbes commiserated. 'The fairer sex they may be, but lighter and flightier too, I'm afraid.'

'No,' Morris muttered, still staring. Any moment now she would give him her sign. He was sure of it. 'No, she died.'

'Ah. I am sorry.'

There was a long pause before Morris said tragically: 'We were going to be married.'

'No one ever seems actually to marry the person they love most,' Forbes said gently. 'It's almost a natural law. Like the impossibility of alchemy or perpetual motion.' The old man became elegiac. 'Life would be too wonderful, wouldn't it?'

'Yes.' Morris appreciated this participation. Indeed although there were plenty of people milling around them, it was as if the two of them were cut off somehow, in a different dimension, standing before this young woman with the naked boys floating about her. The faintest wryness played across the Virgin's lips.

She's making me wait, Morris thought. She's teasing.

'Car accident?' Forbes asked. 'Or illness?'

'They bloody well kidnapped her and killed her,' Morris said fiercely. 'Can you imagine that? The only person I ever loved. They killed her!'

Forbes was taken aback. 'Good heavens!' he said, with an old-fashionedness that again Morris, for all his tension and emotion, was able to appreciate. Out loud he breathed to the painting: 'Mimi!' When was she going to give him her sign? Sometimes she could be so stubborn! As when he had pleaded and pleaded with her to cover the whole thing up with him, not to make him do it, to live happily together for the rest of their lives. Certainly *he* had never wanted it to end as it had. For a moment then he half wondered if he mightn't confess the whole business to Forbes. Hear the man tell him that it was all quite understandable. He had acted as anybody would.

'I'm sorry,' Forbes was saying. 'I didn't realise.'

They stood there. The painting was irksomely frozen in its exact resemblance. Morris felt Forbes might be becoming impatient. To spin it out, he asked: 'Did he use a model, do you think? I mean, was there a real flesh-and-blood girl?'

'Lippi? Well, yes, some of the painters did, for a basic anatomic outline. Though the result was highly idealised of course.'

Of course nothing, Morris thought. It was the spitting image.

'Funny thing about Lippi,' Forbes now remarked, apparently trying to take his young friend's mind off things, 'although he was a monk and did all these devotional paintings, he then went and abducted a nun and later married her.'

'Abducted?' Morris said aghast.

'So the story goes.'

'He abducted her and she was his model?'

'Oh, I wouldn't know about that. But I suppose she could have been.'

'A nun?'

'Yes.'

As Mimi too had been so desperately Catholic! No sooner had he taken all this in than Morris thought it extraordinary that the usually sensitive Forbes had not noticed the obvious parallels. As if he himself had painted her virgin portrait, then married her, which must be a kind of death for a nun. Or not? His mind seemed about to boil. Still the wry smile wouldn't move.

Had she really loved him? Or was it just a ploy to get away from home? Her convent.

'There's a rather jolly poem about the fellow, by Browning, apologising for his lusty instincts,' Forbes went on. 'Somewhat overpraised by Ruskin.'

Quite suddenly Morris had had enough. He had stood there ten minutes and more. He must be going out of his mind, waiting for signs. And if he wasn't, then he was being snubbed. That knowing smile. Damn her! She was only a girl in the end. Madonna or no. He swung round, took Forbes by the arm and headed for the door. 'My stomach,' he complained. 'I can't believe this.'

The voice called exactly as they crossed the threshold into the Botticelli Room. Morris froze. Forbes was clearly afraid his young friend might be going to faint, or vomit, and tried to put a supporting arm round him. Morris turned his head. The room was filling up with a gaggle of schoolchildren, calling to each other in shrill tones. But it was definitely his own name he had heard, and with that unmistakable inflection: 'Morri!' Nobody else had ever called him Morri. The great brown eyes stared across the room. Morris raised a hand to his lips, blew a kiss, turned and, hardly aware that Forbes's arm was still round his shoulder, stumbled down the stairs.

In the car he would have liked to have spoken to her on the telephone, but that was clearly impossible in Forbes's presence. The old man wanted to stop for lunch, but warned that he had forgotten his wallet. Morris felt sorry to see his noble friend reduced to this sort of pathetic scrounging and gallantly insisted they order the most expensive dishes on the menu, his stomach-ache having miraculously disappeared. Afterwards, on the way back, despite his growing impatience to be alone, he generously told Forbes that if ever he needed a loan to tide him over between pensions, he need only ask. Forbes accepted a couple of hundred thousand.

'I know it sounds crazy,' Morris went on, 'but do you think it might ever be possible to buy a picture like that from a gallery like the Uffizi? I mean, they must have about thirty coronations of the Virgin.'

Forbes thought not, but agreed that art was something one needed to have around in one's own environment, rather than merely visit in museums. As with all beauty, the element of possession was important. He frequently felt nostalgic for his old house back in Cambridge and the paintings he had there. But not for the company. Would that he had left earlier and younger.

Again Morris was too engrossed in his own thoughts to accept the invitation to enquire about the older man's private life. Anyway, it was Forbes's culture that interested him, not his personal vicissitudes. When the phone rang he hesitated a moment, wondering if he would ever experience the miracle of *her* phoning him.

But it was Paola.

'Mamma's come to,' she said tersely. 'For God's sake, it seems she's going to recover. I can't believe it!'

Nor could Morris. Still, it did seem tasteless to show one's disappointment so openly.

'The only consolation,' his wife was remarking, 'is that Bobo is more furious about it than we are.'

Putting the phone down, Morris wondered how furious his brother-in-law would be when he realised Morris had confirmed, as he would the moment he got back to Verona, an order for four thousand cases with the tightest possible delivery dates. Quite suddenly he was determined to bring matters to a head.

CHAPTER SIX

TOWARDS MIDNIGHT, WHEN THEY had commiserated together over a good bottle of prosecco and Paola was exploiting Morris's weakness for frozen chocolates to engage in some oral foreplay, the young Englishman remembered his purchase of that morning. Paola pouted around a melting praline. 'A present, my dear,' Morris insisted. In dressing-gown and slippers he walked down the stairs and out into the icy fog of the November night. Quite brazen, the builder had left his excavator parked outside the main gate, making entrance to drive and garages difficult. But some day Morris would find a way to make him pay. There was no hurry. He pulled the package from the back seat of the Mercedes.

It was stopping by his first-floor neighbour's door to listen a moment to the television, that it occurred to Morris that the thing was too heavy. He was hearing the strip music from Channel 7's late show. Surprise, surprise! And yes, it was distinctly audible on the stairs. Which was useful to know. Lifting the package and shaking it slightly, his self-satisfaction began to bleed away into swooning anxiety. Something had shifted inside with an unconvincing thud.

'I've made a fool of myself,' he announced on walking back into the flat. Paola was tummy down on the sofa in just the kind of underwear he found at once exciting and in awful taste. She beckoned with a finger. Morris almost shouted: 'For Christ's sake, I've been a complete and utter prick!'

'Mmm,' she said.

'I hate myself.' He began to tear at the Sellotape around the package with its photo of a Sony Videomaster. 'I meant it as a present for you and instead I just wasted a hundred and fifty thousand lire. A hundred and fifty thousand!'

Suddenly, but not entirely unexpectedly, he could feel the tears coming to his eyes, such a welling of conflicting emotions: self-abasement, anger, forgiveness, humiliation. His nails finally tore open the package, allowing a brick in a polythene bag to slither out and crash down on the tiled floor.

Paola burst out laughing. 'Oh, Mo, you idiot. You didn't buy it from a *marocchino*, did you? Everybody knows they're all fakes.'

The tinkling of her voice seemed to coincide with a sort of bubbling behind his eyes as if blood were flooding to the boil. For a moment even his pyjamas and dressing-gown felt tight around a swelling body. He was so full of rage. He could have picked that brick right up from the floor and smashed it straight down on her sneering, sluttish head. Massimina would never have behaved like this.

'I bought it for you!' he screamed. 'To film ourselves. I was kind to the guy and he let me down!'

Paola got up and came to hold him, trapping his arms in hers. Irritated, he pushed her away, but she came right back and repeated the gesture, arms folding tightly round him, pushing her face into his neck. 'Mo, take me,' she whispered, 'take me. I love it when you're angry. You're so naïve and sweet and strong and violent all together.'

He made a half-hearted attempt to resist, not unaware of the gratifying intensity of these emotions, the pornographic aspect of her sheeny underwear on the dark petite body.

'I love it, I love it,' she insisted, and pulling open his dressing-gown began to tug him by the two lapels.

Later, when she was quietly sleeping, Morris lay awake in a sort of massacred consciousness where every element of his humiliation was kaleidoscopically alive and vivid. Until it occurred to him to get up and go back into the sitting-room. He switched on the light, picked up the brick in its polythene bag and set it down carefully on a rug by the sofa. Then, examining the floor, he found that there was indeed a severe chip in one of the tiles, an ugly, grainy white patch in what was a Bertelli design of delicate geometric greens. So that now the scenario was even worse. Not only had he been fool enough to give money to a man who, due to the way society had treated him, was bound to be a fraud, but then in his foolish hothead anger on realising his mistake, he had allowed himself to damage a tile that had cost in the region of forty thousand lire and would now cost at least twice that to remove and replace.

Returning to bed, it was to find that Paola had invaded his space as she so often would. There was something childish about her luxurious slantwise sprawl under the heavy quilt. The kind of spoilt child who is used to having and taking everything. Morris put on his dressing-gown and sat in the room's one armchair. For about an hour he stared into the dark. Once again he allowed vivid images of his humiliation to pass before his mind's eye: the Moroccan's practised scowl as he squatted down by the car window; his own foolish flush of triumph as he 'brought the man down' to one hundred and fifty thousand; Massimina's painted wryness later on in the gallery, as though looking down on a poor, flailing enmired Morris from the great height of redeemed martyrdom; and then his wife's pealing laughter, her animal grunts and satisfactions, as if her husband were no more than a source of pleasure, something to be enjoyed rather than understood and comforted. 'Call no man happy until he is dead,' Morris remembered from his Moralist Paper Tripos Part Two, and repeated it to himself over and over for much of the night. 'Call no man happy until he is dead.' He almost envied his mother-in-law, so close to the blissful threshold.

CHAPTER SEVEN

PRECARIOUSLY PERCHED ON THE hill above Marzana, it had three stories and a leaky roof with four statues, which Forbes, after standing discreetly in a corner of the terrace for a few moments, promptly pronounced of no aesthetic value, though Morris thought them, if nothing else, picturesque. Apparently they represented San Zeno, San Rocco, Sant'Anna and Sant'Agata, minor local saints of miscellaneous and implausible miracles. But this was the best part of Italian culture, Morris often felt: its fantastical superfluity. Who would ever believe that Mimi winked at him from photographs or called from old paintings? There was a way, he was discovering, in which his mentality was firmly grounded in the Italian religious tradition, and thus in a very profound way legitimised. He belonged here.

Forbes also objected that the place would be desperately cold or desperately expensive to heat. He tapped at a loose pane of glass.

The former, Morris explained, since there was no central heating and the chimneys needed extensive work before a fire could safely be lit. 'Just the right look for a brochure though,' he insisted: 'the hill, the vines, the cypresses, the noble façade with the statues.'

'*Rudis indigestaque moles,*' Forbes commented.

Which meant?

'That I'd hoped for something better, but *quod bonum felix, faustumque sit,* I'll move in tonight.'

It appeared that Forbes's rent was in considerable arrears due to the difficulty of maintaining two separate households on a miserable pension that didn't always arrive. His wife back in Cambridge was being unreasonable, forever writing about the cost of heating oil, public transport, theatre tickets, etc. Obviously she still hadn't accepted their separation. He was grateful to Morris, he explained, for giving him this chance to regain his dignity, for saving him from an ignominious return.

Yes, he was genuinely grateful, Forbes repeated, turning to take Morris's hand and looking him straight in the eye, his own watery between dusty folds of skin. There was a kind of schoolmasterly nobility about him. Morris smiled warmly. Not to mention it. He was glad to be in a position to help someone so worthy. He enjoyed the curious glance the older man shot him as he said this.

They looked the place over. The stucco was coming away in great chunks and the shutters seemed to be held together by nothing more than thick old coats of paint. A cold stone staircase gave way to the rickety floorboards of underfurnished bedrooms: a sagging mattress between gothic headboards, a dresser with marble top (cracked), a painting of St Peter crucified upside down, ruined by damp. In the penumbra of the top landing a young woman knelt weeping by an extravagant tomb, her eyes glinting in canvas candlelight. Forbes shook his head and muttered something in Latin.

But Morris felt supremely confident. Wasn't it just the kind of culture-saturated location they had been looking for? It was going to look splendid on the leaflets they'd be mailing off to Eton and Harrow in a year or so. Meanwhile, to pay rent and renovation, the immigrants would be arriving in the next couple of days. Say thirty per cent of their wages for bed and board? That was hardly unreasonable. He turned on a tap that delivered a trickle of rusty water followed by a long groan. '*Fiat experimentum in corpore vili*,' was all Forbes would comment, and this time he refused to translate.

But no, the real reason he was feeling so buoyant, Morris thought, driving faster than he should back down the Valpantena, the real reason he could be so confident, was precisely because he was so ruthlessly hard on himself when things went wrong. Emotionally, he earned these highs, and of course when, as now, you had everything planned to a tee for once, it was difficult not to be elated and rather impressed with oneself. Life was a game in the end, and Morris was staying ahead of it. Way, way ahead. 'Isn't that right, Mimi, *cara?*' He picked up the phone, then promptly put it down again. There were moments when he felt he should steer well clear of that oddball stuff and keep life as simple and practical as possible. Mimi would be in touch just as soon as she needed to be.

He found Kwame by the main traffic lights outside the cemetery, cleaning windows for small change. The big black knew Morris was a soft touch and immediately came towards his Mercedes, bucket in hand. Despite his eagerness to be up and doing, Morris let the boy sluice the windscreen and then attack it with his sponge. The light turned green. The cars ahead and in the left-hand lane began to move. Kwame worked on conscientiously, scrubbing at encrusted flies. A car behind hit its horn. Morris sat tight. The horns began to chorus. That extraordinary Italian impatience! Kwame looked up to catch Morris's eye through the now glistening windscreen. As on two previous occasions when this had happened, there was a definite hint of complicity in the polished black face, Morris was quite sure of it. He buzzed down the window and instead of offering the customary thousand lire invited Kwame to get in, then waited perhaps thirty more seconds till the light turned to amber, before releasing the clutch and accelerating away. There was simply no need for people to be so aggressive.

Morris had learnt the black's name, or perhaps surname, when he had helped him with his application for a *permesso di soggiorno* at the police station. Then there had been these meetings on the busy circular road by the cemetery, where Kwame and a dozen others apparently slept in the empty grave niches in the walls. Now, as Morris made his gesture of invitation, the black simply left his bucket on the pavement and climbed into the car with a great beaming smile on his face and no questions asked, not a word. As Peter had once dropped his nets when Jesus beckoned, Morris thought; and he was impressed and deeply touched by this demonstration of trust, intrigued too by the other man's simple life. Because for all his love of elegance and class, if there was one thing Morris was not, it was a snob. Indeed, his genius was to recognise class in a boy like Kwame, the way he recognised culture in a penny-pinching fellow like Forbes, and had found such a potent cocktail of virtue, beauty and sensuality in a total non-entity like Massimina.

Silent in city traffic, they inched their way to the centre. Morris found, as somehow he knew he would, the last available parking meter in the approach to Piazza Bra, and again he couldn't help wondering whether there wasn't some kind of destiny guiding his actions. It was the way, whenever he began something, everything seemed to conspire to make events turn out *as they must*. There was a Forbes to keep the hostel for you. There was a crumbling old house to be cheaply rented. There were Kwame and his boys at the cemetery. There was the mammoth order from Doorways. So often, it seemed, he was nothing more than an agent weaving together threads that had clearly been made for each other. It was a topic he might do well to explore with Massimina. Perhaps from beyond the grave the pattern would be clear to her. Perhaps she might even explain to him what seemed at the moment the rift in that pattern, his great mistake in life: his humiliating marriage to Paola. A form of penance perhaps? A constant and mocking reminder of the great wrong he had done? He took the black into a department store and bought him new shoes, new jeans, new sweater, new down jacket.

Kwame was neither overwhelmed nor ungrateful. Tall and remarkably healthy, Morris thought, for his hours collecting small change in the freezing exhaust fumes and his nights wrapped in a blanket in a hole in the wall, he stood easily in his new clothes at the polished granite bar of one of the spiffier cafés in the piazza, and accepted a beer.

'How many of you are there?' Morris asked, speaking English. He rather enjoyed the truculent glances of a clientele unused to having blacks in their bar.

'Ten, eleven, twelve.' Kwame shrugged his shoulders, still smiling broadly. 'Depends on the day, the polizia.'

'And all good boys?'

The thick, black lower lip pouted out in an eloquent expression of 'How should I know?'

'But reliable?' Morris insisted, scooping up a handful of peanuts.

Again the pouting lower lip, quickly followed by the beaming smile, the bright black eyes with their fascinating mixture of complicity and reticence. The boy must be a good twenty centimetres taller than Morris. And so very black.

'Because I want to offer you all a job,' Morris said. 'And a place to live.'

It was more than anybody had done for him when he

first arrived here! Driving the boy across town a few minutes later, he picked up the phone, pretended to dial, and immediately started to tell Mimi about his weaving metaphor. He experienced a curious frisson in doing this in front of somebody else. Like letting someone overhear you flirting without their knowing who with. Though it was cheating a little, choosing somebody as insignificant as Kwame for one's audience. The point being, he explained, that for a successful design one would require a good variety of colours combining together in ways at once surprising and harmonious. Which meant you needed an artist. Only an artist would see as self-evident the congruity between apparently disparate elements, the way for example even Pollo Bobo's hostility and refusal to get involved was now to become part of the pattern, to galvanise it, give it tension, make it more fun, more of an achievement. So that if he had never felt that he really had the talent, and more critically the contacts, to become a writer or painter, perhaps in the end the truth was that he was an artist of *life*. He knew how to make things happen between *people*. 'As they did between us, Mimi,' he finished rather huskily. 'As they did between us. How I miss you and miss you!' Then he had to fight back the inevitable gnawing emotion these phone calls always prompted.

On putting down the receiver, he turned to glance at Kwame. The boy smiled warmly and began to slap his knees in a slow, even rhythm. Pleasant company, Morris thought. Dumb, no doubt, but curiously understanding, and deeply deserving of the help Morris was going to offer.

CHAPTER EIGHT

IT WAS A SORT of village for the rich. Two older but completely renovated villas split up into flats, then four new palazzine with extravagant terrace balconies, expensive window fittings and copper drains. There was a swimming pool and tennis courts. But the most important feature, and one that Morris finally decided was a rather sad comment, was that the whole thing was surrounded by a tall, wire-topped wall, the entrance being guarded by an electronic gate and two video-cameras. As if one could simply cut oneself off from the whole of the world and wallow in one's money! He felt these people deserved the sight of Kwame in their midst, a sort of visual expression of Morris's own spiritual alienation. He rang one of forty bells.

'*Sono io*, Morris.' He looked straight into the camera to the right of the gate and did not say he had come for Bobo.

The maid said she would have to ask, thus allowing Morris to note that he was not among the privileged group of people whom the girl presumably knew to let in at any time of the day or night. A short, but telling wait, then the gate buzzed. Morris turned and only now beckoned to Kwame to get out of the car.

The tiles were polished Sardinian granite, the walls a new kind of waxed stucco very much in vogue, the furniture predominantly antique, but with a curiously modern feel to it, perhaps because the chests and dressers had been so perfectly restored, stood out so cleanly against glossy floor and wall. Rather than suggesting some anchoring in history, the rich composure of an awareness of time, it was more as if everything had been snipped from the sheeny pages of *Casa bella*.

Yet Morris could not help admiring the environment. There was nothing gauche about it, none of Paola's depressing predilection for pastel silks and soft low sofas, her vision of home as some kind of high-class brothel; nor was it the *ad hoc* muddle of the English homes he remembered. Yet one still felt there was something missing. The old family home in the outlying village of Quinzano, where Massimina had first taken him to meet her mother and sisters, had had some magical extra element, something that transformed provincial conservatism into richness and culture: a place that had been tastefully lived in! That was the goal. Well, he was only thirty. There was still time.

Kwame hovered by the door. Morris beckoned for him to come in. The small southern maid did not think to hide her alarm, which Morris studiously ignored. Kwame cut such a fine and Moorish figure against the abrupt surfaces of granite and waxed stucco, as if he, like the antiques, had been cut out of a page. One certainly felt more powerful having him around.

'I'd like to see Bobo,' Morris announced at his most casual. Before the maid could tell him the head of the house wasn't in, Antonella appeared, descending a spiral staircase at the far end of the room, where travertine steps rested on an elegant scaffolding of brushed tubular steel.

The dark-trousered legs coming down behind her gradually revealed themselves as those of a small, bespectacled, elderly priest carrying two bulging plastic bags.

'Don Carlo,' she introduced him, 'my brother-in-law, Morris Duckworth.'

'*Piacere.*' They shook hands. The cleric smiled and moved toward the door. 'I'll presume no longer,' he said with the air of one for whom humility has become a profession.

'We were sorting out clothes,' Antonella explained superfluously, 'for the poor.'

But Morris intervened: 'Allow me to introduce Kwame.'

The priest, though taken aback, turned graciously, as if relieved to have been forced to do his duty.

Kwame muttered something incomprehensible, big black face beaming. But a sidelong glance at Morris carried an exciting mixture of trust, inquisitiveness, concern.

'He doesn't speak much Italian yet,' Morris explained, 'only English.' As the priest left, he added: 'He's one of our new workers in the packaging department. I hoped Bobo would be here. I phoned him at the office but he was out.'

Needless to say, this was a lie.

Antonella stood gawkily amongst her expensive furnishings. She was simply and traditionally dressed, but one of the few Italians Morris had met who didn't appear to know how to hold herself properly. With that speed of intuition he had always prided himself on, he realised now that this high-class domestic environment she lived in must be the product of Bobo's mentality. Antonella would be more interested in a publication like *I miracoli di Sant' Antonio* than *Casa bella*.

'But he's always in the office,' the wife said, perplexed.

'Perhaps he just popped out for a minute.' Morris hesitated, as if genuinely weighing up how best to manage his precious time. 'I suppose I'll have to drive the boy up there,' he decided. 'Kwame,' he said in English, 'this is your boss's wife, Signora Posenato.'

Bowing, the big black came and took her hand. Antonella's fear was evident, as was her distaste for the strong smell the boy emitted. But at the same time she was clearly determined to overcome these negative feelings. Unwilling lips and cheeks were forced into a smile. The corner of the mouth was trembling. After shaking his hand she instinctively began to wring her own together. Kwame continued to nod rather idiotically.

'*Bene,*' Morris announced, looking about him.

Then Antonella at last said what he was waiting to hear: 'Bobo didn't tell me we were taking on any new workers. Why's that?'

'*Davvero.* Didn't he?'

She shook her head, hair tightly knotted above a solid neck. She wore a crucifix, he noticed, in what was actually a rather deep cleavage. More like Massimina's than Paola's. Traditional and maternal. The sort of abundance that made you think of a resting place and source of nourishment rather than a pornographic playground. In the end more rewarding.

Why on earth had he married Paola? Or could it be that everybody's life was just a long slow discovery of all the mistakes one was born to make?

'You see, the fact is I've landed a huge order from a supermarket chain in the UK. We're buying out to make up the numbers and we need some more workers for packaging. There'll have to be a night shift.'

Antonella was now genuinely interested and concerned. The looming presence of Kwame was forgotten.

'But we've never bought out,' she protested. 'That was always Father's policy. And Mother's too. Trevisan wines from Trevisan vines. Nothing else.'

Morris had no difficulty pretending surprise. He cocked his head, a perplexed look on his handsome blond brow, then pulled a rather austere chair from a glass-topped table and sat down. If anything, the problem was not to overdo it. He was having so much fun.

'Oh dear,' he said, 'I hope I haven't said the wrong thing!'

The black, he noticed, was smiling cannily, as if he understood more than he let on. Morris shot him a stern look.

Antonella also sat down. Opposite.

Morris was most candid. 'I'm sorry, it's just that I can never get used to this business in Italy – I mean, of what can be said and what can't, you know? – the safe in public view in the office and the safe behind the fuse box, the accounts in the books and the ones on the computer with the restricted access code. Everybody's in on it, aren't they, but there are only certain people you're allowed to say it to. I find it difficult.'

Her eyes were wide as saucers now. After all, it was her family who owned the place. Not Bobo's.

'No, my idea was, once one's accepted the principle of buying out, which after all most wine companies do – there's even the list of the suppliers on the computer – well, one may as well set up a night shift, use the machines to the full, and if none of the Italians want to work nights, we can give work to these poor people who are crying out for it.'

Before she could intervene, he went on to explain about the house he had rented to set up a hostel. 'Perhaps you could talk to Don Carlo about it. I know some of them would be interested in doing a catechism course. They're simply craving to be accepted into society.'

Antonella was staring at him with the air of one who sees all kinds of unusual objects scattered across the floor and has no idea where to put them away or whether it mightn't be better just to chuck them all out.

Morris smiled his most winning and apologetic smile.

'Actually, Paola and I have got a fair number of clothes that could go to the poor too. I'll get her to give them to you if you're collecting.'

'And Bobo's happy about this, er, development?' Antonella asked, trying to hide her incredulity.

'Look' – Morris began to fiddle with the buckle on his briefcase – 'thinking about it, I don't suppose I will actually have time to get up to the factory before lunch. I should have a copy of the Doorways contract here in my bag somewhere. Just show it to Bobo when he gets back. I mean, you only need to look at the kind of figures they're talking about to understand why he'll be happy about it. And if it means we can help people like Kwame, then I think it's great. After all, capitalism is only good when we draw others into our wealth, don't you think?'

'Sì, sì, sono d'accordo.'

But Morris could see that she hadn't expected this philanthropy from him. The family still had the same prejudice they had had that first day he arrived with Massimina: that in the end he was no more than a gold-digger. They denied him any spiritual dimension, any scrap of altruism. Suddenly he felt determined that the pious Antonella should understand that there was more to him than met the eye. He would pay back for Massimina's death. Somehow he would. Again he smiled warmly. 'Better to give them jobs, in the end, than clothes, don't you think?'

Antonella nodded.

'Oh, I'd better leave a note too.' On his memo pad he wrote in Cartier biro: 'Bobo, I've found the workers. To respect delivery dates we will have to start a night shift within the week. You'll have to be in touch with your suppliers at once. Speak to you this afternoon. Ciao, Morris.'

At the door he turned and enquired: 'By the way, about Mamma? I'm never sure if I should visit or not. I know Bobo goes quite a lot.'

'She's a bit better,' Antonella said. 'Though the doctors say she'll never speak again. Bobo says it might have been better if she had died, but I'm praying for her to recover at least some faculties.'

Morris shook his head sadly. 'I'm afraid Paola doesn't go as often as she ought and I feel odd going when she doesn't. I mean, somebody might get the wrong idea.'

Antonella found her forgiving smile. 'That's just Paola. It wouldn't really be her if she was always visiting Mamma, would it?'

This was a more intelligent response than Morris had expected. Character was destiny. Noticing the rather daintily crucified Christ above the entrance, he left with a better impression of his sister-in-law than when he had arrived. Pious she might be, and gawky and inelegant, but her heart was in the right place.

'And those breasts . . .' he said aloud to Kwame as they climbed into the car.

The black burst into raucous laughter and began to beat a swift rhythm on the thighs of his new jeans. But Morris immediately felt angry with himself. It was just the kind of down-market remark his father would have made. Then, reversing suddenly and viciously from the small car park out into the road, he almost ran down a scarecrow figure toiling up the hill on an ancient bicycle. The cyclist swerved and fell, unbalanced by the tattered briefcase he was trying to hold in one hand as he rode. Morris had already opened the door to dash out and apologise profusely, when he recognised, in wispy hair fluttering about an unhealthy bald patch, the familiar and ludicrous presence of Stan Albertini. 'Shee-et and mother-fuckin' shee-et, man!' a West Coast voice exclaimed. But before it had finished, Morris, safe in the knowledge that he hadn't been seen, was already back in the Mercedes attacking the first hairpin back to town at breakneck speed.

CHAPTER NINE

MORRIS WAS IN THE dark again on the armchair in his dressing-gown. He felt the pressure of the shuttered blackness on his open eyes. Sex had been having this effect on him lately. The more adventurous and demanding Paola became, the more alienated he felt. He watched himself going very efficiently through the motions, but the sense of discovery and conquest was gone, and affection on either side had never been more than cursory. Her avidity had begun to irritate him. Until, afterwards, he felt as though reduced somehow to a state of razor-sharp consciousness. His mind was a sleek panther interminably pacing a cage, dreaming of non-existent prey.

He held his head upright and quite motionless in the total dark. If only she had wanted a child! Something that could have given Morris a sense that all this was leading somewhere, towards some social consolidation, some greater vision of Morris taking his rightful place in the traditional lattice of family ties. Sometimes images of Mimi would superimpose themselves over Paola's squirming body. Maternal Mimi. Her big breasts. The quiet smile on her face when she had told him she was pregnant. After her death he had repressed all this, but now it was coming out. The adventure with Paola was no longer doing its job of suffocating all his nobler feelings. Sooner or later he would have to face the anguish of having lost Mimi, his one true love.

Morris pressed the thumbnail of his right hand deep into the soft skin below his left elbow. For a moment the black room filled with colour.

Was this why he was getting involved with this farce of the wines, Bobo, the immigrants? Clearly, even a plan of this complexity could be nothing but underachievement for someone like himself. Provincial sitcom. But it would force them to notice him. Why, Morris wondered, his mind suddenly quite cool and enquiring, why had they never simply accepted him into the family as they would have done anybody else, let him share things as of right, know everything that was going on? And if they didn't accept him, could they really expect him just to sit around and agree to some subordinate role, as if he were a mere employee, rather than one of the clan? Why was it that they not only rejected him but also failed in some way to appreciate that he was actually there?

Still pressing thumbnail into flesh, Morris laughed, then burst into tears. Only Mimi had ever really taken him into her trust. With the others he was always being forced to punish them for not doing so. He himself would accept those blacks like blood-brothers. Even the *marocchino* who had cheated him. Even Stan, had he not seen him that fatal afternoon. For God's sake, what a scare it had given him seeing Stan again!

Falling to his knees, Morris was suddenly praying: 'Mimi, Mimi, help me to do what is noble and right. Show me the way of acceptance and justice. Let me achieve happiness in the end.'

His lips moved soundlessly in the air. As they must when one prays. And so complete was the darkness with the shutters tightly closed that, away from the chair, Morris experienced a moment of acute physical disorientation. As if he were nowhere, falling through space, or in some remote place of the spirit. Then he became aware of having pressed his hands tightly together before his face, a child again doing his mother's bidding. He felt thrilled, uplifted, purged. He had prayed to Massimina. His saint! Morris had prayed. Surely he was a deep person! After two minutes, perhaps three, he stood uncertainly, felt his way across the black room, and stretched voluptuously on the bed.

An hour later his eyes were still wide open to challenge the staring dark. Because he suffered: that was the truth. Yes, he suffered, he possessed the marvellous gift of intensity. Not like the serene Paola, stretched out in baby sleep after the pleasure she had taken from him. Whenever he thought of Paola now, her body, her sex, the word 'maw' came to mind: more, maw, more maw, the swollen brown redness of her, at once vulnerable and insatiable beneath the teasing, fascist-black pubes. What if he were simply to come into his hand and slither the stuff up inside her? Why not? Morris was stiffening already. He enjoyed the feel of a smile spreading across his face. The truth was, there were all kinds of interesting thoughts to take you through the night. Moving a hand down across the smooth skin of his belly, Morris embraced his insomnia like a bride.

CHAPTER TEN

THEY WERE BY NO means all black. There was a Croat,
Ante; and an Egyptian, Farouk. There was an Albanian,
Ramiz, perhaps only fourteen or fifteen; and an older
Moroccan, Azedine, apparently in his mid-fifties. Forbes
was not pleased with Azedine. Then Kwame and another
three Ghanaians. And a couple of Senegalese who came
and went. They slept in three rooms on the second floor
on the hard wooden boards of the empty house amongst
the paintings of St Peter crucified upside down and the
woman weeping by a tomb. They washed in cold water
in the bathroom, sharing a single towel. They did their
shopping separately and kept their food on different
window-sills which served perfectly well as fridges, eating
in pairs or groups on the huge, stone-topped table in the
kitchen. Forbes cooked simple pastas for Ramiz and
the somewhat pathetic Farouk, which Morris thought
extremely generous of him. It was the mark of a truly
cultured man that he was willing to give time to those
younger and simpler than himself.

In the morning they slept until one or two o'clock.
Farouk and Azedine said their prayers before an east-facing
window on the first floor. The other rooms here were
Forbes's bedroom, study and bathroom. In the late afternoon on the ground floor Forbes offered lessons in Italian
language and culture. Only Ante, Farouk, Kwame and

Ramiz attended, sitting on rusting iron chairs retrieved from the gazebo at the bottom of the garden. Forbes taught them the various tenses of Italian verbs in a splendidly English accent and explained the sad decline in Italian art from the Renaissance on. For which Morris, from his own pocket, paid him enough cash every week to tide him over until such time as the house could be furnished and restored to receive the well-educated, paying pupils Forbes felt his life had prepared him to teach.

Then in the evening the Trevisan delivery van came to pick them up and take them to work in the long shed attached to the office that housed a primitive bottling line. Having seen the size of the contract and appreciated how much Morris knew and was willing to tell Antonella, and presumably Signora Trevisan as well, about the way he had been running the company, Bobo had reluctantly agreed to the purchase of a thousand hectolitres of assorted plonk, from the south, from Algeria, from the Valpantena itself (he had his contacts after all), to cut with their own mediocre produce, plus a fair sprinkling of sugar, and then sell on to the poor English.

'Doorways Trevisan Superiore,' the label said. 'A full-blooded table wine from the sun-baked slopes of northern Italy.' It was priced a good forty pence cheaper than anything else available in the store and apparently sold fast. The immigrants were paid 150,000 lire under the table every Friday night. The van in which they arrived and left the factory had no windows. Anyway the weather was still predominantly foggy. Cleaning up as splendidly as they were, Morris just couldn't understand why Bobo wasn't more cheerful about it all. The whole thing had been a stroke of genius.

'Happy customers!' he said this morning, showing Bobo a fax announcing a further order. The boy sucked in his cheeks, then shook his head. The situation could not be protracted over the long term, he said sourly. It would become *controproducente*.

They were in the main office with the plastic Crucifixion and a Marilyn Monroe look-alike straddling a Fratelli Ruffoli bottle as it zoomed through a Christmas snow-storm. Bobo sat forward in his leather chair and held a yellow pencil so that one end was between his teeth (also yellowish). His hair was limp on his forehead and thin-ning dangerously – at what? twenty-six, twenty-seven? Morris, full of the kind of blond bounce and enthusiasm he paid so dearly for at nights, felt younger somehow. Also his cheerfulness was morally superior. The divinities surely would have no truck with truculence. Especially from those born with a silver spoon. He sat on the desk beside the computer and actually swung a leg.

Bobo took the fax from him and scowled. There was something theatrical about his head-shaking, Morris thought, as if he had prepared himself for this eventuality and was simply following his script. He had been planning some kind of showdown. For the moment the Englishman just waited, enjoying the feeling of firm flesh tensing and relaxing under good wool trousers as his leg went back and forth. There were moments when being handsome was just an immense plus. And if *he* had found acne lurking around *his* jawline like that, then he would most certainly have done something about it. As he was pres-ently treating the fungus that made the top of his right foot so ugly and itchy. Surely there was a way in which those with money had a duty to make themselves attrac-tive. He would write an essay one day exploring the relationship between aesthetics and morality. Something Aristotelian.

'You need me to translate?' he asked Bobo, still poring over the fax.

'I need you to send a polite fax back explaining that this year's supplies are now exhausted and that any further communication will have to wait until next year's harvest,' Bobo said.

Morris had no difficulty being friendly: 'Look, Bobo, we've made more money in six weeks than in the rest of the year. Why don't you relax?' And he used one of his favourite Italian expressions: 'Don't be such an owl' – meaning a misery. But then this reminded him of Massimina that night in Rome when he had refused to dance. *'Non fare il gufo, Mo, balliamo.'* Her winsome smile, her flashing eyes. 'Don't be an owl, Mo.' So that while savouring the forthcoming tussle with his brother-in-law he was also finding time to reflect on the way that for the sensitive person like himself each and every word – *gufo, genio, artista, vittima* – will tend to acquire its own personal history, its own special echoes, depths, associations. How could other people ever know why you chose the words you did? And Massimina wasn't dead at all. It came to him as a sudden and entirely convincing intuition. She had become part of himself: her voice, her essence, absorbed inside him. As Mother had been too. And Father never could.

Meanwhile his brother-in-law had said something.

'Scusami, no, sorry, I was thinking of something else.' Again he smiled brightly. The fact that he was so relaxed as to indulge in a little absent-mindedness must be unnerving for Bobo.

'I said' – the boy's voice had a whiny petulance that somehow went with the hints of acne – 'I said that if the National Insurance catch up with us on one of any number of counts, not to mention the Guardia di Finanza, they'll close us down.'

Still swinging his leg, Morris asked: 'Why should they catch up with us?'

'Some of the day workers are not happy with the situation. They think it is bad that we are exploiting the immigrants. They think there could be more overtime for themselves. It would only take an anonymous letter . . . We are vulnerable on a wide range of issues.'

Morris did what the last few years had taught him to do in these kinds of conversations: sit tight a moment, pace it. Never blurt. Smile. Let the other betray himself. Though he did object to the word 'exploiting'.

'And some of them don't like blacks in general. They want them out.'

Here Morris suspected that Bobo was referring to himself. 'That's hardly Christian,' he remarked. Without changing tone at all, he added: 'Still, if we do get a visit from the INPS or the Finanza I imagine you can always do with them what you did with the VAT people back in June.'

As he said this he deliberately looked away so as not to capture whatever expression of anger or surprise might be crossing Bobo's face. Or rather, so as not to give Bobo the chance to feel that in not showing anger and surprise he had scored a point. Though it was only in the very moment that he looked away that Morris appreciated why he was doing so. This was extremely interesting. The fact was, Morris was becoming a natural, becoming entirely himself. Instinct and design were somehow one. He couldn't go wrong.

Bobo was trying for an unconvincing imperturbability: 'And what did I do, *prego*, with the VAT people back in June?'

Morris laughed. 'Don't tell me the computer has a better memory than you do.' Then, determined to be friendly to the bitter end, because this really was such a far cry from his hangdog, poor-boy-out-in-the-cold, chip-on-the-shoulder days of some years ago, he protested: 'Really,

Bobo, what's the matter? Is it just because *I* thought of it that you don't like the scheme? Think of something better yourself and I promise I'll go along. But you've got to admit, this is a money-spinner. We're building up the kind of capital that will allow us to expand, diversify.'

But Bobo's stare was fierce. There was a distinct redness about the glassy bead-brown eyes. Almost hatred. Morris realised that rather than it being a question of the boy's not liking the blacks, or the risks, such as they were in a country where to pay tax was to offer oneself up as a laughing-stock, it was simply that his brother-in-law didn't like Morris Duckworth. Indeed he loathed him.

But why? Why? What had Morris actually done not to be liked? He was handsome, affable, charitable, clever. What did these provincial plutocrats want in the end? Hadn't he bent over backwards? Changing tone to something more plaintive, because it was time to show he was hurt, he said: 'And then we are helping these people, you know, Bobo. Those poor young men would be freezing in the cemetery if we weren't looking after them. They were complete outcasts and we've given them a place, however humble, in society. Kwame tells me he is actually sending money home. I mean, it's not just us getting richer, but families in the Third World who really need it. That's why I feel we must continue.' He smiled at Bobo's incredulity. 'Which reminds me, please do thank Antonella for the bundle of clothes she sent.'

Bobo stood up as if suddenly, brusquely coming to a decision. '*Va bene*,' he said. 'OK, two thousand more cases it is.' Then pushing lank hair from his forehead he suggested they go out for a cup of coffee. Morris experienced that sudden twinge of disorientation that came with getting what one wanted. Perhaps the boy didn't hate him after all.

The two put on their coats, left the office, walked past

the dog, now thankfully chained, and drove a kilometre or so to a small bar in Quinto where Bobo made a resigned sort of small-talk, spooning the froth off his cappuccino. Never one to crow, Morris was more avuncular than triumphant over a brioche with custard cream. Even in the dowdiest out-of-town bars, he remarked, the Italians knew how to make a coffee and pastry such as you wouldn't find anywhere in the UK. Not to mention the courtesy of the service, 'an innate sense of the *signorile*,' he added warmly, 'of what *civiltà* really means.' Somewhat overdoing it, he said: 'I really envy you Italians your culture and background, you know. I really do. The English are so inelegant.'

There was a slight pause in which Morris savoured this generous humility. Then Bobo said: 'Speaking of English, did you know that Antonella wants to learn?'

'Oh, I'd be delighted to give her lessons,' Morris immediately came back. 'Delighted.' Clearly it would be churlish of him not to show that he was more than willing to make himself useful. As long as they were decent to him. Give and take.

Bobo smiled, but there was a twist to his pale lips.

'Actually, she's already found a teacher.'

'Fine.' Morris shrugged. 'Fine.' After all, the last thing he wanted was to bore himself stupid again teaching a language he was only too glad to have stopped thinking in. There had always been something constraining about English, as if he couldn't really be himself in it. Then it was hardly likely that the moonish Antonella would be a star student, was it? Let somebody who needed the money have the work.

'A funny sort of person,' Bobo said thoughtfully.

'Oh yes? Good.' Morris just couldn't be affable enough. 'I've always said, a bit of humour's a great help when you're teaching.' The only thing that saved one from death by tedium more often than not.

'And he knows you very well,' Bobo added. 'In fact I think you told us a story about him that night when you came to see us all, with Massimina.'

'Oh really?' But Morris's mind was suddenly racing. Who could it be? What unhappy coincidence was working against him? The planets, the stars, always against him.

'His name's Stan,' Bobo said.

'Oh, Stan!' Morris laughed, but almost choked. 'Yes, Stan Albertini!' God, of course. That was why the dumb American had been toiling up the hill on his stupid bicycle, to see Antonella, who no doubt must have photos of Massimina all over the living-room. He racked his brains to remember. The same Massimina Stan had seen calling Morris from across the platform when he picked up the ransom money at Roma Termini. For a moment Morris felt desperately sick, as if he might just throw up the much-praised cappuccino and brioche all over the marble-topped table. At the same time some automatic pilot managed to get out most amiably: 'Still wearing his kaftan and beads, is he? Not a very good teacher, I'm afraid.'

Bobo got up to pay the bill. 'Maybe not, but he does have some good stories to tell.'

Morris, however, was beginning to get a hold on himself by now and simply let that one pass. If anybody had really known anything he would have been serving a life sentence already.

In gaol rather than out, that is.

CHAPTER ELEVEN

LIKE ANY PHILANTHROPIST, MORRIS liked to visit the beneficiaries of his charity, muck in, have lunch with the boys, ask them if all was well, here in the hostel, over at the factory: conditions of work, pay, food. He particularly liked to perch on one of the window-sills at the villa near Marzana, frugally spooning up a *brodo di verdura* he himself had indirectly provided. He would listen to Farouk's pidgin English, encourage the brave young Ramiz, who had lost parents and sister when their boat capsised off Bari, discuss the disgraceful behaviour of the Serbs with Croatian Ante.

Then if he had time on his hands he might sit patiently through Forbes's presentation of the perfection of Raphael, the decadence of Tintoretto. Raphael had died at thirty-seven. *Ars longa, vita brevis*. Tintoretto at seventy-six. Somehow that was always the way with the great and the not quite so great. Shelley and Browning, for example. In his late sixties himself and never without his flowery ties, Forbes projected slides onto the powdery plasterwork of the sitting-room, where the immigrants lit wood fires using sticks they collected on the hillside above. Still unrepaired, the chimney refused to draw, the hearth smoked. Farouk dozed off, his head on Azedine's shoulder. One of the Ghanaians was whittling something. And as Forbes's plummy voice plodded learnedly on and flame-light flickered over the rich colour of St George slaying the dragon or a Last Judgement, Morris could feel himself quite marvellously part of it all, this curious world he had invented: the underprivileged, art, Italy. His family, almost.

This morning, steering the Mercedes up the foggy track to the house, he told Mimi that, given the mistakes he had made in the past, she could hardly deny he was doing his best to atone. Could she? Which surely was all anybody could ever ask of anybody. Constant atonement for the mistakes one was constantly making. Wasn't that the essence of Catholicism? 'Until the mistakes become the atonement,' he surprised himself by inventing, 'and the atonement the mistakes.' Certainly that was the case with Paola. He made his voice more intimate, more sad: 'Every time I have sex with her it reminds me of you. It's the perfect *fioretto*, a constant mortification. I'm betraying you and atoning at the same time.'

Beyond the windscreen, cypresses and palms in milky whiteness traced out a satisfying otherworldliness, perfect backdrop to this bizarre line of thought. Morris put the phone down as he drew to a halt. A figure loomed suddenly from the fog and leant forward to open the door for him. Kwame, his favourite. Perhaps he should have had the black with him when he went to see Bobo.

'Ah, Kwame! All right?' Morris took the huge meaty arm and squeezed it. There was something wonderfully convincing about the Negro's mere physical presence.

Kwame, however, made it clear that all was not right. Then Forbes appeared in a flurry on the steps. '*Res ipsa loquitur*,' he mysteriously explained. 'The thing speaks for itself.'

When Morris just looked blankly at the foggy house, counting the misty statues on the roof (all still there?), Kwame said: 'It don't speak, man, it stinks.'

He was led across the patio to the edge of the terrace, and now Morris became aware of a fierce stench of sewage in the air. Kwame took him by the arm and steered him away from a dark stain on the paving. Looking over the wall which supported the terraced garden above the road, he was shown two long black and clearly unpleasant streaks dribbling down through patches of ivy and capers.

Morris was upset. As with his own house, no sooner had you got hold of something you'd always wanted than you found all kinds of defects. He was reminded of the roguish builder, a score still unsettled.

'The toilet facilities are unusable,' Forbes said rather primly, as of one who wanted to make it perfectly clear that he didn't feel his duties extended in this direction.

'They is overflowin', man,' Kwame said. 'There is nowhere for us to shit.'

'And unfortunately we are, um, without a phone here.'

Morris paced about the stain where the septic tank must be. Azedine and Farouk came out, the Egyptian boy with a cigarette in his mouth, grimacing and laughing. Certainly the stench was awful, but already Morris's annoyance was fading. For the fact was that ten or twelve people were standing around waiting for him, Morris Duckworth, to act; a dozen people relying on him, on his munificence, his astuteness in resolving the small practical problems that inevitably kept one on one's toes in this life. And just as when he sat with the boys by the fire listening to Forbes talking about Palladio and the re-interpretation of the classical, so now, facing the contingency of a clogged septic tank, he felt at home, and what's more, the head of that household, a role that suited him. He prodded experimentally at a paving stone, as if septic tank diagnosis were one of his many talents. What a long way he had come from the pathetic figure of his childhood, the loner of his youth! In the end, perhaps, it suddenly occurred to him, in the end he might just decide to do without Paola and move in here. That would teach somebody a very big lesson. Doing nothing but watch MTV all day and wanting him to lick yoghurt off her fanny.

Morris the patriarch (though still childless) went over to his Mercedes, took his address book out of a handsome Gucci bag, found the address of the man they had rented the place from, called him and got the number of a local mason who had apparently reorganised the plumbing some fifteen years before.

His adoptive family and the ambiguously avuncular Forbes stood in a motley huddle round the car listening to his calls. Really, it was all most gratifying. '*Sì, subito*,' he insisted, 'at once.'

Then they went in to lunch. There was a huge pan of water boiling away on the stove for the pasta, a great brown carrier-bag bulging with bread on the table. Morris placed his own contributions of a kilo of parmesan and two litres of decent Valpolicella beside it. 'No Trevisan Superiore for us,' he laughed.

The windows steamed. Forbes tied aprons round the giggling young Ramiz, the more solemn Farouk, and began to explain about condiments. A wiry little Senegalese with a surprisingly pointed nose and cracked spectacles scrubbed at the wooden table. From the next room came the wail of Azedine's Moroccan pipes meandering through the kind of tuneless Arab music that has neither beginning nor end, but just a sort of urgent, aimless vitality, so healthy, Morris pleased himself by thinking, compared with that Western obsession for getting from A to B, then on to something else. And as Kwame pulled up the biggest chair for him at the head of the table, he smiled straight into the boy's great, soft African eyes. Indeed, he could have washed the lad's big black feet at the thought of how wonderfully biblical it all was, and how New World too, how marvellously post-imperialist and utopian. Had he been a latter-day saviour, these were just the people he would have chosen as his disciples. Salt of the earth. He didn't even say anything when Azedine came down and lit a fierce cheroot. On the contrary, he almost loved him for it.

'Splendid!' he exclaimed as Ante ladled the pasta. Now he was exchanging warm glances with Forbes. For all the older man's slight woodenness and primness, the curiously stiff way he moved and the occasional impression of suppressed disdain, Morris thought he had never seen him so happy. It was as if looking after these young men had been a kind of revelation to him. Even his usually dusty cheeks had a faint glow to them in the smoky bustle of the kitchen. Perhaps in the end Morris would be able to get him to drop the rich schoolboy business altogether. The upper classes would never have the simple vitality and gratitude these lads had. For a moment he was almost going to ask him to say grace, in Latin perhaps, but then changed his mind.

'Solemn announcement!' he suddenly proclaimed, interrupting the general hubbub. Five or six of the boys were already attacking their pasta, heads down. Morris raised his hands and repeated: 'I have a solemn announcement to make.' The boys looked up, watched him, chewing with unshaven jaws, eyes bright under unkempt hair, woolly or wiry. 'I just want to tell you all,' Morris said very slowly, aware of the language problems, 'how grateful I am. Yes, grateful. The whole project, your living here and working for Trevisan Wines, has been an unqualified success.' He paused. 'To cap it all, we signed a contract today that'll keep you here, fed and paid, for at least another three months. Cause for celebration, I think.'

The Senegalese translated for one of his friends. Kwame's smile was brilliantly white, but for a staining of tomato purée. 'No, everybody thank *you*, boss,' he said. 'Everybody goin' to thank you so much.' Forbes bent to whisper something in Ramiz's ear and the boy beamed.

'Now, as far as the toilet is concerned,' Morris continued, brushing aside the chorus of gratitude, 'the mason is coming about the septic tank at three. In the meantime I suggest we dig a hole in the bushes away from the drive. Anyone who wants to use a proper toilet will have to wait until he goes to work.'

He had said this with good humour and was surprised at the short silence that followed. Ante said darkly: 'What toilet?'

'At work, of course. The one in the bottling plant.'

Kwame shook his head. 'That toilet is locked for us, boss. Mr Bobo say we dirty it. We hide in it not to work. And the cleaners not clean black shit.'

There was another silence, tensed by the irritating click of Azedine picking his teeth with a fingernail. Morris was genuinely shocked, then appalled at the thought that nobody had mentioned this to him before, that they had somehow imagined he was a party to this decision.

'You mean you have to go out in the freezing cold?' he asked.

'But no, there is the *chien*,' the Senegalese said excitedly. 'The *chien, on ne peut pas*.'

'The dog,' corrected Ante. 'We can't go out in the yard. The dog, he eat us before we have our pants down.'

'The dog is a demon,' one of the Ghanaians said. 'An evil spirit.'

'So what do you do?'

Kwame explained: 'We use the bottles, boss, to piss in. And no shit.'

'What, but that's barbaric!' Morris turned to Forbes: 'For heaven's sake, did you know about this?'

'I imagined . . .' the older man muttered vaguely. He

looked more incongruous than ever with pasta sauce spilt on a tie of silk lilacs. '*Volenti non fit injuria*, if you see what I mean.'

Morris didn't. Nor did he have time to ask. He was furious. The heat flooded through his body. That this outrage should have been perpetrated on his boys without his even knowing! He felt the blood throbbing in his neck. Getting up from the table he went straight out of the house to the car and drove at breakneck speed through the fog to tell Bobo that he, Morris, would clean the loos himself if necessary, but this racism had to stop. It was a question of the merest sense of fellow-feeling, the absolutely most basic level of *civiltà*. And when Bobo said that one or two of the day workers had protested at using the same bathroom as a bunch of dirty immigrants, Morris went straight down to the bottling line and talked to the workers one by one at their positions in the din of the machines: four middle-aged and elderly women, a Mongoloid, a younger man with a limp who fixed things when they went wrong, a boy in a wheelchair, and five girls giggling together who couldn't have been a day over sixteen.

In a stupefying steam of wine, the bottles jerking on the conveyor, the cheap plastic tops snapping rhythmically down, Morris had to shout to tell them they should be ashamed of themselves. Hadn't one of the three kings been black? Yet Christ had accepted his gift. Hadn't he told Paul to eat the gentiles' food? Everybody had to be accepted: red and yellow black and white. He could almost hear his mother's voice teaching him the Sunday school chorus now. His mind was buzzing, boiling. Father had been a miserable racist. Of course they knew to do it in the bowl and leave the seat clean. They weren't animals. 'The continuity of your jobs,' he wound up, suddenly determined to punish, 'to a great extent depends on the money we are making from the night shift. These are hard times, and don't you forget it. Other companies are collapsing all around us.'

Then, in his eagerness for her approval, he ran back out to the car to talk to Massimina. Surely she would back him up. He may have been a monster on occasion, he might despise bad taste and obscenity, sometimes he had been guilty of unpleasantness and certainly of rashness, but he had never, never, never sunk to this kind of moral squalor.

He poured his heart out into the phone. Massimina was her usual silent self, yet Morris was not discouraged. He sensed that when the time came she would give him her seal of approval. He was not a man whose affection waned merely because not immediately requited.

On arrival back at Villa Caritas, as Forbes had now christened it, a fat figure in his late fifties, dressed in battered hunting jacket and leggings, was using a pickaxe to pull up the paving. He scratched at the bristles on a square head. He could remember, he said, at least within a yard or two, where they had put the septic tank, though why it should have got blocked, he couldn't imagine. The system had been planned for a family of a dozen and more. It was a big house.

They stood around in a circle, watching the man heave and grunt as he pulled up flagstones. Insects fled like refugees in some aerial photograph. Finally the cement top of the septic tank was uncovered. Kwame and another Ghanaian helped the man to prise it up. They got a plank underneath and slid it away, revealing, in the round hole, along with an amazing and quite overpowering stench, a curious surface of shiny bubble-gum pink, scores of bloated rosy swellings in a brown scum. Everybody stared. Azedine and Farouk exchanged glances. Then the young Ramiz burst out laughing. But the mason was shaking his head. 'You don't,' he said, 'put those rubber things down the toilet. *Va bene!*' Looking up, it was clear his gaze was directed at the two blacks present, as if only they could have been so lascivious and so ignorant. 'Not in the toilet!' he said louder, as though volume might help them understand his fierce Italian. 'Not those rubber things in the toilet!'

'You're joking,' Paola said later when Morris told her this and she laughed loudly. 'Those old peasant guys are so Catholic! I bet he's been crossing himself ever since, thinking of all that sin.'

Well, it certainly seemed to be getting her excited, Morris thought, and he remembered noticing a sort of faint awe on her face the day he had got Kwame to help him up the stairs with a rather attractive eighteenth-century dresser he had bought. '*Bel ragazzo,*' she had said, '*bello grande!*'

They were watching television. The lira was falling, the government debt blossoming, a minor politician had been decapitated in a butcher's shop somewhere down south, a major politician arrested up north. Now the announcer was reading out the names of the referees for next Sunday's first-division games. Apparently, some of the choices were controversial. But Morris was still back there with the devaluation and the public debt. Perhaps he should be getting what personal funds he had into Deutschmarks as soon as possible?

'So?' Paola asked. 'Did anyone own up?'

'What?'

'To the condoms.'

'Oh, I wouldn't presume on their privacy.'

She put an arm round him and kissed a blond cheek. 'I do love the way you talk, Mo.'

Morris found this irritating. Watching an advert now

for a local purveyor of talismans (but how could people be so ingenuous?), he told her that what he found gratifying was that in just a short space of time they had obviously found local girls who had fallen in love with them, who didn't disdain them, the way that unpleasant bunch of cripples and morons at the factory did. The younger generation, he said, seemed more willing to accept diversity, indeed welcome it.

'Mo!'

'What?'

'Mo, you've got to be kidding. No, you're wonderful.'

He was perplexed.

'Mo, those immigrants would never find a girl in a place like Quinto. The country girls never even touch a southerner, never mind a Negro.'

Morris stared. In the flickering light of the TV there was something fearfully will-o'-the-wispish about her. At once sexy and frightening.

'They're doing it with each other, Mo. I thought you'd realised that. The only thing that amazes me is that they have the good sense to use condoms.'

Seeing his bewilderment, she began to giggle hysterically – at his expense, he felt. Then to top it all there was suddenly pornography on the television. *Colpo Grosso* had begun. The strippers' game show. A girl on a red couch was rubbing saliva into her nipples. Morris stood up abruptly.

'Oh, come on, Mo, let's watch, we can compare notes.'

But this wasn't, he said angrily, how he planned to spend his evenings. He'd rather read a book. And he retired to bed with the *Divina Commedia*, which Forbes had ordered him to read. Slow going, but the kind of background one couldn't do without if one wished to be thought cultured in Italy. Closing his eyes half an hour later, the brash music of *Colpo Grosso* still swooning and swanking through poor insulation, Morris wondered what punishment the great poet could possibly have invented that would be bad enough for the likes of Paola and Bobo and . . . and . . . but he was already being raised up into the paradise of sleep. Mimi was Beatrice of course, arms open, beatific, cream-freckled smile.

Of course his boys weren't doing it with each other.

PART TWO

CHAPTER TWELVE

IT WAS TYPICAL OF Morris that he would find around midday or mid-afternoon that he was in a different mood from the one he had imagined he was in, certainly a different mood from the one he had begun the day in, and then he would have to spend a great deal of precious mental effort trying to work out how he had come to be there, inexplicably happy or hopelessly suicidal as he might be. Today, it was while sorting out the little library in his own small office in the town centre, putting the art and photography books in order of period and movement, and then the poetry and novels in order of author (because he thought of the place less and less as an office and more and more as a studio), that he suddenly appreciated that he was feeling immensely cheerful, and this despite the mess he had been reflecting his marriage was, and the not inconsiderable difficulty over the phone with Doorways earlier on about some exploded cases of Superiore. The English were concerned about a suspiciously high alcohol content, but Morris had been able to assure them that it was merely a question of a machine having left too little air space at the top of the bottle. Yes, notwithstanding both the deeper structural problems and the average day's little frictions, he was feeling positively optimistic, and he couldn't for the life of him think why. The morning's conversation with Antonella, perhaps, about whether or not they should insist on the immigrants having a medical check-up every now and then. Her voice had a way of soothing him, he'd noticed that. But hardly to the extent of his jumping for joy. Or the business with the parking ticket he'd avoided by telling the *vigilessa* how much better Italy was than England and how he admired people like herself who did a difficult and generally frowned-upon job seriously. That had been fun. A little exercise of the side of his character he liked best: his charm, his powers of persuasion.

But Morris didn't feel that these things, pleasant as they had been, could account for this sense of what, on inspection, was almost elation. Or if they could, then they shouldn't and there was something wrong with him. Grinning, he filed a copy of Leopardi (doubtless he'd get down to reading all the greats one day) and hoped that when he arrived at the truth he wouldn't feel let down. Like the day he'd caught himself feeling cheerful merely because he'd received a birthday card from his father.

In the event, it wasn't until late afternoon, when he was thinking he might pick up a bottle of something halfway decent for the dinner that evening – otherwise Bobo would be saving pennies by having them drink the company plonk, something Morris had more or less vowed he would never do again (and particularly after this news of the exploding cases) – it wasn't until late afternoon that it occurred to him that what had set his mental weather so fair, was precisely this unexpected dinner with the in-laws. Of course! For although he'd hardly registered the fact during his chat with Antonella, the truth was that this invitation marked a very considerable turning-point. Morris was being invited to a casual family gathering. Not to a formal event planned some weeks ahead and from which he could hardly be excluded, but to a simple informal everyday dinner, the invitation having come in the most relaxed of conversations and at the shortest possible notice. So Morris was being accepted as family and friend, his age-old aspiration and indeed the thing that had attracted him to Massimina in the first place.

The fog early February had lifted. There was an extraordinary crystalline quality to the air now. Everything was sharp horizon, serrated: the pointed cypresses, churches and water-towers in the plain to the south, the splendidly bared teeth of the mountains rising above hills to the north. Then when night fell it was the cut and thrust of bright neon through icy silhouettes and scores of white and yellow holes punched at random in the thick black paper of a winter dark. On his way to Residence La Speranza, Morris stopped at the most expensive florist's Verona could afford.

He thus had a huge bouquet of flowers in his hands when he arrived some fifteen minutes later at the video-controlled gate. That would show them who knew how to be gracious. Plus a bottle of Grigolino and another of Trebbiano, and his face was a wreath of the pleasantest, end-of-the-day, time-for-a-chummy-talk smiles. As he climbed the stairs to their apartment, he decided that when the maid opened the door he must ask her in an undertone to put the flowers in water and say not a word to Antonella – surprise them with his shyness. Since she would mention it of course. Yes.

He knocked. *'Può metter' questi in acqua?'* his lips had already begun to form the request, a delicious candour in his wide-open eyes, when he realised that the face suddenly appearing behind the door was not the maid's at all, no, but a ludicrous photofit combination of goatee beard, hooked nose, and balding pate framed in frizzled curls. A burst balloon could not have deflated more quickly than Morris Duckworth's optimism.

'Hi, kid, how you doin'? Long time no see, hey, pal?'

It was Stan. Stan Albertini. Antonella, apparently, had thought how nice it would be for Morris to have someone 'English' to talk to. As if Morris's Italian wasn't perfectly good enough. As if a Jewish Italian-American could in any way remind him of home. Unless it was that he, Morris, had been invited merely to keep Stan company.

'You must get nostalgic sometimes.' Antonella was smiling at both of them, making no comment on the splendid flowers.

To which Morris could hardly say that the only nostalgia he felt was for the time when he had been in a position to wring the stupid Californian's neck.

And at dinner, with the glass tabletop spangling the candlelight, and the waxed stucco walls flickering back their moneyed pinkness over a white porcelain dinner service, Paola actually flirted with the fool. With Stan! Leaning over so that he could see inside her dress! While Bobo talked politics and economics to him, nodding and shaking his head, taking him seriously even, despite the American's execrable Italian and extraordinary table manners, eating with immense rapidity and asking for seconds of everything in an accent that screamed only-child-in-San-Diego. What did he think about Bush, Bobo asked, about the situation in the Gulf? Could it have commercial repercussions? Questions he never asked Morris. Stan spoke with his mouth full, scratching at obviously abundant chest hair beneath a tattered shirt. His jeans were patched and his wispy hair drifted around his bald spot like weeds in water. Meanwhile Antonella asked the maid to get him some more lasagne since he seemed so hungry, while Bobo thoughtfully poured him another glass of the expensive wine Morris had bought that nobody had as yet said thank you for. Then of course Paola had to join in again and say how much she would like to visit the USA – she had never been, she was sure it must be more fun than England – and Stan, almost spitting pasta as he spoke, started to sing the praises of California and to wave a fork in the air to suggest the various beach activities that could only happen in San Francisco. Paola giggled.

So much, Morris thought grimly, for his arrival into the cosy inner circle of the Trevisan family. So much for his triumph, his initiation! No sooner did he arrive in the sanctum – the expensive antiques tastefully laid out in a sharp geometry of modern surfaces; the intimacy of the family, in the sense at once of commercial venture and the wholesome expression of traditional socio-cultural values – than with a carelessness indistinguishable from cruelty, they allowed that sanctum to be violated by, of all people, stupid Stan, hippy-dippy, bisexual, deep-as-ice-cream Stan. Stan, who had seen him with Mimi, first at the bus-stop in Verona, then at Roma Termini the day he picked up the cash.

Mimi! Suddenly all Morris wanted was to be out of there, to be back home on his own – in the bath perhaps – with his memories. His body flooded with a heat that could find no outlet. His wrists were tense as tense hawsers, holding up some tottering edifice. With a clatter of fork and spoon he pushed away the inevitable tiramisu. Faces that had been politely agog at Stan's description of sunset-lit barbecues by the Pacific surf turned toward him in alarm. Morris hesitated. Glowing with an anger that he hoped would pass as embarrassment, he said he didn't feel well.

'Hey, man!' Stan exclaimed, as if only now remembering he was there. 'You look pretty rough, kid.'

Paola raised wry eyebrows and clearly had no intention of going early. Bobo was stiffly silent in a candlelight that turned his bad skin to polished board. Only Antonella showed signs of genuine concern, wondered whether it mightn't be the pigeons they had eaten, invited him to lie on the sofa. Flustered, Morris refused. He'd just have a glass of water. Because he had thought of a better method of escape. He tried to catch his wife's eye.

But they were talking of holidays now. Antonella, Bobo said, had been thinking of going to Turkey, but perhaps it might be more fun, even though a bit more expensive, to go to California.

Unable to get Paola's attention, Morris reached a foot under the table and managed to bring his ankle into contact with the inside of her calf. This could have been a little risky under a glass table with no cloth, except that the light above had turned the surface to a mirror on their well-fed chatter. He moved his leg up and down. In the space of a second Paola's features froze in surprise, thawed into puzzlement, then were soft with indulgence. For Morris had managed to manoeuvre a little higher so that the ankle was on the inside of the thigh now.

'*Povero piccolo*,' Paola immediately said, 'if you're really not feeling well, Mo, perhaps we had better go home, after all. I don't want to be selfish.'

At the very same moment, Antonella leaned across from the conversation they were having with Stan, and said: 'Oh, of course, you went there too that year, didn't you, Morris?' In the rather unfashionable green dress she was wearing, her big breasts were ample and maternal, reminding him again of Mimi.

'*Scusa*,' he said. 'I wasn't following. I was thinking perhaps I'd better go.'

'Yes, I just remembered, you went to Turkey, didn't you, the summer that poor . . .'

Her voice trailed off. She couldn't say it, though Morris was still numbed with shock that she had said so much.

'Turkey?' he almost demanded, in sudden and total confusion. 'Which summer?'

Stan laughed. 'No, he was going to come with me, weren't you, but he backed out at the very last moment.' Smiling through his silly beard across the table, the American said: 'I guess Morris is a bit of an English aristocrat; he isn't the kind to travel in a microbus.'

'But didn't . . .' Bobo had begun to object. Quick as thought, Morris was giving him one of those narrowed gazes that mean: I have something to explain to you that I can't say in front of Stan. At the same time he realised he could barely breathe.

'Lucky for you you didn't come.' Stan was laughing. 'Because of course we crashed the damn thing. Remember, Mo, kiddo, when we met at Roma Termini, and I had the plaster up to my thighs?'

'Come on, Mo.' Paola had stood up. 'You're looking quite white.' Her face bore that inquisitive admiration of one amazed at another's ability to feign something on behalf of a shared complicity. Presumably she imagined he was going to get his colour back and have his hand in her pants the moment they were out of there.

Morris opened his mouth, but nothing came out. Stan was greedily shoving more tiramisu into his. Bobo was staring. Antonella said lightly: 'Oh, but I was *sure* you'd been to Turkey, Morris. I remember thinking how kind of you it was to phone from Ankara about . . .'

Again she couldn't quite bring herself to say it.

'Yes,' Bobo agreed. 'I distinctly remember you calling from Ankara, when Mimi was missing.'

Morris was suffering from that mixture of horror and speech paralysis that so often filled his nightmares. There was a moment's pause, which Stan's vigorous plate-scraping only tensed. Paola had now stood up herself and obviously couldn't understand why Morris was allowing himself to get engaged in this mindless conversation about when he'd been to Turkey, rather than heading for the door and the sack. So little, Morris thought bitterly, did she care, or had ever cared, about Mimi that rather than putting two and two together her whole miserable brain power was concentrated on her cunt. This bitter reflection seemed suddenly to return him to himself. With one of those sudden flashes of the coolest intelligence and a splendid recovery of composure, like a sailboat jerking upright just before the point of no return, Morris said: 'Yes, I did go to Ankara, of course. Just that I never told you,' he turned to Stan, 'because I thought you might be offended, you know, that I had decided to go, but not with you and all the others. There were one or two of them I couldn't stand.'

'Hey,' Stan began to say, mixing Italian with English, 'you went *davvero*? How about that! But you shouldn't have been *preoccupato*, man. Come on!'

Already Morris could see Bobo losing interest.

'I can't advise it for a holiday, though.' Morris turned back to Antonella. 'The place was really filthy and burning hot and I had my bag stolen. Not to mention the trouble trying to get through to Italy on the phone.'

That should sound convincing, and as if to make it more so a phone did in fact begin to trill somewhere. Bobo pulled a receiver from his pocket. His brow knitted in concern. 'I'll have to take this in the study,' he said. '*Arrivederci*.'

They had all said their hurried goodbyes and Morris and Paola were already on their way out, lifting their coats from the pretentious nineteenth-century wood-panelled coat-hanger in the entrance, when Stan, still stuffing himself at table, called laughingly: 'It was that chick, wasn't it?' He was speaking with his mouth full. 'You wanted to be alone with that chick, the one you were with at the station. Hey, kid, I would have understood. That's so funny you didn't tell me. What do you take me for?'

Morris was just about to run back into the room and throttle the fool, hack him to pieces – because if one was going to serve a life sentence for one murder, one might as well serve it for two, or two thousand, and certainly with more satisfaction – when he realised that Stan had spoken in English. Yes, English. Or his version of it. And the only person in present company who might have been capable of understanding Stan's twangy West Coast drivel, shouting obscure words like 'chick' from a mouth full of mascarpone across a space where people were clattering plates and putting coats on, was Paola, but she already had a hand tightly round him and was steering him to the door. While Bobo had retired to the study with his phone call.

In a joke that was not a joke, Morris called back: 'Careful what you say in front of my in-laws, buddy.' Stan burst into giggles, and then they were out.

'*Caro, caro,*' Paola was all over him on the stairs, 'you sexy thing, faking like that. God! Do you want me to blow you in the car? Come on, let's.' She was already unbuttoning his shirt.

Morris, experiencing a huge wave of relief, felt he might do worse than treat himself.

CHAPTER THIRTEEN

TOWARDS EIGHT THE FOLLOWING morning, somewhere
between Ponte Florio and Verona, a phone trilled in an
expensive car. The driver laid a kid-gloved hand on the
receiver but didn't pick up. He was driving slowly today,
enjoying the glassy clarity of the morning, the firm grip
of expensive gloves, the delightful sense he had had,
ever since walking out of the previous evening's dinner
party, of having defused what might have been a nuclear
device at the eleventh hour and then some. So that he
was able to think that perhaps it was rather fun in the
end to have this volcano of a past which gave life a
grand sense of drama, kept you on your toes. Why did
people live on the slopes of Etna after all? The danger
made life more intense. Just as it could be rather fun
on occasion to have a perverse little hussy like Paola
for a wife, who blew you in the car and then brought
herself off on the leather-clad gear stick. He must check
to see if the thing smelled.

'*Pronto?*' Having let the phone ring a little, he slowly
picked up. It would be Forbes, he thought, with the newly
installed phone at Villa Caritas. Or Bobo with some technical detail. There had been problems with the feed device
on the labeller which could slow down the next Doorways
delivery. Bobo was very strict about warning clients of
possible delays.

'Mo!' His wife's voice at the other end was excited and breathless.

'Paola!' He'd imagined that after last night she wouldn't be up till lunchtime.

'Mo, Mo, listen, Antonella phoned. It seems the nurse has just phoned her. Mo, Mamma's dead.'

'What?' Morris immediately geared down and pulled over to the side of the road, hazard lights flashing. 'The nurse phoned Antonella? But why her? Why not you?'

'*Cristo!*' The voice was exasperated. 'It's no time for worrying about details like that.'

Meaning she didn't want to admit to not having spent the necessary time talking to the woman. Which was what wives did, surely, especially when they refused to study or work.

'Mo, look, you've got to drive over to the house in Quinzano, pay your respects and get the will.'

'I'll come back and pick you up.'

'No, you've got to get over there before Bobo does. So get moving. Don't let him see it before you.'

'Hang on!' A brief glance in the mirror showed the local bus approaching far faster than it should have been. But Morris managed to shoot out in front. If the passengers were thrown off their feet it was hardly his fault. The Mercedes picked up speed and hurtled at the morning traffic.

'But do we actually know where the will is?'

'Well, you can try the writing desk in her little study. But the most important thing is the key to her safety deposit box at the *Cassa di risparmio*. It's in a locket in the bottom of the sewing basket in the corner of the dining-room. The will is almost bound to be in the box. Just get hold of the key so we can go to the bank for the first look, to be quite sure that there's no hokey-pokey.'

Morris hit the horn when a van driver in front didn't move the split second the light changed.

'*Va bene?*'

'Hang on a minute.'

As he was trying to overtake the van, the idiot deliberately accelerated, so that Morris found himself head on with an old Fiat coming the other way. He never flinched. He saw the sleepy felt-hatted face of an elderly peasant fill with shocked surprise, then the car swerved away into the kerb. Glancing in his mirror, he saw the van driver waving a fist. So much aggression in the world just waiting to be awoken! He took the next light on red and turned up on the road that snaked over the hills to the north of the city in a long series of hairpins.

'Mo?'

'Just a little trouble with the traffic,' he explained.

'*Allora, ciao.*'

'No, hang on, what if Bobo's already there?'

'He shouldn't be. He's usually at work at this time, and he obviously wasn't there when Antonella called. You have a head start.'

'But what if he is?'

'You just insist on seeing the will together.'

'It would be easier if you were here,' Morris said.

'But I'm not.'

They signed off. Morris was definitely happy now. The adventure and the new sense of complicity with his wife were invigorating. Perhaps in the end it was a perfect partnership. And he wondered at the speed with which he could change his mind, with which the whole shape of that mental landscape that was his life could be transformed from desert to garden, mountain to plain. What a splendid chameleon he was, a maverick, multicoloured, moody Morris.

He drove hard on the tail of work-bound traffic climbing the hill along the city's sprawling walls. His overtaking was more expert than rash now. He even had the presence of mind to spot a carabiniere a few cars ahead and slow down. Then the phone rang again and it was Forbes.

'Bad moment, I'm afraid,' Morris said. 'I'm trying to get somewhere in a desperate hurry.'

'Ah,' the voice seemed hesitant.

On a steep downslope now, Morris overtook a stream of traffic, then had to brake fiercely for the hairpin where the road met the city's medieval walls climbing up. Tyres shrieked and the car strained on its bearings. Then he was back in the suburbs, but on the other side of town.

'Old woman Trevisan just died,' he explained, then thought that this was the kind of thing his father would have said. Thoroughly coarse. But his father couldn't have been wrong all the time.

'Ah.'

'Yep, I'm going to check out the corpse and the will before Bobo gets there.'

He ran a light on *rosso fresco*.

'Yes, I see.' Forbes was clearly taken aback. 'I'm sorry.'

The line was crackling with interference. Unless the older man was now clearing his throat rather elaborately.

'Hm, it's just that, er, something rather dramatic has happened this end.'

'If it's the septic tank again,' Morris said brusquely, 'the bloke's name is Checchinato. Get it from the directory.'

'No, rather more serious, I'm afraid.'

'Look, keep it brief. I'm nearly there, I'll have to fly.'

'Well, your friend Bobo, er, he dismissed everybody last night.'

'What?'

Morris was too surprised at this turn of events even to be angry.

'He came in in the early hours, it seems, during the night shift, and dismissed everybody. Paid them all off too. The Senegalese boys have already packed up and gone.'

'But what on earth for?'

'I gather there was some kind of argument. Something, er, that's been going on for a while. But, er, nobody seems eager to tell me.'

'For Christ's sake . . . I . . . I . . . What am I going to say to . . .' He was speechless for some thirty seconds, intimidating pedestrians on the crossing by the hospital.

Finally Forbes said: '*Aequam memento rebus in arduis . . .*'

But Morris was in no mood to listen to stupid bloody Latin. 'Let me think!' he interrupted curtly.

'I'm sorry, old chap, I . . .'

'Just tell them,' Morris snapped, 'not to leave until I get there and sort things out. Bobo can't fire people without consulting me. I'm part of the family.'

He hung up.

The road slalomed quite steeply away from the town now to the small village of Quinzano, a huddle of peeling stucco in the icy morning light. Morris drove through the central piazza, ruined by its 1950s war memorial, a vertical panel with a stylised and now weather-stained mosaic of an expiring soldier, the kind of thing a suitably benevolent dictator with the right sort of aesthetic sense (himself perhaps) would have had removed immediately so as to keep Italy the perfect place it very nearly was.

Morris had just about a split second to admire himself formulating this kind of punchy, by-the-way reflection at such a dramatic moment in his life, when he found the narrow road up to Casa Trevisan blocked by a *furgoncino* unloading firewood into a cellar window. He hit the horn, then immediately wished he hadn't. It might be unwise to draw attention to oneself. For though he wasn't actually doing anything wrong, he somehow felt as if he was, or as if he might. Morris shook his head – this kind of neurosis wouldn't get him anywhere. Very deliberately, he hit the horn again. The inevitable grizzled peasant head appeared, expressing the inevitable and infuriating unconcern in a shrug of bovine shoulders. *'Porti pazienza, Signore!'* Five salami fingers were held up to indicate as many minutes. Morris reversed sharply, parked in the piazza and began to walk up to the house.

It was two or three hundred undeniably steep metres. His breath clouded thickly in the glassy winter air. But he was lightfooted, full of energy. Perhaps the walk would do him good, straighten him out. Indeed it was a pleasure to feel the air stabbing deep into the lungs, the blood in one's cheeks meeting the chill head on; the sort of moment (ignoring a barking dog straining its chain) when one congratulated oneself for neither smoking nor drinking in any serious way. He said a jaunty *buon dì* to a woman scrubbing at stains in an outdoor sink. Paola, he thought, would have been left gasping, that was for sure. As likewise his father, for all the macho crap Morris had had to put up with on seaside holidays.

Not for the first time (bending virtuously into an ever-steepening road) Morris reflected on this curious fact: that his wife and his father had any number of things in common, and both seemed destined to torment and provoke him. While Massimina on the other hand had had a great deal in common with his mother, who on the contrary had always soothed. Though the most pertinent distinction of all perhaps was the fact that, whereas the first two were alive, dear Mother and Mimi were dead. Quite dead.

As now Signora Trevisan . . .

The big wrought-iron gate stood on the inside of a hairpin. Walking up here reminded him of that first time he had come to court Massimina, frisky and full of hope, of how he had lied about having a car and said he'd left it in the piazza, when in fact he'd waited almost half an hour for the bus. Well, the time was rapidly coming when he wouldn't have to lie any more, when he might even be able to allow himself a little patriarchal nostalgia for the old penny-pinching mendacious days. Morris smiled the able, maturer-man's smile he had been noticing in mirrors of late.

'*Chi è?*' the nurse enquired through the intercom.

You'd have thought that with the old woman dead and the family obviously on their way up to pay respects, the girl would simply have opened to his buzzing. This instinctive caution on the part of Italians always amazed and unnerved Morris. Feeling unnerved he was also suddenly reminded of what he had momentarily forgotten, the news Forbes had phoned through. With disturbing volatility, he now felt extremely anxious, even alarmed, a thousand miles from the cool self-confidence he had always longed for in himself. What if the will left everything to Antonella, if old Signora Trevisan had never accepted his marrying into the family? Was that why Bobo, knowing somehow of the death in advance, had felt free to fire his boys? Could Morris suddenly find himself without a source of income: a potentially penniless Duckworth with a gauche and good-for-nothing wife?

'*Sono Morris*, the son-in-law.' Other people, he was aware, never needed to explain themselves.

The gates swung open, creaking and clanking, eighteenth-century ironwork forced along by two remote-controlled, electrically powered hydraulic cylinders. It was important to register these things. He slipped through and concentrated on the simple pleasure of his even pace crunching on carefully raked white stones.

The nurse was petite and dark and might have done well to have oxygenated the hair on her upper lip. Sardinian probably. Her small quick hands reattached the chain on the door behind him, surely unnecessarily. In a crumpled green uniform she looked exhausted and attractively fragile, a fragility wonderfully set off by improbably large breasts.

'. . . Towards seven o'clock,' she was saying. 'Or that's when I found her. I must have dozed off for an hour or so. It was a difficult night.'

'I'm sure it was.' Morris respected nurses, their practicality and busy modesty. 'Perhaps you should have phoned earlier.'

'I didn't wish to disturb.'

Crossing the hall to the stair, Morris drank in the fusty smell of polished wood and stone, the splendidly straight-backed provincial conservatism that had so thrilled him on that first visit two years ago: lace doilies, coffin-quality furniture, silver-framed photographs, a great pietra serena fireplace, and then, between drape curtains, the view of a travertine balustrade festooned in dark ivy. Yes, it thrilled him precisely because of its archaisms, its theatricality, as if this was a place for acting in, for being melodramatic, in an entirely conventional, predictable way, and with no more responsibility than a melodramatic actor had. His hands ran up a mahogany rail. They were the sort of carved banisters ghosts laid a white finger on as they walked down stone stairs, or lovers hanged themselves from. The gazebo glimpsed through a small window as they turned the corner of the stairs was a set for a romantic rendezvous, the little writing desk in Paola's old bedroom to the left would have the kind of secret drawers where Signora or Signorina kept an elegant gun, or a will. And it suddenly occurred to Morris that if the more yuppie-minded Bobo was happy in his *Casa bella*-inspired duplex, then he and Paola would move in here themselves! With Kwame as a servant perhaps. There was an idea! It was just the kind of tradition-oozing place he would love his children to grow up in.

The small nurse pushed the door. Morris stepped by her, saw the corpse and drew an audibly sharp breath that must have impressed the girl behind. Again it was the marvellous theatricality of the scene that so pleased him: the waxen, open-mouthed face in the four-poster bed, the knotty, thickly ringed fingers at the end of white sleeves resting quietly on a linen sheet. 'I have to wait for the doctor to come before I can tie up the jaw,' the nurse was explaining by way of apology, but Morris was thinking how Mimi had used to sleep here in the same bed with Signora Trevisan, all her life, right up to the day when she had run away with him. In fact, aside from himself, this dreadfully hook-nosed, sunken-eyed, heavy-fleshed corpse was the only other person on this living earth Massimina had ever slept with. 'Mimi,' he breathed. For a moment he had a vivid mental image of her laid out there, dead on the bed beside her dead mother, but in the rich gowns Lippo Lippi had painted her in, deep blue and red. Not Giotto's *Death of the Madonna* at all. 'Mimi, I shall never forget you,' he said.

'*Mi scusi?*' the nurse asked.

'Er, yes, I have to go downstairs and make a phone call,' Morris said. 'Could you please wait here with her until I come back. I wouldn't like for her to be alone, so, er' – he hesitated – 'so soon.'

'*Sì, signore, anche se . . .*'

'What?'

'Really I should have been off duty half an hour ago.'

'Then where's the other nurse? The day nurse.'

The dark little girl shrugged her shoulders. Her replacement hadn't come. Morris realised with a faint sense of weariness that on hearing the news of Signora Trevisan's death, the first thing one of his well-to-do in-laws must have done was to decide what economies could be made. Reaching his hand in his jacket, the more magnanimous Morris pulled out his wallet, found a hundred-thousand-lire note and pushed it into the girl's hand.

'With my gratitude,' he said gallantly, 'for all you have done for the family,' and he hurried off downstairs. Already he could imagine Kwame in a tight white jacket, crossing the *salotto* with a bottle of champagne on a silver tray held high.

The sewing box was an elaborate varnished wicker basket standing beside rubber plants and heavy antiques in the *soggiorno*. Inside, amazingly, amongst cotton-reels and an armoury of needles – some long and suggestively curved, others thin and brightly fragile – was a wodge of threadbare underclothes that needed patching and darning. Morris marvelled. This interminable thriftiness of the provincial prosperous! He would never get over it. Searching for the locket, he pulled out a girdle on its very last legs (as it were), elastic parting company with cotton, then a pair of dull pink panties sad with years of service and irretrievably crotch-stained, a hole half sewn up with needle stowed sideways where the material doubled to absorb what it must, as if she'd been doing just this when the first stroke struck.

Non fortuna sed labor indeed! But for what? He shook his head over an ample bra, the strap almost worn through, and was aware now of a curious sense of arousal. His hands lingered for a moment on the lifeless fabric – surely it couldn't be less sexy. But it had to do with Mimi again, with the fact of her having slept so smooth and fragrantly young beside the sagging flesh of that elderly woman. He pushed a fist into one of the cups, knuckle for nipple, and stared, remembering how Mimi too had been dreadfully parsimonious those first days of their flight, until he had taught her how to spend. Then the first thing she had wanted to buy was new underwear, because her own was grey almost, and rough. Could it have been simply the luxury of new underwear that had finally made her decide to make love to him?

Certainly Paola never skimped in that department.

And now he was remembering the moment when he had packed up her clothes in the pensione in Rome, on the way to pick up the money, how he had wished he had time to try them on, at least her pants and bra, so as to savour somehow the difference between them, himself and Mimi, man and woman, what it must feel like to have a girl's young body, the breasts, the crotch space . . .

But he mustn't let his mind wander like this, pleasurable as it might very well be. Morris rummaged. There was the locket: a small puff of gold on a broken chain. Good! He fiddled with the clasp, then drew a sharp breath. Paola hadn't told him that along with the key there was a photograph of Massimina inside, tinily girlish, poignantly creased in a frame that was too small. 'Mimi!' Would it never end! Oh, for Christ's sake! Banish these thoughts! Morris shivered, grabbed the key, then the underwear too, and thrust the both of them in his pocket.

Yet the sense of her presence here in this house, this room, was overwhelming now. Her perfume too, the perfume she used to use. No! That was impossible! All at once his senses seemed to flood toward fullness, an alertness rising under such surprised pressure it bubbled over into confusion. The room was full of her perfume. His body knotted in tension, but trembling.

Then her voice said: 'Morrees?'

He closed his eyes. His knees almost gave as he rose to his feet, ready to embrace her in any form. In any form. For he had always known this moment must come some day. When they would see each other again, when they would look each other in the eye and know each other in some new and deeper way. Turning slowly round, he found Antonella standing by the sofa behind him, a puzzled look on her face.

How the hell had she got in with the door chained?

For a moment he was a rabbit trapped in torchlight, frozen and desperately disappointed.

'Morrees,' his sister-in-law repeated. She was dressed in black, which oddly made her look rather smarter and younger than she usually managed. Morris pulled something of himself together.

'Paola, er, she phoned me in the car. You know, I came to pay my respects. The nurse is upstairs. Oh, and she asked me to get this key. She, er, thought we should open the safety deposit box in case there were any papers that needed dealing with in a hurry.'

He felt desperately squalid saying this. Certainly it was not part of the elegant, tasteful life he had meant to lead. Not to mention the discomfort of sweat trickling down the small of his back, between his buttocks. And could this really be the same perfume Mimi had used? Baruffa. Sweet and dirt cheap in a trite red box. Paola used Givenchy.

Antonella stood there, perhaps two yards away, a stern puckering about her mouth, as though to show a child she was more sad than angry.

Morris faltered: 'We, we, er . . .' How had the woman got in? Through garden gate and back door? This was unfair.

Quite unexpectedly, Antonella took two steps, opened her arms, burst into tears, and embraced him. She sobbed and sobbed, so that for the first time Morris now had the third and eldest sister's body pressed tight and trembling against his own.

'*Terribile, terribile!*' she was weeping. 'It's so awful. *Povera Mamma, povera povera Mamma*, I'll feel so alone without her, so alone.'

Morris held her, recovering a little of his confidence. And it *was* Baruffa! When Bobo could perfectly well have bought his wife a gallon of Chanel every day had he only had the class! Suddenly he felt deeply endeared to this woman, his sister-in-law, to the quality of her grief. He squeezed her shoulders reassuringly and his soft voice told her that perhaps this was all for the best. It was a miserable existence Mamma had been leading the last year or so.

Antonella only wept the harder. Morris could see no way he might in all decency go and check the writing desk in the next room. However, what mattered was that he was here in case anybody else tried to check it.

'It reminds me,' he said, tucking her face into his neck, 'of when I lost my own mother.' Rather unwisely he added: 'I felt so angry with the world.'

Antonella was calming down. She detached herself, fumbling for a handkerchief in her sleeve.

'Why angry?' she asked.

Of course it wasn't a real request for information, more part of the process of moving from tears to snuffles, from outburst to self-control. There was no need for him to answer. All the same, and perhaps to recover some of the dignity he felt he had lost in being caught rummaging for safety-deposit-box keys the moment the head of the household expired, Morris responded truthfully: 'Because it seemed so unfair to take away the person who mattered most to me and brought out the best in me.'

Even more unwisely, he added, and there was a catch in his voice now: 'Like when Massimina died.'

Antonella looked up. There was a soft spark of recognition in her eyes, of appreciation. '*Sei molto dolce, Morrees*,' she said quietly. 'Very sweet. I'm so glad you are here. Bobo said he couldn't come for a while. He says he has a problem at the office, but it's so mean of him, I think. I was just dreading having to see her on my own.' She wiped her tears. 'Will you come up with me?'

Taking her arm as they crossed to the stairs and getting

another wave of her perfume, Morris once again sensed his old lover's presence. It was almost as if the girl were breathing lightly on his neck from behind as they walked. He felt full of emotion and tenderness, yet it was precisely this intensity which gave him the presence in another part of his mind to remark: 'I suppose Bobo is responsible for getting in touch with the lawyer about the will and so on.'

'The will?' Antonella asked.

'I'm thinking of the company,' Morris lied. And invented: 'I think we're legally obliged to register change of ownership within a certain time.'

'The will?' Antonella repeated. She was clutching his arm very tightly as they turned the corner of the stairs and approached the bedroom. 'Don't worry, Bobo's got it in the safe at home. He'll sort it out.'

'*Bene*,' Morris said. And was furious. Why hadn't Paola known this? How careless! How ingenuous! And how could this charitable, right-feeling, sensitive woman be so incredibly blinkered as not to see through the machinations of her uncharitable, insensitve, wrong-feeling husband! It was unforgivable! As it was unforgivable in the end that his own mother had married his father. How could it have led to anything but disaster? Himself. His useless, pitiable, beaten self! He could have smashed the plaster Madonna on the window-ledge at the turn of the stairs to smithereens. These stupid, inappropriate images of piety! When the truth was that Bobo had no doubt walked off with everything!

'*Grazie*,' Antonella whispered. She had interpreted the involuntary tightening of his arm around her as his caring response to her trepidation. '*Grazie, Morrees*.'

Leaving all self-respect behind (and they were right by the door now) he asked bluntly: 'I presume everything was left equally to both daughters.'

But Antonella, at the thought of what she was about to have come home to her, was beginning to cry. Morris reached out for the handle, pushed the door and repeated quite brutally: 'I presume she left everything equally to both daughters. *Vero?*'

Antonella looked at him through tears with alarm in her eyes. She seemed to be having difficulty even focusing on his face, never mind understanding what his lips had uttered.

'Equally? *Ma sì!*' she finally said. '*Sì, certo.* Mamma never showed any favouritism to any of us.' Turning away, she burst into tears again. For the door had swung open, revealing, as they walked in, the old woman's now ghoulish profile, nose unnaturally prominent as if thrust upwards from the fast-sinking pallor of the cheeks, mouth still agape. The effect was of something at once malign and pathetic. '*Mamma!*' Antonella wailed, and covered her face with her hands. '*O Mamma, cara!*' The nurse turned respectfully away. Morris soothed his sister-in-law with gentle arms and soft voice, elated.

CHAPTER FOURTEEN

WALKING DOWN TO THE square, Morris Duckworth could have hugged the old peasant still offloading his wood into the cellar window half an hour on. Oh, this Wedgwood-blue sky, these sharp, sharp horizons of cypresses and campanili, the silver green of the olives and rose pastel of pitted stucco! Italy, oh Italy! Tiled red roofs and Roman walls higgledy-piggledy in a sparkling Ferrarelle distance! He stopped and breathed deeply. In a yard below the curving road a shawled woman swept at cobble-stones with a twig broom while hens clucked about her. '*Buon giorno!*' Morris shouted down. '*Buon giorno!*' he called to a felt-hatted relic of the peasantry fighting his way up the hill with a stick, dead cigar clamped between wrinkled lips. A dog barked, joyfully it seemed despite its chain, and the bus down in the piazza honked gaily to announce imminent service. Upon which sharp and sudden sound, a cloud of sparrows rose from intertwined persimmon trees. Orange fruit quivered against shiny black bark. Then smells of wood smoke on the breeze. Yes, God is in His heaven, Morris thought, and all is right with the world.

Or rather, Morris was in his heaven. Or Morris was God? In the sense that he was in everything and everything was in him: the delicious wood smoke, the grimly whole-some faces of the peasant folk, the winter tracery of the vines, the pitted road. In everything and accepted by it, as he reciprocally accepted everything. Wholly himself, exactly as he overflowed and emptied into everything else. Rich now and thus free to be happy and generous, a rightful heir to the wide world's abundance.

'Mimi?' As soon as he was in the car, he lifted the phone again, and the number to dial for her, he suddenly decided, was 321 for the circles of the Inferno backwards, then 789 for the slow prosaic ascent of purgatory, and at last a single zero, which was the mystical shape of perfection, of the crown that excludes everything profane – the garland of a soul in paradise. And the shape of a kiss too, her full lips forming a perfect round.

'Mimi, yes,' he got through almost at once, 'no, sorry, I'll have to be dreadfully brief. I just wanted to say thank you. I mean, I know you've been helping me. I know I owe this to you, this inheritance, your inheritance. I want to promise that the money, your money, will be used to help others, to make other people's lives that much happier. I know it is your sign that I must stay with Paola and the company, to point them in the right direction. Thank you, Mimi, thank you.'

Morris shifted on the white leather seat in the stationary car, smiled indulgently at loud adolescents reading *La Gazzetta dello Sport* at tables outside the bar, buzzed down the window to let in some fresh air, then dialled again: the more arbitrary code for England this time.

'Dad? Yes, Dad, it's me.'

There was the problem with this call, of course, that the old man could and no doubt would answer back, that one couldn't, as it were, simply deliver the *fait accompli* of one's message and escape untainted.

'Me, Morris!'

There was a sharp groan. 'Christ, what time is it? Do you realise what bloody time it is?' Morris had forgotten the hour's difference. Still, it was eight-thirty here. He said contritely: 'I thought you were an early riser, Dad. I wanted to catch you before you were up and out.'

There was a fairly long and, at cellular-phone rates, decidedly expensive silence. 'God, Christ, no, heavy night on the boozer, you know. Bugger me, what a razzle!'

Behind the exaggerated tones of morning-after suffering, Morris immediately picked up the bragging subtext: Here I am still living a real man's life, even in retirement, which is more than my wimp of a son ever managed. But rather than irritating, let alone humilating him, as it might have in the past, the mature Morris found his father's misplaced bravado almost endearing. The way one might be endeared to a dog's wagging pride at having stupidly retrieved a flung stick from filth.

'Dad,' he said, at his most demurely respectful. 'I just wanted to say that Paola and I will shortly be moving into a rather larger, er, residence, so if you'd like to come and visit in, say, a month or two, please do feel free.'

Sipping whisky on the wistaria-draped terrace of Casa Trevisan, it would be somewhat difficult for old Mr D to continue to think of his son as a failure.

Nothing. The radio connection crackled.

'Meantime' – for some reason Morris's accent always moved sharply up-market when he talked to his father, as if in necessary compensation – 'meantime, if your pension should need topping up at some point, please don't feel ashamed to ask.'

When his father was still silent, Morris added: 'I was saying to Paola only the other day, I think you've worked hard enough in your life to deserve a comfortable retirement.'

'Oh, bloody Christ!' his father immediately objected. 'Aren't we la-di-da!'

Morris reflected that the man's expletives had never been anything but repetitive. Even in his coarseness there had never been anything to admire. Perhaps that was where he and Paola parted company.

'Beg pardon?' he asked. Pretty well hamming it now. Riding the crest.

Another expensive crackle, unless the man was belching.

'I've said it before' – his father now sucked in catarrh – 'and I'll say it again: it was the ruin of you when your mother wouldn't have it any other way but to call you Morris. The ruin. I could never take a person seriously that got himself called Morris.'

How remorselessly his father always played on this imagined transfer of femininity from mother to son! Morris, however, had skin scaly centimetres thick against this kind of assault now. He fingered the satisfyingly bulbed head of the gear stick and waggled it affectionately, in complete control.

'Well, Dad, the invitation is quite serious, I can assure you, and ditto the offer of funds if you should find yourself in a spot of difficulty. I just wouldn't like you to think,' he added quickly, 'that your son had, er, abandoned you in your old age.' Then before his father could object to this nail so elegantly whammed into his coffin, Morris finished: 'I'm afraid I'll have to leave you to your aspirins and raw eggs now. I've got a pretty busy day ahead of me here.' With fingertip pressure on a delightfully oval button, violet against the subtly contoured whiteness of the receiver, he cut his father off, sent him plunging back down into the outer darkness of east Acton, surely at least the second circle, if not worse.

Then the phone began to ring, or rather trill. Morris looked at it, but decided that Paola perhaps deserved to wait a little longer for the good news. He got out of the car and, jingling various important keys in his pocket, sauntered over to the bar, sat at a table beneath the pergola and, doing his best to ignore the dying soldier in grimy mosaic across the piazza, ordered a cappuccino and brioche.

'Sprinkling of cocoa on top, *per favore*.'

Quite pixily pretty, the waitress, he thought, despite a down-market tightness of the skirt on plump thighs. Nice. And there was something most voluptuous about deliberately wasting time like this when he should have been rushing off to tackle Bobo over this firing business. Bobo, who hadn't even had the good grace to go and pay his prompt respects to his dead mother-in-law. Well! Mmm. Morris savoured time's passing to the taste of sweet coffee in his mouth. With any luck the boy would actually be intimidated by the unexpected delay, for he must be expecting his brother-in-law to rush out there in a rage.

The brioche had apricot marmalade inside, which was pleasant enough. Morris politely had himself passed the local paper. He decided he would not think about his acned in-law at all. No, he wouldn't plan any strategy or even remotely speculate on the coincidence of this unpleasantness of Bobo's firing his boys, his family, cropping up the very night Signora Trevisan had died, the very night after their little dinner party. Because he was home and dry now, co-heir, through Paola, of the whole estate, on absolutely equal terms. If the government had had to devalue the lira again, as the newspaper's headlines made plain, then who gave a tinker's curse (not to stoop to his father's language)? Who gave a beggar's tithe (that was good)? Because exports to Doorways (prices quoted in sterling) would only be all the more profitable. Indeed, Italy might well be witnessing the birth of a great new commercial empire. The truth was that every magnate played hard and fast to begin with, then little by little became respectable as wealth snow-balled and culture followed in its wake.

Morris felt he was already on the home straight. Soon

it would merely be a question of learning how to accept congratulations with the right poise and grace.

Driving back around the north of the city, sedately now, he called Paola at his leisure with the excellent news.

'Everything equally? Are you sure?'

'Sure I'm sure. I mean, the way she said it, it was as if it was something everybody had known for years. Written into the natural order.'

'Mo,' there was a brief pause, then his wife's voice had thrilled to a whisper, 'Mo, I'm going to give you hell tonight. That's a promise. I'm going to make somebody's cock pay and pay and pay for being so rich and fat. Oh, this is such good news!'

Very casually, Morris suggested: 'So, how about making love in her bed?'

'*Cosa!* Whose?'

'Your mother's.'

'Mo!'

Finally, he thought, he had gone one better than her.

'Antonella's going to have the coffin set up in the living-room, for the wake. Somebody's going to have to spend the night there. Our turn to show filial respect, I think. All we have to do is change the sheets.

Paola appeared to hesitate. 'You know, sometimes you're really strange, Mo. I mean, what turns you on.'

'I could say the same of you sometimes,' he said evenly. But what he was thinking was how Mimi had said the exact same words into his dictaphone shortly before she died: '*Che strano che sei, Morri, che strano!* How strange you are sometimes!'

Suddenly he felt desperately excited by the idea that he would be making love in the bed she had always slept in, right where he had felt her presence most strongly. Putting his hand in his jacket pocket, there was the underwear that must have been hers. He clenched it tight in his fist.

'*Va bene, caro mio,*' Paola was saying. '*Va bene*. Mamma was always so strait-laced about sex. Let's do something really outrageous. It'll be like a revenge.'

It would also be the first step in getting his wife to agree to move in there, Morris thought, when he thankfully got the phone down. Or maybe he could even get her pregnant tonight. Hole in the johnny job. Why not? His instincts were so perfectly honed today, it was as if he were snipping out the future with a pair of new scissors (in leather-gloved hands). He would be so thrillingly erotic, he'd be able to get her to agree to anything.

For a moment Morris wondered whether, if he let go of the steering wheel and just closed his eyes, the car wouldn't all the same take him exactly where he ought to be going, so in tune did he feel with the universe round about, the stars, the circling spheres.

CHAPTER FIFTEEN

MORRIS DROVE UP THE Valpantena, turned off at Quinto and pulled in at Villa Caritas. But a sense of urgency was returning now and it wasn't a moment for hanging around and listening to Forbes spouting Latin, however appropriate his maxims might mysteriously be. Fortunately, he found Kwame sprawling on the swing couch in the cold sunlight. Morris told him to put out his cigarette and hop in at once, then immediately was reversing fast back down the drive to the gate. Not that he needed company, quite the contrary, but Kwame, he felt, was the kind of presence who could only be persuasive.

Why had Bobo acted like that?

The bottling plant was humming. The dog was on his chain. So successful was Morris feeling this morning, so sure that everything could simply be worked out by forthright expression of commonsense and legal entitlement, that he decided he might not poison the brute after all. 'Here, Volfi!' he called to the creature, though he had no idea what its baptismal name might be. 'Here, Volfi-Volfi!' He held out a hand as if to caress.

But there must have been something in Morris's voice, genuinely friendly as he meant to be, that gave him away, something that irritated or mocked, as if he could never quite convince anybody, even the dumbest animal, of his good intentions. The same way, despite a certain blond charm and handsome suavity, he had never in the end managed to persuade anybody to give him a regular job. In response to his blandishments, the animal leapt to the furthest reach of its chain, went up on its hind legs, pawing, then bayed quite horribly in a red-grey slaver of teeth and strangled fur. Kwame cowered back, clearly frightened. Morris stood just beyond the animal's range, smiling. In the end, given the robustness of the chain, it was not the kind of relationship one need feel unhappy with.

'Evil, man,' Kwame said. 'He got an evil spirit in him, that dog.'

Morris was wondering if Bobo would put up the same display of animosity, despite the now established chain of legitimate inheritance. With an expression that he hoped balanced sobriety and insouciance while still catching the essential, willing-to-help-but-determined-not-to-sell-himself-short Morris, he pushed open the office door without knocking.

Bobo was on the phone. The unpleasant boy sat round-backed over piles of neatly clipped, tissue-pink-and-blue papers marshalled across the gun-metal desktop in the prosaic glow of the AppleMac. With his correct but, for an Italian, ill-cut suit and one hand both holding the receiver and tugging the lobe of a protruding ear while the other scribbled figures in blunt pencil, the whole scene (right down to the Fratelli Ruffoli bottle squidged between a model's sunbathing buttocks) reeked of tawdry commerce, seemed impossibly far removed from the tasteful setting of yesterday evening's dinner. Morris, thought Morris, would move all the company's offices into the centre of town and spruce them up; that designer look of lush efficiency Italians were so good at. Some expensive furniture from Milan perhaps.

Into the receiver, Bobo was apologising to Antonella

for the fact that he wouldn't be able to make it over to see the corpse for at least a couple of hours. There was a crisis in the factory, he said, raising mousy eyebrows towards Morris (the eyes themselves had the dull beadiness of teddy bears and stuffed birds). No, no, he would explain later. But he certainly wouldn't have stayed out half the night for nothing, would he? A crisis was a crisis.

Sensing that if he seemed too deliberately to be waiting for his brother-in-law to be polite enough to cut his conversation short, he would begin to feel edgy and humiliated, Morris launched into ostentatious chatter with Kwame. In English.

'Everybody OK back at Villa Caritas?'

Kwame kept his voice low. He seemed nervous. 'Everybody pretty black, man.'

Morris chose not to pun on this.

'Yes,' he said, making no concessions to Bobo's phone talk. 'Forbes did sound rather upset about it all on the phone. But don't worry, it'll all sort itself out.'

'He is just *wild* with Azedine, man!'

'Who?'

'The old fellah.'

'Forbes? With Azedine, why's that?'

'I thought you would know that, boss.'

'Not at all.'

Only now did Morris realise that he had spent the ten minutes driving over here without asking one useful question, so mentally busy had he been bobbing about on the geyser of his euphoria, enjoying the vertiginous view from the summit of a frothing pile of imagined money.

'Tell me,' he said, with mature concern.

'Man, that Azedine, him and Farouk, that was the old man's special friend . . .'

But the moment the phone clattered down, Bobo's

voice was a shrill bark: 'I want that dirty Negro out of here. *Maledetto!*'

Morris was shocked. If there were moments when he reasonably felt that other races were inferior, he would certainly never have expressed his feelings so coarsely.

'Out!' Bobo said peremptorily.

'But why? I want him *in* here.' Then Morris said: 'Actually, now that Signora Trevisan has passed on and I'm to become, er, a full partner, I've decided to train Kwame up to be my personal assistant.'

Bobo stared. Why, Morris thought, why wouldn't this wretched boy's elder brothers just die, so he could go away and run Daddy's chicken empire? Something about his plucked beadiness made him painfully suitable. Morris added: 'Frankly I find racism detestable.'

'I said I want that Negro out of here and off the premises.'

Kwame looked uncertain.

Morris said: 'Don't worry, just wait for me outside the door. I won't be long.'

As the tall figure slipped out there was the sound of furious barking again.

'Vicious brute,' Morris remarked, but if he had hoped for a vague ambiguity as to whom this might refer, it went over Bobo's head.

'And I want you out too,' his brother-in-law said. 'Do you understand? I want you *out*.'

The rich boy had obviously been tensing himself for this confrontation. He was both seething and determined to be cold. Probably he was confused too, Morris thought, by what had apparently been a long night.

Still, there was no denying that one had been caught very much by surprise. Morris decided to sit down on a swivel chair by the other desk. He did a complete 360-degree turn, collecting his thoughts. Had Antonella been wrong about the will? Was that possible? Or had Bobo destroyed it, and produced another? Taking possession of the whole estate, he was simply kicking Morris out. But it seemed improbably melodramatic and nineteenth century.

'Tell me about this crisis we've got on our hands,' Morris said reasonably.

Again Bobo was staring at him. Their eyes met, Morris's a clear, innocent, well-slept blue, Bobo's small, red-rimmed. The Englishman felt almost sorry for his brother-in-law and decided to forgive all this unpleasantness just as soon as it had blown over. Bobo opened his mouth. He was obviously having trouble expressing himself. Embarrassed perhaps?

Morris became even more accommodating.

'Just tell me why you fired the entire night shift. Did they do something awful?'

Bobo drew breath. 'You will have to leave the company,' he said. 'I don't want you here. Or your crazy ideas. I'd be grateful if you would leave the room now.'

Morris was perplexed. 'But why did you fire them?' he repeated. 'Any disagreement between ourselves is one thing, but they're quite another. They need the money. It's life or death to them.' He felt that swell of strength that comes from moral rectitude. Not only was he more handsome than Bobo, he was also better, as a person. Certainly the pornographic calendar would have no place in the offices he envisaged. Had he put anything of that nature in his own little cubby-hole in town? Certainly not. Immediately he decided he would terminate the rent contract this very day and move into somewhere more salubrious, or just work from his new Quinzano home.

Bobo sighed. 'When I came in last night, two of them were using this office for obscene acts.'

It was Morris's turn to stare. 'What do you mean, obscene acts? And why did you come here anyway?'

'*S'inculavano,*' Bobo said brutally. 'They were giving it each other up the arse.' He laughed.

Morris didn't know whether to be more shocked by the coarse way his brother-in-law expressed himself, or by what he claimed had happened.

'Who?' he demanded.

'What does it matter?'

'Of course it matters. You could have had those two fired immediately and I would have chucked them out of Villa Caritas and that would have been the end of it. I agree entirely to firing the two you found.'

'They're all the same,' Bobo said flatly. 'That's why the staff didn't want them to use the toilet. All queer. They've probably got Aids. It was time for them to go. I've had enough of this farce.'

Morris was furious, but at the same time pleased to have at least discovered that the problem was nothing more than die-hard provincial racism of the most ignorant variety. He could just about believe the story about the couple in the office – and it occurred to him that this must have been what Kwame meant when he talked about Azedine and Farouk – Forbes was obviously furious with the Moroccan for perverting a minor – but the idea that they were *all* queer, or just in some way dirty, was simply ridiculous, nothing more than the kind of prejudice that had once made his father accuse him, Morris, of being homosexual simply because he read a lot of books and went to art galleries. Again, however, Morris decided to be understanding. He was eager to reach a compromise. Ten minutes and everything would sort itself out. He could relax and celebrate.

'Listen, Bobo,' he suggested. 'Early this morning, Signora Trevisan died. From what I have frequently heard from Paola, and Antonella for that matter, the family business is being left equally to the two sisters. Given that they're not interested in running the show, it would thus seem to be up to us two to do the job on equal terms. Only last night we were happily having dinner together after all. Weren't we? And I must say that I for one enjoyed myself. In the circumstances, then, don't you think that rather than making any hasty decisions it would be wise to finish this contract and then assess the situation?'

'You will have to go,' Bobo repeated. 'And since you're going they may as well go too.' His fingers drummed nervously on the desk. Clearly there was something he couldn't quite decide to blurt out.

Morris became almost avuncular: '*Caro,*' he said, 'I can appreciate that you don't really like me, but from a legal point of view . . .'

Bobo suddenly thrust back his chair. He moved quickly, with the purposefulness of someone who has just changed tack. 'I didn't mention,' he said nervously, going over to the kind of depressing grey filing cabinet which Morris would very soon be replacing, 'why I came to this office in the middle of the night. Did I? Not something I do every day.' He squatted down and from the very back of the bottom drawer pulled out a file.

At last Morris appreciated that something was very seriously wrong. It came not as a vague fear, but as total and desperately sudden conviction. From the base of his spine, heat began to pump up through his body. As on the evening before, the tension in his wrists was suddenly as if wires had been strung to breaking point.

Bobo returned to his desk. Without looking up, he said: 'Last night Stan said you didn't go to Turkey with him that summer.'

'Yes, but, as I explained, I went on my own.'

Bobo snorted. Reading upside down, Morris now managed to decipher the heading typed on the file the boy had got. Immediately, the heat in his bowels dissolved to shivers, then came surging back to scorching point. MASSIMINA TREVISAN. This simply wasn't fair!

Bobo opened the file. 'After you so, er, precipitately left, I asked him what date it was he says he saw you at the station in Rome.'

Morris pretended puzzlement.

'He said it was sometime in late July.'

Bobo looked up. Morris was quite rigid.

'So?'

'So, I have a note here in the diary I kept then in which I record a phone call from you in Ankara on August 2nd, more than a week *after* the ransom was paid and only the day before Massimina tried to speak to her mother but was cut off.'

There was a pause which Morris chose not to fill. His mind was as if scurrying around a holed ship. Could it be repaired, or had the moment come to trust himself once more to waves and storm?

'Stan said that you . . .'

'I can't quite see what you're trying to imply. As I said, I went to Turkey on my own. Having decided not to go with Stan, I told him I hadn't gone at all, so as not to offend him. As for the date when we ran into each other in Rome, you can't honestly expect a cretin like Stan to remember what day of the month it was.'

Bobo waited a few seconds. 'He also said he remembered you were with a girl. Somebody he'd seen you with before in Verona.'

Even as he spoke Morris had already reflected that presumably not a word of this had been said to Antonella, otherwise she would hardly have been so pleasant this morning.

'I'm sorry,' Morris repeated, 'really, but I can't see what any of this has got to do with anything. It's perfectly normal to run into people at a railway station. They are

137

nodal points. People have to pass through them. And yes, I think I was in company with a girl, but just somebody I'd met on the train, not from Verona.'

Bobo rubbed a hand over his chin. Both elated and grim, acne inflamed in pale cheeks, it was as if he wasn't listening to Morris at all. He didn't need to. Making a deliberate effort to keep his voice calm, he said: 'I didn't actually see it all at once, you know, while we were talking, I mean the way it fits so perfectly, but later on everything clicked. I came straight over to the office. I've been here since four.'

Morris shook his head. 'I don't know what you're talking about.' He tried an incredulous little laugh, but it came out painfully forced, and thus became a giveaway. The blood now flushed right to the surface of his face. Why – he ground his teeth – why had nature bestowed so very little talent on him in the way of dissimulation? And how on earth could he have imagined he'd got away with last night merely by saying he had been to Turkey, but not with Stan? Ridiculous complacency. What an idiot he had been not to stay on till the bitter end of the evening, so as to be able to counter and neutralise anything the American came out with. Christ! 'Be sure thy sins will find thee out,' he heard his mother's old warning. Directed at Father, of course. Suddenly he hated himself. He was completely useless, pathetic. No, he was a wretched, miserable, beaten Morris. He deserved to go to prison. And if he had the courage to hang himself there, well then, so much the better.

It was then that her darling soft voice said: 'No, Morri.'

'. . . Of course, the ransom was placed on the Milan-Palermo espresso,' Bobo was saying. 'I put it on the train myself, in a brown holdall on the luggage rack of the most forward first-class compartment. That was July 23rd. Right around the time Stan was talking about. And the

Milan-Palermo espresso stops in Roma Termini, *non è vero*. The money could have been picked up there. Then her body was found in Sardinia. And of course the train from Roma Termini goes straight to Ostia and the ferry.'

'No,' she said. There was her perfume again and, as it were, the swishing of a dress against his leg. '*O, ti amo, Morrees*,' she cooed. '*Sei così dolce*.' He closed his eyes on the sweetness of hearing it. Mimi! At last, her voice, unbidden, not ventriloquy. He was barely listening to his brother-in-law now.

'So I came along here to look at the file. Because I kept copies of the ransom letters, of course. I thought I might compare the handwriting. With yours.'

'But they weren't in handwriting,' Morris murmured, as if in a trance. '*Ti voglio*,' she was saying. 'I want you, want you, want you. *O, Morri*.'

'No,' Bobo said, 'no, they weren't. I'd forgotten. But how would you know that?'

There was a long silence in which the hum of the bottle factory became hypnotic.

'Because I wrote them, of course.'

'*Caro, caro, caro*,' she whispered. Just as when she had sat above him. Her tight stomach and big maternal breasts.

Bobo was staring.

'You see, we wrote them together.' From under the deep ether of her presence, Morris spoke in spellbound monotone. 'We planned the whole thing together to get back at her mother for the way she'd kept us apart. We thought we'd run away and get her to send us money.' He stopped. He was both aware of speaking and unaware, wide eyes unblinking, and the cleverness of what was coming out was her speaking through him. He had never thought of this alibi at all. 'Then we were just ready to come home, after we'd found out she was pregnant and we knew they'd have to let us marry, when Mimi fell, in

Sardinia, from a sort of cliff in the mountains, and killed herself.'

'*Caro*,' Mimi breathed. 'So sweet!'

'Killed herself,' he repeated, and now it was as though something he'd said in a dream was threatening to wake him up.

Bobo was shaking his head slowly from side to side in what must have been a heady cocktail of incredulity and satisfaction. He couldn't believe that what he'd imagined was true.

'It's what Inspector Marangoni suspected, you remember,' Morris went on, monotonous, plausible, bewitched, 'when they found she was pregnant, and that she'd had her hair done, and had a whole suitcase of new clothes with her. He said there must have been some complicity on her part. In fact the truth is that it was her idea in the first place.' As all of this was her idea now, Morris thought, aware that his eyes were staring blankly at the neon light above Bobo's head. As if the white tube were numinous somehow. Her power came from there.

'She was so scared at having to retake her exams. She was in love with me and she wanted us to be married. Yes, but with our own money, so we wouldn't always have to ask her mother.' Morris was aware of smiling, at once more automatically and more naturally than he ever did. He was aware of an unusual persuasive power in his voice. 'That's why I think the best course of action now would be to leave the whole thing be. It would only upset Paola and Antonella to bring it all out again. They'd have to appreciate how much of it was their fault and their mother's.'

Bobo hesitated. For a moment it seemed he might yield to whatever power had made a sort of oracle of Morris. Then with an air of crude commercial decision, as though deciding on nothing more than the size of some order or other, he announced: 'I don't believe a single word of it.'

There was another mesmerised silence, during which Morris found himself thinking again, thinking with a sort of bewildered lucidity beyond conscious control. And what he thought was that the story she had just invented for him to tell was perfectly feasible, and infinitely more attractive than the various alternatives. How much better to believe that Mimi had been happy those last weeks, and death an almost lucky accident at the moment of life's greatest exaltation: first love. But his lucidity and bewilderment came together in his appreciation that this was actually true. Yes, she had been happy, far happier than he'd been, that was for sure. Hence the only problem was that the others had no imagination. All they understood was the newspaper fare of kidnap, rape and murder. They saw only the ugly side of everything. They couldn't imagine the love there had been, couldn't understand that the exact way she'd died meant nothing beside the momentous fact that they had loved each other. But it would be pointless and humiliating trying to explain this to Bobo. Humiliating to himself and to Mimi too. He wouldn't even try.

'Mimi!' he whispered.

'Morri!' she answered so promptly.

Morris felt an immense lassitude sweeping across him. All the nerves in his puppet body had been cut. He could flop. He could sleep. If he was finished, then so be it.

'*Ti amo, Morri,*' she was whispering. 'I love you. You were my only lover ever.' Quite distinctly he felt her hair brush across his face. 'I forgive you everything,' she said.

How wonderful! Morris thought. How wonderful.

Bobo had picked up the phone. 'I was going to talk to Paola about this first,' he was saying. 'But now I think we should just get it over with as soon as possible.' He was dialling.

'Do it,' her voice suddenly said. 'Wake up, Morri. Before it's too late. Do it. Do what you're so good at!'

Do what?

Her voice was childishly urgent. 'Your party piece, Morri. That you're so good at. Do it!'

But he didn't want to move. It was so pleasant listening to her. He remembered how her voice had always soothed. Always, always, always. Such an escape from the tortuous back and forth that consciousness inevitably was for someone of his sensibility and misfortune.

Perhaps the police would swallow his story in the end. It was perfectly feasible.

'Morri!' She became shrill. 'Morri, you know I hated Bobo. If you did it to me, the least you can do is do it to him too! It was him stopped us from being lovers at the beginning. He started all this. He ruined your whole life. He was responsible for my death. He killed me, Morri!'

'*Pronto? Polizia?* Posenato here. *Si*. Posenato, Roberto. I'd like to talk to the *ispettore capo criminale*.'

Still enchanted, moving as if there were no hurry at all, Morris stood up, turned, grasped the back of the heavy office chair, then in a single measured gesture heaved it high in the air. But he wasn't concentrating. His muscles were slack. As the chair reached its apex, the metal revolving section swung round with the momentum, throwing him off balance. He slipped, let go. A castor came thumping into Bobo's shoulder, throwing him sideways onto the floor. But that was all. Then the whole chair clattered over the top against the wall.

Kwame pushed open the door and looked in. '*Maledetto!*' Bobo was shrieking. 'Are you crazy?' He grabbed at the phone.

Morris had finally woken up. The noise and confusion snapped him from his hypnotised state. Like water bursting a dam, all his repressed faculties were suddenly released. He had never moved so fast and purposefully. In a second, he tore the cord from the phone, swung himself over the desk, grasped and lifted Bobo by the shoulders, then banged his head down fiercely on the tiled floor. And again. And again. And again. In uncanny silence. For her voice had gone now. There was just the scuffle of clothes and the thump of the head on the tiles. Bang, bang, bang. The face beneath him contorted as if in orgasm. Again, and again. But it was exhausting. He lifted the boy a fifth time, a sixth. Down crashed the head. Then quite suddenly he couldn't go on. The flood of energy was gone, drained right out of him. He fell back and sat on the floor, shoulders shivering against the wall.

Why had he done that? Or had he known all along that sooner or later it must come to this? Some feeling there'd been between him and the boy, as when you knew that sooner or later a woman would become a lover.

Kwame was staring at him. There was the hum of the bottling plant beyond, freezing air flowing in from the open door.

'You killed him, man.'

Morris had put his face in his hands. There was the dawning horror that he would have to kill the black now too. It was too awful. And anyway, how? The boy was six-six. And he didn't *want* to kill Kwame. His hands would refuse, his body would rebel, because he *liked* the boy. Already he was trembling like a leaf, muscles twitching in arms and legs. With a sense of complete unreality, he announced out loud: 'Mimi, I will not kill anyone I like any more. I won't do it. Whatever the cost.'

'Man!' The whites of Kwame's eyes had expanded to pantomime proportions.

Face in hands, Morris waited a moment, hoping her voice would respond to this, give some acknowledgement. If only he could be sure of a constant dialogue with her, nothing would be too hard.

'This, big trouble!' Kwame was shaking his head.

Enough. Morris had suddenly seen the way. He leapt to his feet, tossed a bunch of keys across the room. 'Go and get the car. Bring it right up to the door and open the boot. OK?'

For some reason it never occurred to him that Kwame would not accept the accomplice's role. He was right. The boy caught the keys and turned. Before he was even out of the room, Morris was on his feet sorting through the file on the desk. But he mustn't touch. Oh shit! Every time you did this business you had to remember everything all over again. Because he wasn't a professional murderer, as in love he could never be a Don Juan. Just a sensitive young man reacting to extreme circumstances. Or a hopeless amateur. Unbuttoning his cuffs, Morris pulled his hands inside his shirt-sleeves and clumsily shuffled the papers back into the file. There were photocopies of the letters he had pasted together with bits of cheap novels and newsprint so long ago. How odd to see them again. DEAR SUFFERERS, WHAT PRICE YOUR LITTLE LOST ONE THEN? So ingenuous, so effective. There was a lesson to be learnt there. Then bank documents referring to the money they had drawn. A single withdrawal from a single account. He should have asked for more.

Morris hesitated. He felt a curious desire to read those letters again, to remind himself of that wonderful time. Oh, but he was going quite crazy now! Anyway, they would still be around later. Hands still in his sleeves, he lifted the whole file, negotiated his way past the body and two fallen chairs, taking care not to look at Bobo's face. The filing cabinet drawer was still open. He got the papers away and pushed the thing closed with his foot.

Now. He glanced round the room. Must wipe the places where he'd grasped the chair. Otherwise his prints would be quite acceptable in this office. He did work here some-times after all. It was *his* company, for Christ's sake. Oh, but this was hopeless. There was an avalanche of evidence to hold back here. It was impossible. He went to the door that led through to the bathrooms and then the bottling plant. No one out by the bathrooms. The hum of the plant was louder. Mustn't look in there. Mustn't be seen. Then he thought: at least he had a challenge worthy of Morris Duckworth on his hands. At least he had killed someone who thoroughly deserved it. Genius and a smidgen of luck and he might just get through.

Kwame came back. Precisely as he appeared, Morris realised how incredibly stupid it would be to use his own car. One hair in the boot and he would be taking university degrees by post for the rest of his life. 'Move it!' he shouted to Kwame. 'Move mine. We'll use his. I'll get the keys.' Kwame went out again. Morris crouched down by the corpse. Assuming it was a corpse. Was it? There was no time to listen for breathing. Somebody might arrive at any moment. Somebody might wonder why the phone was engaged. Would it sound engaged or just as if someone was not answering? Oh God, if he was going to kill the boy he should have planned it. How long would the police take to work out who Posenato was and where he had been calling from? Morris felt, quite sincerely, that he wasn't up to this. At the same time, turning the corpse over, plunging his hand into one pocket after another, he had never been more happily sure of himself, so that even after he found the car keys he kept looking – outside pockets, inside – it was one of those special moments when intuition reigns supreme. It was thus that he found, serendipity itself, a postcard showing Juliet's tomb.

He slid it out of the top inside pocket. There was no stamp or postmark.

All it said was: 'Bobo, *carissimo*, the morning afterwards is always a dream, you, you, you, as if you were still inside me. Your Bimbetta.'

Morris thought for about ten seconds, then he wiped the glossy surface with the elbow of his jacket and slipped the card two or three papers down in the in-tray on Bobo's desk. As with the first time he'd killed, there was a sense, Morris realised, in which forces beyond him used him as an instrument of retribution. Genital Giacomo and Sex-Swap Sandra then. Bawdy Bobo now. Yes, that phone call yesterday evening that he had to take in the other room! These nights when he supposedly had to check up on things in the office! It was obvious. The pig! He grabbed Bobo roughly from under the shoulders and began to drag him to the door. Moving, he was careful to keep his trousers from making contact with the blood-sticky hair. When the head fell back and the mouth opened, he remarked once again on how truly ugly the boy was. Ugly and corrupt.

Barely ten minutes later, giving the white Audi no more than five to get away, he opened the door of his own car and, hesitating between police and carabinieri, he remembered Bobo had called the former, and thus opted himself for the latter.

CHAPTER SIXTEEN

CARNIVAL WAS COMING. BACK in Piazza Bra the children
had their Harlequin outfits, their cowboy suits and Zorro
cloaks. Alone at last towards four o'clock that afternoon,
Morris decided to treat himself to a table outside Bar
Baglioni, whence a slanting sun picked out the nylon
colours of innocent festivity against the stony backdrop of
the Roman arena, where lions had once mauled Christians.

Saddam Hussein leered. A diminutive Dracula turned
and showed his bloody teeth. Morris smiled, and smiled
again at a yet unpoisoned Snow White. With a little sense
of myth and history it wasn't impossible to feel oneself
less monstrous. He wasn't the first to have faced the question of what to do with an unwanted body. Indeed, you
might almost see it as the primeval paradigm of all human
dilemmas: what practical arrangements to make for the
spirit turned carcass, for the putrefying confirmation of
corrupt mortality? Burial, when you came down to it, lay
at the origins of all human culture, was the first step in
the long road to civilisation, to the properly responsible,
fecund, well-ordered and – why not? – sumptuous life
which Morris must believe he would one day achieve:
harmony, elegance, culture. Otherwise he might as well
give up now and confess it all, because at the moment he
felt no better than a drunken tightrope walker in thick fog.
Lost. Nauseous. God only knew where the wire wobbling

147

beneath him was connected, or whether there wasn't an executioner waiting for him at the end of it, or simply sawing through strand after strand at this very moment.

Morris took a deep breath, then blew out, as if one could just exhale one's angst. He frowned. Burial. It was such a depressing hurdle to have to overcome, such a stiff test of one's cultural and criminal credentials.

The truth was he had felt far more exhilarated when he had killed Giacomo and Sandra eighteen months ago, and so deeply moved when the story had ended for Mimi. Because these things had been intimately related to his being in love, to the noblest and deepest of emotions, which had bathed the whole terrible adventure in a rich light.

Whereas now life was no more than an interminable 'in memoriam', a constantly self-perpetuating sense of bereavement, a search to repeat the lost impossible. Farce after tragedy.

He had been a hero when he carried off Mimi: Theseus in complicity with Ariadne, Paris abducting Helen. Brutal stories, but glorious. That summer kidnap had been his Trojan War, his epopoeia. Splendid profiles in Homeric light. After which came the long, weary centuries of tawdry chronicle. Living in the memory. The shadow. Summer then, winter now. He felt nothing for Bobo at all. Neither guilt, nor satisfaction. The whole business had been entirely casual, an *incidente di percorso*, as they said here. Like running over a rat on the road.

Though it had to be gratifying, he reflected, sipping a light Custoza, watching witch and fairy queen gather around a trestle table with soft drinks – it had to be gratifying that he was able to see his actions in these terms. Of how many murderers could it be said that they had a sense of historical perspective? Of how many of his victims? So that if ever he needed to look for justification it was straightforwardly there, in the superior quality of his mind. Indeed, he wouldn't put it past himself to write a book about it all one day: diaries of a thinking man's murderer, for posthumous publication only of course. But there was a long way to go till he got there.

And a fair bit even till tomorrow morning, with the carabinieri combing the countryside, grilling the workers at the bottling plant, fingerprinting the office, calling for witnesses. Plus the galling business of having to rely on somebody else. He had never done that before. On a twenty-year-old black boy of whom one knew exactly nothing. Indeed who might perfectly well feel it was in his own personal interest to turn Morris in. But there was also a sort of delicious penance here, in this having to rely on the lowest of the low. A thrill of risk and humiliation. It was picking up the crumbs after what he had had with Massimina, but it would have to do.

Morris stood up and made a point of winking to the waiter and leaving the kind of handsome tip that would be remembered if ever he were asked to account for his movements. Then, moving away from his table across the square and back to his car, he collided with a tiny skeleton being chased by a bear. The painted bones tumbled over and began to weep. Morris leaned down to help the little boy up. How much he wished for a child of his own! A father appeared and laughed: '*Povero scheletrino*, he should never have left the cemetery!'

At which it occurred to Morris that of course cemeteries were where one buried people. Particularly if you wanted to bury them with style. And if anybody knew the cemetery, it was Kwame.

Signora Trevisan was in the *salotto*, watched over by Antonella. Stepping in discreetly, Morris noted how extraordinarily well the coffin blended in with the rest of the room, as if only now the inspiration behind the heavy mahogany décor, the marble door surrounds, grim credenza and gloomy chandelier was at last revealed: to host a wake, to welcome a great black-lacquered casket with bellied sides and brass fittings. Perhaps, Morris thought, a whole tradition of Latin furnishings had been developed around the wake. Perhaps no provincial *salotto* was truly complete until it had its coffin. Certainly he felt a sense of propriety and repose, taking one of the rigidly straight-backed chairs and bowing his head in silent prayer, face in hands. Going through the motions had always been one of his greatest pleasures.

Then it would do no harm of course to impress poor Antonella, to whom at some point he would be obliged to report on the way he was managing the company. For a moment he tried to use the breather to make the necessary plans. If the body was found before he could bury it? If it wasn't found, how to bury it? Was this cemetery idea feasible? But as in the café an hour before, serious decisions proved impossible. His mind just would not focus on the sequence of actions and precautions necessary to get him through. His intelligence was not of that variety. All he could really do was to react, to feel the rope trembling beneath his feet and take the next step, while what he had of wit was engaged not in the action at all, but in watching himself doing it, in reflecting upon it, in hoping all would turn out for the best. The fact was, Morris thought, that the qualities you most despised in yourself – whimsy, spontaneity – were also the things you were most proud of.

Restless, he peeped out from between his fingers as he always had in church with Mother beside him. Antonella stood up and went to draw the room's heavy curtains against the last of winter twilight. Shadows rushed as candlelight stabbed out in the dark by head and toe of the deceased. Dropping his hands and glancing up as if after prayer, Morris noticed how Antonella's face as she returned to her seat looked truly fine in the softly lambent glow, noble in her suffering. Apparently bereavement became her. He smiled sadly at his sister-in-law across her mother's corpse.

Antonella burst into tears.

'*Povera Mamma, povera Mamma,* and now I can't even mourn her properly for worrying about Bobo. *O Dio!*' The young woman sobbed, voice a little slurred (from sedatives they'd given her perhaps?). '*Povera, povera Mamma,* she was such a wonderful woman.'

'*Sì,*' Morris gravely agreed. '*Sì,* a truly wonderful woman.' But it was interesting, he reflected, that nobody else was in the room. For being so marvellous, old Signora Trevisan had hardly made a great deal of friends, had she? The more fool her, then, to have rejected Morris's friendship when it had been offered, to have spurned his perfectly appropriate courtship of her youngest and by no means brilliant daughter. No doubt the old bitch was now plummeting down to the first circle, where crimes of arrogance and presumption were most properly dealt with.

Antonella looked up from her tears. They exchanged glances, and it seemed the day's constant see-saw of exaltation and despair had left Morris hyperaware of every detail: the honest, untrimmed bushiness of her eyebrows; the lank modesty of her hair, just pinned back behind one rosy ear. He felt he had never really looked at her before, and the very intensity of the looking, rather than its object, somehow excited him.

Of the three, should he perhaps have married Antonella?

'Was there any blood?' she now forced herself to ask, voice trembling. 'In the office, I mean.'

Morris hesitated. 'Only a little,' he answered truthfully.

'On the floor, by the desk. Just a smear really. As if somebody had scraped their elbow there or something.'

'*O Dio. O Dio, Dio, Dio!* Why does everything have to happen at once?'

'I know,' Morris said, and couldn't have agreed more. If Kwame ratted on him he was quite dead.

'The inspector's talking to Paola in the kitchen.'

'I know,' Morris repeated. To cheer her up, he said: 'Bobo must have put up quite a terrific fight though. You ought to be proud of him. The office was complete havoc.'

Antonella burst into tears again. She bent forward and sobbed in her hands. The candles flickered, as if in response to her emotion. Shadows slithered back and forth across her face, caressing her slim forearms, the heavy bosom of her black dress. In her coffin Signora Trevisan's stern wax nose seemed to rise and fall.

Morris stared, mesmerised by the visual richness of it all. He was an artist in the end, that was his problem: the carnival, the wake, the nuptial bed. They were all the same to him.

'Comfort her,' Mimi whispered then.

Immediately there was the smell of her perfume, and the vision before him was as if transformed into a completed picture: Antonella, the coffin, Signora Trevisan, they were oil on canvas. The perfume made him part of it.

'You must comfort her, Morri.'

Mimi! Morris pushed his chair back. Moving round the coffin on its trestles, he was already lifting his hand to lay it on his sister-in-law's shoulder, when Paola called him from the door. The picture disintegrated into mere people and places, faces and furniture.

'They want to talk to you.' His wife's eyes glinted in the pool of dark beyond the candle.

'*Va bene.* I'm coming.'

When he got to the door, she whispered: 'I told them you phoned me at nine-fifteen. This morning.'

Morris stared at her. 'Why do you say that?'

She opened her brown eyes in a sudden intense complicity. 'Nine-fifteen,' she repeated. Half an hour later than the truth.

Unnerved, Morris shrugged his shoulders and crossed to the dining-room, where two men in light raincoats were sitting around the huge wooden dining-table in the way people will when they wish to emphasise their outsideness, to maximise a sense of official intrusion. Even before the bulky figure to the right turned to greet him, Morris recognised Inspector Marangoni. Of old. For a second he closed his eyes. He simply couldn't believe it. It was like drawing the hanged man from a seventy-two-card tarot pack. For heaven's sake, surely the Verona police force must have more than one inspector!

'*Buona sera*,' Morris said at his most ingratiating, but knowing his skin had drained to paper. Beside the inspector, the same thin, olive-skinned assistant was already scribbling in a notebook.

'I'm truly sorry,' Marangoni said, 'to have to meet you once again in such sad and dramatic circumstances.'

'*Sì, sì, è vero.*' Then, too quickly, Morris added: 'Actually, as you must be aware, I've already told all I know to the carabinieri, this morning on the spot. I don't, er, see what else . . .'

Marangoni, Morris noticed, still had the kind of bad teeth that suggested either that police salaries were too low, or his personal priorities all wrong. Unless it was some form of intimidation by grossness. The lower left incisor was completely black. Lighting a cigarette in a room where the absence of ashtrays made it clear nobody indulged, the heavy man explained: 'The carabinieri in Quinto are responsible for the *territorio extraurbano*. The polizia are responsible for the city. Given that this may be a kidnap aimed at a family resident within the official confines of the city, both forces will naturally be involved.'

'Ah.' So not only, Morris thought, did he have a corpse on his hands, a stolen car and the kind of accomplice who was probably visible from satellite photographs, but there were now actually two police forces looking for him: carabinieri and polizia. Still, he was suddenly pleased it was Marangoni again. Any *déjà vu* was welcome if it brought him close to Mimi.

'I have to repeat everything then?' he said wearily, and wearily aware of the irony.

'Sit down.' Marangoni gestured condescendingly to a chair which very soon would be Morris's own. 'Actually, we have the main facts from our colleagues. My interest is in just one or two small additional questions.'

Morris sat opposite the inspector, while his impassive assistant continued to write with a rapidity quite unjustified by the very little that had been said. For a moment Morris began to wonder whether something in clothes or behaviour wasn't visibly giving him away. He looked down at his hands on the table to check there was no blood in the fingernails.

Only to find, much worse, that wrists and fingers were trembling.

'Two questions, to be precise. First, shortly before whatever happened happened, Signor Posenato telephoned the police.'

'*Davvero!*' Morris was almost too quick to be surprised. 'The carabinieri didn't tell me that.'

'Because they don't know.' Marangoni grinned fatly. He had certainly put on weight since the Massimina business. 'Because Posenato called us, the police, not them.'

'To say what? Presumably this solves the case.' Only as he said it did he realise what a trap he had just avoided.

'No, you don't understand. The call was interrupted.'

'Ah, ah, I see. That would explain why the phone had been smashed.'

'Yes, but the odd thing is that the operator who took the call said that Posenato's voice was not particularly urgent.'

Marangoni paused, and his piggy eyes were staring straight into Morris's now. But to no avail, for Morris was beginning to relax. It was like riding a bicycle in the end. Once you'd got the hang of it, you never forgot. Even after years, it all came back in a moment or two. His features slowly arranged themselves into a perfect image of puzzlement. 'He wasn't urgent. And so?'

'Then when the call was interrupted and something in the room happened, Posenato shouted out: "Are you mad?" or something of the kind, indicating that he was more surprised than frightened.'

Morris shook his head in apparently bewildered reflection. The inspector's assistant had now stopped writing and was rather unnervingly smiling at him through glasses that caught dim light from the chandelier. Morris noted that the man had a ridiculously tropical tie on, all lemons and bananas, the kind of thing you only wore to scream that you didn't consider yourself the loser you obviously were. Feeling on top again, Morris decided he would install wall lighting and never buy a bulb of less than sixty watts.

'This would seem to suggest that he knew his assailant,' Marangoni concluded.

Morris offered a pantomime of hesitant agreement. 'Could be.'

The inspector leaned suddenly and heavily across the table: 'Now I want you to tell me who that assailant was, Signor Duckworth.'

Morris was alarmed. He hadn't been expecting such

sudden confidence and aggression. To gain time, he said: 'So you don't think it is another kidnap?'

This left Marangoni a little exposed in his position of attack across the table.

'No,' he said. '*Per niente.*'

'In which case it would be a case for the carabinieri, not the police,' Morris managed, as if surprising himself with this irrelevant thought.

But Marangoni was having none of it. 'Signor Duckworth' – he put all the stress on the second syllable – 'I asked you who the assailant was.'

Morris took a deep breath, appeared to hesitate, then seemed to make up his mind: 'You see, Ispettore,' he said; 'by the way, it is Ispettore, isn't it, not Colonnello, or something like that? I got very confused with the carabinieri this morning.'

'Ispettore,' Marangoni said patiently, and obviously felt the moment had come to retreat across the table. 'Don't concern yourself about that, Signor Duckworth. Just tell us what you think.'

'I didn't want to offend. No, the point is, Posenato, well, he's the kind of person who has all sorts of enemies. Also he is conducting his business – or rather the Trevisan business; his family, you see, are keeping him out of their own – in the kind of way that, well, I feel disloyal saying this, being part of the set-up myself and so on now, but if it can help Bobo in any possible way then I suppose it has to be said, in the kind of way that could lay him wide open to bribery.'

Having said this, Morris felt like someone who has just run across an entire canyon on nothing more than a washing line.

Maragoni leaned back on his chair and drew on his cigarette, staring intently at Morris, who, irony of ironies, now had to fake his nervousness.

'There are various, er, well, illicit practices in the company,' he explained.

The assistant scribbled. Again Marangoni waited, but this time Morris wouldn't oblige.

Patronising and avuncular, the inspector said: 'That is not entirely unheard of in Italy.'

Morris shrugged his shoulders. 'I have very little experience of these things, apart from what one reads in the papers.'

'Just tell me what these illicit practices were.'

Morris took a very melodramatic breath, then didn't plunge. 'If I say this, does it mean the company will be investigated? Because, I mean, that could lead to its failing.'

'That depends.' Marangoni's voice appeared to mix leniency with severity, then came down on the side of the latter. 'But if you don't tell me what you have to say, you can be quite sure it will be investigated.'

Still Morris wavered. 'Can I at least have your word that, if it is investigated, you will not inform the rest of the family, and particularly Bobo, I mean Signor Posenato, that it was me who put you on to this.'

'Yes,' Marangoni was almost too eager. Morris could only reflect what a genius these situations always proved him to be. The only problem now was overkill.

So then he explained that Trevisan Wines had been evading both company tax and VAT for very considerable sums (paying off the officials in the respective collecting offices), that there was also a significant amount of false invoicing, and worst of all that they had been using immigrant labour at night-time for completely unrecorded business, paying neither taxes nor health contributions. To complicate matters, Posenato had been treating these immigrants so badly that Morris had felt obliged on purely human terms to set up a hostel for them to live in, something in which fortunately he had been warmly supported by Signora Posenato who, together with the Church, had kindly supplied a considerable amount of cast-off shoes and clothes. 'Then last night . . .'

'*Sì?*'

'*Mi scusi*, I just thought I should let, er, your colleague catch up with his writing.'

'Just tell me what happened last night.'

'Last night – and I find it odd that this happened on the very night Signora Trevisan died . . .' Morris stopped as if this curiosity had only just occurred to him. 'Yes, it is odd, isn't it?'

'*Per favore*, Signor Duckworth, last night . . .'

'Last night Bobo fired all the immigrant workers.'

'Ah, and why?'

Morris had no difficulty appearing embarrassed.

'Apparently he found two of them engaging in, er, homosexual practices in his office, early in the morning.'

'And he fired all of them?'

'It seems crazy to me too, but he was an irascible person. Or perhaps he felt there was only so long you could continue to get away with something like that.' Morris hesitated. 'The truth is he had a great aversion to black people.' Then, to his horror, he realised that he had been talking about Bobo in the past tense. For Christ's sake! There was an almost total rebellion of all the muscles about the spine. For a second it was truly as if he were going to crumple. His breath wouldn't come. Looking up, he was perfectly ready to see the handcuffs already opening. Instead, what he read on their faces was merely impatience to hear more. In their imbecile eagerness, neither policeman had noticed. Nor were they taping him. Morris sighed quite audibly, almost theatrically, as though giving them a second chance, the way at chess one might invite an inferior opponent to study the board more carefully before making a hasty move. Had he been their superior he would have fired the both of them at once. Just like that. Never mind the poor immigrants.

Pulling himself together, Morris explained; 'I had the story from one of the immigrants and from somebody called Forbes, Peter Forbes, another Englishman and a friend of mine, who runs the hostel. I went to the hostel where they live this morning, because Forbes had telephoned me in the car, and they explained the situation: that Posenato had found two of the boys, well, buggering each other, in the office, and that this had proved to be the straw that broke the camel's back . . .'

When the assistant raised a puzzled face at this expression, Morris explained indulgently with the Italian equivalent: '*La goccia che ha fatto traboccare il vaso*, the drop that made the bowl spill. Though somehow,' he added blandly, 'the English idiom seems more appropriate here.'

'Quite.' Marangoni was impatient. But . . .'

'So I went on to the office,' Morris continued, 'to discuss the matter with Bobo. I was concerned that without the immigrants we wouldn't be able to honour a contract that I myself had recently negotiated with an English company and hence felt responsible for. And that, of course, was when I found what I found.'

He looked directly at the policeman, eyes mild with studied artlessness.

'But, Signor Duckworth, what I asked you was, did Signor Posenato go to the factory in the middle of the night expressly to fire them?'

'I've no idea. He couldn't have actually gone to fire them if the problem was his finding them, er, well, I've already said it, buggering in his office.'

'No. That is precisely why I asked my question.'

Morris managed to pull the face of someone to whom something has just occurred. 'You're right. In fact, you know, I can't imagine why he went to the office. Perhaps he checked the factory regularly, you know, the night shift I mean. He was very suspicious of these immigrants, always afraid they weren't working well, or would steal things. Perhaps he made checks like that quite routinely, though he never mentioned doing so to me. You'd have to ask his wife, I suppose. I remember just as we were leaving last night – I presume you know we dined together – yes, just as we were leaving he got a phone call; maybe it was something to do with that.'

At this Marangoni and his assistant exchanged the kind of knowing glance that Morris had always found so distasteful, the sort of nudge-nudge-know-what-I-mean look his father had endlessly exchanged with the friends he brought home from the pub when they were finally thrown out. Immediately he objected: 'No, I don't think it could be anything like that.'

Marangoni raised thick eyebrows: 'Like what?'

Morris steadied himself. 'I don't think he was the kind of man to be having, erm, an affair.'

The inspector smiled, then pushed back his chair and got to his feet. 'The two main immigrants who were the cause of the problem, are they available for interview?'

'I imagine so,' Morris lied with increasing fluency. 'You'll have to go along to the hostel to speak to them.' He explained where it was.

'You didn't tell any of this to the carabinieri.'

'Any of what exactly?'

'The irregularities in the company. Signor Posenato's firing the immigrants.'

Morris looked apologetic. 'I suppose really I should have, but to tell the truth I was in a bit of a daze. I mean, with finding the office like that. All they asked me about was how I'd found the place. What time. Where I'd phoned from and so on. It was all rather cursory, I thought. They only kept me about an hour, and most of the time they were busy taking photographs and measuring things.'

'Quite, quite.' Marangoni and his assistant exchanged satisfied smiles.

Morris offered: 'Really it was only a couple of hours later, you know, that it came to me that it might have something to do with the people he fired.'

In fact it had been exactly two minutes ago, and the solution was ideal: the immigrants had done it. He could have spat in a contrary wind for not having told the carabinieri the same. Anyway, the thing to remember was that, however someone was really murdered, there was always another completely feasible way in which they might have been, because in the end so many of us have such excellent reasons for wanting to do away with each other.

The two policemen were heading for the door now, taking their leave, but Morris was on such a rollercoaster of virtuosity, he stopped them: 'Sorry, didn't you say at the beginning that there were two things you wanted to talk to me about. I mean, I don't want to have to go through this again.'

They were standing in the hall, with its polished black-and-white stone floor, the lacquered portraits against dusty plaster with ironwork candelabra above. There was certainly a lot of work to be done on Casa Trevisan before one could feel happy here.

'Ah.' For a moment Marangoni looked puzzled. The assistant consulted his notebook. Then they remembered. 'Yes, yes, our only other question was: what time exactly did you leave the house here after paying your respects to your mother-in-law? What time did you set off for the office?'

'No, the hostel first,' Morris corrected, 'and then the office. Well . . .' But he caught his breath. 'Oh, I *see*, you mean where was I when the, ah . . .' He appeared to think. 'Well, as I said to the carabinieri, you know, I really wouldn't know exactly what time it was. I mean, first I raced over here – we're talking about something like seven-thirty or eight – because of Signora Trevisan; then going back I stopped at the bar in the square, I mean, I was so shocked by it all. It reminded me of my own mother dying.' He balked a little at the unfaithfulness of that. 'Then I drove over to the hostel, where I spoke to an immigrant called Kwame. Do you want me to spell that for you? I don't know his surname. Or maybe that is his surname. In any case, you can ask him when I arrived, because I've no idea.'

'Did you phone anyone from the car?'

Morris thought. 'No, oh yes, wait a minute, my wife, Paola. To discuss funeral arrangements and so on.'

'What time?'

Again Morris shrugged. 'Really, I've no idea. I'm afraid you'll have to ask her. The whole day has been a complete whirl for me. I can barely believe it's happened.'

Then as the policemen were fretting to go off and pick up Azedine and Farouk, he continued garrulously: 'You know, I feel a million miles away from where I was when I woke up this morning, with my mother-in-law dying and then this thing, and the situation at the company to sort out and the funeral and . . . I mean, have you ever had the feeling that things are completely unreal and . . .'

The portly Marangoni was staring at him through the domestic gloom with such piercing eyes that he stopped short. 'In fact, I'd better hurry,' he said. 'There are all the people to invite to the funeral.'

CHAPTER SEVENTEEN

'MO,' HIS WIFE WHISPERED through the candlelight. He raised his head and, before turning to the door, exchanged another of those looks of intense sympathy with Antonella. Between them, the corpse now held flowers in her hands and had been doused in a scent that mingled promiscuously with the wax of polished floor and furniture. Then a gloriously pompous clock began to chime out midnight. Already it was another day.

'Mo!'

Remembering to cross himself as he moved out of the presence of the corpse (or was that rather overdoing it?), he went to her at the door. She was in her night-dress already.

'Haven't you forgotten something?' Paola's small eyes were bright in candle-gloom that just picked out a sacred ceramic heart bleeding from a watching Christ on the wall, the kind of bric-à-brac that would be in the bin just as soon as was decently feasible.

'I've been waiting more than an hour,' she protested. 'I mean, that's why we're staying here tonight, right?'

There was a bloom, Morris noted, on her young skin which quite possibly suggested she had already brought herself off once or twice, an idea that both depressed and excited him.

'I didn't expect your sister to stay.'

'Who cares if she does? You don't have to impress her, do you? What's wrong with you?'

'But . . .'

'You're not planning to sit up all night with a stiff, are you? Mamma's dead. It makes no difference to her.'

While Morris was still some way from actually believing in God, he did feel that a certain respect for tradition (as distinguished from its cheap wall-hung souvenirs) was both decorous and, in a young woman, becoming.

'I don't want to offend anybody,' he said.

Across the thickly odoured room, Paola called: 'We're going to take a short break now. We'll be down later.'

Antonella didn't so much as respond. Again, Morris reflected that given the extraordinary double whammy she'd been hit with today, his sister-in-law was behaving with remarkable poise, even nobility. Climbing the stairs ahead of him, his wife lifted her night-dress over a perfect backside, wiggled, and whispered: 'Lick it.' Morris flinched.

Stress, of course, is supposed to inhibit sexual performance. Apart from his growing desire to be close to Antonella, one thing that had stopped Morris from leaving the corpse and rushing upstairs was his concern that he might not be able to satisfy the expectations that in a different mood earlier on in the day he himself had so frivolously aroused. But in the end the old four-poster bed in the deliciously sombre room did for him what Paola's buttocks pressed into his face halfway up the stairs could not. The thought of the years Massimina had slept in this heavy feather mattress beside her mother, first as a little girl when her father died, then as an adolescent; the thought of those breasts slowly budding, hairs softly forming, while the old woman beside her, now dead downstairs, gradually withered and decayed; and then the thought that he in some marvellous way had appropriated all this, had almost swallowed it up somehow, as Zeus had supposedly swallowed the whole universe, or been swallowed up by it in some ultimate form of communion and sacrifice – these ideas could not help but give him the kind of erection that was all in the end dear Paola – so innocently really – required of him.

On his back as she laboured away above him, he sucked in the dusty smell of the old coverlet and stared at the family photo on the bedside table where Mamma was only forty-odd, the elder sisters in their teens, and dear Mimi a rather chubby prepubescent schoolgirl. How he wished he could have known her then! Everything innocent and all ahead of them. It wasn't so much a regret he felt as an intense desire to be other, which was somehow gratifying in itself. Approaching orgasm, he remembered that the first time he had ever made love in his whole life had been with Mimi immediately after killing Genital Giacomo and his girlfriend, as tonight he somehow felt it was her he was embracing after dispatching Bobo.

Except that with that first love there had been no contraceptive, but a fuller, more trusting intimacy.

'Mimi!'

In the moonlit afterwards, Paola asked: 'Mo, what did you do between eight-thirty and ten o'clock?'

'Sorry?' He had just remembered he was supposed to be up early to meet Kwame. The truth was there was just too much going on. He needed a secretary.

'You called me about quarter to nine. You called the police about ten. What were you doing in between? You know he was assaulted or abducted or whatever around nine-thirty.'

'Heavens, you don't think I did it!'

She said nothing.

'I went to Villa Caritas,' he said indignantly. 'And if you must know, the police already have their suspects.

Apparently Bobo fired two of the immigrants last night. The inspector obviously thinks they were responsible. He says it would explain why they took his car.'

'*Oddio!*' she said quietly.

Then nothing. He had expected she would want to talk more about this, to hear the details. But she was strangely silent and while this disturbed Morris, he didn't feel it would be wise to volunteer any information. What, after all, could she know?

Just as he was drifting into sleep, she rolled over to him and whispered: 'It was pretty weird you calling me Mimi, by the way.'

'What!' It took a moment for alarm to sharpen in the mists of gathering drowsiness.

'Actually, I rather liked it. There's something, I don't know, sexy about thinking the other person is imagining someone else. Next time I'll call you something different. I'll pretend I'm having it off with Bobo or something. What do you think?'

What Morris thought was that no fate could be bad enough for someone with a mind like his wife's, because if he had been able to marry his first love he would never, never have left her or betrayed her or played these kinds of sick games with her all his life long. Turning away, he snuggled down in the sheets where Mimi had once slept and again tried to imagine her smell, her voice. Perhaps salvation lay quite simply in making her a constant presence, to advise and guide him in what looked like being a very long road ahead.

Tomorrow he would tell Paola they were moving here permanently. He felt closer to her here.

CHAPTER EIGHTEEN

THERE IS AN EXTENT, of course, to which flagrancy is the best method of concealment, a sort of hiding things in the light itself, while the suspicious parent, partner or detective pokes about in the shadows. So one does not look for one's husband's billets-doux in the papers on top of the sideboard, because one imagines he will have the good sense, and shame, to keep them tucked away in the bottom of some trunk somewhere. Nor does one search for stolen car and corpse in the line of tightly parked vehicles directly opposite the police station along a busy riverside road.

Or so Morris hoped. For that is where he had told Kwame to park the thing. Only after the burial – itself to be an act of exquisite flagrancy – would the car be abandoned in a more conventional hiding-place deep in the country, where no doubt it would promptly be found.

So just as he had once concealed his kidnap victim on the crowded beach of Rimini, Morris now hoped to slot this again unfortunate and certainly unpremeditated crime into two of the classical focal points of Italian life: the car park and the cemetery.

Coming downstairs at six o'clock, he made a coffee for poor Antonella and took it into the darkened *soggiorno*. He looked into the coffin, sighed at what he saw there, said it was important to find the will in case there were any particular instructions for her funeral, and heard Antonella promise she would get it from the safe at home. Good. First thing, though, he suggested, was that she should phone the police to hear if there had been any developments. Pushing wisps of unwashed hair from her face, she came out into the hallway and, in what was a still-uncracked dawn, phoned. Morris waited beside her, hoping she would interpret his anxiety as sympathetic concern. Putting the receiver down, she began to weep.

Morris had his arm round her.

'They've found him?' He held his breath.

'An anonymous phone call,' she sobbed.

'What?'

'Saying he'd got what he deserved.'

Still holding her, Morris simply stared through the gloom of his future home. How could there have been a phone call? Why was there always a wild card in every pack, always someone more perverted than oneself?

In the car, he called directory enquiries and dialled a number, forgetting of course that Stan would never be up at this hour. There was the shamefully poor Italian of his answering machine. Morris had just started to leave a message when a sleepy voice said: 'Hi, gee, it's early.'

Morris excused himself. He'd been up all night and it hadn't occurred to him. Then he explained that Signora Trevisan, Antonella's mother, had died and that Antonella had asked him to tell Stan that they would have to suspend lessons until further notice. He himself would pay off any outstanding lessons. How much was it?

Stan apparently consulted a diary, improbable though this seemed. A hundred and forty thousand for four lessons.

Outrageous, Morris thought, hanging up. Thirty-five thousand an hour! Incredible! When he himself had never asked more than twenty-five, despite being an infinitely better teacher.

'Wasn't I, *cara*?' he asked. He had started talking to her even before he picked up the phone. But Mimi was silent today, and it occurred to Morris how feminine this was, this only talking when she wanted to, this wilful muteness followed by unexpected interference, this making him miss her for so long, then whispering something when he least expected it, so that, like a god, she had complete control.

'You do appreciate,' he said, 'that I would never have killed Bobo if you hadn't told me to.'

Still he got no reply.

'It was you I made love to last night,' he went on. 'I was looking at your photo. I called your name.'

Apparently she was unimpressed. The hell with her then. Morris put the phone down. At the same time, he thought that if he couldn't actually buy or steal her portrait from the Uffizi, then perhaps he might be able to commission some passable artist to do a copy. Certainly it was the kind of painting that would look well in Casa Trevisan, and infinitely preferable to bleeding Jesuses. He would mention the matter to Forbes.

'What' – he picked up the phone again, driving fast up the Valpantena – 'do you actually think of your sister? Come on, Mimi, I mean, we would never have got into any of that kinky stuff, would we? We were such simple lovers. Why can't she just have a child and settle down? The way you wanted to. I would love to be a father, Mimi.'

Very faintly, through the receiver, the voice said: 'Morri, she is having a child.'

Morris was so shocked he had to pull over to the side of the road. For a moment he stared at the phone, then thought that in the remote event that the police were following him they might find this suspicious, think he'd dumped the body here, or was meeting somebody or something. He pulled out again in the path of a truck, and glancing in his mirror at the irate driver realised it was Doorways coming for their wine, which might well not be ready with the immigrants fired. But Morris was so excited he hardly cared.

'How can she be?' he asked. 'Since when? She always insisted on using contraceptives.' Then he remembered the times he'd played various games with his fingers.

But like an oracle Massimina was not to be quizzed. In fact it was precisely in this cryptic, sibylline style that the voice's authenticity lay. Who would ever believe in a ghost, an apparition that just chatted to you? The Madonna, the goddess, appeared and disappeared – a sort of distillation of one's experiences with the world in general, here now, gone now. The Lord giveth and the Lord taketh away. Her words were fragments plucked out of the gale of contingency, fragments from which one constructed the implied whole. Morris, Morris thought with some satisfaction, was thus plugged in to a long and honourable cultural tradition.

And Paola was pregnant. Very soon Morris was going to be a very happy fellow indeed.

Forbes was writing on the big table in the kitchen. He wore at least three sweaters and an overcoat against the freezing cold, while the young Ramiz shivered opposite, munching stale bread. On entering, Morris experienced the feeling of the father who has been absent precisely when needed. These people had been cut adrift yesterday morning and he hadn't been there to give them help or guidance. Immediately, even as he crossed the threshold, he dictated three sharp beginning-of-the-day orders to himself: he must sort out these people who depended on him; he must get things straight with his wife about living in the Trevisan household and having a decent family; most of all, having committed this murder, he must exploit it to the full to establish a successful, generous, well-ordered and solidly based life, both social and commercial. He must become a public figure.

Good.

If ever he, Morris Duckworth, lost sight of these goals, he would be no more than flotsam in a storm, dross in a slip-stream, tossed and blown from one police interrogation to the next, lost in the maze of his paltry misdemeanours.

Worse, he would have killed Mimi for nothing.

Leaning over Forbes's shoulder he read: 'For the serious and sentient student eager to absorb Renaissance culture *in situ* . . . Just five miles from the splendid city of Verona, Professor Forbes's School of Italian Art is situated in the suggestive Villa Catullus, where the motto that rules our daily life and vision of human creativity is *gratia placendi*. Students attending the four-week courses will . . .'

Morris asked: 'Where are the others?'

Forbes was tired and clearly out of sorts. His paper was full of blottings and erasures. He explained that Azedine and Farouk had disappeared yesterday night. The Senegalese had taken fright when the police came and searched the place. The others were now upstairs packing and trying to decide what to do.

Morris asked where Forbes intended to place the ad.

'Various publications,' he said rather vaguely, 'in the, er, private education sector.'

'Put the name of the school in caps,' Morris told him, with that tone of authority that was coming so naturally these days. 'You can say that the starting date is July. We should have the place ready by then. Meanwhile, I'd be grateful if you could get everybody downstairs for breakfast and have a fire lit in the study. I'll be back in ten minutes.'

He then went out to the car again, drove to Quinto, bought twenty croissants from the *pasticceria*, a new pack of coffee, milk, sugar, butter and jam. He already had his hand on the ignition key, when the kind of indulgent, generous idea he could never resist crossed his mind. He got out of the car, walked back to the local tobacconist's and asked for two hundred of the best cigarettes they had. 'Not for myself, you understand,' he explained, for he hated to be thought of as a smoker. Smoking was so ugly. The sleepy young woman, however, was clearly entirely indifferent to Morris's habits. She climbed on her chair and tugged at packets on a top shelf, allowing him to see a fair way up the skirt of what was no more than a flimsy night-dress with woollen jacket worn over. People, he reflected as he watched, were so used to each other's shortcomings, each other's shamelessness, that he might perfectly well have picked up one of the awful porno-graphic magazines they were selling (something he had never dared to do), or even told her he was a serial killer, and she wouldn't have batted an eyelid. What could you expect of people in such an age? Any kind of respectability had to be fought for tooth and nail.

Ten minutes later, when he had those destitute immi-grants all gathered round a smoky fire with their *caffè latte*, croissants and Phillip Morris cigarettes, he explained that he was now personally in control of the company. Everything depended on him. They were thus being imme-diately taken on again, and this time officially. Their papers would be put in order, taxes and contributions would be paid and they would have proper contracts of the standard union-subscribed variety. So long as they behaved them-selves, they would have permanent jobs and need not fear for the future.

Sitting on the corner of the room's big table, informally, like the teacher who likes to eliminate the distance between himself and his eager students, Morris was moved in the silence after he had spoken to observe the incredulity on their dusky faces, the faintness of the smiles on sullen black and brown cheeks, the extent to which they were clearly so used to things going wrong they couldn't actually believe their good fortune, their having found a benefactor.

'Permanent jobs,' he repeated. Already it was as if killing Bobo had been the right, no, the necessary thing, and terribly worth while, and if they arrested him it would be them committing the real crime, putting a spoke in the wheel of interracial co-operation.

After a short pause, Kwame asked: 'What if Mr Posenato, he come back?'

Some of the others nodded and muttered, but Morris was thinking: how brilliant, what a perfect accomplice the boy was, and he said that they would deal with that problem when it arose. 'For the moment the police are working on the theory that he has been killed or kidnapped by Azedine and Farouk.'

It was remarkable how lightly one could say this kind of thing.

Forbes, however, who had been sitting a little to one side, staring dreamily at the fire, started quite violently: 'But that's ridiculous!'

'Oh, I don't know.' Morris was a little ruffled.

'Farouk is such a gentle boy, he would never . . .'

'Well,' Morris came in hard, 'I would never have imagined he was a raving homosexual who would let himself be buggered over his boss's desk.'

Forbes winced.

'Once you know that somebody's perverse,' Morris insisted, 'they are clearly capable of anything, aren't they? I wouldn't be at all surprised to hear that people like that had killed Bobo. I'm just sorry we ever let them in here, or didn't weed them out after that business with the septic tank.'

Forbes opened his mouth, whether purely in disbelief or intending to object wasn't clear. In any event nothing came out. His eyes were wide with a moist mixture of concern and amazement. Then it was as if he muttered something in Latin, but nobody heard. Anyway, Morris was already ploughing on, because it was so important all of a sudden to have a plan and a sense of purpose. Otherwise he might just lose the will to go through with all the gruesome details ahead. Like those cancer patients who need something to live for before they can make a miracle recovery, and so go and climb Kilimanjaro or open a handicapped children's home in Bucharest.

'From here on,' he was saying in a voice now noticeably louder, 'I am in charge of Trevisan Wines, and as long as the company can make money, I will be guaranteeing you all a decent job. As for the practical details, you will be housed here in Villa Caritas until the end of March, when major renovations will take place and you will be expected to find your own accommodation and take your rightful places in Italian society.'

Upon the mention of major renovations, Forbes's anxious features smoothed. The blacks and Slavs were dumbstruck.

'So, you go back to work this evening. OK? Because we have quotas to meet.' If necessary the Doorways truck could stay overnight. 'Meanwhile . . .' – but here Morris hesitated. When he began to speak again his voice had become quieter and more intimate. 'Meanwhile, I would like to share a piece of happy news with you. My wife, Paola, told me this morning that she is pregnant with our first child.'

Forbes immediately said: 'Oh, my good fellow, I'm so happy for you!'

'Good news, man!' Kwame shouted. The others just murmured incoherently amongst themselves, cross-legged on stone flooring in the smoky room. But Morris was not the kind of person who expected a formal display of gratitude or congratulations (though doubtless he would have offered those things himself had he been in their position). 'Kwame, come with me, please,' he said briskly and, turning on an almost military heel, left the room.

There were faxes to be sent to England. There were the workers to talk to. There were papers to be got in order, sums to be calculated, the last details of tomorrow's funeral to arrange. At last Morris was a legitimately busy man.

CHAPTER NINETEEN

THE WILL SAID NOTHING more than that Signora Luisa Trevisan's goods and chattels should be divided evenly between her surviving daughters and that she herself wished to be buried in the family tomb along with her dear husband, Vittorio, and her much-mourned daughter, Massimina.

Could anyone have ever imagined otherwise?

Morris folded the two sheets of protocol paper and looked up gravely. Antonella had her face in her hands on one of the antique chairs by the crystal-topped dinner-table of only two evenings before. The dusty old priest, always ready to collect cast-off clothes, stood beside her holding her hand, rather awkwardly, Morris felt, for someone who should be used to this role; while Kwame, erect in the corner against waxed pink stucco, looked for all the world like the kind of primitive statue that has become so popular amongst the thinking bourgeoisie: a sort of appropriation and exorcism of that alien world that suffers on the television and threatens you in the street.

As long as Morris could formulate thoughts that were intelligently redundant, then he needn't think of himself as merely the creature of his farcical crime. That was the struggle that lay before him: always to be more than what he had merely been obliged to do.

He said: 'I suppose, since the funeral is early tomorrow, they will have to open the family tomb today?'

Antonella began to weep again. Beside her were a stack of freshly printed copies of *Famiglia Cristiana*, which presumably it was her duty to deliver to the other luxury flats. But now she simply put her face on them and shook with emotion.

The priest moved softly over the parquet. 'She's very upset,' he whispered to the brother-in-law. 'The police just came and asked some very unpleasant questions.'

'In what sense unpleasant?' Morris had no difficulty feigning alarm.

'About her husband being out at night.'

'Ah.' Morris could now nod understandingly, and did indeed feel very sorry for her. Though in a sense he had done her a huge favour relieving her of a creep like Bobo. Presumably having a sordid affair with some factory girl – your Bimbetta indeed! 'Yes, yes, I see. It's just that someone has to, er, think of the practical side,' he explained. 'And unfortunately I don't know how things work *vis-à-vis* graveyards here. I mean, what the family's supposed to do and what the authorities do.'

The priest led him to a window that looked out over one of those views one can only hope console the rich for the heavy responsibilities they have to bear: blue covers over the swimming pool, lavender hedges and rosemary, the wistful statuettes gesturing in the shrubbery, and beyond that a cypress-lined drive framing the city's finest towers and campanili: Sant' Anastasia, il Duomo, La Torre dei Lamberti. The sort of view that might more success-fully have tempted Christ, Morris thought, had it been available at the time.

'The cemetery authorities do it all,' Don Carlo was saying. 'They remove the other coffins in the grave today and put the new one on the bottom tomorrow. It will all be looked after.'

'Why put the new one on the bottom?' Morris asked what he already knew, hoping he would be told more than he had asked.

'So that when it's time to remove the oldest *defunto* to make room for another, they'll be on top.'

'Ah, when they put them in the ossuary?'

'Yes.' But the priest would say no more.

'By the way,' Morris continued, as Antonella could be heard blowing her nose behind, 'I'm trying to get the *extra-comunitari*, you know, the immigrant boys at the hostel, er, *in regola*. Papers and everything. I haven't had time till now, but with the police suddenly, you know, on the scene, I'll have to do it, otherwise the poor boys will be back on the streets again, starving and thieving.'

He paused. Don Carlo politely said: 'I understand.'

'Anyway I was wondering,' Morris went on very quickly, as if it were difficult for him to ask this, 'if you could help, *padre*, when it came to, well, smoothing things over with the powers that be. I mean, explaining to them that we're talking about an act of charity.'

How Italian Morris had become! '*Un atto di carità*' sounded so exactly right in Italian.

The bespectacled Don Carlo disturbed the wrinkles round his mouth with a smile and said of course. He would put in a word.

All Morris would have to do now would be to make the expected contribution to the roof repair fund.

'*A proposito*,' the priest went on, moving back toward Antonella. 'I met your Signor 'Orbes when we took the clothes out to your hostel. *Un uomo meraviglioso!*'

'Yes,' Morris agreed and immediately warmed to the fellow.

'Very cultured. He said he would come to Mass at San

Tommaso just as soon as he has some form of transport.'

'Oh, I'll bring him myself, if that's all the problem is,' Morris said, and he and Don Carlo exchanged the kind of warm, mutually respectful smile he had never been able to share with his father. The truth was he should have started regular church attendance ages ago.

'Wonderful idea he has for a *scuola di cultura*,' the priest said. 'He asked me if I wanted to conduct some of the lessons.'

'Excellent,' Morris enthused.

'*Palmam qui meruit ferat*,' the cleric said modestly.

'Quite,' Morris agreed at random.

The priest had to go now. Very gently, the older man asked Antonella if he should give the copies of *Famiglia Cristiana* to someone else to deliver. She found a snuffle of a voice to say no, no, it would distract her a little delivering them, and it had been so kind of him to visit and pray with her.

Morris moved over and sat opposite the young widow. Their reflections hovered on the glass-topped table between them, as if in a wishing-well, and when she looked up from another attack of tears he took her pudgy hands across the polished surface, remembering how small and quick and white they had seemed when she had arranged the flowers on her father's grave in November.

He said: 'Listen, Tonia' – and it was the first time he had called her that – 'the only reason Bobo went out at night was to check that all was well on the night shift. *Va bene?* He frequently told me he felt it was his duty to put in an appearance every few nights.'

She lifted her rather blowsy face and half smiled through her tears. Morris smiled back. Again, he was thinking how there was something exquisite about her dowdiness, her obvious honesty: an emerging quality, if there was such a word, of 'genuinity'. So that not only had he done her a favour in ridding her of an inferior and unfaithful partner, but also in giving her the suffering that would bring her best qualities to maturity. Already she was a finer woman than she had been forty-eight hours ago.

Gently, he said: 'Now, let me just give you the practical details. The wreaths will be arriving in Quinzano this afternoon. Somebody will have to be there to receive them. I've got the authorities to put up death notices round the village, so don't worry about that. The hearse will be at the house at nine tomorrow morning. In the meantime, frankly, I would just tell the police to leave you alone. I'm sure you've told them all they need to know.'

She nodded. Her fingers were torturing a small crucifix round her neck now. Otherwise she wore a black blouse with a very serious brassière injudiciously white beneath.

'Oh, and by the way,' he remembered, 'Stan called me earlier on. Apparently he tried to call you yesterday evening. He said he'd have to suspend the lessons for a while because somebody's given him a course to teach in Vicenza. I said I'd pay him whatever you owed.'

Antonella stared at Morris blankly.

'When you want to go on I could always do the lessons myself,' the brother-in-law said.

Again she could only nod, but as Morris turned away and signed to Kwame to go, she got enough control of herself to say: '*Grazie, grazie, Morris. Sei davvero simpatico.* Truly sweet.' She stood up, and came round the table and kissed him softly on each cheek, holding him a little, as one who finds comfort above all in the gesture of comforting others.

'*Grazie*,' she repeated. Her plum-dark eyes glistened.

All qualities, of course, invite you to possess those who embody them, but Morris found this trustfulness of hers quite the supreme attraction. It reminded him of Mimi. Whereas Paola didn't trust anyone an inch. Let alone her husband.

'Don't worry,' he said. 'I'm sure it will all work out.'

For a moment he almost wished he could have given the woman her husband back. No, he *did* wish it. He was profoundly sorry. Not to prolong the poignancy, he gave her rounded shoulders one small squeeze, gestured to Kwame, and was off.

In the car, Morris told Kwame to drive. Which gave the Englishman a chance to observe his Third-World accomplice with more care. That curiously grainy skin real Negroes have, a cortex almost. Thicker, surely, than his own too-delicate peach-drying-to-parchment. Though he had begun to use Paola's formidable array of moisturisers; not purely out of vanity, but because of the small thrill he always got from fiddling through the mysteries of a woman's cosmetics bag.

He thought again of Mimi's darned pants that he had found in Signora Trevisan's sewing basket. Could he reasonably ask Paola to wear them sometime? Would she get off on that?

Then he remembered she was pregnant now, and this made him feel calmer and more respectful. All could yet turn out for the best with Paola. It was pointless hankering after Antonella's piety. Perhaps it was his appointed duty to make a good woman out of Paola. A sort of trial. Life might yet settle into something decent and honourable.

'From now on you drive me everywhere I need to go.'

'OK, boss.'

Taking a bend coming down from Avesa, the car wandered dangerously into the middle of the road. Kwame had to swerve to avoid an oncoming motor bike. His round cheeks remained impassive, as though nothing had happened.

Morris's likewise, though the blood had clearly drained from his face. And when Kwame simply ran the light where the country road joined the main *statale* from Trento, Morris realised that this was the right thing. This humble submission to contingency must guarantee one luck.

'You will also become my secretary and learn how to run the company when I'm busy elsewhere,' Morris went on determinedly. 'In particular, you will be responsible for the other boys at Villa Caritas, you will refer any needs to me and above all you will make sure that none of them is involved in the kind of behaviour that could cause trouble with the Italian workers or in any way pollute the atmosphere. I don't want a repeat of the Farouk-Azedine business. I find that kind of thing disgusting.'

Even as he was speaking, Morris reached forward, picked up the phone and, in an extraordinary act of memory, phoned the number he had last phoned from Roma Termini almost two years ago when he was about to pick up the ransom, about to run into Stan.

'Inspector Marangoni here.'

Not unsurprisingly, the man had not been promoted in the meantime. The office was the same, the phone number the same.

'*Sono Morris,*' he said. 'Morris Duckworth.'

There was the kind of brief pause that suggests that a call is unwelcome.

'And how can I help you?' The inspector's voice was, if possible, both avuncular and cold.

Not to be outdone, Morris left a pause himself.

A little more uncertainly the inspector asked: '*E allora?*'

'I'm not really sure if I should tell you this,' Morris said, and at the same time saw a smile forming on Kwame's face. But then he had to shut his eyes as, painfully slowly, the newly appointed chauffeur turned left across a hectically advancing stream of traffic.

'Listen, have you found those two, er, gays yet?'

'No,' Marangoni said sharply, sniffing criticism.

It was curious, Morris thought, but the man had seemed more friendly two years ago. For a moment he wondered if he mightn't be having problems with his marriage. It was a common complaint.

'I can imagine,' he said consolingly, 'it must be difficult not having photographs and documents and so on.'

'What did you want to tell me?'

'The fact is,' Morris said, 'that Bobo, er, Signor Posenato, kept, er, I suppose you would call it a second safe. I mean, apart from the main one in the wall behind the desk.'

He paused.

'For, well, illegal payments,' he added, just as Marangoni had begun to speak. So that then he had to repeat because the other hadn't heard.

'It's behind the fuse box next to the door.'

They both waited. Kwame was now cruising quite safely in light traffic along the river towards the very police station from which Marangoni was talking. The black braked sharply and gestured with his thumb. Bobo's white Audi was jammed between a Cinquecento and a German VW bus in which some Kraut hippies were clearly camping out illegally. Morris nodded and waved him on towards the cemetery.

'Well, I didn't think to look in there until this morning. I mean, it just didn't occur to me.'

'And?'

'It's empty,' Morris said. 'About two million lire gone, I should say.'

In his briefcase to be precise. The money would serve to keep Kwame sweet.

After a long pause Marangoni could say nothing more than 'Ah.'

'That's all,' Morris said, but he was struggling to ignore

what was a growing sense of the other's hostility. Then, quite suddenly, he had one of those awful moments of physical fear, when he felt with every cell in his body that he was making mistakes, that he was going to be *caught*, and it wasn't so much the consequences of such a capture that turned his muscles to water, as just the idea of being discovered, of being revealed as false. He felt deeply that he was not false. In some part of himself he was *not* false.

'Please keep me up to date on developments,' he managed to finish, and thankfully got the phone down in the middle of the other's *arrivederci*.

Kwame parked outside the cemetery. Morris's mind was still lost in a fog of things to do, things to remember, a dark turbulence where fear and confidence were constantly confused, colliding or even somehow superimposed over each other. Then the black's deep voice came rumbling through:

'Boss?'

Though he had never actually asked for it, the word was heartening.

'We're here, boss.'

Morris looked out across the pitted tarmac to the florist's stall, yellow and gold with chrysanthemums. A man was selling the local paper to those Italians who can't get by for more than a day or two without visiting their dead; and with yet another start of weary nerves, Morris realised that he hadn't read the papers yet, hadn't seen how his exploits were being described. Perhaps there was something there that would explain Marangoni's scepticism.

'We're here. What we gonna do?'

Morris drew a deep breath. 'Listen, Kwame, I want you to tell me what you think. I mean, about the whole thing.'

Kwame shrugged his shoulders. 'Big trouble,' he said. 'But boss very smart.'

It was more or less Morris's own analysis. But not enough.

'No, I mean, your advice. You see, if these two, I mean Azedine and Farouk, get, well, arrested . . .'

Kwame said nothing. His face had that purity of intelligence some inarticulate people do have, as if rather than lacking education, life had given him so much he knew there was nothing to say. He hadn't even asked, for example, why Morris had killed Bobo. Morris felt quite jealous.

'Though, I don't suppose even in Italy they could really convict them for anything, I mean, without the evidence of the body, or without actually finding the money on them . . . No, as I see it, it's just a convenient red herring to establish some distance between, between . . .'

Kwame slapped his hands in a dense rhythm from thighs to steering wheel. Despite his humble origins, he seemed perfectly at home in a Mercedes coupé.

'And then, they are homosexual, and promiscuous, and with Aids and everything they're really a peril to society.'

The rhythm that had set in – back and forth from pants to leather wheel – had that sullen knowledge of jungle drumming in films whose designs on their audiences are all too obvious.

Uneasy, Morris cast about for something that would make the black utter the words of comfort he needed. There were times when he could well convince himself he was nothing more than a poor boy whose mother had died too young.

'Listen, Kwame, I am going to be moving into the family house in Quinzano in another week or so. It's bigger, and of course Paola, my wife, is expecting a baby, so we will be needing more space. When I do that I'd like you to have the flat I've been living in till now, in Montorio. I mean, obviously you'll have to be rewarded for your help.'

Kwame nodded slowly forward and backward as he drummed, though whether in assent or gratitude, or in some instinctive response to the rhythm flowing from his fingers wasn't clear.

'I thought it was terribly clever when you asked what would happen if Bobo came back.'

Only the faintest of smiles crossed the big Negro's features as he stared through the windscreen at the stone-hooded statues over the gate. Then the drumming stopped abruptly.

'You know what I think, boss?'

'What?'

'I think there is easier ways of dumping a stiff.'

'Like?'

'In the river. In the mountains. Easy.'

Morris pondered. But whenever challenged, he tended to feel confident again. 'No, this is the right way,' he said. Then conjuring up something that was a mystery even to himself, and thus doubly pleasing, he added: 'This is the way that fits.'

To his credit, Kwame didn't question any further. 'Let's check it out, then, man,' he said. Morris, watching him stride away to the cemetery gate, thought that the black man's appearance in Via dei Gelsomini would doubtless bring down the price of the surrounding property, thus finally getting back at the builder who so far had taken him for a very long ride unscathed. Leaving the car to follow him, Morris stopped at a booth and picked up all three local papers.

Ten minutes later, as Kwame was pointing out the ossuary and the corner where coffins would be stacked, Morris leaned against a pillar and read the, he felt, inept and certainly racist headline: MASSACRED BY GAY IMMIGRANTS? MYSTERY OF MISSING BUSINESSMAN. There was no mention, he noticed with interest, of the billet-doux they had obviously found among Bobo's papers, but this just underlined the fact that you could never trust the media, or the police, to give you anything like the full picture. He must never forget that there might be things they knew that he didn't, or that he knew but didn't know they did.

Like who had made that anonymous phone call, for example.

CHAPTER TWENTY

AFTER THE BITING NIGHT air, after the smell of death and its clammy touch, the weird red pinpoints of the grave-lights and thud of the body falling from the wall, after the tight screws in old wood, the bones and skull and rags of fine clothes, after the muttered exchanges, the screws driven back over a blind face, the long drive up into the hills, where snowy tracks lost themselves in precipitous woodland, Morris felt that his crime had been more than sufficiently expiated. He had muttered a brief prayer over the closing coffin: '*Requiescat in pace.*' He had kissed the wood hiding Mimi's dear dead flesh. Then, having forgotten to squeeze them back in with Bobo in the old coffin, he had tucked Signor Trevisan's *Non-fortuna-sed-labor* bones into a capacious dry-cleaning bag and dropped the bag in a bin. A mere wash of the hands now, surely, and all evidence against him would be gone. And with the evidence would go what sin there might have been.

But that was hardly for him to judge, Morris thought.

When Kwame climbed back into the Mercedes after dumping the Audi, Morris embraced the boy and held him tight. The black's skin had a powerful live smell and his arms round Morris's shoulders were reassuringly robust. They held each other close for some time, until, disengaging, the two of them burst out laughing. They laughed and laughed in the dark of the car, far up in the pre-Alps, where snow glowed on stone walls in a moon-less night.

On the way back, Morris stopped at the bottling plant to let Kwame get back to work. They decided on the excuse that he had been outside counting carton supplies. Driving off again into the clear cold night, Morris felt at once elated and desperately eager to be generous. Could things feasibly have gone better in the end? For everybody concerned? Could those poor boys have hoped for a better master than himself? As he approached home, towards three in the morning, he actually burst into song, swinging the wheel to left and right on the empty road. The song he sang was 'John Brown's Body'. Burial really was such a weight off one's mind.

Five minutes later he was still singing when he opened the car door outside the family villa in Quinzano and stepped directly into the arms of a waiting carabiniere. Handcuffs appeared, and snapped. A voice with a strong southern accent explained, superfluously, that Signor Duckworth was under arrest.

His first thought, in the cold night with the metal clamping painfully round his wrists, was to tell all. So completely did nerves and spirit dissolve into some fetid, evil-smelling liquid, that the best thing to do seemed to be to have it all ooze out at once, to purge himself, to feel at least that it was all over. For a moment he was even eager to tell, to justify himself, to point out how reasonable and how clever he had been, to explain that his crimes were more things he suffered than planned, things that simply happened to him. And he wanted to tell them that Massimina herself had forgiven him, often spoke to him, that it was she who had told him, ordered him, to kill the boy!

But the two young carabinieri merely bundled their prisoner into the back of their Alfetta and without so much as a polite request for a confession, never mind the kind of violence that would doubtless have extracted all kinds of information from someone as fearful of physical pain as Morris, set off to drive him back to their headquarters at Quinto. One of them lit a cigarette. Morris asked if he could please extinguish it, as, in the present emotive circumstances, cigarette smoke might well make him vomit. The young carabiniere immediately acquiesced, and somehow this obedience and implied respect lifted Morris's heart. Perhaps it wasn't all over yet. Or even if it was, he had nothing to lose in playing as if it wasn't.

'How long were you waiting there?' he asked tentatively. 'You must have been dreadfully cold.'

At least he might find out how long they knew he had been absent. But for all the force's fame as blockheads, the two carabinieri merely muttered that explanations would come later.

'Can I phone my wife?' Morris asked. 'And a lawyer?' (Though the truth was he knew no lawyers, since any contact with the legal profession he had always thought might bring bad luck.) 'I mean,' he added, looking for a little of the male complicity he had always despised, 'I wouldn't like her to get the wrong idea.'

The one driving half chuckled. The other said: 'All in good time.'

Another five minutes of this and Morris began to feel like someone who, having fallen from a great height into a dark place and briefly believed himself dead, was now testing his manipulative skills with a little wiggle of this toe, a careful clenching of that hand. Just how much damage had been done?

'In fact, I only heard today,' he said, 'that she is pregnant. My wife. I wouldn't like her to imagine I'd just run for it.'

He got another chuckle. The more sober fellow grunted: '*Complimenti.*'

Suddenly at his most uncharacteristically chatty, and with a rapidly rising feeling of hilarity, because this was all quite unreal in the end, Morris asked: 'And are you folks actually going to charge me with anything?'

The driver who had been chuckling stopped. There was a short silence. Then his colleague said: '*Omicidio. Premeditato e pluriaggravato.*'

They drove in through the sliding iron gates of the carabinieri's barracks. The balloon of Morris's fragile confidence could not have burst faster. Sitting on the back seat, he brought his knees up and hugged himself tight, a desperate gesture of self-love in deflation. He took trousers and a lump of skin between his teeth and bit them hard. *Omicidio!* With malice aforethought! When the car door opened it was two or three minutes before they could persuade him to get out.

The cell was whitewashed concrete with a barred window. There were two bunk-beds, one of them occupied by a corpulent figure with tousled hair who didn't so much snore as sigh heavily with every drawn breath of dry, centrally heated air. Over the iron door with its Judas window hung the inevitable crucifix, which, curiously, Morris noted, when they turned out the light, must be of some luminous plastic material as it appeared to glow in the dark. Sleepless, self-pitying, Morris gazed at it: that pathetic twisted figure, at once put to death and master of the universe, that figure worshipped and prayed to by the two people who had meant most to him in his life: his mother, Massimina. But this thought only provoked another less pleasant. Did the carabinieri know something about Massimina too? What had they found out? For a while, Morris's mind churned over the details of the last two hectic days. What concrete piece of evidence could they have? What motive had they unearthed? What were they going to present him with tomorrow morning? Had they already found the body in old Trevisan's coffin, lying there under the tarpaulin, or had they followed Kwame and him up into the hills where they'd dumped the car?

And what alibi could he possibly give for the evening without first consulting Paola? How stupid, how hatefully stupid he had been just to rely on her sleeping through his absence, on getting back unnoticed!

Morris loathed himself when he was stupid. He deserved prison!

The other occupant of the cell sighed heavily in his sleep and groaned.

Or had Massimina told him to kill Bobo precisely so he could be arrested and punished for her death too? Could the whole thing simply have been a ghostly trap?

Footsteps passed along the corridor and for a moment it seemed their heavy, even tread must stretch away to the utmost limits of Morris's existence.

'Mimi,' he breathed out loud. 'You are all I ever cared for. Mimi?'

There was no answer of course, but, as if in compensation, the small crucifix over the door seemed to glow a little brighter. Morris stared at it. There was the head fallen to one side, the studied contortion of the body, the crown of thorns. The figure seemed to be inviting him to forget his worries in a shared gesture of resignation. 'Are you weak and heavy laden, burdened with a load of care . . .' Mother had always sung that over the dishes. Morris stared at the little crucifix, and for the first time in his life – in a carabinieri cell at four in the morning – he became lucidly aware of the possibility of the religious option as a real solution to his problems: complete sacrifice of miserable self to a greater truth and good, sense of one's allotted and humble place in a divine pattern, redemption not through works – that was beyond him now – but through faith.

He made a pact: 'Mimi,' he prayed, 'Mimi, if you get me out of this, I will give my heart to God, I promise.' The words coming from he knew not where, he added: 'I will be born again in Christ.'

Thus conscious that he had reached a major turning-point in his life, Morris Duckworth at last fell asleep on this his first night in captivity.

CHAPTER TWENTY-ONE

THEY CAME FOR HIM at six. He was forced to dress in front of them under hard fluorescent light, scrambling on his trousers, getting shirt-buttons mixed up. A deliberate humiliation. With the fluorescent Messiah still in mind, Morris wouldn't have been surprised had they jammed a crown of thorns on his head. Only when he sat back on his bed to pull on his shoes did he notice that the cell's other occupant had already gone. And there was a crumb of satisfaction here in reflecting that he must at some point during the night have slept through a disturbance similar to the one he was now experiencing. For a dazed moment, with the carabinieri standing over him and a stale smell of morning breath and dusty concrete, he thought he was going to make some remark of the variety: 'The clear conscience sleeps sound.' But no sooner had he opened his mouth than he realised how pathetic this would seem. He must not appear to be clutching at straws. He must not allow himself to be either brutalised or intimidated. On the contrary, he must aim for that perfect combination of dignity and indignation.

So in the interrogation room with its ludicrous poster – 'Hands Linked across the World for a Better Future' – he sat down in front of a tall, thin, bespectacled man and immediately told him: 'I do hope you appreciate how ridiculous all this is. Why wasn't I given some opportunity to explain myself last night and go home?'

Attack would be the best form of defence. He would create his own luck. At the back of his mind he heard his own voice whisper: 'Mimi!'

And he had a new reason for getting through now. He would become a Christian. He would undertake a mission.

The colonnello could have been no more than forty and had the unhealthy, thin-nosed pallor of the diligent. Slowly twining long fingers together, he looked at Morris for no more than a second through glinting lenses. His eyes were large and disturbingly colourless. '*Allora*, Signor Duckworth,' he said in a voice that was surprisingly clipped, 'explain away. Before you begin, though, could you just say who you are and give date and place of birth and address of present residence.'

They were sitting either side of an undistinguished desk where a rather bulky out-of-date tape-recorder on top of a pile of local newspapers had already been switched on. The room was institutional prefab, white walls and posters showing uniformed men embracing children and helping pensioners. The lighting was fluorescent.

Morris said: 'I believe it is my right to insist on having a lawyer here with me.'

'It is indeed, Signor Duckworth' – the carabiniere neither smiled nor looked up from his notes – 'under clause 223, section 2 of the *codice penale* you are entitled to have a lawyer present at all police interrogations. However, if you wish to call one and then arrange a time that suits both him and me, you can hardly complain about us keeping you until such an appointment is possible.'

Morris pulled a frowning face, apparently reflecting on this, whereas in fact he was merely registering how much more at home he had always felt with Marangoni. There had always been an atmosphere of banter and amicable challenge with the police inspector, as if they were acting out the kind of story that couldn't really end too badly. Here, however, the genre seemed of quite a different variety.

'Ask away then,' Morris said. 'I've nothing to hide.'

'If you could just begin by stating your particulars,' the pale man asked, again without so much as looking up.

'My name,' Morris said resentfully, 'is Morris Albert Duckworth, born 19/12/1960, Acton, London, Gran Bretagna, at present officially resident at Via dei Gelsomini 6, Montorio, Verona, though I am in the process of moving into my wife's family home in Quinzano, Verona. I am not guilty of any crime and am ready to answer any reasonable questions I am asked.'

'*Grazie.*' The colonnello was silent for a moment, during which time Morris was pleased to notice two rather ugly mole formations beneath his mushroom-white left ear. Cancerous? Either way, anybody truly intelligent would have had a blemish like that removed some good long time ago, as he himself had recently had a wart burnt out of the back of his hand, at not inconsiderable pain and expense. Then he heard the man say: 'I don't really have any questions, Signor Duckworth. All we need is a state-ment of confirmation or denial of the facts as we see them: that is, the manner in which and the time at which you murdered Signor Posenato.'

Morris froze. Certainly Marangoni had never talked like this, even when things had been very sticky indeed. There was an extremely unprepossessing efficiency about the young man with the death-white complexion, moles and spectacles, and something fearfully Teutonic in his voice. He pronounced the 'w' in Duckworth with a strong German 'v', while the 'th' was almost an 's'.

But Morris was determined not to confess till he at

least knew how much they knew. He would not be thrown by a simple accusation. That was child's play. Probably they accused everybody who walked in here of something awful just to see how they reacted. You never knew your luck. With a calm he wouldn't have imagined possible in such circumstances, he asked: 'You're not from around these parts, are you?'

The carabiniere frowned at something on his desk.

'I was trying to place the accent,' Morris said amiably.

'I'm from the South Tyrol,' the colonnello said half under his breath, intent on turning a page of his notebook.

'Ah, of course, Alto Adige. And your name?'

At last the man looked up. Morris experienced a flicker of triumph. Now he could work on him with his eyes, his big frank blue eyes.

'Signor Duckworth, I don't think we need . . .'

'Oh, as you will, as you will. Just that it does seem to me to be common courtesy to let another person know who they are talking to. But of course if it's a question of official secrecy, I . . .'

'Fendtsteig,' the man said evenly.

'Ah,' Morris smiled frankly, full of sympathy. 'Yes, the South Tyrol. Fendtsteig. Almost as bad as Duckworth really. Don't you find that with names like ours one can never really feel at home in Italy? There's always a gap between us and the others.'

Instead of warming to him, the man's colourless eyes were unmistakably gelid now. The lips, too, were pressed almost white. A sparse prickling showed he hadn't shaved yet, perhaps had been up all night. Morris went on quickly: 'I mean, do you ever wonder if people's characters aren't influenced by their names? I remember when I was younger . . .'

'Signor Duckvorse,' Fendtsteig cut in, and his Italian

seemed to be growing more German by the minute, 'I have no intention of having a pleasant chat with someone I believe to be a murderer. I shall now present you with the facts as we see them. You will then deny or confirm those facts, or refuse to do either as you wish, adding any extra particulars you feel should be taken into consideration. Our interview will then be over. *Capito?*'

'Of course, Colonnello,' Morris said in pantomime obedience; then just as the other was opening his mouth to read from a notebook, he put in: 'The fact is, I suppose, that for some of us the social graces die hard.'

But the pale man had already started to read, impervious, Morris realised, to either charm or shame; and as he read, his voice was completely flat, and as sure of itself as a recorded message.

'On the morning of Wednesday, February 28th, you left your house at seven-thirty to proceed to work as was your normal habit.'

Morris pushed back his seat, crossed his legs, propped his right elbow on his knee and took the knuckle of a forefinger between his teeth. His brow knitted in concentration. His left hand grasped his right foot. The pose he had once assumed in university lectures.

'During the journey your wife, Paola Trevisan-in-Duckvorse, phoned and alerted you to the fact that her mother had died. She asked you to drive immediately to your mother-in-law's house, where you arrived at seven-fifty. You spoke to the nurse, then immediately went downstairs, saying you needed to make a phone call. You were then discovered by your sister-in-law, Antonella Trevisan-in-Posenato, searching through her mother's belongings and spent ten minutes with her asking questions about the inheritance.'

Morris was on the point of interrupting here. Clearly words like 'discovered' and 'searching' were heavily loaded, as if he had already been doing something wrong. It wasn't fair. It was like *L'Étranger*, where the poor fellow was accused of having smoked a cigarette at his mother's wake, as though this in some way demonstrated that he was guilty of shooting the Arab. But even as Morris opened his mouth to object, he was unnerved by the reflection that actually it *was* outrageous for a man to smoke a cigarette at his mother's wake. It was terrible. Certainly Morris never would. Though it was frankly unkind of the caretaker who had given him the cigarette to present it to the police so negatively. As perhaps it had been unkind of Antonella to tell the police that he had asked her about the inheritance. Unless she was simply being candid and didn't realise that a fact like that could be used to smear his character. But now he had lost the thread of what Fendtsteig was saying.

'I'm sorry, could you go back a bit. I lost you at the inheritance business.'

Like a tape-recorder wound back, Fendtsteig repeated in exactly the same monotone: '. . . asked questions about the inheritance. You then drove off to the family company's headquarters outside Quinto, where you had an argument with your brother-in-law, Signor Posenato, with whom you have long had a difficult, not to say stormy, relationship.'

'Stormy', Morris thought, was far too attractive and passionate a word to describe his dull exchanges with the miserable chicken magnate, but he let it pass.

'The argument of the morning in question presumably had to do with the Trevisan inheritance and a will apparently in Signor Posenato's possession. The argument became heated, on which you fell to blows and killed him – no, please, Signor Duckvorse, can you save your comments until I have finished reading this account.'

'My apologies,' Morris begged, for he had rather impolitely burst out laughing. 'I was just . . .'

Fendtsteig raised his eyes to treat Morris to one of his rare Gestapo gazes of unblinking eyes behind cold lenses; lenses, Morris now noticed, which were not as clean as they might have been.

'I was just thinking what a funny collocation "fell to blows" was.'

Fendtsteig looked down again. Probably the poor fellow didn't even know what 'collocation' meant. Then exactly as the man began to read, Morris said: 'Sorry, please do go on.' Fendtsteig ignored it.

'. . . killed him, perhaps by accident, given the kind of scuffle indicated by the disarray of the furniture and the lack of blood that a conventional weapon would have caused. But perhaps not. Perhaps that was set up. Certainly a number of items had been moved before we arrived, despite your claims to the contrary. In any event, your fingerprints were found in a very unusual position on the upturned chair, on the desktop and on various file drawers.'

What, Morris wondered, was a very unusual position for a fingerprint on a desktop? The kind that Farouk and Azedine would have left? He wouldn't have been surprised if Bobo and his improbable Bimbetta hadn't left a good few themselves.

Could Bobo have actually fired the immigrants because *they* found *him*!? It was becoming harder and harder to concentrate on what the carabiniere was saying.

'You then put Signor Posenato in his own car. You drove a very short distance and hid the vehicle. Perhaps in a local garage. You then walked back to the scene of the crime and, seeing that nobody had as yet discovered it, called the police from your car phone. It was now ten o'clock. The following night, you left the house in Quinzano after your wife was already asleep, returned to the car and drove it away somewhere to dispose of the body. You then drove it back to its nearby hiding-place, got back into your own car and returned home. That is the end of our version of events. I would now like to invite you to confirm or deny them.'

Good. Morris waited.

'*Per favore*, Signor Duckvorse.'

'Colonnello Fendtsteig, please don't feel you have to hurry things for me. If there are one or two other crimes you'd like to accuse me of at the same time, do go ahead.'

The pale man waited, then said quietly: 'This is a serious matter, Signor Duckvorse. I would be grateful if you could treat it as such.'

'Worth,' Morris said.

Fendtsteig looked up from his notes but only to gaze past Morris through the window.

Morris sighed. For a moment he almost wished he smoked, since apart from the histrionic effect and the opportunities for playing for time, lighting a cigarette would now have given him an excellent chance to show that his hands weren't shaking one bit. Because they had nothing on him at all! It was all pure speculation, and quite wrong for the most part. Your argument 'presumably had to do with the Trevisan inheritance'! Indeed! Perhaps in a local garage! Perhaps! Not to mention the fact that they couldn't have found his prints on the chair. It was impossible. Or did they think he was going to be so stupid as to say: Look, I wiped them off with a wet-wipe?

Eventually, he said: 'Colonnello Fendtsteig, do you ever actually communicate with your colleagues in the polizia? You know? I mean, it would save a lot of time and I wouldn't have to try to remember what I've already said and to whom.'

'Signore Duckvorse, I asked you to confirm or deny what I read out to you.'

'Because, as I explained to the polizia yesterday, Bobo fired two of our immigrant workers the night before he was killed . . .'

'You admit, then, that he was killed?'

'What?' But Morris knew he had slipped up.

'You know that he is dead?'

Morris made his eyes wide and puzzled. Speaking, he was very aware of how his tone of voice would come over on the tape-recorder. 'Oh, I *see*. No, I imagined that since you were so convinced he'd been killed you must have found the body or something.' He waited, but had begun to feel nervous again. Sometimes the ice was so desperately thin, and if he went through it he knew there'd be no coming back up. He breathed deeply, forced himself to think. 'There is also quite frankly the fact that these two men disappeared immediately afterwards and all the petty cash along with them. From Bobo's office. The safe behind the fuse box.'

Fendtsteig didn't immediately reply. He studied his notes. Morris forced himself to be patient. The man obviously cultivated this disturbing habit of avoiding all eye contact and generally refusing to engage in a properly personal conversation. The thing was, Morris thought, to treat it as the pathetic ruse it was and not to be thrown by it.

'Naturally,' Fendtsteig finally remarked, turning a page, 'naturally the police informed us of all this. But we are not impressed. The two men were seen leaving the area of Villa Caritas at five in the morning, whereas Signor Posenato spoke to a number of workers arriving for the morning shift at seven. So he was still alive then. As for the petty cash, we have only your word for it.'

It was intriguing, though, Morris thought, that the police hadn't yet told their colleagues that Bobo had called them at nine. Should he? For a moment he hesitated, then suddenly felt impatient again. Enough was enough. It was time to put an end to this charade and get on home for breakfast. He said: 'Colonnello Fendtsteig, I, Morris Duckworth, categorically deny killing my brother-in-law, Roberto Posenato. I deny being on bad terms with him. On the contrary, we had an excellent business relationship. Over the last few months we have turned the business round and we were extremely pleased with ourselves. I deny going straight from my mother-in-law's house to the company. I stopped in the bar in the piazza in Quinzano, and then went to what we call Villa Caritas, some way beyond Quinto, where I spoke for some time to one of the immigrants, a certain Kwame, before going on to the company. I categorically deny being engaged last night in anything but my own very private business.'

And that, Morris thought, or at least until they did a little more homework, should be that.

The colonnello left another long pause. Again he consulted his notes, leafing through pink-lined pages. To Morris's left, the window was suddenly less black and glossy. A first filtering of winter light found the profile of a car, the outline of a low building beyond. And something of the institutional squalor of it came home to him: grey lines in grey light, the sort of rectangles and compounds they would be trying to trap him in for ever now. Suddenly he felt deeply afraid. For what he wanted was to be free. Free to drive through the countryside, to help the immigrants, to look at art, to make love to his wife, to bring up his child. Were they unreasonable ambitions? Under his breath, he whispered: 'Mimi!'

'*Mi scusi?* You wanted to say something?'

'No,' Morris said.

Fendtsteig ran a tooth over a thin lower lip. 'First: we have no confirmation that you went to the bar in Quinzano. Nobody remembers you going in there that morning.

Second: the witness who is supposed to have talked to you at Villa Caritas was not convincing. He was unable to say how long you spoke together, or what about. Third: we have it from your wife, sister-in-law and various workers at Trevisan Wines that you were not on good terms with Signor Posenato. Fourth: there is your long absence of yesterday evening to account for.'

To avoid eye contact this time, Fendtsteig examined the tape-recorder, turned a volume control. It was almost as if they were communicating by fax. Yet the tighter the corner Morris seemed to be getting into, the more determined he became to fight his way out of it. And he began to feel the growing warmth of self-justification. He *had* sat in that bar. He *had* gone to Villa Caritas. And if he had killed Bobo afterwards, he certainly hadn't planned to do so and certainly did not deserve to spend the rest of his life languishing in a prison cell for the fact. He was himself a more attractive and better-educated person than Bobo, or Fendtsteig for that matter, and one presently engaged in various acts of charity, not to mention the religious crisis he was going through. What's more, he had tried to reason with the boy and offered him a perfectly acceptable and even aesthetically pleasing version of the Massimina story which Bobo had refused even to consider.

Morris said: 'I would be more than happy to go to the bar with you and identify the waitress who served me and describe the boy who passed me the local newspaper. Presumably, you asked if an Englishman had been there and they said no, because my Italian is so good.'

Morris put not a little stress on the word 'my', as if to suggest that his accent was in fact rather better than Fendtsteig's, the colonnello having doubtless grown up speaking pidgin Kraut in some God-forsaken, snow-buried village above Bozen. As a result of which he quite probably suffered from that appalling Austro-Germanic superiority complex. Morris felt combative. Italian justice would never allow some mean-minded South Tyrolean to condemn him. And ugly to boot. Those moles definitely looked malignant.

'As for the boy I spoke to at Villa Caritas,' he added, 'he had been working all night, and in any event, they're all on drugs. Actually, I'm amazed he can remember speaking to me at all. Obviously, what we talked about was the business of Bobo having fired these two workers and then everybody else.'

Fendtsteig pored over his papers, allowing the tape-recorder to pick up nothing more than Morris clearing his throat and the sound of another car pulling into the yard outside. Daylight, mingling with the room's sad fluorescence, was doing nothing, Morris reflected, to improve the colonnello's unshaven complexion. The passing time irritated him. They should put a time clock on the man. Like in chess. Into the silence he tried: 'Are you ill, Colonnello Fendtsteig?'

'*Prego?*' The man had an ugly 'r'.

'You look so pale.'

Fendtsteig chose to ignore him. He looked up and folded his arms, thin face to one side, glasses flashing neon. 'Please, explain last night,' he said. 'After which, we have finished.'

Morris hesitated, then thrust back his chair. 'No, I've had enough of being treated like this. I won't say a word more until I have spoken to a lawyer.'

'So, we have arrived at the unanswerable question.' Fendtsteig at last managed a smile and looked directly, coldly into Morris's eyes. 'Or is it that you need time to remember where you were only eight or nine hours ago?'

Meeting that freezing gaze, so perfectly timed, Morris was distinctly aware of having lost the initiative, of having made some awful tactical mistake. He wavered, stood up.

'Not at all, Colonnello. But if you are so convinced I am guilty, then everything I say will be turned against me.'

Then, as he was getting to his feet, his whole body was swamped with scorching heat. It came up from his groin, fast and prickly, the skin on his hands and cheeks tingled with blood. There was even the thickening of an erection. *If only he could just solve the whole damn stupid problem by wringing the little rat's neck!* At the same moment a voice deep inside, as if calling from the bottom of a well, screamed no. The sound swelled and echoed in his head. *No, Morri, no! Don't!* Accompanied by an oppressive darkness. Curtains were being drawn in on either side of the world. Vision was narrowing and narrowing to the last bright glint of Fendtsteig's spectacles.

Swaying on his feet, Morris leaned forward and grabbed at the desk. His hand closed on a great glass paperweight in the shape of a whale. He clutched at it. *No!* her voice was screaming. His head spun.

PART THREE

PART THREE

CHAPTER TWENTY-TWO

FROM A SHEET OF paper, his fourteenth day in gaol, Morris cut out a cross. More difficult was crucifying Our Lord on it. But he remembered the curious twist the body must have, the curve following through from hips and torso to the head leaning on the left shoulder and then the undulating arms, sinking at the elbow, rising to cruelly nailed hands. Not unlike, he thought, the trained contortions of vines stark in winter sunlight on the Veronese hills. When he turned the hands to leaves his serial-murderer cellmate was most impressed. The face, as it must be, was hers. Androgynous, but identifiable. Morris stared at the nth effort and saw he'd got it right. Perhaps he did have a talent for the visual arts after all. He tucked the top of the cross into a crack above the room's small mirror, then folded the rest of the paper down so that it seemed to divide his reflected face into four small segments around its twin axes of torment. IHS. Certainly Catholicism was more satisfying than his mother's austere Methodism, infinitely richer; and staring at the face he'd drawn, Morris muttered the words he'd learnt at catechism when preparing for his marriage: '*Ave Maria*; hail, Mary! full of grace, blessed art thou among women.'

'And blessed,' his psycho-cellmate chimed in, 'the fruit of your womb, Jesus Christ.'

Morris looked up. The fruit of her womb? He had

forgotten that part. The other man's eyes, looking round from the window, were glassily empty. But for Morris the message was only too clear. He had killed the fruit of her womb. In his dear Mimi, he had crucified Christ, even before he could be born. Upon reading the radiant alarm on his face, his cellmate, who it seemed had done away with his whole and remarkably extended family, burst into raucous laughter. The man had a frightening way of blowing out fat cheeks and chuckling for too long over things that weren't funny. Morris, before the cross he had made himself, crossed himself, and fell to his knees. Somehow he would make amends. Indeed, his only real reason for wanting to get out of here, for being alive at all, was to make amends.

But when would he get out? The lawyer, when they finally let him see one, had explained that he hadn't been officially charged as yet, was only being held because if released he might pervert evidence pertaining to a crime. Apparently they could do that for up to six months, though in Italy, Morris often felt, they could do more or less whatever they wanted anyway. And what they wanted most of all of course was for him to tell them what he had been doing that night; indeed they wouldn't let him out until he did, because that would give him the chance, they said, to cook up a story with someone else. His wife for example.

This, the lawyer explained, was why a guard had to be present throughout their interview. This was why he wasn't being allowed any visitors.

Morris had objected strongly to the notion that he might cook up a story. And he made it clear that he would never, never, never tell what he had been doing that night. It was his own private business. Anyway, there was no need for him to tell them anything when it was quite clear that whatever had happened to Bobo was the responsibility of the two immigrants. Why hadn't they caught them yet?

Delicately, the lawyer had hinted that his wife might not mind so much if he said he had spent those missing hours with another woman. Or even a man. Morris had dismissed the fellow at once. Both for impertinence and incompetence. For not only had it never occurred to Morris to be unfaithful to his wife, but he felt it must be perfectly clear to all and sundry that he was just not that kind of person. Nobody would believe such a story. He himself barely believed it of Bobo.

Then gaol was not without its consolations, for the moment. The humiliations of prison clothes, prison food, prison companions, Morris quickly decided, offered the sort of mortifying experience that set one apart, gave one a more human perspective on things. As if, like Dante, one had been allowed to make a brief visit to hell, check out everybody's sins, their punishments, their state of mind, but always in the knowledge that one was not oneself one of the damned. For, consolations or no consolations, Morris had no intention of staying very long. It was just that, since Mimi had promised she would tell him how to get out, he simply didn't need to worry about it.

In his prison cell he drew his crucifixions and kept his Mimi journal: page after page of philosophical dialogue, fulsome affection, bizarre narrative. It was she who invented all the wonderful inaccuracies there. She was so clever at that. Or if time hung heavy, he liked to psycho-analyse his cellmate, which he did rather well, he thought. Certainly the man seemed much improved by the kind of attention Morris was paying him. It even occurred to Morris that if they did ever manage to put him away for any length of time, he might do worse than take a degree and doctorate in psychology. It was something he was well equipped for and doubtless the prison would throw up analysis fodder in abundance. At mealtimes he was careful not to overeat, he must stay in trim. There would be so much to be done when he got out: completing the move to Quinzano, planning the renovation of Villa Caritas, developing the company into something rather more serious than it was at present.

In the evenings, on closing his eyes for sleep, Morris would lie back in the blissful peace that came with conjuring Mimi: Mimi as she had been on the beach at Rimini: the raven hair, the smell of her lotioned skin, the smooth length of her; Mimi in a bar drinking Coca-Cola, head tipped back, lips parted, eyes smiling; and now she was with him in the hotel room that moment when he turned from washing blood from his hands to find that she had let her night-dress slip down over those huge breasts. The first time he ever saw her naked, that splendid slim, full body. Morris was in paradise. What a rich life he had had!

But he didn't masturbate. He just held her smiling image perfectly there before him, not unlike the way he used to remember his dead mother, holding some image still and full in his adolescent mind. And it was during one of these pre-sleep reveries that she came to him and very simply explained how it was to be done. There were parallels, he later thought, with the angel who threw open the prison doors for the Apostle Peter, who loosened his chains and took him past the guards. Just that Mimi was a shade subtler. Who would ever have thought it of her?

The priest, when Mimi decided it was time he should ask for one, was young and suave and clearly liberal, which unfortunately did not fit in at all with Morris's vision of how their conversation should be. However, making do with what the Lord had provided seemed very much the story of his life. He explained to the man, who wore fashionable, gold-rimmed glasses, that although he, Morris, wasn't guilty of any crime, his imprisonment had brought on a sort of religious crisis. All this time he'd had to think and to see other people suffering had led him to appreciate that the life he had been trying to live till now, his modern, businessman's affluent existence, had no meaning at all, was merely the voracious mouth of materialism chasing the arid tail of hedonism.

The priest no more than blinked at this gem.

Plus there was something else weighing on his mind, Morris said. Something that would give him no peace.

The priest watched intently as he spoke and, being watched, Morris noted that the man had cut himself shaving too closely to a small snub nose.

The fact was, he said, that when he had converted to Catholicism something over a year ago, he had done so merely out of convenience, in order to marry. In truth, he had lied before God when he had spoken of his penitence, since the whole thing had been merely form to him, like getting some bureaucratic document stamped or something. In fact he hadn't even believed in God at the time, he had been so bitter about this other thing in his life, this other thing that weighed on his heart, and that he had never mentioned. Morris looked the man straight in the eye, then bowed his head. Now he wished to make a proper, full confession and receive the Host and feel he had been accepted into Christ's church.

From his cassock the priest produced a diary with the Reader's Digest logo, and a further appointment was fixed. So that during the recreation hour of two days later, Morris knelt in a prefab confession box in a small cement chapel and began to tell, among other things, how he had been in love with and had had sex with his wife's sister, Massimina, before she was kidnapped and killed some years ago, and how he had then married his wife only because she reminded him of her sister, with whose soul in paradise he was still in love, and whom he regularly saw in sleep and sometimes even awake in the form of the Madonna and other saints, and whom he thought about quite constantly, with the result that he lived in a state of profound alienation from his wife, as if he wasn't really with her at all. Of course he made hundreds of simple material decisions with Paola, about furniture and meals and means of transport and suchlike, but really it was as if he never spoke to her at all, because that bourgeois outward aspect of his life, the practical accumulation of wealth and so on and so forth, was completely meaningless – and when they made love it was Massimina he saw, Massimina he imagined, even calling out her name sometimes, so that he felt desperately guilty and at the same time blocked, paralysed, unable to move forward in his life, unable to be generous or even true to himself.

Morris spoke for about twenty minutes like this, responding to a question here and there, some small request for clarification, but for the most part pressing on blindly, or rather cleverly and passionately inventing, even as he spoke, what was after all the inescapable underlying truth, the deep structure of his unconscious mind, this profound mental malaise into which life had plunged him and from which he earnestly desired to escape. Yet his obsession was such, as he explained, that recently he had arrived at extremes of perversion he would never have imagined possible in his saner days. Terrible, impure things.

'Tell me, *figlio mio*,' the priest said softly.

But Morris felt too embarrassed, he said, too deeply ashamed.

It was through the unburdening of shame that the soul achieved liberation, the priest said persuasively.

Morris fell silent. The truth was his knees were hurting on the hard floor, although at the same time he realised how appropriate this was.

'*Figlio mio*, all have sinned. There is nothing the Lord has not heard and forgiven before.'

This reminded Morris of his reflections on the carnival crowd in Piazza Bra, the Draculas and Saddam Husseins, though all that seemed a very long time ago now.

'*Grazie, padre*,' he said, then let a good thirty seconds pass before offering: 'Shortly before I came into prison, my mother-in-law died.' He stopped.

'That was hardly your fault,' the priest remarked.

'In order to bury her in the family grave' – there was an edge in Morris's voice now – 'they had to . . .'

'Yes, my son?'

He shifted his weight to shake a cramp out of his right leg.

'They had to pull out Massimina's coffin. That is the girl I loved. I love.'

The priest now filled the considerable space Morris left here by remarking that this was perfectly normal procedure.

'When I . . . when I heard that her coffin would be left out the night before the burial, I went to the cemetery. I went after it was closed. I climbed over the wall' – here Morris faltered – 'I climbed over the wall and found her coffin and sat by it for hours.'

'Again that is hardly a sin, my son.'

'I sat by it, in the dark, and I masturbated. Twice,' Morris said.

The priest was silent now. Morris became acutely aware of his breathing just the other side of the small grille. 'But it's not so much what I did that was bad. It was what I was thinking.'

There was a pause. 'And what were you thinking, my son?'

'My heart was full of bitterness,' Morris said.

This was true.

'You had thoughts you are now ashamed of?'

'I thought,' Morris said, enunciating very carefully, but as if against all the odds, 'I thought that I . . . I wished it was my wife who had been kidnapped and killed, not Massimina, and I wished I could have sex with Massimina, even dead as a corpse, even decomposed as she must be in that awful box.' He hesitated, wondering if this wasn't going rather too far. 'I wished I could pour my sperm into her, even in the state she is in now.'

'*Figlio mio*,' the priest said, clearly finding this heavy going, although, working in a prison, Morris thought, one must get to hear some pretty ugly stuff. The man could hardly afford to be squeamish. He waited.

After a moment the priest asked: 'Is that all, my son?'

Wasn't it enough? Morris thought for a moment, then said: '*Sì, padre, sì*, except . . . you see, ever since then I've been unable to get these thoughts out of my head. I think of nothing else. It's humiliating. Totally humiliating. My mind is completely blocked. I mean, they've put me here for something I didn't do, and I don't even care. I'm even happy to be here. Because my mind is so blocked and paralysed I wouldn't know what to do if I got out. I can't bear the thought of seeing my wife and feeling so guilty with her all the time. Then to make matters worse she's expecting a child, which should . . .'

Quite unexpectedly, quite genuinely, Morris began to cry. It was the third or fourth time in just a few days. His ugly infant sobs filled the enclosed space. And what he was crying for, he thought quite lucidly, was all the lies he had to tell, and what a true picture those lies nevertheless painted of his perverted soul.

After a few more minutes of this, of Morris trying to stem the tidal wave of his self-pity and the voice the other side of the grille murmuring words of comfort into the tempest of his tears, the bell sounded for the end of the recreation period and hence the time had come for ecclesiastical authority to announce the required penance.

Morris was hoping for something dramatic, something that might quite convincingly confer forgiveness, but in the end and after what was, when you came to think of it, remarkably little reflection, the young priest betrayed his liberalism by offering nothing more than a modest dosage of *Ave Marias* and *mea culpas*.

'But . . .' Morris began.

'Your sins are not sins of wilfulness,' the priest explained. 'They are sins of sickness, a sickness so profound that I do not imagine any penance, however extravagant and well meant, could resolve it.' He paused. 'On the contrary, this is a case where even penance itself might become a perverse form of indulgence. You must understand that your heart and your soul are sick. You must pray to God to cure your sickness. Above all, you must learn to want to be cured.' The priest hesitated. 'Frankly, if you will let me advise you, my son, I believe it is your duty both to God and to your wife to see a psychiatrist.'

Morris made a noise of protest. If he had come to a priest rather than to a psychiatrist, it was because he believed that help lay only in God and in a complete turning away from the life he had been living. He had been having strange visions in his sleep recently, he added quite truthfully, visions that seemed to him profoundly religious in nature. He saw the Madonna.

'*Figlio mio*' – the priest got up and began to move – 'so long as it remains obedient to His will, learning is a blessed virtue. I suggest that I get in touch with the prison psychiatrist and arrange a meeting for you as soon as possible.'

Again Morris appeared to object, upon which the priest's voice hardened. 'Consider it, if you like, an integral part of your penance. I repeat, the Lord has given us skill in medicine precisely in order to deal with cases like yours.'

This was a fair comment, Morris thought as he emerged from the cramped confessional to shake the man's hand and return to his cell. But far more importantly it meant that some three or four days later he would be able to hand over to that prison psychiatrist the scores of pages of notes he had been writing under her dictation ever since they had put him in prison. After which, assuming the man actually read them and had checked up some file or other on his case, it should be nothing more than a matter of time before they let him out. Because they could hardly accuse him of reticence after reading that lot. If it was a story they wanted, then they had got one, and far more convincingly than if he had just told it to them: a brilliantly concocted alibi, and brilliant precisely because it had been *she* had thought of it. Though when in sleep Mimi returned to him as the *Vergine incoronata*, he insisted that, fabrications apart, the conversion part of his story was real. Truly it was. But Mimi said of course she knew that anyway, since she could read inside his soul. She knew he believed, just as she always had, in the almighty God and in Christ crucified and in the transubstantiation of the bread and wine into the blessed body and blood. It was just that if he were to make good use of the life and talents God had given him, if he were to help those poor immigrants and be a good father to Paola's child, then there was no point in his getting himself put away for the rest of his life, was there? So she had had to invent this rather unpleasant story of the cemetery and the coffin, to get her lover out of here.

Having said this, the blessed Virgin removed her holy crown, and opening her long blue robe on the most perfect wax-white nakedness, stretched out beside him. Waking in the dark light of the small hours, Morris found himself as it were borne upwards out of sleep on an extraordinary tide of well-being, the air around him dense with her perfume, the prison darkness throbbing with her presence. Footsteps passed, plodding slowly down the corridor, keys jingled, his cellmate groaned in his nightmares. Apparently nothing had changed. But Morris knew that he was in the best of hands now. All would be well. 'Mimi,' he breathed into the dawning of another day.

CHAPTER TWENTY-THREE

DESPITE MOURNING, PAOLA HAD applied Marlboro-red lipstick and Baci-blue eye-shadow. Which was somewhat injudicious, Morris thought as he emerged from the prison gate into hard, bright winter sunlight. For sure enough, a small knot of pressmen were waiting, in search of fresh fuel for a story that had been smouldering on the inside pages of the local papers for more than a month now.

'Scandalous Revelations Imminent,' had been the line throughout. Was Posenato really dead, or had he been kidnapped? Could it, perhaps, have been a mistress's husband who had made the anonymous call to say he had got what he deserved? And why was the English brother-in-law refusing to co-operate? But with so many questions and so few answers, the affair had never quite managed to match up to the editors' expectations, was in danger of becoming, like Mimi's story of two years ago, just another saga of ungratified speculation.

The photographers stepped forward. Embracing his wife with simplicity and restraint, Morris was careful neither to hide his face nor to pose, in short to offer nothing that might encourage those paid to daydream on behalf of a jaded public. His expression, for the brief moment he faced their flashlights, was that of someone who has survived a difficult ordeal with dignity. On being asked for comment by a man with a microphone, he said politely that he hoped his release meant that the police now had some kind of idea who the real culprit was. No, for his own part he bore no hard feelings about his imprisonment, despite its manifest injustice. On the contrary, the experience had been instructive, had brought him to a deeper understanding of himself.

A moment later he was in the Mercedes, with Paola pulling quickly away into traffic. For a minute or two, they were silent, then at the first crossroads she burst into laughter.

'*Dio santo*, you're so funny!' she said.

Morris was still in something of a daze, his head full of plans, people to see, vows and resolutions to be honoured.

'What do you mean?'

'I don't know, it's the way you always say exactly the right sanctimonious thing to these people. You're such a beautiful hypocrite. I do love it.'

Morris said crisply: 'I meant every word of it. I bear no hard feelings at all towards anyone.'

But again his wife was laughing softly. 'My old Mo,' she said in her sardonic English. '*Dio Cristo*, I've missed fucking you.'

Morris winced. It occurred to him that one of the factors that had made his prison cell less of a misery than he had expected was the absence of his wife and this peculiar way she had of interpreting his character and then damning herself by appearing to appreciate the devil she mistakenly saw in him. No, he hadn't missed her at all. Although now that she was to be the mother of his child there was nothing for it but to settle down and do his best to love her, hope that motherhood would mellow her. Because this was one of the important decisions he had taken in the last few days in prison. Marriage would be a sort of alternative life sentence. After all, Morris had never pretended that he hadn't sinned ('all had gone astray'), only that it must be he who decided on the appropriate form of expiation.

A life with Paola seemed more than sufficient.

Steering with her left hand, Paola put her right on his thigh and began a fingertip massage down the inside of his leg. Morris took the hand and lifted it chastely to his lips. Again she burst out laughing.

'*Che romantico!*' she said. Then, without any apparent change of tone she asked: '*Allora*, what did you tell them in the end?'

'How do you mean?'

'Come on. About where you were that evening. I couldn't tell them anything in case you'd told them something different. I said I thought you were having an affair maybe. I tried to get the lawyer to suggest it to you, but when he told me about your little scene, I realised you must have something else in mind.'

Morris was silent. The extraordinary thing, he thought, was how he could be at once so clever and so stupid. Having accepted Mimi's complicated plan for getting him out of gaol, giving an alibi and at the same time explaining why he hadn't given it before (how well humiliation could stand in for authenticity), he hadn't even begun to think of what he would say to the pregnant wife he was supposed to be spending the rest of his life with. The fact was of course that if the carabinieri hadn't gone and arrested him that night, she would never have realised he wasn't by her side. Since between falling asleep in the evening and rising in the morning, Paola had never been known to wake up once. So deeply complacent was her spirit.

It occurred to Morris then that somebody who never lost sleep would likewise never be able to begin to understand him. They were utterly incompatible.

'*Allora?*'

'I am not having an affair,' Morris said coldly. 'I am not the kind of person who has affairs.'

Braking for a red light, she said: 'It wouldn't be the end of the world if you were, you know, Mo. One understands that these things happen.'

'I beg your pardon?'

'I mean, people do have affairs, you know. It's not something to lose one's head about.'

Morris said firmly: 'As I see it, faithfulness is the basis of any relationship that involves complicity. Being married means being faithful.'

For some reason saying this made him think of Kwame. More and more his brain seemed to make connections all its own, while that part of him that was most consciously Morris experienced a vague and not unpleasant sense of vertigo.

Paola was laughing again. Almost everything he had said this morning seemed to have made her laugh. She shook softly, holding the wheel with two hands again now.

'*Sei comico*, Mo.'

Morris began to feel angry. It was this way she had of never taking him seriously.

'I imagine,' he said, 'having read yesterday's newspaper, that they've let me out, not because of anything I told them, but because they've finally arrested those two *marocchini* who presumably did whatever it was that was done.'

Paola nodded: 'According to the police, yes. But that man Fendtsteig with the carabinieri obviously feels differently.' After a pause she added: 'He still thinks it was you.'

Folding his arms, Morris said: 'Clearly I'm the victim of some sort of ridiculous rivalry between the police and the carabinieri. Both of them want to solve the big local crime first. And since the police are on to the right people,

223

the carabinieri have to find someone else.' But in the silence that followed, Morris was careful not to ask whether his wife shared Fendtsteig's suspicions. Even to show that such a suspicion was imaginable on her part would be a considerable error.

Paola was accelerating now, driving up the city's circular road to where rugged hills loomed from the plain. A late fall of snow was sharply white in the blue distance of the pre-Alps, and Morris was pleased to realise that in his absence she must have completed the change of households. They were going to Quinzano. He'd be able to sleep in Mimi's bed again tonight.

'All the same,' she came back, 'you must have told them something, since whatever they say, you were really being held for reticence. They could have kept you another five months if you hadn't told them something.'

When he didn't reply, she laughed: 'Not much complicity here for anyone to want to remain faithful to.'

But Morris bit the inside of his cheek. He would not speak. He would not be told what he could and could not say to his wife, whose duty in the end was simply to trust him willy-nilly. 'Honour' and 'obey' were the words as he recalled them. Then noticing the shrine of La Nostra Signora di Lourdes perched on the first hilltop above the city, he suddenly remembered a vow. 'Turn right at the lights,' he ordered. He was determined to be a more head-of-the-household Morris.

'Why?'

'Turn right, I have to go to a church,' he said.

'*Scusa?*' She honestly thought she had misunderstood.

'I have to go to a church,' he repeated.

Ten minutes later, in the disappointingly modern surroundings of San Giovanni Fuori, he lit a four-hundred-lire candle. Bowing his head on a small seat beside an incredulous Paola, he was briefly reminded of that time he had gone into a church with Massimina, the first day of their elopement, of how eager she had been to convert him, how cynical and superior he had felt. Well, she had won in the end. The wheel had come full circle: Morris was at last learning humility. But what wouldn't he have given to be back there now! Back with that breathless, eager young girl at his side in the house of God.

Standing to face a poorly executed Deposition above the altar, Morris crossed himself and muttered a determined prayer of gratitude.

Behind him, Paola whispered: 'Have you gone crazy, Mo, or are we being followed by the press or something?' At the threshold, coming out, she pulled her cigarettes from her bag and thrust one between bright-red lips. It wasn't clear whether she was irritated, or just plain nervous.

Morris turned and rather dramatically put his hands on her shoulders, determined to give her a chance. His eyes found hers, his own glassy and blue, hers flightily quick and brown. 'Seeing that you're pregnant, *cara*,' he said, speaking very slowly, 'I really do think you should stop smoking. I mean, I think we should try to settle down now and concentrate on having a healthy, happy family. That's all I've ever wanted.'

His wife's pretty features froze. For a moment it seemed she might burst out laughing. Then the colour drained from her face.

'Whoever said I was pregnant?'

'I know you are,' he said. 'I was told in a dream.'

Returning to the car he realised the phone was ringing, and since Paola had already buzzed the door open, Morris hurried to pick up the receiver before the call was lost. But on hearing his '*Pronto*', whoever it was must have realised they'd got a wrong number and hung up.

CHAPTER TWENTY-FOUR

LATER ON THAT DAY, Morris made a list. There was the company to get running again (state of order book, possible investments), the immigrants to keep happy, Forbes to mollify, the Quinzano house to get in order (furniture and one or two paintings to buy), his wife to deal with (how?), and above all his own back to watch. Sitting at the seventeenth-century writing table in the small room he had decided would be his study, this attractive young Englishman was at once daunted and excited by the prospect of the coming weeks. Clearly, however, if one were to arrange one's responsibilities in order of priority, then watching one's back would have to be the first; since the success of all other tasks depended on that.

Morris sat erect at the elegant table, very aware of himself, of his new-found liberty, and sucked on a Parker pen. Could they really have lost interest in him, or was Morris Duckworth still a (the) prime suspect? It was hard to tell. As far as Fendtsteig was concerned, it had been enough perhaps to have a story to go on, however bizarre and bizarrely presented, so that he could then get to work to show that it was false. Indeed it was quite possible that they had let him out without officially charging him simply in order to catch him when he made some mistake. Was he or wasn't he under surveillance?

The problem, of course, Morris reflected, was knowing anything. Above all, knowing how much they knew.

Was it possible, for example, that they hadn't found the car yet? Was that really possible? When he had put it there on purpose to have it found! In precisely the kind of place criminals did put cars. Pinewoods way up in the hills. The problem was, you couldn't even rely on these people to know the things they ought to be ashamed of not knowing. You threw red herrings into a tiny pond and they didn't even catch them. Certainly the papers had said nothing about the car.

Or did they really believe now that those two dumb immigrants had done it? Was Fendtsteig's posturing mere sour grapes?

Morris contemplated one of Signora Trevisan's supermarket Sacred Hearts on the wall above him and wondered if the choice of such ugly bric-à-brac hadn't been a deliberate act of mortification on her part, a refusal to sublimate humble religious contemplation in the arrogance of the aesthetic. Probably not, knowing Signora Trevisan and her peasant origins. But it was certainly an excellent reason for keeping the ugly things now: a mortification of Morris's essential good taste, and thus all the proof anyone could ask for of the profound nature of his conversion. Tomorrow, Sunday, he would go to Mass at Don Carlo's church in the village square, which should give him his first chance to see Antonella again, to assure her that he was in no way involved in what had happened to her husband. Just the thought that she might suspect him hurt him deeply. Whereas with his wife it was more a question of his determination to outsmart her, and to defend an area of privacy for himself.

Morris allowed himself to dwell on this subtle difference for some time. Yes, he was looking forward to seeing Antonella, looking forward above all to sharing the news of his conversion with her, his whole-hearted commitment to Christ and Christianity, the chapel he was planning to build in the grounds of Trevisan Wines. Because she wouldn't be scathing the way his wife had been. She wouldn't make comments about whether they'd have to eat fish on Fridays now, whether grace would have to be said before every meal, whether workers would be fired if they didn't attend Mass and genuflect before the altar. Morris smiled weakly. Paola was going to prove a penance and a half, that was for sure.

Considering his list again, he opened a sublist beside the entry WATCH YOUR BACK, and wrote:

1. Bobo's car: send Kwame to check if it's still there?
2. Kwame: has anybody been asking him any difficult questions?
3. Azedine and Farouk: don't sound too eager to condemn them.
4. Mimi: remove file in office. Priority!!!
5. Stan: Antonella's conversations with? Avoid or tackle?
6. Coffins: possible exhumation? Refuse permission on grounds of emotional damage to family.
7. Miscellaneous tell-tale evidence: fingerprints, witnesses, flakes of skin, blood and the like. Reflect at length.
8. Anonymous phone call: try to find out if man or woman?
9. . . . .

But it was hopeless. Morris stopped. How could he even begin to control everything? How could he know what Fendtsteig knew or might find out, or even what the man needed to find out to get a conviction? A body? A witness? It was simply amazing, he thought, his mind flitting rather dangerously from the sensibly practical to the philosophic, amazing how one – anyone – could live so blithely in one's ignorance, one's unknowing, until such time as one knew something, did something, that others mustn't know. At which point it became necessary to be almost omniscient, to know everything about what everybody else was doing and thinking, simply in order to make sure that they remained ignorant of what you knew, of what must be for ever hidden.

The truth was, you had to become a sort of god when you committed a crime. 'In the day ye eat thereof,' he remembered, 'then ye shall be as gods.'

Standing up, straightening his tie as he watched himself in the glass of a bookcase (it was so nice to be able to wear his own smart clothes again), Morris phoned Inspector Marangoni and offered his congratulations on the policeman's having arrested the two immigrants. And thank God he had! Because that man Fendtsteig or Fennstig, or whatever he was called, at the carabinieri just hadn't seemed to be interested at all.

'I hope,' Marangoni said, cautious as ever, 'that you didn't find prison too trying.'

Morris was aware that it would be as well to appear consistent. Yet he must not seem to be flaunting consistency. He hesitated. 'From a commercial point of view' – he spoke slowly – 'it was something of a disaster, I'm afraid, with Bobo gone and me out at the same time. The company's just been drifting. By the way, I don't suppose there's any chance of compensation over that?' But then, before Marangoni could tell him the inevitable no, Morris added somewhat vaguely: 'In personal terms, though, I don't know, I suppose it proved quite a watershed. I mean, I had time to think about a lot of things.'

Marangoni managed a sort of sad chuckle. 'I often think I wouldn't mind a month or so in prison myself with all the work I've got to do here.'

'I can imagine,' Morris said politely.

'Anyway, I'm sorry, but there can be no question of

compensation,' Marangoni went on, 'since I gather that you were in fact choosing to be reticent in a situation where there was the apparent danger of perverting the course of justice.'

Morris left a brief embarrassed silence, before saying: 'I suppose I should apologise if I held up investigations, but it was a very personal matter. I was confused.'

'So I gather,' Marangoni said, but non-committal.

'Anyway, yes, I just phoned to offer my congratulations, I mean, I'm sure it isn't easy to track down these people.' He hesitated. 'And then to say that if I can help in any way, I'd be delighted to do so.'

'We'll be in touch,' Marangoni said.

But Morris had other ideas. 'You see . . .'

'Yes?'

'Well, you see, there's something I remembered while I was in prison, only I don't know if it can really be corroborated, so I don't know if there's any point in mentioning it.'

Was Marangoni's voice a trifle weary as he said: 'Tell me'? Morris decided that it was.

'Forget it,' he said. 'It's probably nothing.'

'Signor Duckworth, if you . . .'

That was better. 'No, I just wondered if, when you did your forensic tests on the office, you might have found, er . . .'

But at this precise moment, without even knocking, his wife put her head round the door. It was something that was definitely going to have to stop.

'What?' Marangoni enquired, clearly getting interested.

'Guests for you,' Paola said, but then stayed to listen. When the art of marriage, surely, was learning to give your partner the kind of breathing space even a saint would need.

'Yes, whether you'd found,' Morris continued, 'er, any particular kind of cigarette ash in the room.'

There was a brief pause. 'Signor Duckworth, even if you were not yourself in a difficult position in this case, it would hardly be professional of me to reveal details of our forensic investigations to you, would it? Now why don't you just tell me what you have to tell me.'

'It's precisely because people insist on considering me a suspect,' Morris came back, 'that I didn't wish to appear to be too forward.'

His wife, he saw, was shaking her head, a smile at once intrigued and sardonic playing over painted lips. One could only hope, once again, that imminent motherhood would give her something else to think about.

Morris knitted his brow: 'The fact is that when I walked into the office, you know, that morning, and found everything turned upside down like it was, I remember there was a strong smell of cheroots. You know, that really acrid sort of cigar tobacco. I mean, it was only later that I remembered it. I thought it might be worth checking whether one of these two immigrants you've arrested smokes that kind of thing. Though of course if you don't have any forensic evidence to corroborate the fact . . .'

Inspector Marangoni said he would look into the matter. Any information was always useful. So long as it really was information.

'Definitely a smell of cheroots,' Morris confirmed, and in a mixture of nervousness and euphoria got the phone down.

Paola was still shaking her head. 'Don't you think it would be better to leave well alone?'

Morris was blandly quizzical. 'How do you mean? I'm only trying to get this horrible business behind me. The more I can tell them, the more likely they are to settle the thing. Now, who are these guests?'

Forbes and Kwame were standing in the hallway amidst the antique furniture and the smell of wax. The bespectacled

Englishman was small and shabby beside the splendid stature of the black. Kwame was clearly flourishing, a brilliant set of teeth blossoming in a great white smile between fleshy lips.

'*Quod bonum, felix, faustumque sit,*' announced Forbes in the same accent public-school masters no doubt used to say grace at Eton and Harrow. Turning to the wall he picked up a large flat parcel wrapped in brown paper. 'A small token of my affection, Morris. When I discovered they wouldn't let me visit I decided to prepare something for your return.'

While Forbes was speaking, Kwame stepped forward and embraced Morris tightly, kissing him on both cheeks.

'I is so glad the boss is back,' he said.

In a low voice, though he was perfectly aware that Paola was watching, Morris whispered: 'Thanks for not running for it. We must talk.'

The black was still hugging him quite fiercely and with genuine joy. 'You is the best, boss, everything going to be all right now.'

Paola's eyes had opened wide indeed. This would show her, Morris thought – his body filling with a pleasant warmth and sense of security – this would show her the kind of affection her husband was capable of inspiring in those he had helped. Then disengaging from the black's embrace, he found he was looking directly at Massimina.

He froze. These moments of sudden and complete disorientation were so frightening! But it really was her: her face, her hair, her faintly wry, rosy-lipped, lightly freckled smile. And wearing, as in his dream, the blue-and-red robe of the *Vergine incoronata*. What had she come to tell him? Was it a warning? Did he have to kill somebody?

'Two weeks' work,' Forbes smiled. 'As you requested. Remember? A token of my thanks. By the way, I've had a contractor in to get a quote for the renovation work at the villa.'

Morris had turned to paper.

'Mo!' Paola said.

Darkness flooded the brain. He almost passed out, then with an immense effort somehow forced the shadows back. From being her living face in flesh and blood, the image receded to indifferently painted canvas.

'Hey, boss!' Kwame's hand was round his shoulders.

Morris managed a weak smile. 'Sorry, it's nothing. Just a bit overwhelmed,' he murmured, 'by all your kindness. Can't tell you how glad I am to be back. We'll hang it in the bedroom.'

Where, later on that evening, Paola protested that just because he claimed to be converted there was no reason for them not to use a condom. Morris reminded her that since she was pregnant there was hardly any point. Paola shook her head. How could she be pregnant if they'd always used something? Where was he getting all these crazy ideas? When was her last period? Morris asked. Oh, but she frequently skipped a cycle or two, he knew that.

She stared at him. She was wearing the suspender belt and extravagant underwear she sometimes masturbated in, in front of the mirror.

'Perhaps you should buy a test,' he suggested. He had never felt less excited, at least sexually.

'This bed will have to go,' she said. 'It's too old-fashioned and soggy. It turns me off. We'll bring the other one over from Montorio.'

Over my dead body, Morris thought, exchanging glances with Mimi over her shoulder. Looking at the picture more calmly now, he noticed that the face was rather more boyish than in the original. The effect was not unlike that of his androgynous Christ crucified that had so impressed the prison psychiatrist.

Paola said: '*A proposito*, don't you think it's a bit extravagant giving that big black boy the flat?'

'I saw it as a gesture of kindness.'

'So why not give it to one of the others? Or to all of them. That would really piss the builder off.'

Morris was silent. Surely the thing about a wife was that she was supposed to trust you without requiring explanations. Paola sat cross-legged on the bed, clearly trying to impress her physical presence upon him, one hand resting lightly on her furriness. When Morris still showed no interest, she said: 'You know, if you did do in Bobo, this religious conversion thing is not such a great idea. People tend to convert when they feel guilty.'

'What do you mean, if I did in Bobo!' Morris sat bolt upright.

She laughed. 'Just testing.' At the same time she was shaking her head. 'There's something so weird about you, Mo. I sense it. So many odd things you've done lately. It's scary. Anyway, what did happen to Bobo?'

'The obvious explanation is that those immigrants did him in.'

But Morris was reaching the conclusion that, like it or not, he was going to have to distract the woman, the only way he knew how. So to resolve the difference of opinion over contraceptives, since he didn't want to go back on having sworn not to use them, he lured her into their first anal adventure, and to his surprise found the procedure not ungratifying.

CHAPTER TWENTY-FIVE

THE FOLLOWING MORNING WAS a Sunday. Morris rose bright and early, just registering the predictable swell of superiority one got from seeing someone else, and particularly one's wife, still clinging on to sloth. What everybody else seemed to lack was a proper sense of purpose. In this respect – and the thought came as a surprise to him – he couldn't help feeling a certain affinity with the odious but undeniably purposeful Fendtsteig. Which was interesting. Then the mere fact that he had thought this new thought cheered Morris up. He pulled on an Armani silk dressing-gown, crossed himself briefly in front of Massimina and explained in a loud voice, just in case either of the two women present were listening, that he had things to look over at the company, after which he planned to go to Mass. As indeed he would every morning of his life from now on. Like the present Prime Minister, Andreotti. Morris smiled, because he recalled having read somewhere that Andreotti had been accused of more or less everything, from embezzlement, to *associazione mafiosa*, to murder. And never been caught. Never, never, never been caught. Italy, it was heartening to think, was that kind of place.

Stepping through to the bathroom, Morris washed and shaved, reflecting that in due time the dated ceramics here might profitably be replaced with a good white marble. And though he would never be seen dead with mixers or gold-and-ivory taps, something would have to be done about the fittings, which had that public-lavatory feel of the kind of unfortunate renovations people used to make in the mid and late fifties.

He had wiped his face and was unlocking the door when something occurred to him: a tip a rather pleasant young man had given him in prison and that he had promised he would act upon just as soon as he had the opportunity. Turning back into the bathroom, he picked up a small yellow sponge on the ledge over the tub, wrung it dry and slipped it into his pocket. Downstairs, he removed a plastic bag from the roll in the kitchen and spent all of five minutes trying to get the damn thing open. Or was he fiddling with the wrong end? So much for modern convenience. Looking in the fridge, he pushed the yellow sponge into a pool of greasy juice swirling about the remains of yesterday's celebratory roast beef (not so much an unusual culinary effort on Paola's part, as the work of Signora Trevisan's old *donna di servizio*, who appeared, most acceptably to Morris's mind, to have come with the house). As soon as the sponge had gained a bit of weight and turned suitably brown and meat-like and sticky, Morris slipped it into the plastic bag, tied a knot at the top and put it in his jacket pocket. This was going to be fun! Quite apart from throwing another red herring into the already muddy water. Feeling light-hearted for the first time in weeks, he found his coat and stepped out into an air that smelt appropriately spring-like.

It was around eight and there was already a brisk stream of traffic heading off for some last Easter skiing in Fendtsteig country. Morris drove carefully, relishing his freedom, the extraordinary wide whiteness of the landscape with its snow-peaked mountains to the north and the sun-bright haze of city and plain to the south. After a brief chat with Massimina on the subject of Paola's pregnancy, which she again assured him was for real and at least two months on, Morris stopped and bought the local newspaper, where yet another pleasant surprise awaited him. Among the usual trivial tales of officials accepting bribes, babes tossed in bins and drug addicts meat-axing their parsimonious parents, was the marvellously uninspired headline: MAROCCHINO AND EGYPTIAN CHARGED WITH MURDER OF LOCAL INDUSTRIALIST.

Morris went back into the newsagents, bought himself a bar of Swiss chocolate, then relaxed into the leather seat of the Mercedes to read at leisure.

Perhaps he would call Father again if it was really promising.

The charge, admitted the newspaper, had been made despite the absence of a body. Thank heaven. But a pocket-knife had been found in the possession of the *marocchino* with traces of blood of the same group as that of the missing Posenato. How very interesting! His young accomplice, on the other hand, was carrying an expensive silver paperweight which was known to have been on Posenato's desk (though Morris could remember no such thing), while both men were in possession of a modest quantity of banknotes which were found to have serial numbers similar to those in one of the company's safes. The immigrants' improbable story, that they had returned to Verona to file a petition for illegal dismissal and knew nothing of Bobo's disappearance, was not felt by the polizia to carry any conviction. On the contrary, it was thought that the real reason for their return was to recover items they had hidden during their flight, perhaps even the industrialist's Audi 100, which remained as yet undiscovered and could well contain the body. Given the seriousness of the crime, both the *marocchino* and his

Egyptian accomplice would be tried *per direttissima*. That is, as soon as possible.

Morris swallowed his chocolate and wiped his hands carefully on a handkerchief. He was at once delighted and perplexed. What, for example, was he supposed to make of 'one of the company's safes'? Clearly this was not the one behind the fuse box, which he had emptied himself, leaving the police nothing to match the banknotes with. While the main safe notoriously never had any money in it at all. The only explanation was thus that Bobo had given the two men some small pay-off (how unexpectedly generous of him!) from yet another safe, about which he, Morris, knew nothing at all, but which someone, presumably Antonella, had been able to tell the police about, otherwise how would they have found the notes in there? Apart from the confirmation, if any was required, of the low esteem in which Bobo had held him and the extent to which the boy had been determined to hang on to all the power in the company (how many things were there Morris still didn't know?), there was now the further problem that the police might believe that he himself had been witholding evidence from them, if nothing else, about the extent of the company's illicit operations. And how could they believe that Azedine and Farouk would have taken only *some* of the money in the safe? That was ludicrous.

Still, on the whole, it had to be excellent news, particularly the blood on the penknife. Indeed, it was news that more or less set Morris up for life, turned him into a successful man with his hands on the springs of wealth and his heart set to use that wealth wisely and generously. But then: 'All things work together for good to them that love God, to those who are called according to his purpose.' It was merely a question of having faith. In a sudden swelling of innocent excitement, Morris picked up the phone to share his enthusiasm first with Massimina, then in some more indirect way with Father. Forgetting that he hadn't dialled her *paradiso* number for the routine call he always gave her on getting in the car, he simply pressed, for authenticity's sake, the repeat button, and was already expressing his gratitude for the guardian angel role she was so effectively playing, when somewhere a phone began to ring.

In heaven?

Morris hesitated, trying to remember whether he had actually dialled any numbers on this phone himself since getting out of prison yesterday. He thought not. Then a deep voice, which was clearly not Massimina's, yet at the same time immediately recognisable, said: '*Pronto.*'

Morris was taken aback.

'*Pronto?*' the voice repeated into what was a particularly disturbed line.

'Kwame!' Morris said. 'Yes, look, I'm on my way over to pick you up. We've got stuff to do.'

Oddly, it was as if he'd never meant to phone anybody else.

Ten minutes later, parking in Via dei Gelsomini, Morris was pleased to see fresh graffiti on the garden wall of his old condominium. FORA I NERI DAL VENETO, it said in metre-high letters. BLACKS OUT. A neighbour coming down the short path from the main door scowled at his *buon giorno*. Morris smiled almost too broadly. When he got upstairs, Kwame showed him a letter that had been pushed, unsealed, under the door a week or so before.

Egregio Signor Duckworth,
  My most sincere condolences on the loss of your mother-in-law. I hope that the unhappy event has not been too painful and upsetting for you and your wife.

I gather from other members of your condominium that you have decided to leave Via dei Gelsomini to live in your wife's family house. Since this is the case, I wonder if, rather than installing a tenant, which is never a welcome development in a condominium of owner-occupiers, you mightn't perhaps find it more convenient to sell your flat back to me at whatever price you feel is fair.

In fede,

SILVANO CASTELLANI

Got him! Morris was on cloud nine. Especially when he saw that Kwame was *not* turning the place into a pigsty at all! On the contrary, he seemed to have a far greater sense of tidiness than Paola had ever had. The rugs were all square to the wall, the spines of Morris's precious books were perfectly flush in the shelves, and there seemed to be none of the flotsam and jetsam drifting about that one had had to get used to living with Paola: odd shoes kicked in corners, nail-file cards between the sofa cushions, etc. No, the boy was treating the place like a museum. And if it smelt faintly different than it had when he and Paola lived there, then that was simply because blacks did smell a bit different, and cooked different food and probably liked different-smelling products, cleaning agents, perfumes, shampoos and the like. The way they apparently (incredibly) liked menthol cigarettes. But then wasn't difference the spice of life in the end? What were the neighbours so worried about? Why had the Trevisan family worried so much about *him*? No, there could be no doubt about who was being inhuman here! Morris himself had *never shown prejudice*, nor indeed done harm to anyone who dealt with him reasonably. He embraced Kwame and slapped him hard on that huge back. Presumably Paola had phoned the boy to deal with some practical issue over moving houses.

Kwame wore a fashionable pale-blue tracksuit and a good cashmere coat, a sign that he wasn't squandering his wages on booze and cigarettes. It occurred to Morris that, of all the people he had ever known, this big black, strangely enough, was probably the closest to himself in psyche and behaviour: an outcast who in the end was more civilised than the society which he aspired to enter, and which constantly rejected him.

Kwame showed where somebody had thrown a stone against a shutter. Morris promised he would talk to the police about the matter. Walking back out to the car, he made a point of taking Kwame's arm and leading him off the path for a stroll around the big condominium garden where spring flowers were just peeping through the dewy grass. Show the boy around, show the others that he had Morris's full support. Sure enough, turning suddenly, he saw a curtain twitch. Lucia in number three. Spying. Excellent!

They climbed into the Mercedes and once more Morris gave Kwame the keys. 'From now on,' he said, 'you keep the car. Just make sure that you arrive at our house in Quinzano no later than seven-thirty every morning. You then remain in my company or parked outside whatever building I am in until I go to bed in the evening.'

'Yes, boss.'

'You don't have trouble waking up, I hope. I hate people arriving late.'

'No, boss.'

'OK, so now straight to Trevisan Wines, then Villa Caritas, then church.'

Morris shut his eyes as Kwame overtook at a leisurely pace on a completely blind bend. But he admired the boy's aplomb, and he admired the amazing reticence he showed *vis-à-vis* the crime they had committed together, the way he asked nothing about what Morris might have said during questioning, offered nothing about what he himself had said, as if entirely unconcerned about his fate. Or rather, entirely trustful that Morris had everything under control.

In the way, Morris thought, that Massimina had been entirely trustful. It was so fascinating comparing people, contrasting them. For about two minutes, perhaps, he felt immensely gratified.

'By the way,' he said, 'they've charged Azedine and Farouk. They're going to be tried quite soon.'

Kwame only nodded, driving too close to a three-wheel van piled high with scrap metal. A small dog sitting on a swaying heap of rusty bed springs looked as if it might leap onto their smooth white bonnet. Which had Morris thinking of the sponge in his pocket again. It was going to be quite a morning. First the builder, then the dog.

'I don't think they'll ever really be able to nail them on the evidence they've got. What do you think? But it does rather take the pressure off us.'

Kwame, however, seemed entirely unconcerned. And this was perhaps a little callous of him. For Morris was perfectly aware that there was a moral issue here. Somebody else was suffering for what they had done.

'They've probably both got Aids anyway, poor guys, with what they were up to.'

The black took a sharp corner, in third.

'Don't you think?'

Finally Kwame grinned. 'Is a pity about that big Audi, boss,' he said. 'Man, I like that big, big car.'

Morris promised: 'All in good time and I'll get you one.'

Clearly he was not going to get much change out of Kwame when it came to weighing up moral issues.

* * *

When they arrived at Trevisan Wines, the Dobermann was as hostile as ever, snapping and slavering about the car door. Presumably one of the workers was under instruction to let the thing off its chain at weekends. Now he had his paws on the car window, black lips drawn back on a well-fed snarl. Morris found the plastic bag in his pocket, pulled out the meat-soaked sponge with two fingers, ordered Kwame to buzz down the window a snout and pushed it into the brute's maw. Thus demonstrating how incredibly naïve it was to keep animals as guards, for the dog immediately set about gobbling the thing up, letting them by to unlock the office door.

An agonisingly slow death, the veterinary student turned pederast had explained.

Time would tell.

And how curious, Morris thought, as he stepped through the door, to be back in this squalid office, just four or five months after that other holiday morning (*il giorno dei morti* of all days!) when he and Bobo had so ominously clashed. He glanced around, checking that nothing had changed: the desk, the filing cabinet, the safe, the fuse box, the crucifix . . . nothing. Except that the girl, who had been suggestively licking around the top of a Fratelli Ruffoli bottle in early February, now in mid-March appeared to be trying to open two of them at once with nothing more than both gloriously hard, dark nipples. Morris stepped briskly across the room, removed the calendar and was going to put it in the bin where it belonged, when it occurred to him that he might, quite charitably, and without offending either Mimi or the sad crucifix over the door, offer it to Kwame. After all, one could hardly expect everybody to convert at exactly the same moment.

The black grinned appreciatively and flicked through

the thing, rather oddly turning it this way and that, as if the vertical was not a position that inspired him. And while Morris was now pulling open the drawer with the fatal Massimina file inside, his accomplice's deep voice chuckled and said: 'You know where I stick dis 'ere bottle, man?'

Quickly folding the various letters and papers, Morris hardly needed to ask.

Kwame was laughing. 'I stick it right up her sweet white fanny, that's where.'

Although this was the kind of conversation he had spent most of his life trying to avoid, Morris felt it would be churlish to criticise, having just been responsible for giving the boy the miserable thing. Anyhow, if it kept him out of more serious sin, there was a lot to be said for it. Better the hand than the gland, so to speak.

Fearing the waste bin was too risky, he slipped the offending papers into his inside coat pocket and turned to go. 'We haven't got time now,' he explained, 'but over the next few days, I want you to go through all the files in the cabinet, paper by paper, so as to get to know the company. And if you find any notes in handwriting, or anything obviously personal, I want you to get in touch with me right away. OK?'

Outside, the dog was coming to terms with the fact that the sponge was not exactly what he had expected. Throat stretched upwards, he was opening and snapping shut his all too impressive teeth. For the last time, Morris hoped. In any event, occupied as the creature was with swallowing the unswallowable, there was plenty of time for them to walk the few muddy paces to the Mercedes undisturbed.

'Drive,' he told Kwame.

Nobody was up on their arrival at Villa Caritas. At nine-thirty now. It made Morris wonder how Forbes would fare when he had to run a school and have the boys at their lessons or other activities in reasonable time. But he was pleased to see that the big house was being kept quite tidily with spring flowers (narcissi) on the big table in the dining-room-cum-lecture-room and some drawings, clearly attempted by the immigrants under Forbes's instruction, pinned up on the wall. There were some rather rough sketches of the garden with its pergola and pomegranate tree, one or two of the surrounding hills to the north, a frank set of life drawings of a young man sprawled on a couch, and then a remarkably delicate production of a young Slavic face, features almost melting into the soft pillow he lay on. Morris recognised Ramiz. Forbes's work presumably. Very impressive.

But now Morris was staring. Was there something of Massimina in it too? Could it be? No. He was just becoming paranoiac, or psychotic or whatever it was. Seeing her in everything. Unless it was that, not having the more promising subject of a woman to hand, Forbes's work had imbued the boy with something of the transparent loveliness of the subject he had recently been copying from the Uffizi. Her beauty was infectious.

Morris was pleased with this reflection.

He was just setting off up the stairs to remind Forbes that he had asked to be taken to Mass at Don Carlo's church in Quinzano, when Kwame called him back. Rather urgently.

'You let me go get the old man, boss!'

'No, no, it's OK.' Morris was at the turning of the stairs.

But Kwame shouted: 'No, I mean, I thought, man, maybe, we could wake the poor old fellah with the cup o' tea. He like that.'

Well, this was a generous idea. Once again Morris was impressed by the boy. He came back downstairs. 'I used

245

to wake my mother with a cup of tea,' he remarked, perhaps unwisely, because now he was remembering how furious his father had been when an adolescent Morris had refused to continue this courtesy for himself and his various fancy women after Mother died. Immediately he was aware of the old poison in his blood, that bitterness you could actually feel in your bowels. For a moment it occurred to him that his father might have heard from some tabloid rag about his being in prison on a suspected murder charge. Well, good, that should show the old lecher who was a mother's boy.

In the kitchen Kwame was bustling about. 'Just going to get something from my old room, boss,' he said as soon as he'd got the kettle on the gas. He hurried off, long legs taking the stairs three at a time. So that when Morris took up the tea ten minutes later, his discreet knock drew an immediate and very plummy: *'Veni Creator Spiritus!'* and Forbes was already wide awake, sitting up in bed, alone, reading a book. The rather sweet smell came from a lighted joss-stick on a surface crammed with medicines and haemorrhoid creams. Morris had the good manners to avert his gaze.

'Wonderful to see you, my lad,' the old man said loudly. 'Splendid!' When Morris dutifully complimented him on the excellent artwork he was doing with the boys, Forbes, in the most cheerful mood his benefactor had ever seen him, spread his striped pyjama arms and announced most lyrically: *'Virginibus puerisque canto.'* As he spoke, he was shaking his head slowly from side to side and looking Morris directly in his blue eyes. He seemed terribly amused by something. Morris thought he had never liked his cultured friend more. He immediately told him about his conversion, how he planned to spend the rest of his life in an orgy of philanthropy, of which Forbes's school was to be the corner-stone.

'At least two of the pupils,' he insisted earnestly as the old man shook his head in what looked very much like wonder, 'must be from poor families, their fees being paid directly by myself.'

CHAPTER TWENTY-SIX

THE SERVICE COULD BEST have been described as a long rhythmical murmur. Don Carlo's voice was low and toneless. The responses came as soft waves, barely breaking on the stone floor of San Tommaso in Organo. The undertow was a shuffle of shoes, a rustle of expensive clothing. And already Don Carlo's voice was gently drawing his congregation into another '*che Gesù vi benedica*', another '*ave Maria, madre di Dio*', another '*amen*'. In the small church, the thickly smoking incense was soporific, wafting this way and that, coiling and melting in a shaft of sunlight that lay like a great bright girder across the chancel pulpit while, deep in shadow all around, the frescoed figures of the Passion beckoned like ghosts on the fatal shore.

In short, nothing could have been more congenial. Morris genuinely regretted not having made this a habit years ago. If only he could have persuaded Paola to come! What a happily married family life they could have, standing proudly together here with two or three innocent little children. Why couldn't he inspire the woman with this healthy vision? It was a goal to work toward.

Morris contemplated the Crucifixion. For the first time in a long time he found himself deeply relaxed, placed as he was beside the impeccably genuflecting Forbes and the towering Kwame, who stood, sat and knelt just a fraction of a second after the others like some awkward black flotsam bobbing and dipping on the smooth surface of their communal piety. And when it came to filing out to take the host, Morris managed to time things so that he was alongside Antonella, who was sitting in the opposite row of chairs. But he didn't look at her, didn't search out her gaze or even try to follow the practised grace of her devotion. He kept his head bowed and, standing at the chancel steps, immediately closed his eyes in prayerful concentration, lips moving ever so faintly as the body and blood melted on his warm tongue. '*Cara Massimina,*' he prayed, 'intercede for me with the saints and the blessed Virgin, that I may redeem my soul and be forgiven my many sins.' It was a heartfelt request. Somehow the ransom letters in his pocket made him feel desperately close to her.

Morris lingered a moment longer than the other communicants, lips faintly moving. Until, as if in a sort of divine version of instant feedback, Antonella, turning to go back to her seat, whispered in his ear: 'I'm so glad that misunderstanding has been cleared up, Morris. I was so upset when they arrested you. I never believed it could be true.' Morris was only disappointed to register that on her other side she had Bobo's more handsome elder brother.

Later, on the steps overlooking the piazza with its miserably modern war memorial, they all chatted together for some minutes in the spring breeze. Bobo's brother was grimly pleased that the police had finally charged the immigrants. The important thing was to have this horrible business behind them so that they could begin to live again. He looked to Antonella for approval. But the young woman had tears in her eyes, and in an attempt to correct the other man's fatuous insensitivity, Morris said that he for one still chose to believe that Bobo was alive, and that some explanation would soon come to light. It was all too easy for the police to arrest people and then accuse them of the most appalling things merely to appease a voracious local press, and probably for no other reason than that the poor boys weren't white. Heavens, they'd even accused *him* of murdering poor Bobo at one point, just because he and his brother-in-law had occasionally disagreed about how to run the company, as if everybody who disagreed necessarily ended up killing each other. When there wasn't even a body! He smiled sadly. Forbes, however, returning from a trip to the lavatory, was hearing the news about the murder charge for the first time, and had turned to chalk.

'*Quid hoc sibi vult?*' the old man whispered. 'It can't be true! Not Farouk!' For a moment it seemed as if he might faint, so visibly was the blood draining from his face. He clutched at the basin of a fountain where grubby marble cherubs were not performing. Morris was moved then to observe how the tall Kwame, who had been standing respectfully outside the group, now leant down to mutter some words of comfort to the old man. For a few seconds he was thus able to enjoy the extraordinary image of the black's big blood-dark lips softly moving beside a tuft of white hair sprouting from Forbes's waxy ear. It was the kind of thing that had he been a painter he would have painted. Or perhaps Caravaggio already had.

Don Carlo emerged from the church and, taking Morris to one side, assured him that he had done what he could to smooth over the bureaucratic problems they had spoken about the previous month. The immigrants would all be granted the appropriate papers, so long as Trevisan Wines gave them official employment and paid their health and insurance contributions. Morris asked what he could possibly do to repay such generosity, to which Don Carlo replied that a good work on behalf of the poor could never be construed as requiring payment; on the contrary, it had been a duty, but if Morris should ever feel a debt of gratitude towards his Creator, he was always welcome to make a contribution to the Church. The most pressing concern for San Tommaso at this particular moment was the sad state of the stonework on the campanile. Far from making the gauche gesture of simply pulling out his cheque-book, Morris nodded sagely and decided to make an anonymous cash donation sometime in the next week or two, perhaps with some tiny mistake in the Italian on the envelope announcing the campanile as the benefactor's desired destination for the money. Feminine for masculine should be sufficient. Or he could spell '*milione*' with a double 'l'.

'*Padre*,' he said, as the priest was about to turn.

'*Sì, figlio mio.*'

But this reminder of his prison confession was too poignant. Morris simply stared the old man in his honest eyes. For a moment he was aware of that feeling he had felt the one time he had been in love, of his soul lying just below the surface of his face. Mimi was near.

'Is something troubling you, my son?' the priest asked.

Morris waited perhaps fifteen seconds. Then clearly making a considerable effort, he said: 'I'm seriously concerned about my sister-in-law, *padre*.' This was true. 'I'd like you to try to be close to her.' In a lower voice, he added: 'I'm afraid it is probably true that her husband was seeing someone else.' Again he stared at the deeply lined old face before winding up: '*La ringrazio*, Father, for all your help. You have been a great support to the family.'

'May God bless you, *figlio mio*,' the priest said. 'These must be hard times for you.'

It then occurred to Morris that if he hadn't married with such foolish haste, he might himself have made an excellent priest. Certainly he had plenty to teach people and was always willing to listen to their little problems. The strict observance of ceremony would have been a pleasure for someone of his aesthetic leanings. Nor would the detail of a vow of celibacy have presented a serious obstacle. Indeed the more physical enjoyment he got from the whole charade that was sex these days, the more it disturbed him. Only with Mimi had sex been something holy.

Tears filled Morris's blue eyes as he bid the priest good day and called to Kwame to buzz open the car.

Then, wanting to check that the dog was indeed dying the atrocious death he believed it must, Morris asked the black to make a detour on the way back to Villa Caritas. 'Just a couple of files I forgot to pick up,' he explained to Forbes, who was still bothering him in the back seat about the plight of Azedine and Farouk, something Morris genuinely found difficult to understand when he remembered how reluctant the older man had originally been at the idea of having anything at all to do with any immigrants. Presumably it was just another way in which he, Morris, had influenced those around him for the better. He assured Forbes that such a charge was just part of the interminable farce of Italian public life, where everything was announced and nothing ever done. If they invariably let *Mafia* bosses out on the most minor of technicalities, was there any chance at all that they could condemn two men for murder without a corpse to show and on the most slender of circumstantial evidence?

Forbes said glumly: 'The real murderer must be laughing.'

'On the contrary,' Morris was in a position to insist with sincerity, 'he's probably not even relieved. I mean, he will already have seen me accused of everything under the sun and then summarily released. He can't imagine the charge will stick on these two.'

'*Fiat justitia, ruat caelum.*'

To which grimly delivered and incomprehensible pronouncement Morris had just deigned the usual polite enquiry for enlightenment, when, rounding the bend beyond Quinto, they saw a patrol car with flashing light drawn up outside the locked gate of Trevisan Wines.

'Let justice be done, though the heavens fall,' Forbes explained.

But Morris wasn't listening. The heavens were already falling. Somebody must have called the carabinieri. And the reason was all too obvious. Beyond the gate the huge ugly guard dog Bobo had bought for reasons that to Morris were still obscure (had the company ever needed a guard dog in the past?) was sprinting up and down by the factory wall, barking quite insanely and occasionally leaping up four or five feet to hurl itself against the cement. Fearing their car might already have been seen and recognised, Morris told Kwame to draw up behind the flashing blue light.

The carabinieri were perplexed, unsure as to whether they should break down the gate to see if an intruder was in the factory, or proceed more cautiously, so as not to damage the property. For his part, Morris had no difficulty appearing concerned. And all the more so a moment later. For no sooner had he gone back to the car for the remote control, thanking the carabinieri for their promptness and wondering aloud why on earth the dog was behaving so wildly, than another car pulled off the road. Turning briefly from buzzing open the gate, the dog howling behind them, Morris found himself face to face with Fendtsteig. And at precisely the same moment he remembered that he still had all the Massimina ransom letters in his inside coat pocket.

What a hopeless, hopeless fool!

'*Buon giorno,*' Fendtsteig announced, but it might as well have been *Guten Morgen*. Or *Arbeit macht frei*. A shiver of danger flickered up Morris's spine. He was a hair's breadth from discovery.

'It is a pleasure to see you again, Signor Duckvorse,' Fendtsteig insisted through the dog's tortured baying. At least the animal was suffering for its sins.

Morris merely nodded, almost as if he hadn't properly recognised the man, and, as the opening mechanism now began to whine and the big iron gate to slide, he shouted desperately: 'Somebody must be in there! They're stealing something!' Squeezing through what seemed an impossibly small gap, he made a mad dash towards the factory building, fearfully aware of the carabinieri and Kwame hard on his heels, of those ransom letters stuffed in his pocket.

He was some ten metres from the office building when the animal turned. Forty or fifty kilos of Dobermann came bounding at his chest. Morris scarcely had time to register a fury of fangs and fur, snarling black gums, mad eyes, then a terrible tearing of flesh, his own, before he was plunged into a violent blood-tossed dark that had more to do with nightmare than consciousness.

CHAPTER TWENTY-SEVEN

IF THERE WERE AWAKENINGS over the following forty-eight hours, Morris did not remember them as such. Later, discussing the matter with Forbes, he would suggest that Dante would have had a whole new range of punishments to mete out had he ever undergone modern anaesthetics: combinations of suffocation, nightmare images and nausea, intense lights in oppressive darkness, consciousness only of the impossibility of regaining consciousness, induced passivity of sickness without reference to a before or hope of an after, and total, total anxiety – in short, an excellent punishment, for those whose crime involved the presumption of being in control of their existence, of believing they could organise their lives and the lives of those around them.

The only solace was that so long as one was still alive one could look on such sufferings as penance. Clearly God was purging Morris for the long years of service ahead, the hundreds of hungry souls he would feed and clothe in a much-expanded Duckworth Wines, gently drawing a Third World fraternity into the Catholic fold.

But the punishment, while it lasted, was a painful one. Indeed it now seemed that the rubble he was buried under, or rather, the viscous liquid he sank and floated in, at once bright and dark, loud and silent, smooth and abrasive, must soon crush him into itself: a lurid purée of pain, both mental and spiritual.

From nothing, he heard a muffled voice say: '*È straordinario!*'

Another voice, equally muffled, said: 'Paola, Paola, *cara*, I can scarcely believe it. If only it were true!'

So that now Morris knew it must be his wife who was enquiring: 'But what did the polizia say about it?'

Upon hearing which word, he was suddenly catapulted into a state of the most intense, the most nerve-raw consciousness: aware of the darkness, aware of a sort of institutional humming and rustling behind the voices of his wife and sister-in-law, aware of his supine position on a bed that was too hard to be his own, aware of fierce pain in the right ear and neck, aware of the thick bandages round his face that were blocking out vision and dulling sound, but aware most of all that he was no longer wearing his winter coat . . .

'For Christ's sake!' he shouted. 'My coat!' His head jerked up, his arms lifted and groped, and the most indescribable pain seared through his face: lightning struck him on the scalp, ran down across his right ear and then exploded in the soft nerviness where shoulder met neck.

'Mo!' Paola exclaimed. '*Stai buono!* Don't move!'

'I'll call the doctor,' Antonella said.

Now he remembered the dog, the teeth, the blood that must have been his own. Had they at least dispatched the thing? But it was still the coat that was uppermost in his mind. The old ransom letters of years ago. The proof and key to everything. He had been discovered, despite his conversion. Be sure your sins will find you out. It wasn't fair.

'Mimi!' he cried out, most, most unwisely. But already the needle was in his arm. As suddenly as he had awoken he was asleep again.

There followed another great lapse of darkness, though less oppressive this time, a mere eclipse of consciousness, however prolonged, behind fleecy clouds of analgesics. Then he was aware of a hand caressing his own as his soul stirred within him, stirred and gathered anxiety as it rose to the surface of his face, his eyes, until, as he opened the latter, the hand pulled quickly away.

The bandage across his face had gone now, though something tight ran under his chin and around the top of his head. In any event, he couldn't move, only stare at a fluorescent-lit ceiling.

'Paola,' he said.

The reply was gravelly and low: 'Morris, my boy.' Forbes stood up and leaned over him, a benign, dusty apparition carved out of neon above, tears in watery eyes.

'God, what happened?'

But already Morris was acting. Already Morris knew perfectly well what had happened. The dog had got his throat. Whereas what he needed to know was who had got his coat.

'Somebody tried to poison the dog,' Forbes was telling him. 'It went crazy and tore up your face. You remember, when we all went to the office together. The day before yesterday?'

Morris hadn't expected this. 'Tore up my face?' He was silent a moment. Then alarmed. '*Tore up my face?* For God's sake, how do I look?'

Forbes had sat back on his chair and thus disappeared from Morris's field of vision. Before speaking, he took the younger man's hand once more, holding it with infinite lightness and tenderness. He cleared his throat. Then still didn't speak.

Quite horrified, Morris struggled to sit up, only to be overwhelmed by the pain of skin that refused to stretch. Forbes put a hand on his good shoulder to hold him down.

'I cannot tell a lie,' he said, the unavailability of a Latin tag perhaps betraying the extent of his emotion.

'Oh God.' Morris got his other hand free from the sheets and found the thick padding that went from the top of his right temple down as far as the neck. Touching the exposed part of his cheek close to his nose, it was to find the alien coarseness of wire threading. Yards of it. For Christ's sake! Criss-crossing everywhere from forehead to lips.

'I'm scarred for life,' he whispered.

Forbes, still invisible, said nothing.

'Scarred for life!' Morris repeated. He could feel the tears welling painfully in his eyes. Immediately he wanted to be alone, alone to bewail his misfortune, to call upon Mimi and upon God, to know the meaning of this immense calamity. Merely because he had tried to do away with a stupid dog! The irony of it! When sometimes you felt you could slay half the human race and get away scot-free! The saltiness of a tear scalded fierce wounds. In the space of one stupid Sunday morning, everything had gone wrong.

'*Ne cede malis*,' muttered Forbes. Then, as Morris closed his eyes and showed signs of beginning to sob, Forbes added tentatively: 'At least there is one piece of good news.'

Morris fought through self-pity to some reasonable state of alertness, and was immediately suspicious.

'What's that?'

'It seems Bobo may only have been kidnapped.'

'What?' Morris opened his eyes and again made the mistake of trying to turn his head.

'Antonella has received a letter asking for a ransom.'

It took quite a few seconds for this to sink in. A letter, asking for a ransom? Morris's mind was reeling. For Christ's sake! The least thing and there were a whole bunch of nuts flocking round ready to exploit it, to turn it into a fast billion lire, as if other people's suffering was nothing at all! It dawned on him then that this letter was what Antonella and Paola must have been talking about ('I can scarcely believe it'). Yes. He took a deep breath. Though for the life of him he couldn't understand why on earth Forbes might think such an outrage was good news.

'The fact is it's going to make it that much more difficult for them to convict Azedine and Farouk, isn't it?'

Again it took a moment or two for Morris to register this. Then he was furious. He tried to sit up again, again fell back. 'What the fuck do I care about two murderous queers, when my face has been torn apart? I don't give a damn. I couldn't care less. My life has been ruined by a stupid dog and you come and bother me with the fate of a couple of queers.'

This outburst was followed by a long silence. Morris stared dumbly at the ceiling, as if mesmerised by the immense misfortune that had overcome him, at precisely the point when he had sworn to be good, too.

Finally, in a tone of quiet rebuke, Forbes said: 'Morris, you have been very generous to me, setting me up at Villa Caritas and paying for all the renovations and so on.' He hesitated. Morris was hardly listening, having suddenly remembered his coat again. Surely the game was up. Innocence and beauty both lost at a single blow. 'But the fact is,' Forbes continued, 'that I have a very soft spot for Farouk. He is a lovely and very gentle young man. As to his sexual inclinations, they are surely a matter for his own personal discretion. After all, Michelangelo was homosexual, and likewise Socrates. The important thing is that I don't believe for one moment that he could have been involved in killing anybody and I will do everything I can to make sure he is not convicted.'

There was a second long and portentous silence. What could Forbes mean by 'do everything I can'? What could he do? Still the silence. Morris waited, then began to quiz the old man on exactly what had happened after the dog knocked him to the ground (his coat, who had taken his coat?). Only when there was no answer did he realise that Forbes had gone. To the bathroom most probably, Morris thought. But having said his piece in defence of Farouk, the Englishman did not come back.

Morris had very little experience of hospitals. Apart from the sad occasion when he had pressed his boyish face against the glass of Acton Memorial's Intensive Care Unit to watch dear Mother die, he had never been in one at all. He was thus surprised, on sitting up at last a couple of hours after Forbes had so abruptly disappeared, to notice that the nurses were predominantly men and wore green pyjamas for uniforms and clogs for shoes. Otherwise the mixture of institutional greys, fire extinguishers, bed screens, enamel-white cabinets, plus a crucifix caught in cobwebs over the spring-loaded door, was all that one might have expected.

Rotating from the waist to avoid the pain in his neck, Morris observed the man in the bed beside him. With his right arm reduced to a bandaged stump, the fellow was understandably having difficulty turning the pages of his *La Gazzetta dello Sport*. Newspaper, Morris thought. He must get hold of a newspaper to check the state of play. At least as the media saw it. Though the truth was the police were probably just waiting for him to be sufficiently *compos mentis* to understand the full weight of the charges they could now lay against him.

Kidnap. Multiple murder. The scenario seemed less surreal than it might have done before he had been to prison, where one had realised how normal, not to say decent, many of the other kidnappers, multiple murderers and pederasts were. Just people for whom opportunity had collided with predisposition. Most of them suffered their crimes as though they were some unfortunate illness against which they had not been properly inoculated at the appropriate age. Certainly he had met nobody as obtuse as Bobo in prison. Nor as profoundly perverse as his wife.

Two women and an older man were gathered round the next bed, preventing Morris from seeing whatever misfortune had befallen its occupant. But it was clear that his fellow inmates, bedmates, were all severe accident cases. Mutilation, amputation, disfigurement were all on parade. Plastic surgery candidates perhaps? Did this explain why his slow survey of the ten beds and four walls revealed not a single mirror? The patients had to be carefully prepared. Patients like himself.

Oh, Mimi, this beautiful, clear-skinned, persuasive face! Ruined. The cheeks you kissed so avidly!

And what with this on his mind, plus the missing coat, plus the nagging anxiety of the ransom letter (who in God's dear name could have sent that? The same person who had made the earlier phone call?), Morris was roasting in a sort of exquisite mental hell. From which, he thought, he could do little more for the moment than turn his eyes upwards to paradise and beg that his guardian angel might dip her fingertips in the soothing water there and wet his flaming wounds, his no doubt grisly jowls and swollen lips, his suppurating soul. Having no other expedient available, Morris pressed his hands together and bowed his mutilated head in prayer. For he was determined not to abandon his beliefs at the very first let-down, however considerable it might have been.

''Allo,' a voice said. ''Ow arrre you, Meester Duckwart. Ees the lunch-time!'

Looking up, Morris saw a squat, diminutive southern figure with toffee-brown face and bright, squinting eyes. 'Is good we 'ave the Eengleesh *paziente* so I can practise my Eengleesh, no?' Taking a tray from a trolley and laying it on the bedside cabinet, the small man explained: 'I live two years in the Earrrls Court, you know. That is 'ow I speak so good the Eengleesh.' A broad smile showed broken teeth.

Still absorbed in his supplications, Morris experienced a sense of the entirely surreal. He blinked, then saw how this vision might have been sent him to illustrate that there were indeed people more pathetic and ridiculous than himself. However badly things went, however ugly he became, he would always surely be afforded more respect than this ludicrous mixture of clown and gnome.

Looking at a piece of chicken in thin broth with floating grains of rice, he said: 'Thank you, thank you, nurse. By all means speak in English.' And immediately he asked: where were his clothes, where was there a mirror, where could he find a copy of the local newspaper?

The nurse squinted brightly. 'I'm Dionisio,' he said. 'Call me Dionisio.'

'Pleased to meet you, Dionisio. I'm Morris.'

It must be some kind of divine test of his patience.

'Your clo-thes is in the *armadio* that 'as the number of your bed. It is the eight. The mirror is in the toilette in the corridor.' The nurse cocked a small Sicilian head to one side. 'But is better you don't look before the operation. The newspaper is in the *soggiorno* at the end of the corridor.'

'And when can I leave, Dionisio?' Morris asked. His mind had simply refused to register the word 'operation'.

'Ah, Meester Duckwart, we are in such a 'urry to go before 'ardly we 'ave arrived!' Dionisio shook his head and went to the end of the bed, where he consulted a clipboard. 'You 'ave the operation the Friday. There will be many tests to do before then. They take the, 'ow do you say?' – he put down the clipboard and pinched a fold of hairy olive flesh on the back of his hand.

'Skin,' Morris said, already wincing.

'They take the skeen from the leg and put it on the face.' The little man patted his own cheeks as if making up. He consulted the board again. 'Then they 'ave to – 'ow you say? – *rimodellare* the ear.' Again, he shook his head. 'You can leave next week maybe.'

He now arranged a table affair that attached to the bed across Morris's knees, and placed the tray on top. Then, since he had apparently completed his rounds and all the other patients were already eating, each after his mutilated fashion, the nurse stayed to talk.

'Meester Morris!' he announced. 'An Eengleeshman! I am so 'appy. Is a long time I am not speaking Eengleesh.'

It was one of the staples of existence, Morris thought, that people you didn't want to talk to always wanted to talk to you, and that at all the truly important moments of one's life one always had to deal with somebody ridiculous: that idiot PhD. fellow, for example, in the pensione in Rome, explaining his structuralist theory of ghosts as no more than a literary technique, when Morris had known even then that they must exist, they must, as events since had all too clearly demonstrated. Yes, no doubt on his deathbed they would send along some interfering halfwit to see him on his clownish way. The cosmos's eternal love-affair with the ridiculous. But Morris felt more amenable and resigned since his conversion. Perhaps the whole point of this was to punish him for his vanity. He wasn't so morally blind as not to appreciate that he sometimes strayed in that direction. With Mimi's help, he thought, he would do his best to put a brave (if no longer beautiful) face on it.

'You know the Earrrls Court?' Dionisio was asking. 'I work in the hotel there.'

Morris spooned up the broth, only to discover that the right corner of his mouth was extremely painful.

Meanwhile, his eyes sought out and found the block of ten grey lockers at the end of the room, sliced in half by the diagonal of somebody's leg in traction.

Remodel his ear! The truth was he was in a sort of swoon of disbelief.

'You don't know Earrrls Court?' the nurse insisted.

'I went to the Ideal Home Exhibition once,' Morris confessed (when Mother was still alive, of course – it was with people like Mother and Massimina that you went to venues like that).

'Ah, Olympia,' Dionisio remembered. 'Olympia. The Idea Lome. Verry, verry beautiful.'

Morris almost choked. There probably wasn't a decent home within a mile of Earls Court, never mind an ideal one. Certainly the miserable Duckworth ménage had never even been an also-ran.

'Why don't you go back, then?' he asked, getting another fierce stab of pain from stitches in the corner of his mouth. 'If you like it so much.'

Dionisio got to his feet and smiled rather sadly: 'I must for the moment look after my old mamma 'ere. She is sick. Then I go back.'

Lucky to have a mother to look after! Morris watched the small man push his trolley away. As soon as the ward door swung to behind him, he lifted the tray from off its support, extricated himself from the bed, found uncertain feet, and stumbled across to the lockers.

Thus, over the next ten tumultuous minutes, Morris discovered: first, that, no, his coat, and hence the ransom letters, was not in the locker; second, that, yes, his face looked far worse than anything he had ever done to any of his victims; and third, that, amazing but true, the police, or rather carabinieri, appeared to be paying serious attention to the ransom note Signora Posenato had received, if for no other reason than, as the local paper put it, 'its curious similarity to letters sent after the kidnap of the missing man's sister-in-law, Massimina Trevisan, some two years ago'.

Morris almost passed out. Finding Dionisio in the corridor as he tottered back to the ward, he begged the little man for a tranquilliser. But after consulting the clipboard at the end of his bed, Dionisio assured him that he had already been given the maximum permitted dose. He was already tranquillised. That was normal in disfigurement cases. He smiled apologetically. 'I tell you the what. No sooner I am feenished with taking the medicine, I come back and we keep everybody other the company. What you say?'

Kindly, Morris said nothing, but headed for his bed, his horror, his self-pity.

CHAPTER TWENTY-EIGHT

EARLY AFTERNOON OF THE fourth day Paola arranged the screen around his bed and wanted to indulge in some kind of activity there and then. First the three weeks in prison, and now this. With only one night at home in between! It was sufficient cause for divorce!

Was this kind of jolly jolly talk intended to cheer him up? Ever more obsessed with the missing coat, Morris watched her face, and came to the conclusion, even as she slipped an arm into the sheets, that there was something wrong, something not quite Paola, perhaps precisely because of this exaggeration of her Paolaishness.

She had penetrated his pyjama now, but was clearly disappointed.

The drugs had wiped out his libido, Morris explained.

'Put your hand up my skirt,' she said. 'God, but you're sexy, all bandaged up like that!' She was pressing her knees against the edge of the bed. Sure enough she had no knickers on. Morris's thumb slid neatly into her. In a sort of pantomime of her erotic self, she rocked slowly back and forth on his wrist.

'Pull it out,' she ordered, 'suck it, then kiss me.'

Morris did as he was bidden, her hands already forcing his thumb back in as she kissed the cuntiness on his lips. Quite definitely, he thought, this was an act. But to cover for what? Did it mean that she knew? And if so, how much? Just Bobo? Or Bobo and Massimina? Was it that she had found the coat, the letters? Did she imagine he knew she knew? Was she showing him she could use that power to turn him into a sex slave for the rest of his days?

And when would her belly start to swell with their baby? Mimi had assured him she was pregnant. The child, Morris felt, would mark the beginning of his reformed life. His wife at that point would surely ease up, become someone one could imagine spending one's life with. It was simply a question of hanging on.

Then her face had just begun to take on the rather coarse contortions it always did at this point in the proceedings, when Kwame's woolly head popped up above the screen behind her.

For Christ's sake! What squalor! He tried to ease out of her, but she grabbed his arm, thrusting herself hard against him to squeeze out the titbit. Her breath was coming quick and deep.

Above the screen, Kwame grinned broadly. Morris could do nothing else but hang on, her hand clutching his under her skirt, her thighs squeezing and squeezing his wrist. He felt deeply humiliated.

'*O Dio!*' Paola gasped. '*O Dio, Dio, Dio!*' Then opening her eyes, she asked: 'Why on earth did you do that, Mo? *Antipatico!* I almost missed my slot.'

Retrieving his hand and wiping it on the sheet, Morris said: 'We were being observed.'

Paola glanced over her shoulder. Kwame's features had settled back into an enviable impassivity.

'Hello, boss,' he said.

'Oh, Kwame.' Paola was straightening her skirt, an unembarrassed flush on her face. 'I thought you were going to stay in the car.' Rather than seeming upset she even managed a smile, which was the kind of whore she was of course.

'I wanted to see the boss about the work,' the big black said. 'And this is the only time for visiting.' He came round inside the screen. 'I want to tell him about the threats I am getting.'

Apparently there had been messages under his door, telling the black to get out or else. A brick tossed through the *soggiorno* window. '*Veneto per i Veneti*' scratched on the side of the car.

Morris promised he would inform the police. He then gave them both a series of instructions about what must be urgently done at the company: messages for Doorways and other clients, clarifications of orders, an explanation of how Bobo had managed to account for the money paid under the table to suppliers. Because if they didn't get things moving, he said, Trevisan Wines would simply wind down and die. Paola complained that it was all too complicated, that Morris would have to do it himself when he was out. But Kwame rather surprisingly took a small diary from the pockets of quite fashionable trousers and made careful notes, asking the boss to repeat everything very precisely. So that despite the embarrassment of what had come before, not to mention the huge repertoire of worries he was currently engaged with, Morris experienced the genuine pleasure of having a worthy pupil, a good apprentice. When his eyes met the black's across the length of the bed, a dark and reassuring complicity passed between them.

'*Povera faccia selvaggia,*' Paola was cooing. 'My poor savaged savage!'

Did she know or didn't she? And if she didn't, why that strange determination to be more normal than normal, bringing herself off like that?

'By the way' – addressing both of them at once, Morris tried to be completely offhand – 'after they killed that bloody dog, you don't know what happened to my coat, do you? I think I must have had my wallet in one of the pockets.'

There was a very brief silence.

'You was all covered in the blood, boss. That big dog, he was tearing you up like a demon.'

'Then the police shot him,' Morris said. 'Or so Forbes tells me.'

'First we try to pull him off, then they shot him. Man, was he crazy!'

'But why?' Paola asked. 'He'd never done that before.'

'Police said somebody try to poison him, lady,' Kwame explained.

Once again, Morris was impressed by the boy's talent for lying, or rather for telling the innocent half-truth, for saying exactly what he would have said if he hadn't known the half of what he undeniably did. Also it pleased him that, despite having watched as he had, he still addressed Mrs Duckworth with the utmost respect.

'I just wondered what happened to my coat?' Morris repeated.

Kwame shook his head. 'You still had it on when I help with the stretcher, boss.'

'You didn't have the credit cards in it, did you, Mo?' Paola wriggled a little inside her skirt and mixed a grimace with a smile.

Very well, Morris thought, if it came to playing it hard and long, he was as good as the next man. But that coat and the letters inside it must have ended up somewhere.

The following morning, only twenty-four hours before the operation now, Antonella came to visit, and after a few moments' hesitation agreed to read to Morris from his English Bible. She was demurely dressed in brown and black. Morris had explained to her about his conversion, his desire to serve, his intention, as long as she agreed, to combine Trevisan Wines' commercial operations with a charitable organisation, to build a chapel in the grounds. Now she sat beside him, her hands pale on the black book, her long black hair falling forward to brush an ample bosom.

'What do you want me to read?' his sister-in-law asked.

'Anything,' he said. 'Your favourite passage.'

'I'm afraid I'm really rather ignorant,' she flustered. 'Catholics don't tend to read the Bible that much.'

Her fumblings were endearing.

'Perhaps when I get better we could study it together,' he suggested. 'It would be an adventure. Perhaps it would help you to take your mind off things. Or we could even study it in English. Mix learning and devotion. That would be a good way to start lessons again. Now Stan can't do them any more.'

He sincerely hoped nobody had told the American he was in hospital. The last thing he needed was for the fawning Californian to come and visit and for Antonella to go and meet him in the lift.

She smiled gratefully, while Morris reflected that the very fact his sister-in-law had come to see him at all meant that, even if someone had found the coat and put two and two together, the cat was certainly not out of the bag yet. Otherwise she would have been gouging his eyes out.

'Open it at random,' he said, nodding to the gilt-edged pages. If he ever wrote a book himself he would like it to have gilt-edged pages.

She did so, and finding reading glasses (he hadn't known about those, but made no comment) in a black handbag, began to read: '"Oh, that I were as in months past, as in the days when God preserved me."'

She looked up at him from the pages, the briefest glance,

her features brimming with a pain made all the more noble by those wonderfully serious glasses.

'"When his candle shined upon my head, and when by his light I walked through darkness."'

Morris sighed.

'"As I was in the days of my youth, when the secret of God was upon my tabernacle."'

He watched her intently. There was a fine trembling about swollen lips, a splendidly womanly intensity, which in Paola was mere voracity.

'"When the Almighty was yet with me, when my children were about me,

'"When I washed my steps with butter, and the rock poured me out rivers of oil."'

Antonella burst into tears. 'Oh, Morris,' she cried. 'Why did it have to happen to us?'

He sat up and put a hand on hers. He felt genuinely upset and desperately attracted, quite in spite of himself, since he was committed to Paola now.

Washed my steps with butter! He should have started studying the Bible long ago.

Suddenly, Antonella was sobbing. 'First with Mimi and now Bobo. You know we've had this horrible letter. Just like the ones for Mimi. I was pleased at first, I thought it meant he must be alive, but then I remembered what happened to her. *O Dio*, it's so awful. I can't understand why God would let it happen twice in the same family. And now I go and open the Bible right at Job!'

She wept.

Cautiously, Morris asked in what way this letter was similar to the ones they had got for Mimi. He had never seen them, he reminded her. And himself.

'Cut out of novels and newspapers,' she said, taking off her glasses to wipe her eyes with a tissue. 'Not a word of handwriting. Full of strange threats.'

Morris was concerned. 'Could I see it?' he asked. It turned out she had a photocopy of the thing in her handbag. She leant down to the floor and rummaged. Morris spread the paper open on his sheets.

Immediately he started, his whole body stiffened, so complete a *déjà vu* it was.

DARK PRINCESS OF THE SEVEN KINGDOMS!

The thing had obviously been cut out from some third-rate translation of an even worse novel. Gothic, for young teenagers.

IT IS MY BEHOLDEN DUTY TO APPRISE THEE THAT NUMBERED ARE NOW THE DAYS OF THY EVIL REIGN OVER THE LONG-SUFFERING PEOPLES OF ZORN. EVEN AS MY HAND SETS FORTH THIS MISSIVE, I DIP MY QUILL IN THE BLOOD OF THY MALEFICENT SON, BLACK THOMAS, WHO WRITHES TORMENTED AS ONCE HE TORMENTED OTHERS IN IGNOMINIOUS SHACKLES. GNASH THY TEETH, CHRISTENDOM'S FELL OPPRESSOR! IF BEFORE SUNSET OF THE SECOND SABBATH THOU DOST NOT LAY ALL THY ILL-GOT GAIN AT THE FEET OF GENTLE KNIGHT RUDOLPH AND SWEAR ALLEGIANCE UPON HIS MIGHTY SWORD, THEN HE ONLY THAT THOU LOVEST, HE ONLY WHO IS DEAR TO THY FOUL HEART AND FOULER SOUL, SHALL BE DISPATCHED SANS SHRIVE OR MERCY TO MEET THE MOST JUST WRATH OF HIS ALL-HOLY MAKER.

Gnash thy teeth indeed! Morris thought. What miserable prose! But the exact same ruse as his own first ransom letter. The teasing horror of the absurd. Some stupid adventure for retarded adults turned into reality. It was signed: RODOLFO IL ROSSO, DIFENSORE DELLA FEDE, PROTETTORE DEI POVERI, FLAGELLO DI SATANA E

TUTTE LE SUE OPERE. Beneath the cheap publication's caps a small piece cut from a local newspaper said: 'The authorities promised that technical details relative to the payment of the new tax will be released over the next few days.'

Morris let out a deep breath. Actually, it was pretty damn clever: a perfect imitation of his own earlier pastiche, at once daring the recipient not to take it seriously while allowing the sender to pretend, above all to himself perhaps, that for all its horror it was no more than a joke. Morris was just about to look up and comfort Antonella and insist that she absolutely must not pay – since, after all, nothing had been gained from paying all that money for Massimina, had it? – when a male voice asked:

'*Allora*, your opinion, Mr Duckvorse?'

It was the first, but by no means the last, time that Morris would appreciate the advantage of having had his face half chewed to pieces. For however keenly he sensed the blood draining from his cheeks, his eyes widening to a stare, surely no one could have read anything from the mess of stitches and bandages his once handsome features had now become. He shivered and, turning his eyes to the apparition of a Fendtsteig more Gestapo-like than ever in full uniform and rimless spectacles, told him truthfully: 'Colonnello, I'm afraid it's a complete mystery to me.'

'If you could leave us alone for just one moment?' Fendtsteig said to Antonella, rather coldly, Morris felt, given all that the poor woman was going through. However, the carabiniere's uniform was impressive with its white holster strap and red-striped trousers. Aesthetically a considerable improvement on the rather workaday uniform of the polizia.

Antonella slipped away, fumbling reading glasses into

an open handbag. Morris appeared to gaze at the spot where she had disappeared.

'Signor Duckvorse,' Fendtsteig began at once, 'I'm afraid we must have yet another talk.'

The Englishman's face was a mask of resignation.

'Signor Duckvorse, a man has disappeared, for more than a month now, apparently after a struggle.' He paused, bit at his lips, brought the tips of his fingers together. 'In terms of opportunity to kill or abduct we have three suspects: you and two rather pathetic *extra-comunitari*.'

'Homosexuals,' Morris said.

Fendtsteig ignored this. Could the carabiniere be a homosexual? Morris wondered. He would not be surprised. The world seemed to be swarming with them and their sad diseases just at the moment.

Fendtsteig continued to consider his fingertips, as if deep in thought.

'On the evening following the crime, you were absent from your house until two in the morning. I repeat, two in the morning. You refused to clarify your whereabouts. Because of this, firmly believing that you were the murderer or abductor, I had you imprisoned to prevent you establishing any alibi with anybody else, a provision available to me under *decreto legge* of the penal code 776/91.'

Tedium. Morris's eye strayed to the cobweb-caught crucifix above the door. It surely suggested something of a breakdown in ward hygiene, both practical and spiritual. And when was this obnoxious, nit-picking Tyrolese going to tell him whether or not they had found the letters in his coat? So that Morris could know whether he needed to keep fighting his corner or whether he mightn't do better just to relax and resign.

'You then contrived,' Fendtsteig went on, using the same dull, machine-like tone he had used on their first meeting, 'I repeat, *contrived*, and only after three weeks'' hard thinking at that, to create the most bizarre alibi for your absence on that evening. In interviews with the prison psychiatrist you claimed that . . .'

'*Per favore, Colonnello,*' Morris interrupted. 'It really is too painful. I know perfectly well what I said, please let's not talk about it.'

Fendtsteig hesitated, though without appearing to acknowledge Morris's interruption, then continued: 'However, it was sufficient for me, under the terms of the above-mentioned *decreto legge,* to have a story, however unlikely, just so long as I could later, if necessary, prove it to be wrong. In fact the weaker and more ridiculous the story, the better.'

He paused, but again without exchanging glances with Morris, who muttered into the silence: 'If I had known the man would tell people about what I'd said, I would never have told him. I imagined any discussion with a doctor was in confidence.'

Fendtsteig's thin, bespectacled face above the high military collar showed how little he was convinced of this. Which Morris genuinely felt was unreasonable. Especially since the description he had given of the point at which he had climbed over the cemetery wall, and the way the coffins were stacked and so on, had been extremely accurate and, presumably, verifiable. Let them think what they liked, quite clearly he *had* at some time or other in his life climbed over that cemetery wall. And for what other reason if not to moan over the coffin of his dead mistress, which, again, *had* been available for weeping over only on that one special evening?

Burying Bobo there would prove a winning card yet.

'As you know,' Fendtsteig continued with that air of inexorability he clearly cultivated and which was leaving Morris steadily less impressed, 'immediately before your release, the polizia arrested two *extra-comunitari*, charged them, I believe erroneously, with the murder of your colleague, and then proceeded to arrange for trial *per direttissima*, on the slimmest of circumstantial evidence.'

Mimicking the other man's official tone, Morris said: 'Two young men whom I had helped in every possible way and who repaid my kindness by engaging in lewd and perverse activities while under my employ. For which my colleague very rightly fired them. An excellent motive for their doing away with him.'

For a moment he couldn't remember whether he had taken this line with Fendtsteig before, or with Marangoni, or whether he hadn't taken some other line, or even the opposite line. He stared defiantly at Fendtsteig, who was apparently still engrossed in the tips of his fingers.

Morris said nervously: 'Given their general behaviour, I myself wouldn't be at all surprised if they turned out to be the culprits.'

The carabiniere's long silence was becoming ominous.

Morris talked on: 'The sort of people who will sell a man a video-recorder in a *stazione di servizio* that turns out to be nothing more than a brick or a block of wood. You know the kind of thing? You open it in your house and it falls on the floor and chips an expensive tile. A breach of faith towards the very people who have attempted to make their lives here less miserable.'

Saying this, he contrived to colour nervousness with a convincing flush of anger. For a moment he enjoyed imagining himself a sort of chameleon, constantly changing shape in Fendtsteig's bewildered and defeated grip.

'Biting the very hand that wishes to feed them,' he concluded with genuine self-righteousness.

Fendtsteig at last looked up. He measured his words. 'As to the exact character of the two unfortunates, Signor Duckvorse, I will not even hazard a guess. You may perfectly well be correct in your impression. However, it is not an important element. Far more interesting is the fact that no sooner was this development – the arrest and trial of these two persons – announced than we, or rather the family, received this most unpleasant note, which Signora Posenato has just shown you, a note, I might say, exactly similar in style and content to the first ransom note received by the Trevisan family when their daughter was abducted some two years ago. Now how do you explain that, Signor Duckvorse?'

Signor Duckvorse clearly did not explain that at all – he wished he could – and hence felt it wiser simply to stare. Glimpsing, through a gap in the screen, a small brown figure pushing his drugs trolley down the ward, he shouted: '*Ciao*, Dionisio, how's life?'

'*Ciao*,' Dionisio called. 'Everything well!'

'See you later,' Morris called, and as if it were an after-thought, which it was, added: 'I was thinking, there's a friend of mine has a hotel in Shepherd's Bush you might be interested in getting in contact with.'

'*Benissimo!*'

Had his teeth been a little better looked after, Dionisio's smile, as he poked his face for a moment through the screen, might have been described as radiant. The cara-biniere, on the other hand, frowned rather severely, with a sort of small child's pique.

'*Mi scusi*, Colonnello, but you have to humour people in the hospital here if you want good service.'

Fendtsteig, however, would not be drawn. Very matter-of-factly he insisted: 'Now, Signor Duckvorse, I would be grateful if you could explain that circumstance, the arrival of this letter, only three days after the other two are accused of murder. About the fastest our post office could possibly operate in my experience. And sent espresso too.'

Morris felt it only reasonable to show irritation at this point.

'Colonello, if you cannot explain what has happened, I don't see how I can be expected to. Especially when you consider that I've been ill in hospital for upwards of a week.'

'Oh, but I can explain it.' Fendtsteig had regained his composure. 'I was merely hoping that you might save me the trouble.'

'Well, then I'm sorry to have to disappoint you,' Morris said, but he was having to hold on to his nerve for dear life now. What did he mean, he could explain it?

Fendtsteig waited, then when he began to speak it was with the sort of sinister background tone a vacuum cleaner or electric razor makes. 'My explanation, Signor Duckvorse, is as follows. Very simply, given the nature of this letter, we can say that the man responsible for the kidnap of Signorina Trevisan and the man responsible for the disappearance of Signor Posenato are, must be, one and the same person.'

There! Morris took a sharp breath. The game was up. They had finally seen the obvious. Already he could smell the mixture of cheap disinfectant and human staleness that had been his prison cell. Definitely a tang of urine. Yes. And vaguely he wondered whether he would be able to ask them to put him back in with the same cellmate, whom he had rather taken a liking to after a while. In the end a murderous schizophrenic had more to offer as an object of long-term study than your average embezzler or hitman.

'However, upon seeing that two innocent people were to be tried for murder, this' – Fendtsteig hesitated and knit his Tyrolese brow – 'this most curious maniac, Signor Duckvorse, as I think clearly transpires from the bizarre tone of these letters, has a fit of conscience and decides to use his knowledge of the ransom note he sent in the past to convince the police that they have made a mistake, and that this is a kidnap not a murder. In the end it was a provident move on the part of the polizia to charge these two. It drew the real culprit out into the open.'

Morris sighed deeply. One could only thank the Almighty God that these people weren't just a scintilla, a scantling, a soupçon more intelligent. He strived to look as humbly puzzled as he could.

'Colonnello, I'm sorry, but it does seem somewhat unlikely to me that' – he hesitated – 'yes, though of course I have far less experience than yourself in such matters.' He stopped, hesitated, wondered if his brow was registering knitted or just carelessly sewn back together. 'As I was saying, it does seem unlikely that someone responsible for the callous murder of a beautiful young girl and a charming young man would worry immoderately about the fate of two miserable Third-World homosexuals. I can tell you for one that were I the murderer I most certainly would not.'

This was almost true. But not quite.

Fendtsteig said nothing. Absurdly, it occurred to Morris that if by any chance Antonella were listening behind the screen, she would be appalled by his racism. Though such considerations hardly seemed relevant at this point, like worrying if one was looking one's best for the firing-squad. Suddenly, irrationally, feeling the game must be up, he asked: 'In any event, who would this heinous person be?'

For the first time Fendtsteig looked him straight in the eyes. It was not a pleasant experience. Behind their polished, rimless spectacles the carabiniere's watery orbs gave the impression of some rather unpleasant vegetable species inexpertly preserved under glass, one could only imagine in the interests of science.

'Once again I was hoping, Signor Duckvorse,' the carabiniere said, with the air of one who finally has his quarry cornered, 'that you, with your rather morbid attraction to cemeteries and young girls' coffins, would be the person best qualified to tell me that.'

If there were moments in his life upon which, however things ultimately panned out, Morris would be justified in looking back with nothing short of immense pride, then this was to be one of them. Brought most cruelly to bay in this squalid municipal hospital bed, his back to the wall, his handsome features disfigured, and not even in possession, as he had been on other occasions, of all the nasty facts that now needed to be juggled into some plausible illusion, Morris Duckworth, as Morris would later have occasion to think, nevertheless performed most perfectly. Indeed, the word breathtaking would hardly be out of place, though Morris was not such a fool as to arrogate all the credit for such a performance to himself. For quite definitely it was *her* voice he heard prompting him now, *her* perfume he smelt. Quite definitely it was Massimina who simply dictated what, dancing at the end of a plank over tumultuous seas, he now contrived to repeat.

And behind Mimi, presumably, was . . . well, God.

'Colonnello' – he took a very deep breath, as if expecting to go under for a long time – 'Colonnello, it is unkind of you to make fun of an obsession that I appreciate is horribly morbid, even aesthetically distasteful, but which my analyst assures me is one of the most common the world over. At least among those, Colonnello Fendtsteig, who have had the good fortune to love someone and be loved by them in return.' He paused, then with dreadful assurance simply talked on into the unknown, went right over the end of that plank, expecting the very worst of course – the billowing waves, the suck of the undertow – only to find that, like his dear Saviour before him, the monstrous waters calmed beneath his feet, the storm responded to his rebuke, allowing him quite serenely to stroll across the deep, to walk, to talk his way to the other side.

Mimi was holding his hand.

'My version of events, if you will allow me to offer an amateur's humble opinion, is as follows; and if, as you will no doubt protest, I haven't offered it before, this was merely, as you shall see, out of a sense of loyalty to my colleague and a genuine affection for his poor wife.'

He paused, amazed to discover that he wasn't even seasick, though quite how he was going to step over the next wave was not as yet clear. As usual, he had planned nothing. But this was his genius.

Mimi was beside him.

'Bobo, that is my colleague, Signor Posenato, had for some time been very, er, how shall we say, restless about his life. He felt trapped, nervous. He was afraid that the imminent death of Signora Trevisan would condemn him to what he felt was a miserable existence running a tiny company with little hope of expansion. And' – here Morris lowered his voice, looking up hard at the screen curtain, as if his eye might penetrate it and discover Antonella's hearkening ear – 'although in previous interviews I may, as I said, have denied this for reasons of loyalty, I do have reason to suspect, though I cannot be sure, that most of all he was restless because *there was another woman in his life*.'

Fendtsteig was rubbing two fingers back and forth on his chin waiting, expecting another mere diversion, such as that with Dionisio. He hadn't realised as yet that Morris was acting under divine afflatus.

'The truth is that Bobo was frequently in the factory, or rather the office, at night-time. Yes, at night-time. He frequently seemed flustered and distracted. He often spoke harshly or excitedly to people without their being able to understand why. Hence these ridiculous stories of his arguments with me.'

'Signor Duckvorse, if I may interrupt, these are the kind of subjective impressions which it is all too easy to invent and which no one could ever possibly verify.'

281

'If necessary,' Morris sailed on, 'chapter and verse can be added at a later date. The purchase of a savage dog, for example, was no doubt intended to discourage interruptions when he was with his mistress in the office at night.' There was an idea! 'His opposition to my suggestion that we set up a night shift probably had a similar basis. But for the moment I will give you just the broad outline of what I have long suspected is the true state of affairs.'

He had no idea what this might be, but at the same time was quite convinced that, even as he spoke, it was about to reveal itself.

'I got my first inkling when Ispettore – is he an ispettore? I get so mixed up – Ispettore Marangoni informed me that the police had received an anonymous phone call suggesting that something drastic had deservedly happened to Bobo, Signor Posenato. But when I realised the other day that our guard dog at the factory had been poisoned I became sure of it.'

He nodded his head twice briskly, despite the pain, like one who is at last saying and at the same time discovering what he knows must be true. 'Yes, when I saw that poisoned dog I was convinced, and I would then have told you my suspicions – I mean, Colonnello Fendtsteig, I was myself concerned that these poor *extra-comunitari*, however inappropriately they may have behaved prior to the event, were being wrongly charged – yes, would have told you myself, if I hadn't heard that Bobo had already solved the problem by sending that letter.'

In a state somewhere between ecstasy and vertigo, Morris suddenly realised what his dear Mimi had quite probably been trying to get through to him for days now: that they would *never* discover the corpse. That was his trump card. That was the plank that extended to an infinite horizon. Without a corpse one could simply go on speculating *ad infinitum*.

'*Mi scusi*,' Fendtsteig interrupted, but at last with a hint of genuine interest and concern now, albeit coated with irony, '*mi scusi*, but I can't follow you. What exactly are you trying to tell me?'

A reasonable question.

'Bobo faked the whole thing and ran off with his mistress,' Morris invented abruptly. Then, like an animal who has given birth after considerable and painful effort, he immediately proceeded to lick the little creature he had produced with love and amazement. 'Consider, Colonnello: his body hasn't been found; not even his car has been found.' Morris began to fill in, even caress, the details, already quite sure that they must all, without exception, fit. Otherwise Mimi wouldn't have told him to say it, would she? 'In fact, Colonnello, the only indication we have of there being any foul play is the mess in the office, a bit of blood that anybody could have produced, an easily staged interrupted phone call to the police, then an anonymous phone call, and finally a ransom letter, which, as you point out, was probably written because Bobo, who as I said is a charming person, was most upset to find that two people were being unjustly accused of his murder. But most conclusively for me,' Morris said, though he still wasn't quite sure why, 'there was this business of the poisoned dog.'

'Ah,' Fendtsteig sighed. 'You are now going to explain to me the poisoned dog. I am most impressed, Signor Duckvorse.' But his eyes narrowed dangerously.

'You see, when he first planned his escape,' Morris began a long and winding uphill slope, not sure if the ridge ahead was the last or just one of a series, 'I can't imagine that Bobo foresaw the problem of having to write that ransom letter and the other ones that will doubtless follow. That is, he couldn't suppose that the police, as you so rightly pointed out, would be so stupid as to accuse these two poor immigrants on the slimmest of circumstantial evidence.' Out of deference to Fendtsteig, Morris did not say, though he felt it was implied, that equally Bobo could not have imagined anybody would be so stupid as to suspect Morris himself. 'Now, the fact is that in one of the filing cabinets, there in the office, under, let me see if I can rightly remember, yes, what was it, "Trevisan, Massimina", quite simple, in one of the filing cabinets, there is, or rather' – and here Morris took an immensely deep breath – 'I suspect we'll find *there was*, a collection of the documents regarding Massimina's kidnap. Do you see what I am trying to get at now?'

Fendtsteig did not.

'If the person,' Morris said, discovering the truth even as he was inspired to pronounce it, 'who wrote that letter was not Massimina's kidnapper – and why should such a person wish to draw attention to a previous crime by repeating the same ruse? – then it must have been someone who had immediate access to those letters. Bobo, as I said, had them on file in the office, since it was he who acted on behalf of the Trevisan family during the whole horrible affair, ignoring, may I say, all the sensible advice I tried to offer. My guess is that if you go back to the office you will find the file, but not the letters. *He needed them to fake the one he wrote.*'

Fendtsteig stared glassily through his spectacles. At least Morris could be sure now that the carabinieri hadn't found the letters in the coat, although at the same time, what he had just said convinced him that somebody else had.

And it wasn't Bobo.

Fendtsteig said: 'The dog?'

Morris opened his mouth, but for a moment Massimina seemed to have deserted him. Why on earth would Bobo have killed the dog in such circumstances, for Christ's sake?

'The dog?' Fendtsteig repeated.

'Obviously he couldn't risk breaking into the office

himself,' Morris realised. 'He paid somebody else to do it. Who was duly warned about the dog. Or maybe it was his mistress even. How can I know? Since the damn thing was so fierce they tried to poison it.'

There was a long silence between them. Dionisio pushed his trolley back up the ward. Came the low moan of some patient or other trying to get used to his mutilation. Finally Fendtsteig stood up. He straightened himself to his full slender height in the proud uniform. Once again he submitted Morris to a cold and penetrating stare.

'Signor Duckvorse, everything you have said to me will be meticulously checked. Let me warn you here and now, however, that I believe not one word of your absurd inventions. On the contrary, I am more than ever convinced that this affair can only end with your being charged and convicted of the murder of your brother-in-law. It is merely a question of time before the crucial evidence falls into our hands.'

Watching him out, Morris couldn't help feeling that the man was probably right. Either that, or he himself would have to *invent* some evidence that simply wrapped the whole thing up once and for all in some other way . . .

But quite what and how, he had no idea.

PART FOUR

CHAPTER TWENTY-NINE

MOTHER HAD ALWAYS CALLED him 'her beautiful boy'. It was one of the reasons she was so wonderful. She always, always made him feel attractive, adorable. Mother adored Morris. Morris adored Mother. Each to the other was entirely beautiful. So that if Morris was for ever to remember his encounter with chickenpox, it was not so much because of its belated coincidence with a miserable puberty, as because of the time, coming down the stairs for the cream that was supposed to stop the itching, he had heard her voice over the television saying to his father: 'Yes, he looks like a scrofulous little monster.' And that beloved voice was laughing.

Morris had stopped shock-still on the stair. Not only was she laughing, but her laughter was mingled with the cruder, deeper cackle of his father, who said: 'Serve him right for a week or two, vain little pansy.' To which his mother, with a complicity Morris could never forgive her, replied: 'Perhaps you're right, Ron. Anyway, it can't do him any harm.'

Couldn't do him any harm! To look scrofulous! Monstrous! And she had called the old pig by his name! An obscenity Morris hadn't heard for some very long time. 'Ron.' If there was one thing worse than being called Morris, it was being called Ron. Though the old beer swiller would never have appreciated that. He wasn't sensitive to such things. Turning abruptly, Morris had rushed back to his room to find himself in the mirror in the wardrobe door. Under the forty-watt pallor his father always imposed as part of the long war of attrition against Morris's 'reading habit', his features presented a lurid battlefield of acne and pox spots. The clean, fresh blondness of his normal self was quite lost, quite unimaginable. But Morris had forced himself to look all the same, forced himself to savour his ugliness, to appreciate exactly what it was that after all these happy years had caused his mother to betray him like this. And with Father of all people! For the problem with ugliness, Morris realised as he stared it in the face, his own face, was not so much that it rendered one unattractive, both to oneself and to others, but that it encouraged a complicity, or even conspiracy, amongst others against oneself.

Looking in the bathroom mirror now, with the wraps finally off and the truth at last taking something of its shockingly permanent shape, Morris's first reaction was not rage, horror or even plain sadness at his lost beauty, so much as fear, fear that these livid scars, this unnatural skin texture and the general if elusive loss of symmetricality could only stack the cards the more heavily against him. Wouldn't Paola be eager to be rid of him now? Morris had always sensed how much her being attracted to him depended on his physical beauty. Might she not start to air some of the suspicions she quite clearly had. Fendtsteig, after all, needed only the barest whiff of evidence to be setting his teeth into the grisly truth.

And Antonella? Would she be so sympathetic still? Mightn't she see this ugliness as the revelation somehow of an inner spiritual ugliness? Did Morris see it that way himself? (Up to a point perhaps, though he had never subscribed to anything quite so ingenuous as Platonism.) And Forbes? Why should Forbes love him any the less merely because he had lost his fair complexion? Yet Morris felt he might. He might. Perhaps even Kwame would be less amenable, and reasonably so, especially if he sensed that all the other vermin were abandoning the good ship Duckworth.

The truth was, Morris himself felt less confident without the talisman of what had been an undeniable beauty, those moments when he glanced in a mirror over somebody else's shoulder, or perhaps only in a plate of glass, a window, a tabletop, and saw that he was fairer than they, brighter than they, younger and healthier than Marangoni, infinitely more composed and attractive than the likes of Fendtsteig and Bobo.

Moments that would be no more! For in the blurred and broken mirror of the squalid hospital bathroom Morris found only an unprepossessing stranger with flattened patchwork cheek and lopsided ears under a shaven head of concentration-camp poignancy. Lifting a finger he ran it ever so gently across the skin, which felt nothing. It was the gesture of a lover, a mother. His eyes filled with tears.

'Mimi,' he mouthed. 'Mimi, *you* won't turn against me, will you?' Still gazing, tears still falling, it occurred to Morris that the advantage to be drawn out of this, as experience taught him there was always some kind of advantage to be drawn out of every débâcle – otherwise where would he be, for whom life had been nothing more than one débâcle after another? – the advantage to be drawn was that his disfigurement would bring him into even closer communion with Mimi. As prison had, as hospital had. For he needed her more than ever now. And she – unlike the others, who flattered, pestered and accused – she could live only through him, comely or hideous as he might be. For he was the only person who truly remembered Mimi, truly wanted her inside himself.

Their destinies were locked together for all eternity, and far more convincingly than if they had merely married.

Morris had entered hospital on Sunday, April 10. The trial of Azedine and Farouk was to be celebrated (Morris hoped the term would prove appropriate) on April 28, which was also the day (obviously quite deliberately) that the second ransom letter had set as the deadline for payment of a thousand million lire. The police, however, despite pressure from the carabinieri, were refusing to consider the affair as anything more than a squalid hoax and would not have the trial postponed. The immigrants, Marangoni was convinced, were guilty, and would doubtless be very popular victims of the judicial system. The press were happy with the solution and playing down the ransom letter business. In any event, Morris, Morris felt, should get out of the hospital as soon as he possibly could.

But Dionisio explained that the doctors always kept skin-graft cases for a further four days after removal of dressings, for observation. It was important to see how the operated area reacted to the air. 'In what sense?' Morris demanded. He was growing impatient. In an inexplicable reaction to his inertia of the past week, every second seemed vital now. He must, must, must find out what had happened to his coat! He couldn't afford to become a creature of mere speculation.

'The skin, it can become very, very loose. Is important.'

Morris shrugged his shoulders. It was not as though he didn't recognise a lost cause when he saw one.

Then he was aware of a new feeling: he suddenly felt desperately, almost maliciously eager to see how all the others would respond to this truly ghastly face of his. If nothing else he would have the pleasure of judging them, of appreciating how wise or otherwise he had been to put his trust in them. So, having fobbed Dionisio off with a little chat about the improved situation on the District Line since the installation of new trains with passenger-operated doors, Morris waited till the idiot nurse was out of the ward, grabbed his clothes from his cabinet, dressed quickly in a distressingly dirty loo and walked right out of the hospital, exactly ninety-six hours before anybody expected him to.

Good.

His first move was to take a cab to the town centre and sit at one of the tables that made such a brightly coloured chequerboard of Piazza Bra. When the waiter came and Morris looked quickly up from his newspaper, he was able to gauge the exact level of shock suppressed in a sudden lowering of the eyes and a moment's hesitation. He ordered an *aperitivo* and appropriate munchies and turned his dog-ravaged face to the April tourists thronging the sunlit esplanade. Squinting in the bright light, Japanese and Germans would turn away from the elegant ruin of the arena to the sparkling hedonism of the café tables, weighing up for a moment the nuanced pros and cons of the various bars, the blue tables, the green, the red, the yellow awnings, the white, the pink, a paradise of pastel shade and splashing brightness, until – perhaps on the very brink of choosing this bar rather than another – their eyes came to rest on Morris's shaven head, the livid darkness of those scars, the gashed patchwork of ill-matched skins. At which there was that sudden involuntary recoiling from something that offends a common sense of niceness, as when one sees a spastic child push food into its eye. A passing priest quickened his pace, right hand instinctively moving to his breast to sign Our Saviour's Passion. A tall woman tried to pretend she wasn't looking away by staring at something just over his shoulder. Only a little boy stopped to gape, and was quickly hauled off by his mother.

Morris grinned. Grotesquely, he supposed. Dialling her

number on the mobile phone purchased for his hospital stay, he said: 'I have become a *memento mori*, Mimi. How apt!'

The thought that his very presence might in the future serve to shock people out of their complacency was not, now one had the first inklings of getting used to it, an entirely unpleasant or inappropriate one. Wasn't this, after all, one of the roles that Morris had always cast for himself, especially *vis-à-vis* the silver-spoon-fed elements of society – Paola and Bobo to name but two? 'You know, Mimi, now I come to think of it, perhaps this was exactly what God had in mind for me when he sent me charging so madly at that mad dog . . .'

He broke off and, on instinct, dialled his father's number. But the pig was out, and anyway had doubtless forgotten all about Morris's chickenpox. Any memory more than a week or so old was quickly drowned in the swill of alcohol. Perhaps it was just as well. Morris seemed to be getting sidetracked so easily these days. He must concentrate on the matter in hand.

He had just dialled Antonella's number and was waiting for the connection, when he caught a glimpse of Forbes across the square, tie visibly blossoming even at a good hundred metres.

'*Pronto?*'

He was in the company of a young man, though not, it seemed, one of the immigrants, since Morris had the impression, through milling Orientals, of a beard. Why did this fill him with disquiet?

'*Sono Morris.*'

His sister-in-law's voice was quiet, but brittle, as though barely repressing sobs. Something up. Keeping half an eye on Forbes and his oddly familiar bearded companion, Morris forced himself into alertness, sensitivity, only to be struck by the similarity with Mimi's voice.

'I'll be a little late this evening,' she was saying. 'And I'll only have time to read a chapter or so.'

Morris said not to worry. He felt quite resigned in his bed today, because they had told him he would be out of hospital soon. Immediately he reflected that it had required no reflection to tell this untruth. The only problem was to remember he had told it. She'd be in the hospital looking for him this evening. He'd have to be back.

'Listen, I just wanted to warn you absolutely not to pay this money,' he said. 'The ransom.'

She was silent for a moment. Again he had the impression of restrained emotion. At the same time the waiter brought his *gingerino* and white wine with *noccioline*. Morris coughed theatrically into the phone to cover anything the man might say. And where the hell had Forbes and that bearded bastard gone? It was so painful twisting one's head round. Morris drank. 'Medicine,' he explained. And added: 'The fact is, I just don't believe they've really got Bobo. I mean . . .' He let his voice tail off. 'Although of course I only know what the papers have been saying.'

Waiting for her to speak, he drank another sip of *gingerino*, then offered: 'It's only that if I were you I wouldn't want to throw away a *miliardo* for nothing.' Clearly Forbes and co. had popped into one of the bars. Probably in need of a bathroom.

Still she didn't speak. Then when Morris decided just to wait, she swallowed and said flatly: 'Morris, I found some letters. Just this morning.'

'What!' His heart missed a great deal more than a beat. What letters?

Antonella could contain herself no longer. She wept freely into the phone. 'Oh, he was having an affair. He was! And it's so awful! He'd hidden them in with his old first Communion photos!'

'Tonia,' Morris said. 'I'm so sorry.'

How naturally that lovely *diminutivo* had risen to his lips!

'*O Dio*. They go back months and months, it's awful.'

Quite spontaneously, Morris said: 'Oh, I wish I could be there to comfort you.'

'Morris.' The voice had cracked completely.

Respectfully, he waited a moment before telling her: 'I'm afraid you'll have to tell the police of course. I mean, I know it's unpleasant, but really you rather owe it to those poor immigrants. His disappearance could be something to do with this woman.'

'Yes, yes, I know.'

A passing thought suddenly alarmed him. 'I take it' – he hesitated – 'I mean, that you, that you have spoken to her? The girl. Whoever . . . I mean she might be able to tell us . . .'

'But that's just the point. I don't know who it is,' Antonella wailed. 'She just signs herself, "Your Bimbetta".' The poor woman could barely speak. 'Or "Your Sexy Girl".'

'But I mean, there must be some detail, some reference to somewhere . . .'

'They talk about nothing but sex,' Antonella said brutally. 'They're disgusting. They're . . . oh . . .' For a moment she lost control of her voice.

'I'm so sorry,' Morris consoled, consoled. Because the elopement scenario had yet to be disproved. If anything, indeed, it was reinforced. The truth of the matter was that whenever something happened, a person's disappearance, traces of a scuffle, you name it, there were always a hundred, a thousand ways it might have happened. All perfectly acceptable. There was no reason at all why Bobo shouldn't simply have eloped with his young lady, faking a kidnap to tide over illicit nuptials.

Or somebody had been blackmailing them. Why not? Forcing them to disappear together.

There was a nose-wiping sound to Antonella's voice now. Morris decided that silence would offer the best combination of condemnation and discretion.

'How could he have done that to me, Morrees? How could he!'

'People either do these things or they don't,' Morris told her truthfully. 'I know I never could. But the thing is now that you must tell the police. It might affect the trial of those boys.'

How kind he was being.

'Yes.'

'And don't pay the ransom until you have absolutely cast-iron evidence that it is a kidnap.'

Apparently attempting to recover her pride by adopting a businesslike voice, his sister-in-law said: 'No need to worry about that. I mean, I'm not supposed to tell you, but the carabinieri have told me to take the money, only they're going to be there to arrest whoever it is. It's the morning of the trial, early. Then I have to go and give evidence. It's all so horrible. I just want to get it over and go away.'

Morris barely had time to open his mouth, though he had no idea what might have come out, when he saw Forbes and, yes, Stan wending their way over to his chair. Shutting his eyes to avoid any tell-tale flashes of recognition, and in the vague hope that with his new face they might not recognise him, he hurriedly told Antonella that the nurse had just arrived with the injections – he would see her for Ecclesiastes towards seven – for the moment, *coraggio*.

Just as he switched the line off, a gratingly loud voice announced: 'Man, has some poor bastard been in the wars! Oh boy!'

Morris had never liked Stan. But it was one of those perversities of life that, however rarely they met, however curious the circumstances, Stan appeared to like Morris. Genuinely. The stupid American was all grins and solicitude. God damn, how had it happened? When, where? Jees, what incredibly bad luck! But not to worry, remember what bad shape he'd been in himself that time they ran into each other in Rome, or 'hobbled' might be a better word as far as he was concerned, yeah, half his goddam body in plaster after the car accident on the station . . .

Addressing himself to Forbes, Morris said extremely coldly: 'I didn't know you two knew each other.' At the same time he was thinking what a perfect fool Stan was: as if a disfigured face could ever heal the way a broken leg would. You could be dying of cancer and Stan would cheerfully remind you of some toothache he'd had.

'I've been interviewing people for positions at the college,' Forbes said, though why this should explain their walking across the square together wasn't clear.

There was a moment of mildly embarrassed silence. From dusty eyelids, Forbes appeared to be watching Morris rather more sharply than of yore, unless it was merely his unwillingness to appear unwilling to look disfigurement in the face. Disconcerting, Morris thought, how all his calculations *vis-à-vis* people's facial expressions would have to take another variable into account from now on. Except in cases, like Stan's, of total insensitivity.

'Pete is going to give me a post teaching A. H. in this school thing he's setting up.'

Morris had never heard Forbes referred to as Pete before. Nor was he sure, off the cuff, what A. H. might be. Arse-holery, quite probably.

'Stan has a degree in art history,' Forbes explained, a little apologetically. Certainly there was an awkwardness in the air, which presumably had to do with Morris's face. But maybe not.

'I thought,' Forbes went on unnecessarily, 'it would be

good to get an American voice in the school to give it variety. It doesn't do to be too exclusively English these days.'

At this point, Stan actually looped an arm round Forbes's tweed jacket and gave the older man an affectionate squeeze, reminding Morris of an appalling discussion some years ago, in the days when loneliness had humbled him into frequenting the feckless expat community, on the supposed virtues of bisexuality. What impressed him most of all, however, was how the gentlemanly Forbes managed to disguise the distaste he no doubt felt at such mateyness. Clearly Stan was not worthy of the man's friendship. When he got half a chance Morris would explain to the older man that there was no need to stoop to local third-rate teachers just to save money, since Morris would be quite willing to finance the salaries of a decent staff, at least for the first year or two.

He stood up. 'I have to be getting back to the hospital. They only let me out for an hour or two to clear up a couple of things with the' – he almost said the police – 'to do with the old Signora's will.'

Both Stan and Forbes promised they would come and visit. Tomorrow perhaps. Assuaging their guilt complexes at still being whole and healthy no doubt. Just as he was about to turn away, Morris said: 'By the way, when it happened, you know, with the dog, you don't remember who took my coat off, do you?'

Not so much as a speck of dust stirred in Forbes's deep wrinkles.

'Your coat?'

'My wallet was in the pocket,' Morris explained.

Entirely inappropriately, knowing nothing about the affair, Stan said: 'Yeah.'

Could he be on drugs?

Forbes shook his head. 'I remember Kwame and one

of the carabinieri bending over you, after they shot the dog. Maybe they pulled your coat off. But afterwards . . .' He pouted what were surprisingly damp lips in the papery old face. '*Nec scire fas est omnia.*'

Stan burst out laughing. 'Oh boy, isn't he just a darling with his Latin?' Again the American gave the older man a squeeze. Morris hurried off, more thoroughly disconcerted than he could have explained.

CHAPTER THIRTY

IT WAS TWELVE O'CLOCK. Walking across the splendid square, the porphyry fans spreading before his feet, the well-dressed children pedalling their tricycles among tourists bewildered to find themselves in a place so beautiful, it occurred to Morris that really the best thing would be to go to Fendtsteig and confess it all. For now that he had become so ugly, within and without, what could freedom possibly mean? It was freedom only to be spurned and condescended to. For of course that was the only conceivable reason why Forbes was replacing his friendship with Stan's? Wasn't it, Mimi? Wasn't it? Should he confess?

His guardian angel was silent. No point even in pulling his phone out. Morris stopped by the statue of Vittorio Emanuele. How volatile his moods were becoming! On impulse he hailed a taxi. Before confessing, before deciding whether to confess, he would go home and have it out with Paola. He would demand to know why she was pretending she wasn't pregnant. He would demand to know how much she knew. Perhaps he would even tell her what she didn't know. Most of all, he would demand to know himself whether she planned to abandon him, what future lay before him should he escape their clutches. Perhaps, he thought, at the root of his depression lay the fact that his marriage was a burden to him. Hospital, and even prison, without her, had proved such a wonderful release.

But he could hardly confess to Paola, then ask for a divorce so that he could marry Antonella.

The taxi snaked up to Quinzano, took the first hairpin after the village, stopped at the iron gate. Utterly confused, dangerously excited, poised more delicately than ever between sanity and madness, ruin and triumph, Morris went in to clear things up with Paola once and for all, perhaps to tell her he was about to give himself up, perhaps to enlist her help on his behalf. He really didn't know.

'Paola!' He stood in the hallway and called her, but got no answer. He went into the sitting-room, where the local paper was open on a solid oak table. At the headline: STILL MORE MYSTERIES IN POSENATO CASE. Morris didn't even bother to read it. The days of caring what the papers said were over. He was older and wiser now.

At a loss for a moment, looking around the room, he was struck by its polished peacefulness of chequered tiles and antique furniture, filtered sunlight on elegant surfaces, dark plants. It was exactly the kind of conservative place he would have chosen to live in, to be part of, to construct his identity around. If only he hadn't had to do everything he had done to get it.

Unthinking, he crossed the room and opened old Signora Trevisan's sewing basket, still rather picturesquely decorating the hearth. The patched underwear was still there, where he had returned it after twisting and torturing it in his pocket for days. Pulling it out again now, holding it up to the light, he tried, not for the first time, to imagine Mimi's adolescent body wriggling into it. How black her pubic hair had been! How glossily mussed and bushy!

Five minutes later, stretched on the old double bed where she had always slept, glazed eyes fixed on the *Madonna incoronata*, Morris was approaching orgasm, courtesy of Forbes's brush-work and the patched underwear, when the telephone rang in the hallway. Immediately his hand was stayed. For although there was no question of his answering the thing, it was clearly a message from Mimi that she didn't want him to do *that*. He had never done *that* before, thinking of her. He had never allowed himself. Closing his eyes Morris experienced a tortured voluptuousness in letting pleasure subside, a curious mastery in denial.

Then quite unexpectedly, a voice began to speak.

'*Ci dispiace, ma siamo momentaneamente fuori casa* . . . I'm sorry, but we're out at the moment . . .'

Morris was already on his feet, pulling up his pants and stuffing Massimina's into his pocket, when he recognised his wife's false tones made more brittle than ever through the cheap electronics of an answering machine. He stopped and breathed. That was a novelty, an answering machine. Why hadn't she told him about that? He stood still in the hallway listening. Came the beep, followed by a faint crackle. 'Paola?' There was a pause. 'You there, *signora bella*?' Another pause. 'Guess I'll hang on a bit longer, baby.' Then the machine was beeping and whirring again on its own.

Morris stared. He put a knuckle in his mouth and bit it. For heaven's sake! Then buckling up his belt, he simply flew downstairs and out of the front door. He fiddled with the key and lifted the huge door to the garage, where sure enough both the Mercedes and Paola's Lancia were missing. Leaving only Signora Trevisan's ancient Fiat Seicento. That bizarre snobbery of the genetically rich, driving the oldest possible pieces of junk. But at least the keys were in the ignition. '*Fiat lux,*' he muttered grimly, climbing in.

It wouldn't start. The battery was dead, if not exactly buried, like its owner. Morris had to push the old rust box across the white stones to the gate and then jump in to steer it round the hairpin and down the steep hill. It exploded into life, thank God, just before he had to brake for a tractor toiling with a trailer of dung. What a country! Morris revved the thing mercilessly, whether it meant being noticed or not, and found, as he crossed the city, that in traffic the combination of his reorganised face and the ancient car was most effective indeed.

Ten minutes later, he had just cleared the last lights the other side of town, when the phone in his jacket rang.

'*Pronto*, Morris?' Forbes's voice, so far as Morris could make out in the roar of the small saloon, was unusually tense. But he had no time for nuances now. He didn't even try to pretend he was back in hospital, just demanded point-blank what the matter was.

Before Forbes could continue, he added acid: 'Stan Albertini will not make a good teacher at your or any school. I'm amazed that you're wasting time with him. In fact, seeing that I have a considerable investment in the place, I'd be grateful if you consulted me before you made any firm appointments.'

Forbes said: 'Look, Morris, I've found the car. Just this minute.'

Attacking the bend at Ponte Florio, halfway there, Morris didn't understand. 'I've always said you needed a car,' he conceded. 'Though, if you've called to tell me I'm paying for it I think you should at least put it at the disposition of the boys when they want to go out for a night on the town.'

Forbes needed reminding who was boss.

'No, Morris, I've found *the* car.'

'What car?'

'Listen, I was showing Stan round the place, the school. Just now. And I opened, I don't know why, you know the old stable thing round the back of the house, with the derelict tractor.'

Morris could hardly be bothered to follow, so eager was he to get the confirmation of her Lancia parked outside number six.

'What I'm trying to tell you is that behind the tractor there was a car. And I think it must be Bobo's.'

'Bobo's!' Immediately Morris pulled the Seicento over to the side of the road, but remembered to keep his foot softly on the accelerator. The ancient bodywork rattled.

'What colour was it, what make?'

Forbes told him.

'Did you mention it to Stan?'

'No, it was just in there beside the tractor. He had no reason to comment on it.'

'But surely the police must have searched the place.'

'In the first few days,' Forbes said. 'But not afterwards. Somebody must have brought it here afterwards.'

Morris's mind was working so rapidly now, he barely knew what he was thinking.

Forbes said: 'I fear it means they did do it, Farouk and Azedine. They must have hidden the thing here when they came back, or they were in collusion with the others.'

His voice seemed to be both asking for and fearing confirmation. But it was curious then how Morris immediately saw and rejected this apparently convenient construction without needing to pass through any conscious lucubration whatsoever. Perhaps it was simply that anything offered by way of an obvious solution he had learnt to treat as a trap.

'On the contrary,' he said, 'it looks to me as if somebody is setting them up.'

There was a pause on the line, which, Morris was perfectly aware, might be bugged. Though the peculiar thing about the police, he had often thought, was how little, for all their vehemence when they questioned you, they really tried. Not checking that stable every now and then, for example. All he could assume was that, unlike the detectives in films and books, the poor fellows had other, easier cases to be getting on with, or were more interested in their sex lives and broken marriages than in Bobo Posenato's disappearance. Quite reasonably so, when one came to think of it.

'Who though?' Forbes asked in a whisper.

Morris said very pointedly: 'Are you sure you don't remember who took my coat that morning? Because it seems to me it must have been Kwame.' When Forbes appeared to be struggling to come out with the inevitable confession, he immediately went on: 'Anyhow, for the moment, don't say anything to anybody. OK? I'll come over myself as soon as I can.'

'*Splendide mendax,*' Forbes muttered.

'*Ciao,*' Morris said. He thought that, in the end, even if he had to spend the rest of his life saving souls behind bars, nobody could say he hadn't enjoyed himself, hadn't stayed in the saddle of one of the wildest horses for some considerable time.

CHAPTER THIRTY-ONE

THE CHERRY TREES WERE in bloom on the hills above Montorio. Their white blossoms gave a fluffiness to the landscape's dull continental greens. As Morris quietly closed the car door some fifty metres from the house, the only sounds were the thick buzzing of bees and sharp croaks of the frogs descending the slopes to the valley's ditches.

Another beautiful place, Morris thought, appreciating his ability to appreciate things at such a harrowing moment. For, yes, her Lancia *was* there. It was true. All true.

Suddenly the rural peace was shattered by some piece of equipment starting up. Building work was proceeding behind the house. Morris's entry would not be heard.

Arriving at the gate, he noticed that one of the line of six letter-boxes on the railings was no longer brushed stainless steel but charred black. Yet a fresh piece of white paper had been stuck into it. Morris pulled the paper out and read. The recipient was accused of being as out of place in number six as was the one charred letter-box in the neat row of winking bright steel. The message finished with a vague but nonetheless unpleasant threat. Beautiful surroundings, evidently, did little to civilise, and replacing the paper in the box, Morris stored this information in his mind, as one puts to one side a jigsaw piece that as yet has no partner to make it part of the whole. 'Very soon,' he said out loud in a flash of intuition. 'Very soon, this will all be over,' and as his lips moved he had the impression that this was not his voice speaking, nor Mimi's either, but as it were something, somebody, they were both listening to.

Morris was close to a solution, a resolution.

The piece of machinery – it was an excavator – clattered just beyond the fence. Morris opened the gate quietly, walked up the path and gained the door. The supposedly marble stairs, he noted, were already chipping in several places. Nothing more than polished limestone. Key in hand, he listened, but the only sound was the throb of the building site. This was problematic, since the door opened directly into the front room. How could he know if they weren't right behind the door?

Still, it was *his* front room. Even if they were doing no more than exchanging useful information about company business, it was Morris's prerogative surely to enter at will, there where his legal and pregnant wife was talking to a man he had employed, clothed, fed and housed.

At the same time, Morris knew from the heat in his body, the sweat trickling between his buttocks, the trembling of his fingers as they slotted key into lock, that they would not just be chatting. Also, he sensed that Mimi was close beside him, and obscurely, once again, that the whole affair was almost over.

The door opened on perfect domesticity, furniture as neatly aligned as tombstones. The only alteration in the place since Morris had lived there was a small woodcarving of an African tribesman with spear in hand and a ludicrously large erect penis. On the floor by the sofa Morris noticed the chip in the tile caused by his dropping the brick sold to him by a man he had tried to help. This time, he thought, the damage had been much more severe. No wonder his marriage wasn't working.

Now his ears were accustomed, he caught the sound of music in the lulls of the excavator. From upstairs. He recognised the appalling Sade. Or 'come music' as his wife called it. The case was closed. Even the phone, under her Gustav Klimt poster, was off the hook. What more evidence could one need? Yet Morris's disgust and curiosity were so intense that he couldn't stop here, even though it was ludicrous, even though he was planless.

Softly, he climbed the spiral staircase. He hesitated, listening, treading softly on the step that creaked. Then as his head poked out above floor level between banister supports, the first thing he saw was his wife's brown eyes staring straight into his own.

In the centre of the room, under four skylights, and arranged so that it faced away from the stairs and toward the television, was a fashionable low red sofa. The black's naked shoulder-blades and woolly head rose massively, unshakeably, above the back. Bobbing fiercely beside that head, face toward Morris, features unpleasantly distorted as on her knees she rapidly approached the last station of the libido's *via crucis*, was Paola.

Immediately her eyes fastened on his, but with no indication of surprise, either at his presence or his redesigned face. Instead her greedy gaze seemed just to be begging him not to interrupt, at least until it was over. Morris stood transfixed, watching, together with Mimi he felt, this rape of his marriage. And while at one level he had never been more deeply shocked, at another and deeper level he felt profoundly satisfied, liberated. He need make the effort no more. The family was dead.

Sade crooned in that bitch-in-heat way she had. A bee buzzed about the open skylight. The riggish wench's face broke up in a howl of pleasure, as though torn from the very heart of life itself, followed by nothing more than a few bass grunts from the man.

Climbing to the top of the stairs, Morris said: 'I trust you both enjoyed that.'

Paola was panting hard.

Kwame turned his head, lifting the slight woman to one side. 'Boss,' he said. Then without lowering his head or in any way expressing shame, he explained: 'We thought you is still at the hospital, boss. God, your face is bad.'

There was a short silence, in which Sade moaned about Frankie's first affair, while the excavator could be heard attacking the hill again. Kwame had twisted round, but his nakedness was hidden behind the sofa. Only the powerful chest was evident, muscles glistening. Morris hesitated. Perhaps because there was clearly no way of killing two people at once, one of whom was infinitely stronger than himself, he found himself icily calm. Though his gelid outrage, he sensed, was Mimi's too, and thus pregnant with purpose. Pregnant . . .

He said: 'I wouldn't mind so much if she wasn't pregnant with my child.' My daughter, he should have said. Your reincarnation, Mimi!

Having got her breath back, Paola folded her arms on the back of the sofa, pert breasts peeping over slender forearms. She cocked her head to one side and her features settled in a sly smile. 'Your poor face,' she said. Then she said: 'Mo, instead of filling your head with these crazy ideas, why don't you just get your clothes off and join us?'

It was one-thirty. Back in the hospital, Dionisio would be collecting lunch trays, wondering where on earth his English patient had got to, where the next exchange of views on suburban London was coming from. And how could Morris ever know whether Fendtsteig or Marangoni would be able to demonstrate that he had left the hospital? And where he had gone. But clearly this was the end. Paola had touched bottom now.

'Come on,' she said.

He stared at her.

She laughed. 'Mo, I know it must seem bad, but in the end, why not? I've always wanted to suck and fuck at the same time. Come on, Mo, treat yourself. Enjoy it. Don't make life such a tragedy.'

Kwame said: 'Yeah.'

Morris was seeing red. But at the same time and at another level, he continued to experience an extraordinary lucidity and calm, as if another were thinking for him. For it wasn't like the old days, in the hotel in Rimini, the villa in Sardinia, when he had been so desperately alone. In his mind's eye he saw her round calm face, with the holy crown, *La Vergine incoronata*.

'After all, we know all about you, Mo.' Paola's voice was wheedling now. 'Kwame told me what happened. And we're not going to let you down. What more faithfulness could you ask for than that?'

Morris opened his mouth. But it was premature. Mimi still hadn't spoken.

Paola held out her arms. Kwame was smiling his healthy, strong-teethed smile. '*Coraggio*, Mo. Don't be shy now. Why should we limit ourselves to just one partner in the end? Otherwise life is just a bore! You know you've felt that yourself.'

'Yeah,' Kwame repeated. 'We not going to let you down, boss. We love you.' His black skin seemed perfectly appropriate on the red sofa. He appeared no more shocked or ill at ease than he had been when he found Morris battering Bobo to death on the office floor.

'So you're not pregnant,' Morris faltered.

'You poor sweet thing,' Paola said, arms still extended. 'Let me kiss your poor face.'

'She's lying,' Mimi said. Very loud and clear. 'She is pregnant.'

Hearing the voice, so ringingly hers, Morris experienced

a slight attack of vertigo. The room and his wife and the big black all slipped out of focus for a moment, blurred to grey light. (Was it Paola, already having the affair with Kwame, who had made the phone call? Was it?) By the time everything had recomposed itself he was suddenly decisive, and operating under orders now.

'I'll go down and fix a few drinks,' he said. 'Give you time to get your breath back and me to wind down. Then I'm going to make you pay for this,' he laughed unnaturally. 'In pleasure.'

Paola's eyes were half closed in cheerfully sultry lust. 'Anything, Mo,' she said. 'Just get your cock up here.'

Excited, horrified, determined, elated, Morris hurried downstairs. It seemed that other hands mixed the drinks for him. Two tall glasses full of ice, three inches of gin, three of tonic. Half a lemon in each. And where was the Lexotan? Was it still here? Her tranquilliser for when she felt under stress. She felt under stress! Because she was betraying him of course. Where? Got it. Behind the huge jar of KY she had brought back from England. Morris waited while thirty drops dripped painfully slowly from the nozzle.

'Are you coming, Mo? Don't change your mind now.'

'Couldn't find the lemons,' he shouted, and while one hand held the Lexotan over the second glass, he filled a third with nothing but cool tonic water. Then he wiped the tonic bottles and threw them away, wiped the handle of the fridge, the handle of the knife he'd used, and the glasses after he had set them on a tray.

Sade was serving up 'Cherry Pie', voice oozing with moneyed lust, the saxophones sophisticatedly sleazy, those elements of black culture Europeans have distilled into aphrodisiac. Listening, Morris hesitated a moment on the stairs and closed his eyes. 'Mimi,' he prayed, 'give me the strength to go through with this filth.' And he added: 'It will be for everybody's benefit in the end.' For quite suddenly, despite his nervousness, she had allowed him to see the sense of this, its necessity almost, and a clear path right through to the happy ending.

'Mo, *che dolce!* You darling.' Paola was cross-legged on the carpet. Smoking. Her hair bubbled on thin shoulders. Her little stomach was flat and tight. From amidst the tawny fuzz so frankly displayed between gently rocking thighs, peeped a gash of blood pink. How could Morris have married such a whore? And how could he ever bring himself to turn his head and look at the nakedness of the street Negro who had just penetrated her, poured his filth and diseases into the womb where his baby daughter was growing.

Morris bent down, put the tray on the floor, picked up his drink and sat back on the sofa. Paola took hers, and to Morris's right Kwame reached down so that his long ebony arm came into vision, closing a huge hand round the glass. At which point Morris finally turned to look. And what he saw, to his surprise, was almost a vision: the huge torso tight with muscle under satin-dark skin, the lean waist, and between the powerful thighs, thick but slack, and tipped with red, his black man's long dark sex. Drinking, Kwame began to laugh. 'This is more fun than working, boss. We let the others work.'

Almost in a trance, Morris was reminded, as if seeing everything in negative, of that marble-white Apollo he had viewed and touched, caressed, with Forbes in the Uffizi. 'The only way to learn the *gratia placendi*,' the old man had said. And here there were no guardians to stop them. Only Mimi as a witness.

For Mimi's ghost had appeared now. She was standing behind Kwame in a shaft of sunlight boiling from the skylight above. Her long hair was loose and the gauze gown she wore transparent over high breasts, so much bigger and rounder than Paola's, with a golden crucifix hung between. Likewise a light chain was draped around her hips, gently sagging under the weight of another holy image that winked and shone over the wiry darkness beneath her belly.

. . . *Like a heap of wheat,* Morris remembered, *set about with lilies.*

He wanted to leap from the sofa and rush over to her. But the apparition had raised one finger to softly frowning lips. Then over the music and the drone of the excavator, he distinctly heard her whisper: 'Enjoy, Morrees. Enjoy! But keep your heart and mind on me throughout, and you will stay pure.'

Then came the shock of an ice-cold hand cupped and pressing on his crotch. He looked down to find Paola laughing. 'Isn't he beautiful? Our Negro!' Kwame joined in the laughter. 'But remember you promised you would punish us,' Paola said. She was unbuckling his belt now.

'I do anything you tell me, boss,' Kwame said. 'Anything.'

Looking at his watch as it was taken off, Morris saw it was only five past two, and his rapidly calculating mind reassured him that the schedule wasn't even tight. As his wife's gin-cold lips came down on his underwear, Morris averted his gaze across Kwame's splendid stirring to where, standing immediately behind, Mimi's eyes were half closed now, staring boldly, intently, with complicity, one hand lightly caressing a breast. Her lips pouted in a kiss. With a sense of supreme sacrifice Morris reached across and grabbed the black man's sex.

Some fifty minutes later he was free. They were both asleep on the big bed in the guest-room, drugged, sated, exhausted. Mimi too had gone now, though her orders were very much on his mind as he moved quickly about the house, shirt in one hand to polish away fingerprints, matchbox in the other for the items he must collect (he had emptied the matches in his pocket): pubic hairs from sofa and bed; head hairs from the pillow; one nail-paring from the bin in the bathroom; one used condom, most carefully wrapped in toilet paper, and then so arranged in the matchbox as not to lose its precious burden. What about an earring? He went back into the bedroom where they lay together, she curled on one side and he curled about her, quite romantically, protectively, his dark skin against her soapy white, his thick lips in her hair. Morris lifted her curls to discover an earring, tiny diamond in the lobe. But she twitched when he touched it, suddenly and quite strongly. Kwame breathed more deeply. Morris backed off. With any luck he would find one in her handbag. Yes. On the floor. The big gold hoops. Just one. And a used tissue. And perhaps a couple of cigarette stubs too, now he came to think of it, from the ashtray, with her sex-red lipstick on the tips.

Then it occurred to him that before doing any more of this he should already have closed the windows and turned on the gas. God only knew how long it took to fill a house with gas. God only knew how long they would sleep. He found the pole for the skylights, banged them shut, then hurried downstairs, turned on all the rings, opened the oven door and turned that on too. Another five minutes, washing the three glasses, then rinsing two with a bit of gin and tonic while putting the third back in the cupboard. Good. Now the last fingerprints: as soon as he'd wiped those off he could get his shirt back on and fill his pockets with one or two last items of detritus: a piece of dead skin spotted on the bathroom floor, a damp pantie-liner. Until at last he was – was he? – yes, ready to leave, yes. Morris had just put his eye to the Judas hole these suspicious Italians could never live without, when the buzzer went.

Somebody was at the front gate, buzzing their buzzer. The sound was so brutally loud in the relative silence of the big flat that Morris felt he must be close to a heart attack. Not to mention the possibility it would wake the sleepers. And he'd been *so sure* Mimi had got this sorted out for him. So sure. How could she have let someone come to the door? He held his breath. In the space of thirty seconds he was absolutely sodden with cold sweat.

Morris waited, his mind shuffling through the possible visitors. A *marocchino*? A Jehovah's Witness? It was too late for the postman. But perhaps the local *vigile* had come to warn him he hadn't paid some council tax or other? The ridiculous business about right of way from garage to street. Had he paid it? Had he paid the TV licence? He thought not. But the smell of the gas was overpowering now. If they got inside the palazzo and came to the front door, they couldn't help but notice.

There it went again. *Buzz!* Incredibly loud. He'd never realised. Surely buzzers didn't need to be this loud. And it couldn't be a *marocchino* or Jehovah's Witness, otherwise he would have heard the muffled buzz of the doorbells in the other flats. Because people like that tried everybody. If only the buzzer could be taken off the hook, like the phone. But then there was the further problem that he would have to get out of the palazzo past whoever it was down at the gate. The gas was beginning to make him feel sick now. Of course if he'd simply been living there he could have gone out on the balcony and looked, something one could usually do without being seen. But not always. Not always.

Or could it be the police? Or the carabinieri? Forbes perhaps, knowing what Morris, if only by elimination, now knew he knew – for it had been he who had taken the letters of course – had phoned the police. They had come immediately.

Again the buzzer sounded. Morris was frantic. His head was splitting. He might vomit at any moment. It even occurred to him he might just lie down with them both on the bed and die, after all the humiliation he had been through. There it came again, for God's sake! Except this time the noise was followed by a distant voice screaming: '*Sporco negro*, we know you're in there. Come out and look what's happened to your fancy car.'

Morris breathed, if the word can be used of someone in a gas-filled room. Of course! It was just Mimi's way of reminding him! Running back into the kitchen, arm over his mouth, he grabbed a felt-tip, came back to the sitting-room and began to write in crazy block caps on the whitewashed walls: DEATH TO THE DIRTY NEGROES. *VIVA* the northern league. *VENETO PER I VENETI*.

No more than a minute later he was stumbling down the stairs, gasping for clean air. At the main door to the palazzo he stopped and listened. Sure enough there was the sound of some motor bike or other accelerating away into the distance. Presumably they had knifed the tyres of the Mercedes, or tossed brake fluid over the bonnet, which, though annoying in one sense, could hardly be more convenient in another. In any event, he wouldn't be stopping to look.

Morris had already stepped out onto the front path when he remembered the keys. Oh, but this was so amateur! So hopelessly careless! Did he still have his own? Yes. He rushed back up the stairs, hearing the sudden explosion of a vacuum cleaner behind a door on the first floor. Certainly the builder had cheated shamelessly on the insulation. He deserved a scandal like this to lower his prices. Before inserting his key, without quite knowing why, he untucked his shirt and stuffed it in his mouth.

Inside the air was sickly now. Where would her keys

be? There must be some explanation for that writing on the walls, for how the murderous racists had got in, how they had opened the gas jets. And if he smashed a window the precious poison would escape. No, it must seem as if she had left her keys in the door, a carelessness not beyond her.

In her handbag? He couldn't remember feeling them there.

And how long was he going to last in here without throwing up? Morris dashed up the spiral staircase and straight through to the bathroom, where he pulled the shirt from his mouth, opened the window a moment and breathed deeply. Only to find, directly opposite him on scaffolding that had risen with obscene rapidity, a worker sitting on a plank, drinking from a wine bottle and presumably looking straight at him. This was simply unfair. He got the window closed, went back into the main room and began to root through her clothes in a heap in the corner. Suspender belts, no less. Obviously she'd brought all the gear. Wet with drool too. But there was no time for this indulgence. Her jacket, they must be in her jacket.

Still holding his breath he found the thing over the back of a chair and pulled out the keys. Good. But, as so often, curiosity got the better of him. Instead of rushing back downstairs he returned to the bedroom and the two naked bodies on the big modern bed with the Armani-upholstered oval backboard she had paid so much for. Even now, he thought, even now he could turn back. They weren't dead yet, were they? He bent down and kissed his wife's pale cheek just beside the ear, then crouched and kissed a rubbery nipple, so shy and vulnerable in sleep. The paps that would never suckle Morris's child.

No more than a minute later, mustering all his sang-froid and city man's invisibility, Morris left the palazzina.

Looking neither to right nor left, he walked to the tiny Seicento, and climbed in. Thanks be to God and His guiding and guarding hand, the ancient piece of junk started first time. Morris smiled. *Fiat justitia,* as Forbes would say.

CHAPTER THIRTY-TWO

'OH, ECCO, 'ERE YOU are, Mr Morrees!' Dionisio pushed the drug trolley into the ward. It was almost five o'clock. Morris had not gone to seek him out. That would be too obvious. Anyway, there had been Forbes to attend to first. A confession to wring from him. Strict orders to give, backed up by threats. And promises. The matchbox and assorted detritus were in his jacket pocket in his locker. Nothing ventured, nothing gained, was the motto there.

'It is some hours I am looking for you.'

'I thought your shift was over,' Morris said politely, raising his eyes from his Bible. He had been marvelling at the work that must have gone into cross-referencing his Authorised Version, a labour that had so far allowed him to track down thirteen uses of the word 'vengeance', and notably: 'For he put on righteousness as a breastplate, and an helmet of salvation upon his head, and he put on the garments of vengeance for clothing, and was clad with zeal as a cloke.'

Morris particularly liked 'an helmet' and the spelling of 'cloke', though he feared there would be vivid dreams to come. Beneath an enforced calm and interest in curious detail, his mind was still reeling from the degradations he had been forced to submit to. One clung on to Mimi, to one's religion, one's God, as to identity itself.

'You are not 'ere for lunch.'

He had gone down into the garden, Morris said, and fallen asleep on a bench. He thought it must be the relief of finally having the dressings off and his face fixed (here he smiled falsely). He was feeling good. 'I'll be able to leave the day after tomorrow, won't I?'

'If the doctor is agreed there is no infection,' Dionisio said.

The ward was quite busy at this hour, with worried relatives coming to inspect the kind of monstrosities they would have to learn to put up with over the years to come, and pretend were nothing. The nurse was about to move on with his bountiful selection of tranquillisers. But Morris asked: 'Are you a Christian, Dionisio?'

'A *cattolico*,' the nurse said, showing no surprise.

'I was just reading this passage, and I was wondering,' Morris asked, 'do you think that the Lord wreaks vengeance on those who do evil? I mean it's an old-fashioned concept. But the Bible does say it.'

'"Wreaks"?' Dionisio was puzzled. 'I thought this means the bad smells.'

'No, takes vengeance,' Morris said patiently. 'Vengeance, vendetta. Do you think God would do that kind of thing?'

The nurse's gnomish southern features were endearingly concentrated. At least Morris had got him off the subject of his five-hour absence. Quite probably one thing simply superimposed itself over another in that tiny brain. 'When I first arrive at Earrrls Court,' Dionisio said at last, 'we 'ave the landlord that asks too much, but too much money and 'e never mends the toilet flush and never the heating works properly. Then 'e say he will throw us away because we are too many in the flat.'

'No sense of charity,' Morris agreed, thinking how many feckless foreigners he had given a roof to in Villa Caritas.

Dionisio was stumbling on with his story. 'One of the boys with us 'e is very religious and 'e pray that something will make that the landlord change 'is idea.'

321

Morris waited, mildly bored.

'Well' – Dionisio paused for effect – 'the same day after 'e say we 'ave to go 'e is knocked by the bus.'

'Really?' The coincidence was so interesting it actually took Morris's mind off things for a moment. 'And died?' he asked eagerly.

'No,' Dionisio said. 'But he can't walk. For a long time.'

'Ah, so you mean he relented and let you stay in the flat?'

'No,' Dionisio shook his head very seriously. 'No, 'e threw us away anyway. What you want? In England there is not enough protection for the foreigner in these situations. But we find a place in 'Ammersmith that is nicer.'

'Oh, yes, that was lucky.' It did seem to Morris that there was a lack of biblical clarity in this story. He much preferred Sodom and Gomorrah. But he let it pass. 'By the way, I really want to leave tomorrow morning,' he announced. 'Is there any way . . . I feel I should get out and face the world.'

'The *primario* visits at nine o'clock,' Dionisio said. 'And he will say if the skeen is ready.'

A couple of hours later, Antonella was sitting on the side of Morris's bed, sobbing. She had been trying to talk to Paola all day and hadn't been able to find her. She'd gone to the company, but there was nobody in the office. Anyway the moment she'd walked in she'd had to walk out again, thinking what Bobo had quite probably done there. It was awful, with the police looking at the letters and asking her all kinds of personal details, and with a list of phone numbers called from the house and whose they were and why and who could this woman be. She felt so upset and she just wanted all this to be over. Over. She didn't even care how it finished now, well or badly. The day the trial of these immigrants was over and they had caught this horrible person trying to extort a ransom, she would just get on a plane and fly away, she didn't care where. Or she would go to a convent or something. She'd always wanted to go to a convent when she was a girl. She wished she had done now. But then she had wanted a baby so much and she had loved Bobo so much. Only now she would never, never have a baby, and never love anybody ever again because of the way Bobo had treated her, the horrible things that had happened. She was living in hell.

Propped up on his pillows, Morris thought what a precious and beautiful woman she was, so rich in sincere emotion. Paola could never have cried like this. It wouldn't even have bothered Paola if he had been having an affair with somebody. Probably she would have been quite pleased. Without thinking he reached out across the bed and caressed her hair.

'Don't say never,' Morris said softly. 'Never is a long time. You're such a lovely woman, Tonia.'

His sister-in-law rubbed her knuckles all the more fiercely into her eyes. Her whole body trembled.

'And don't go away,' Morris whispered. 'Because I need you. Who's going to help me run things if you go away? Paola never helps. I've been trying to phone her all day, but she's never there. And I have all kinds of projects you could join in with, giving a hand to these poor *extra-comunitari*. I'd like to open a proper centre for them, you know. Not just make them slaves.'

His fingers were stroking her hair very lightly. Then, as she still hid her face in her hands, though her body had stopped trembling now, he rather injudiciously said: 'I think I'm in love with you, Tonia. I've been in love with you a long time. You remind me so much of Massimina.'

She turned and looked sharply at him, her red eyes straining to focus. 'Morrees.' She shook her head, features brimming with confusion. '*Morrees, sei così strano,*' she whispered. 'So very strange sometimes.'

So that made her the third of three sisters to have said those exact same words. Morris nearly passed out. 'Let's read the Scriptures together,' he muttered.

He had already woken towards three and was vomiting copiously when the police arrived. In his dream they had been filling his mouth with filth and dead flesh: Paola, Kwame, Bobo, Forbes. He had been struggling, fighting, calling for Mimi, calling on God. Then suddenly he sat up sharply and ejected it all in a stream of vomit: the worms and wormwood, gall and dung, even bones. He was screaming for a priest. Then the ward was flooded with a light so brilliant that he imagined a vision, a splendid apparition of Mimi, or of Christ. His mind reeled after sight and focus, his stomach still retching, his skin shivering with cold and sweat. And as he raised his eyes it was to find, more nightmarish than his nightmare, the angular Fendtsteig approaching across the room, a nurse on one side, a carabiniere on the other. They had got him at last.

The nurse broke into a run, found cloths and cleaning equipment. Morris continued to retch and was helped from his bed. 'I had a dream,' he gasped between convulsions. 'My face. They were carving up my face.' A junior doctor had arrived and was kindly explaining that this could well be a delayed reaction to the prolonged anaesthesia of the operation. Morris was helped into a dressing-gown and led off to a consulting room. Fendtsteig came with them, waiting, watching, though actually it was taking Morris some considerable effort to keep retching now. Finally, when he had calmed down and sipped a little water, he turned to the carabiniere with a wan smile. 'Can I help?'

Fendtsteig leaned over to the doctor and there was a muttered exchange. The doctor shrugged his shoulders. 'How do you feel?' he asked.

'A bit weak,' Morris admitted. 'But if the colonnello has some questions, I suppose . . .'

Then they sat him on the examining bed and broke the news. Quite brutally, Morris thought. Not the way he would have done it at all. Just told him straight. Wife dead. In arms of black lover. Gas. Racism. Not a scrap of sensibility. Allowing Morris to respond with the appropriate incredulity, head shaking, staring eyes. Then a barrage of questions, of disbelieving questions – when, where, why, who, how had they got in? – until suddenly he buried his ruined face in his hands, swaying gently from side to side. He waited perhaps a minute. Finally in a low voice he said: 'I'm exhausted, it's too much. It's too much. Why does everything have to happen to me? Why do people die all around me?' He shook his head. No, he couldn't identify the body now. He just couldn't. He wouldn't. He refused! And he begged for tranquillisers and to be allowed to go to sleep. He stood up to go, stumbled, but at the same time saw in the mirror above the washbasin that Fendtsteig's eyes following him to the door were cold and curious. The man was inhuman!

Turning abruptly, Morris screamed: 'Now that you've seen what kind of woman my wife was, maybe you'll understand why I was spending my evenings moping over my dead girlfriend's grave! But your sort never believe people until the truth is rammed in your face. The next thing you know I'll have to hear that I killed my own wife. And mother and first love and colleagues and everybody who's ever died in the vicinity.'

A flicker of guilty uncertainty crossed the carabiniere's face. But stumbling back down the corridor, Morris suddenly wondered whether he had remembered to put away the bottle of Lexotan. Oh, for God's sake! Had he? Or was it still sitting there tell-tale in its little brown bottle on the draining board? No. No, please, Mimi! And at the same time as he found this new source of worry, he was immediately worried about worrying about it, about losing his nerve. For he was vulnerable on so many sides. If they were to search his locker during the night, for example, find the nail-parings, dry skin, pubic hairs. Or to ask people in the hospital where he had been yesterday when absent from the ward for upwards of five hours. Or to grill Forbes, who would doubtless break down, as he had broken down at the merest phone call from Morris. For how long was he going to have to rely on their total lack of imagination, on his being the artist, the conjurer and them almost willingly, yes, willingly, deceived? Hadn't that American in Milwaukee gone and killed twenty and more people because the police just refused to put two and two together and arrest him, even after seeing the murdered flesh in his fridge? It was appalling! May they rot at the very bottom of the bottom of hell. When the night nurse brought out the Diazepam, Morris begged for the maximum dose possible, begged for it and got it and so slept the sleep of the just.

CHAPTER THIRTY-THREE

AZEDINE AND FAROUK LOOKED miserably abject as they were led into the Palazzo di Giustizia. The older man seemed at once hardened and resigned in the way the oppressed classes so often are. He wore jeans and a black smock. In a white shirt, the handsome young Farouk had an elegiac Pre-Raphaelite despondency about him, his hair long, his face olive thin. Passing them in the corridor, Morris wanted to catch them by the arm, tell them all was well. It was merely a question of time. God had sorted everything out, he would say. Allah, if they liked. Morris's religion was in no way sectarian. They need have no fear. The guilty would be punished, had been punished already, the just would be freed. 'Evil pursueth sinners: but to the just good shall be repaid.' Antonella had read that to him only yesterday, shortly after the funeral. Her determination to comfort him for his loss, almost forgetting her own, seemed itself a confirmation of the sacred text. 'Azedine!' he called. '*Coraggio!*' But they were already disappearing into the courtroom, while Morris himself was ushered off to the room where the witnesses must wait to be called. Never mind, he reflected, a bit of tension wouldn't do the two queers any harm, was chastening rather. God knows he had been chastened enough himself.

Chastened was a nice word, he thought, allowing

himself to be led through bustling corridors where journalists tried to catch his arm or stick a microphone in front of him. Its implications of a recovered virginity were refreshing. And such ideas seemed far more feasible now that Paola was gone. In fact one way you could see it all was that he had only undergone the awful degradation of that afternoon in order to be freed from such filth for ever, to be chastened. Certainly for a week now he had been chaste as white snow. And felt the better for it.

Outside the witnesses' room, somebody from some scandal mag was lying in wait with a tape-recorder and huge camera. They were after dirt on Paola and the Negro of course. The press had loved that. Morris made it abundantly clear he would neither talk nor pose for absolutely anyone. He would answer the questions he was asked in court and that was that. Covering his scarred face with both hands, he plunged into the guarded room.

Forbes was already there, looking distinctly more nervous than he need be, Morris noticed, while three or four of the other immigrants were confabulating together on a low bench. Then there were the shop-floor foreman and two of the daytime bottling workers. With the press off his back and the door closed behind, Morris saluted them all affably. Out loud, to no one in particular, he mentioned that he was planning to expand the bottling hall to meet the new orders the company was getting, mainly from England. He tried to draw them in, black and white alike, to give them a feeling they were being consulted, they were part of a large family and he had their future at heart, but both immigrants and natives hung back, awkward and hostile, clustered in their little groups. Perhaps because of the armed policeman standing at the door, Morris thought. In any event he felt no qualms about despising them, their cautiousness and perverse lack of spirit. Even Forbes could manage nothing more than monosyllables when asked how the restoration work at Villa Catullus was getting on. 'Or perhaps we should just call it Il Collegio, what do you think?'

Smiling his brightest smile, Morris sensed how his eyes must now shine all the more blue and bright in the sad field-hospital his face had become (perhaps it was his face that made the bottling staff so uneasy – he kept forgetting). Forbes's own dull orbs fluttered uncertainly under the dusty pelmets of his eyelids. Morris winked at him and grinned, though frankly this flowery tie business was beginning to seem awfully mannered.

The witnesses sat quietly in the waiting-room as Azedine and Farouk were tried for murder. The bottle-plant foreman was smoking, but Morris decided not to object. One by one the immigrants were called to testify. Then the factory workers. No more than ten minutes each. Forbes came over to complain that it was going so much more quickly than he had expected, that Azedine and Farouk would be condemned and sentenced in no time at all. Perhaps even today. Morris told him in no uncertain undertone to keep calm. Even if sentenced they would be let off later, when the truth came out. There would be an *amnistia*. That was what Italy was like. Nothing was *definitivo*. It was merely a question of putting up with a few months of prison while the bureaucracy ground to its inevitable conclusion. Nor could he and Forbes blame themselves if the police were so damn slow at finding the kind of evidence any other police force would have turned up before you could say life sentence. They'd done everything they could to get the boys off. In fact Forbes had done rather too much, Morris said, had complicated the situation unnecessarily out of mere infatuation for a handsome Arab who had anyway betrayed him. *Rodolfo il rosso* indeed! He must have been mad. At which the old man began to moan that he should never have got into this mess. He put his face in his hands and rubbed his fingers into his eyes. Morris felt distinctly superior. It was he who would have to face the most savage cross-questioning in the end, he who the defence lawyers in collusion with the carabinieri had doubtless identified as an alternative scapegoat. Glancing up at the poliziotto at the door, he reminded Forbes quite sharply that, far from being a mess, what he had in fact got himself into was an excellent situation where he could have all the stupid little boys his heart lusted for under the same splendidly restored roof and then teach them the things he was such an expert on. Before he met Morris he had been more or less on the street, with no more than Her Majesty's state pension, *n'est-ce-pas*, and he better not forget it. The truth was that although Forbes could have destroyed him with the slightest disclosure, it somehow seemed to be Morris who had the knife by the handle. As soon as one knew the man was queer – and really Kwame and Paola had given him a fund of information before their decease – all feelings of respect or intimidation were quite lost. And what a hash he'd made of his letters!

'*Audentes fortuna juvat,*' Forbes muttered.

'That's better,' Morris said. Then he asked with a tone bound to remind the man of the relationship they had lost: 'What does it mean exactly?'

'That you're right,' Forbes said, and he got up and asked the guard if he could use *la toilette*.

After a break for lunch Antonella arrived. Morris hurried towards her with concern on his face and they embraced.

'*E allora?*' he asked. 'They came? The police got them?'

'Nobody came,' she explained. 'Obviously. I waited an hour and a half.'

'Perhaps they realised the police were coming.'

'I can't imagine how,' Antonella said. 'I mean, I was really the only person to know about the plan.'

Forbes, on a bench at the other end of the room, had his face in his hands again. He hadn't even had the decency to greet the woman.

'The way I see it,' Morris said, 'it was never anything but a hoax to try to switch attention away from these immigrants. They never had Bobo at all or they would have given some proof.'

Rather encouragingly, if somewhat less sensitively than Morris had expected of her, Antonella said: 'Frankly, with everything that's come out about Bobo, I'm not unhappy about that.' There was something desperately bitter in the way she spoke, something that was going to require a lot of kindness and proven goodwill to heal.

Then the poliziotto called the name Morrees Duckworrth.

Morris got up from the bench and was led through stone-paved corridors into a large bare room with high-vaulted ceiling where memories of a fresco survived in scattered fragments, faces and feathers in the grainy stucco, bellies and buttocks looming at random like some wittily appropriate testimony to the difficulty of reconstructing any comprehensive vision of things. Squalid plastic chairs scraped on a marble floor and there was the clack of a keyboard from a desk in the corner. Modern culture had apparently taken up residence in here like a miserable little hermit crab in some noble old shell. Three judges – an elderly man presiding and two disturbingly young women accompanying – sat in their robes behind the dais, while, on the wall above their heads, beside a broken light fitting and plastic crucifix, the words LA LEGGE È UGUALE PER TUTTI were in need of a touch-up.

Morris was ushered to what might have been a mere kitchen chair with microphone stand beside. But he made up for this mortifying lack of ceremony by announcing 'I swear' with great sonority and solemnity when the judge proposed the oath. As soon as he had sat down he directed his eyes to all the various protagonists one by one, and found no difficulty in conveying both confidence and comprehension: he had nothing to fear, and nothing against these two poor boys who sat paper-white but for their dark faces behind a table, each with his defence lawyer beside him.

Yes, he admitted, he was Morris Albert Duckworth, born in Acton, London, Regno Unito, 19/12/60. Yes, he was resident at Are Zovo 10, Quinzano, Provincia di Verona. Yes, he did recognise the two accused though he only knew their first names. Farouk and Azedine. Both were casual workers in the factory of which he was presently the joint owner. Both had been resident in the hostel that he himself had set up as part of a charitable attempt to help the many *extra-comunitari* living on the streets with no hope of either work or shelter. As an immigrant himself in a way, he had always felt close to those trying to make a new life in an alien community.

This was true. There was a murmur of hypocritical approval in the typically Catholic audience, none of whom, doubtless, had ever done anything to help a miserable immigrant.

So much for the preamble. Now the *pubblico ministero*, the prosecution, began to ask about the morning of the crime, the supposed crime. What time had Morris gone to the office, what had he found, how much money had been missing from the safe? Morris replied efficiently and factually. He reconstructed the scene in the office exactly as it had been: the upturned chairs, the scraping of skin and blood on the floor, the broken telephone. He told of Forbes's phone call earlier that morning explaining that the immigrants had been sacked. He admitted that he had only connected the two facts sometime later, he was so bewildered by the situation, especially coming as it had so soon after his mother-in-law's death. His mind had been in a daze.

Not a word of this in any way broke his oath. Except perhaps his mention now of the strong smell of cheroots.

Had there been, the lawyer asked, any previous conflict between Roberto Posenato and the immigrants in question? Anything that might have created a feeling of resentment on the part of the immigrants. Morris hesitated, he bit his lip for a moment as someone obliged to say something damaging where loyalty would have been more congenial. He made sure that for the moment his eyes crossed no one's. Then he explained the business about the use of the lavatories, how they had been locked during the night shift. 'There was a certain amount of racism,' he said, 'amongst members of staff, and unfortunately Bobo, Roberto Posenato, did nothing to combat it. The night shift, all of whom were *extra-comunitari*, were only allowed to use the toilet facilities after my determined intervention. At the time, I must admit, I had no idea that any of the workers were engaged in homosexual practices, otherwise my own prejudices might have been awakened.'

'You are prejudiced against homosexuals?' the prosecution asked.

The witness appeared to think about this seriously. 'Put it like this,' he finally said, 'I can perfectly well understand Bobo deciding to fire two men found to be having anal sex in his office when they should have been working. On the other hand I can well imagine that they had developed the kind of victim mentality, due to their earlier treatment at the hands of whites in general, which might have led them to believe they were being unfairly treated.'

333

'You believe they reacted by killing him?'

'Not at all,' Morris said, determined to sail as close to the wind as logistics would allow. 'I think nothing at all. One just has to recognise that such things are possible. The two are fired, they go away and talk to the others, as they did. They pack their bags and say they are leaving the area immediately. Then maybe they decide they will have one last try to change Bobo's mind. They go back, an argument begins and . . .' Morris shrugged his shoulders, making it clear he found the whole thing most unpleasant. But feasible.

'That is all,' the *pubblico ministero* told the judges. 'I need nothing more from this witness.'

'*La difesa?*' the presiding judge asked. There was a shuffling of chairs as one man sat and another stood. Apparently one of the two defence lawyers was going to do the questioning for both. At the back, someone got up and slipped out. Inwardly bracing himself, Morris allowed his eye to stray over the forty or fifty people in court to see if there was anyone really dangerous there. Like Stan. No, thank God. Though Morris was surprised to see the ageing Don Carlo in his cassock and crucifix. He shot the man a quick smile of scars and sorrow and got something wearily understanding in exchange. Then he turned his attention to the new voice addressing him.

The defence lawyer was tall, young, rather handsome actually, in that Roman way of hooked nose, proud forehead and dark eyes. And this was annoying because Morris generally found it easier to feel on top and score points with the ugly and unfashionable – Bobo, Genital Giacomo back in Rimini, Marangoni. But never mind. Apparently the man was asking about Morris's arrival in Italy, his first contacts with the Trevisan family. Replying, Morris made sure to be at his most disarming, his voice charmingly smooth and as correctly Italian as he could make it. One of the young lady judges, he noticed, dyed blonde and with the features of a precocious child, was looking at him with some interest, despite his mauled face. Or perhaps because of it. When an usher drew the microphone close to him, he had the pleasing sensation of being at the centre of attention, even sympathy.

'*Naturalmente,*' the lawyer suddenly went on the attack, 'when you first went to see the Trevisan family you told them a whole pack of lies.'

Morris was silent, wondering if his stitched-up face was properly conveying the amiability and lack of concern he felt.

'*Allora?*' the lawyer insisted.

'I'm sorry, but you didn't actually ask me a question. I can't answer if you don't ask me a question.'

'Is it true that you told a pack of lies, about your job, your family, your financial situation, when you first went to visit the Trevisan family?'

'Yes,' Morris said, and added slyly: 'You can assume I would have objected, if it wasn't true.'

The more pertinent truth was that he was almost glad they hadn't found the car yet with its treasure trove of dead skin and used johnnies, courtesy of Paola and Kwame, since it gave him this opportunity to shine, though it might be unwise to let his enjoyment become too obvious.

'From which we might infer that you frequently tell lies.'

'You might, but you would be mistaken,' Morris said, but stopped there. He was in no hurry to justify himself. He would wait for the lawyer to insist on knowing why he had told those lies, and then very politely, sweetly, he would tell him. In fact he would turn to the prettier of the two young lady judges as he did so, his eyes shining.

Now.

'*Signori giudici*, I was at the time deeply in love with the youngest sister of the family, Massimina Trevisan. In my eagerness to please the mother so as to be allowed to keep seeing the girl, I rather foolishly told her the kind of thing I thought she wanted to hear. I was younger and rather naïve. She found out and I was, quite understandably, er, rejected.'

A ghost of a smile passed, against her will, over the pretty judge's face. Morris made no attempt to look at other people in the courtroom to see what effect this testimony was having on them. Rather irritatingly the prosecution stood up at this point and complained that he couldn't see the relevance of these questions. The defence should not stray from what was pertinent to the crime in question.

The other judge, presiding, overruled the objection. It was clear, he said, that the defence was calling into question the reliability of one of the key witnesses and initial suspects, the person who had come across the scene of the crime and informed the police. This was perfectly legitimate. Morris looked up at the ceiling and inadvertently caught a glimpse of painted buttocks as if seen by someone about to be sat on. It brought back a shiver of unpleasant memories. But on the far side, above the busy court typist, there was a bosom worthy of Mimi's (and Antonella's): nipples cream and chocolaty, emerging from a fleece of cloud, though cut off at the neck. Morris waited.

'And do you know how the family found out you were lying?'

'I presume they checked up on something I said.'

'To be exact, Roberto Posenato "checked up" and you have resented it ever since.'

'No,' Morris said, 'no, at this point, I'm afraid I must object. I have no idea who checked up. I didn't even think about it. Nor did or do I bear any grudges towards anyone.

After all, it was only a matter of weeks later that the family was to be shattered by the tragedy of Massimina's kidnap. It would have been churlish indeed to bear a grudge against the family after such a terrible thing had happened to them.'

His Italian, he thought, was remarkably eloquent today. He hadn't made a single mistake yet as far as he could see.

The defence lawyer said drily: 'Meester Duckworrth, it would seem that a remarkable number of "terrible things" have happened to the Trevisan family since they met you.'

Morris closed his eyes. He kept his face perfectly impassive, but at the same time managed to communicate all the self-control required to keep it like that, to accept this gibe without reacting. He felt a scar tingle and tremble above his eye. Eventually he said: 'Yes, Massimina, with whom I was very much in love, was kidnapped and killed. Her mother died almost two years later at an old age and of natural causes. Bobo Posenato, my brother-in-law, with whom I had a very successful working relationship, as the accounts of Trevisan Wines can plainly demonstrate, disappeared shortly after firing the two men now being tried. More recently my wife died of gas poisoning in unfortunate circumstances which the press don't seem to be able to get enough of, victim of a racist attack on her lover, one of the immigrants I had tried to help.' He paused. 'I must apologise to the court if I do not appear to be as moved by all this as they would imagine, if I am not expressing my grief openly, but the truth is that the whole series of events of the last months, including, I may say, my own arrest and then again the accident which led to my face being mauled, has left me in a state of total shock, completely drained. I simply do not know how to react any more. In fact I am only able to be here at all thanks to the help of considerable doses of tranquillisers.'

This was not actually true, but one had to be willing to lose a little pride if it served. Anyway, he could hardly imagine them giving him a blood test.

The defence lawyer said: 'As your catalogue suggests, there are still a great many mysteries to be resolved in the Trevisan family, Meester Duckworrth.'

Morris said sadly: 'I'm afraid I couldn't agree more.'

There was a brief pause in the fray. Morris smiled at his judge, waiting for the ball to be thrown back in.

'Signor Duckworth,' the Arabs' defence pressed on, 'both your wife, Paola, and your sister-in-law Antonella Trevisan made statements to the police to the effect that your relationship with Roberto Posenato was not of the easiest.'

Morris was unperturbed. 'We disagreed about certain aspects of the company's management.' He tried to explain: 'Of course, it's difficult in a company when it's not clear who is boss. Obviously there's a certain amount of jockeying for position. However, apart from this we got on famously. The *barista* at the *pasticceria* in Quinto will testify that we frequently went there for our cappuccino and chatted quite happily together.'

'Meester Duckworrth, on the morning of the crime, your mother-in-law died; you rushed to her house, where, as your sister-in-law has testified, she found you looking through various drawers. Perhaps you could tell us what you were looking for, Meester Duckworrth.'

Morris found that the repetition of his ugly name was beginning to grate. But he was determined to show no signs of irritation. He had often noticed that, not having the sociolinguistic context in which to put it, Italians had no sense of how ungracious a name it was. As to an Englishman a name like Chiavagatti would mean nothing at all. Perhaps in the end that was why he had decided to live abroad.

He sighed. 'To my shame,' he admitted, 'I was looking for Signora Trevisan's will. Immediately Antonella, my sister-in-law, came into the room, I appreciated how awfully insensitive of me this was.'

'Perhaps you could explain to the court why you were in such a hurry to find that will.'

'My wife had insisted I find it.'

'Ah, you were not looking for it for yourself.'

Morris hesitated. Then he said: 'One of my great mistakes in life was that I was always too concerned to please my wife.'

'Who, if I may remind the court, was the sister of the girl you were "in love with" only a year before you married her.'

Morris closed his eyes. There was a definite hush in the room. Quietly, blindly, between gritted teeth, he said: 'When I spoke about this to my psychoanalyst, he explained to me quite feasibly that my problem was that I was trying to make up to my wife for the fact that I had loved her sister more.' He paused. 'However, if this information is not entirely central to your line of questioning I would much rather it wasn't discussed in court.' Then his voice almost broke. 'I feel I have been humiliated and mutilated quite enough in these past weeks.'

Opening his eyes again he deliberately did not look at the young blonde judge, but up at the ample breasts on the vaulted ceiling. For a moment he managed to visualise a big crucifix dangling between them. Perhaps being mauled would turn to his advantage in the end.

'And why, Meester Duckworrth,' the defence asked, 'was your wife so eager to see that will?'

'She was afraid that Signora Trevisan might have left everything to her sister and her husband.' He added: 'My wife was not on good terms with her mother. They had argued about almost everything.'

'And so you too were concerned.'

'Quite concerned,' Morris agreed. 'As well I might be. But, to repeat, as soon as my poor sister-in-law came in crying, I realised what an insensitive fool I had been. I felt like a worm.'

'Quite,' the lawyer said with handsome condescension. Morris was perfectly aware that the man was playing on his superior physical beauty, though it was actually Morris who was getting the attention of the more attractive of the judges. Perhaps precisely because of this willingness to wear sackcloth and ashes, to admit mistakes.

'And did you find the will?'

'No.'

'Why not?'

'I admitted to Antonella that I had been looking for the will and she told me that Bobo had it.'

'You then immediately rushed off to argue with your brother-in-law.'

Morris drew a deep breath, again suggesting the quality of his self-control. 'Not exactly,' he said. 'On the contrary, first I stayed to comfort Antonella, who was most upset. Then I stopped in the bar in Quinzano, as I believe has now been established after some earlier misunderstanding. I wanted to think things over calmly. Then I went to Villa Caritas, the hostel where the immigrants were staying, this in order to find out what had happened about these sackings. I spoke to one of the immigrants, a boy called Kwame.'

'Later found dead in bed with your wife,' the lawyer interrupted. There was a considerable titter from somewhere at the back of the room.

Morris clenched his teeth. 'I see,' he said, turning to the judges, 'that as far as insensitivity is concerned, I come a very poor second to the *avvocato per la difesa*.'

The older man presiding remarked sympathetically that

a certain amount of insensitivity was unfortunately inevitable when trying to clear up such ugly matters. 'You must be patient, Signor Duckworth,' he concluded.

The defence lawyer began to speak, but Morris interrupted. 'If you would let me finish my account of that morning,' he said. 'As I was saying, I did a variety of things, and then, yes, I went to the office to talk to Bobo, both about the sackings and the will.'

'And found the office as you later described to the police?'

'And to this court, yes.'

The defence lawyer slapped down his papers in what was really a rather unimpressive attempt at drama. 'Meester Duckworrth, perhaps you would like to explain to the court why shortly after these events you were arrested and imprisoned for a number of weeks.'

Morris gave the impression of someone determinedly following the advice the judge had given him a moment before. He would be patient. He raised his eyes and let them linger on Mimi's ample breasts high up on the indifferently restored Renaissance ceiling. Since they were only fragments, it seemed absurd to have recoloured them so vividly. A buttock sailed out in total detachment, as if cut from the pages of the kind of magazine his father so enjoyed. Or Kwame for that matter. He looked down, half smiled and began to speak. Yes, well, there had been some rivalry, he said, or at least that had been his impression, between police and carabinieri, as to who would catch the culprit. With the result that when Morris had been unwilling to explain what he had been doing the evening of the day after the crime, Colonnello Fendtsteig had immediately had him arrested and, when he still wouldn't explain, protesting that it was a private matter, imprisoned. Fendtsteig believed that since he had been out until after two in the morning, he might have been disposing of, well, of Bobo's body. Eventually, however, after some weeks in prison, what he, Morris, really had been doing that evening had come out – and come out via the psychoanalyst, he might add, for he himself would never have told – after which Fendtsteig had let him go. 'Though,' Morris added, 'I will say, because I'm sure that if I don't you will, Avvocato, that Colonnello Fendtsteig continues to believe that I was responsible for Bobo's disappearance. He has told me that he is merely waiting to find the evidence which will demonstrate my guilt. This is the kind of atmosphere I have been living in these past few weeks and I can assure you it has been most trying.'

Sure enough this stole a little thunder. There were people in the court who must be admiring his frankness and courage. But the defence lawyer was canny. He said: 'So, Meester Duckworrth, perhaps you can now explain to the court what you *were* doing that evening after your brother-in-law disappeared.'

For the first time Morris allowed a little alarm to invade his scarred features. He turned abruptly to the judges. '*Signori giudici*, you have all read the police reports. You know what I said to my analyst. You know that I only said it after being advised to do so by a priest. Do I really need to repeat it in public? Don't I have a right to silence?'

The older man and the two lady judges put their heads together. A blonde curl fell over the childish cheek. Pushing it back an eye flickered up to glance at Morris.

'The right to silence,' the presiding judge eventually said, 'refers above all to information that might incriminate either yourself or a member of the immediate family, which is not the case here. To remain silent would thus be in contempt of court. Certainly the court would appreciate, if only to dispel all doubts in your regard, a statement as to your whereabouts on that evening, if not your exact activities.'

Immediately and very swiftly, as if to get the thing out and over with, Morris said: 'I was in the cemetery weeping over the coffin of my ex-girlfriend, the coffin having been brought out from the communal family grave to accommodate the burial of the mother the following day.'

Again there was a stir in the court. Morris looked determinedly at the ceiling. Nobody could say he wasn't going through the worst possible humiliation here. He was earning his freedom.

After waiting for the stir to subside, the lawyer asked quietly: 'And you expect us to believe this?'

'If you expect me to treat that as a serious question you are clearly the more impertinent,' Morris snapped back most convincingly, but then immediately recovered himself. '*Mi scusi*, I appreciate that you are only doing your job on behalf of your clients, with whom I have every sympathy' – how Italian encouraged this kind of wonderful pomposity! 'No, I'm afraid that ever since Massimina's disappearance and death I have been obsessed by the idea that I had lost the one great experience of my life. In a way it's as if I had been left behind, marooned with her. I speak to her every day in my mind, I feel she is close to me, I feel she guides me. Perhaps it was this sensation of already having someone that allowed me to continue with what can only be described as an arid marriage.'

Morris looked straight at the lawyer and reflected that there was nothing like admitting the unpalatable to gain a little credence. Certainly the sincerity in his voice must have been undeniable. At the same time he distinctly heard a voice whisper: '*Morrees, grazie, grazie*. Thank you for saying in public that you love only me.'

The lawyer was understandably irritated. 'Meester Duckworrth, let me put it to you that, rather than these two young men having killed or abducted Signor Posenato, it would have been perfectly possible for you to have killed him, to have driven his car away some short distance with the body inside, to have returned, called the police, then disposed of both car and body the following evening, inventing this farcical business of weeping over an ex-girlfriend's coffin only after three weeks of racking your brains in a high-security prison.'

Again the court responded with a ripple of interest, though the two accused seemed to be having extreme difficulty following the whole thing. Azedine was chewing his nails.

Morris said: 'This, as I suggested before, is Colonnello Fendtsteig's theory. Though how I could have done all this car-shuffling and body-burying without an accomplice is beyond me.'

The defence lawyer had begun another question, but Morris ploughed on: 'It must be said, however, in favour of Colonnello Fendtsteig, that given the circumstantial nature of the evidence available, whether against the two accused (apart perhaps from the bloody knife) or against myself for that matter, it is quite amazing to me that this case has been brought to court at all. After all, in circumstantial terms third and even fourth solutions are available. That Bobo was killed or abducted by his lover's husband, for example, if only we knew who that was. Or that Bobo staged the scene in the office and ran off with his mistress. What I'm saying is that without the body, or even the missing car, I don't see how anybody can be tried for . . .'

'Please,' the elderly judge interrupted, but kindly. 'You are here to be cross-examined by the defence for the two men being tried, not to engage in fantasies and personal reflections.'

'*Mi scusi, Signor Giudice.*' Morris was properly self-abasing. 'What I was really trying to say is that the fact that I am obliged to defend myself does not mean that I wish the two accused to be found guilty willy-nilly.'

The defence lawyer turned abruptly to the judges. 'Your honours, let us come to the point. In my summing up later on, I shall be trying to show not only that the evidence against my two clients is pathetically thin, but also that it is far more likely that if a murder were committed it was carried out by Signor Duckworth, who had both motive and opportunity. Of course, as he himself has said, it seems improbable that he could have acted alone. I will thus be suggesting that he was aided by the tall Negro known only as Kwame, who later died together with Paola Trevisan, Signor Duckworth's wife. Signor Duckworth admits that he spoke to the Negro at the so-called Villa Caritas imme-diately before proceeding to the office. For the next two hours the black's movements are unknown. Then only a few days after Posenato's disappearance, Signor Duckworth allowed this young black immigrant to move out of the hostel and into his own private flat. He also rewarded him with the gift of his Mercedes and gave him administrative control of the company in his absence in prison, a development which inevitably brought the black into close contact with Signor Duckworth's wife, a woman whose marital infidelities appear to have been well known to all members of the family and indeed many people outside it. What I am suggesting is that this circumstantial evidence is considerably greater than that being offered by the prosecution against my clients, who are guilty, I suspect, of nothing worse than not being Caucasian.

I will therefore be asking that the case be dropped and that investigations continue into the activities of the present witness.'

If there was immediately an explosion of chatter at the back of the courtroom, the effect on Morris himself was devastating, not unlike that of a great artillery shell missing by a hair's breadth. Or perhaps not missing at all. The livid red of his scars turned with electric quickness to white while his hands trembled visibly on his knees and for the first time in his life he felt an involuntary twitch seize the left corner of his mouth and drag it violently downwards.

'There is also the curious fact,' the defence lawyer went on, 'the curious fact that as his fellow workers have explained to the court, though at the time the fact did not perhaps seem relevant, the Negro Kwame actually turned up to his night shift four hours late on the second night after the crime, with the pathetic excuse that he had been outside rearranging stacks of bottles, something nobody did at night, since at night the guard dog was freed from his chain and would attack anybody coming out of the building. Hence the whereabouts of the Negro Kwame must be considered unaccounted for on the very night that Signor Duckworth was allegedly weeping over the remains of his lost beloved. In short, the two of them together had ample time to dispose of a body.'

This certainly was a direct hit. The only miracle was that it had been so long in coming. 'Mimi,' Morris croaked, though happily his voice was lost in the general hubbub of people finally seeing a whole picture come into focus. 'Mimi!' All at once Morris felt as though he had not a scrap of energy left. Clearly he was finished. If he wasn't going to confess now it was merely in order to have a few last days of semi-liberty so as to put his papers in order and read the Bible a last time or two with Antonella.

'Meester Duckworrth,' the lawyer turned to him, 'I put it to you that you saw the sacking of Azedine and Farouk as a cover for killing your partner when an argument broke out between you as to the future of the company and your shared inheritance.'

Morris opened his mouth. No, wait. He snapped it shut, then shut his eyes too. They were so harrowingly close to the kill now that he simply would not and could not speak for fear of saying the wrong thing. No, he would not answer until Mimi appeared to him, until she actually told him word for word what to say. And what was God's will for him. Even if it meant waiting a thousand years. Thirty seconds passed. A minute. 'Meester Duckworrth,' the lawyer said, 'would you please respond to my question.'

Nothing. The court had fallen silent, waiting. Behind his closed eyes Morris was seeing deep red while the silence began to throb with blood draining down and away from consciousness. Another moment and he would faint. Someone shuffled a chair nearby. At the back of the room there was a whisper, the slightest rustle of paper. Until, into this silence pressed full of passion, the sudden sound of a door opening and footsteps running came as a liberating explosion.

'*Signor Giudice! Signor Giudice!*'

Opening his eyes, dazed by nausea, Morris barely made out what seemed to be Inspector Marangoni's assistant of old hurrying across the courtroom. He went directly to the judges' bench and began to talk to them in a low voice. Glances were exchanged. The judges looked up and called over the two lawyers. People in the courtroom began to talk. The older judge called them to order. And Morris finally came back to his senses just in time to hear the words: '*Signore e signori*, due to the discovery of a new and apparently conclusive piece of evidence, this court will be adjourned for an hour while the prosecution decides whether he wishes to continue the case against the accused.'

CHAPTER THIRTY-FOUR

MAY HAD BROUGHT THE poppies back, a brilliant red dapple in the green patchwork of the countryside. Riding up the Valpantena for his mornings in the office, Morris was reminded of the pointillists and pictures he had seen at the National Gallery as an adolescent. On two occasions he called his father, first to invite him to the funeral, second to point out to him the misfortune they now had in common. Both had lost a young wife. Both in terrible accidents. Though unlike Ron, Morris didn't have the consolation of a child to remind him of his spouse.

Morris was moved by how genuinely upset his father was on his behalf. In the first phone call. In the second, the man seemed more dismissive, more himself. The burden of it was that Morris should pull his socks out of the spilt milk and get on and find somebody else. He'd always tended to be a bit of a crybaby.

'She was pregnant,' Morris whimpered. 'It only came out in the autopsy.'

'I,' his father was already saying, 'didn't wait long after Alice died, because I couldn't see that anybody had anything to gain out of me being a miserable old bastard. Not your mother, not you and not meself. Or am I right?'

Morris hung up. He resented his father taking his mother's name in vain. At cruising speed, he admired the thick freshness of everything, the vine leaves racing along their wires and poles, the stark verticality of the cypress, the waving silver of the birches (like light on water, his artist's eye told him). 'How everything grows back and back,' he told Mimi on the phone.

'Like our love,' she said. For she often answered now. She seemed to have lost the reticence of earlier days. She asked: 'Where are you going now, Morri?'

'But you know where I'm going,' he laughed, 'you know everything, Mimi.'

'Yes, but I like to ask, and for you to answer.'

'Fair enough.' He smiled, taking his hand from the wheel one risky moment to push it through blond hair that was growing back. Though he didn't try to catch a glimpse of himself in the mirror on the sunshade as once he used to. 'I'm going to see Forbes,' he said.

There was a brief silence. The car purred past the ugly industrial developments outside Grezzana. Morris drove more carefully and sedately these days. Then she said: 'I still think Forbes is dangerous, Morri.'

Morris couldn't help but agree. There were indeed all kinds of problems.

'He knows so much,' she said.

'But he did give me the letters back,' Morris reminded her. 'And he doesn't so much *know* everything as imagine it. I mean, he doesn't actually know *I* wrote those letters, just that I had them in my pocket, and he doesn't know what I did to Paola and Kwame. By the way, it seems they were never apart while I was in hospital.' Into a brief space he added: 'Actually, I miss Kwame.'

'Forbes knows,' Massimina said sombrely, and with something final in her voice.

But Morris was quite relaxed. 'He doesn't *know* I put the pubic hair and so on in the car, does he? Only that I drove it off into the hills. And in the end it must have been Kwame who brought it back to the villa, not me.

Right? Probably planning to spray it and resell it or something. I wondered why the police hadn't found it. So the idea that it was them who killed Bobo must seem quite feasible to him. Even if he suspects otherwise. The logistics of it are a bit tight, but just about possible.'

'I love your voice,' she said. Her own was soft in the elegant phone. Though when Morris put the receiver down it was intriguing that she kept on talking to him just the same. You only needed the phone to get things started these days.

'Really, still?' he asked.

'Still,' she said. Her voice had a way of filling the whole car, as if it were on every side of him, coming out of the four-speaker stereo perhaps.

'The thing is,' Morris said, 'that I know he wrote those two ransom letters to try to save Farouk.'

'But you can't prove it. Whereas he could tell the police that he and Stan saw you in Piazza Bra that day.'

Morris laughed: 'Thank God Stan's so incredibly out of it.' He waited patiently to get past a girl on a bike being pulled along by boyfriend on moped. The kind of thing the police incredibly never stopped people for.

He added: 'You're right about that. But the question is, would it ever be in his interest to go to the police? I mean, I'm financing his little dream there, all the little boys he's always wanted to seduce.'

'He might go to them, if he was afraid of you.'

'But why should he be?'

'He might think you're so afraid of what he knows that you will try to kill him.'

Stuck behind the inevitable tractor now, Morris had to admit that this was feasible.

'Or he might think you'd kill him because he was homosexual, the way you've spoken about homosexuality sometimes.'

'Oh, I wouldn't do that. I mean, I'm hardly a mad mass murderer or anything.'

'But he doesn't *know* that. When I think of some of the things you've said to him.' She laughed. 'I was furious with you. I was dying to tell you. You were so blind.'

Morris rather liked that use of the word 'dying'. 'So why didn't you?'

'I was shy, I suppose. I hadn't found my voice.'

'Whereas now you've become quite a little chatterbox.'

'Yes.' There was a brief silence. 'Perhaps the truth is,' she went on softly and her voice seemed to breathe through the air vents now, 'that I hadn't made up my mind whether to forgive you or not.'

'Ah.' He felt a rush of warmth and emotion. 'But now you have?'

'Yes.'

'You're so sweet, Mimi,' he said. 'So sweet and so important.'

'Morri.'

Then with genuine concern he enquired: 'Do you think Paola will ever forgive me?'

But perhaps it was a mistake to ask this, because now there was a very long silence indeed. The Mercedes cruised on between country ditches towards Villa Caritas. At last she said mysteriously: 'From the place where Paola has gone, no word comes forth. Remember Dante: *"Lasciate ogni speranza voi che entrate."* We shall never know whether she forgives you or not. You must forget all about her.'

Morris felt chastened. He drove intently.

Massimina went on: 'But you still haven't told me how you're going to settle this problem with Forbes.'

'Because I've no idea,' Morris said. 'I mean, I don't see how I can. The last thing I want to do is hurt him. I like him. Very much. And then there's Fendtsteig. The truth

352

is, I shall have to keep my head down for years now. Which is only what I ever wanted anyway.'

'Well, I've got an idea,' Massimina said. Her voice was suddenly at its most soft and seductive.

'Yes?'

'But I don't know if you'd be willing to go through with it.'

'If you tell me to I will.'

'Would you?'

'I promise,' Morris said. 'If you give me an order, I'll do it.'

'But I don't want to give you orders, I want you to do it because it's the best thing.'

'Anything you so much as suggest is an order for me,' Morris told her. He was curious to know what it was now, what he was letting himself in for.

'Look, you're almost there,' Mimi said. In fact they had just passed through the village. 'I think you should pull over so we can discuss this before we get there.'

How death had changed her! Matured her! She would never have spoken like this to him when she was just a sweet little girl.

'Of course.' Morris pulled over to the side, so that now he was hard against a stone wall mottled with sunlit capers, though the plane tree beside, he noticed, had two syringes stabbed into its bark. Nothing was ever, he had time to reflect, quite idyllic.

'Make love to him,' Mimi said.

'What!'

'Make love to him. To Forbes. Or rather, let him make love to you.'

For the first time Morris was furious with his guardian ghost. How could she even suggest such a thing? How . . .

'First because it's logical.' Her little voice spoke with a bluntness he would never have expected.

'But . . .'

'It would show that you've come round to his way of thinking as far as homosexuality is concerned, so that he needn't be afraid you're going to do anything to him just because he's gay.'

'Mimi . . .'

'And it will form a bond between you that would make it very unlikely that he would ever do anything to you. Also . . .'

Morris was in a state of shock, breathing very deeply, trying to control a sudden rebellion of various inner organs. And one outer one too. Despite the Mercedes's controlled environment, it was as if there were no air in the car.

'Also, because it's something you've always wanted to do. That's why you're feeling so excited now.'

'But, Mimi, it's against my faith, it's against . . .'

'St Paul was homosexual,' she told him. 'I know that for a fact.' When he still protested, she went on: 'Anyway, I'll shrive you, Morri, I'll forgive you the way I did when you were with Paola and Kwame. Just as long as you watch me throughout.' Her voice was positively oozing sex now. 'Like last time.'

'Yes,' he said, faintly.

'You know that was wonderful for me too, Morri,' she breathed, 'the way you looked at me. With your poor hurt face.'

There was a moment's silence. An elderly woman passed by, labouring at the pedals of an ancient bicycle, huge shopping bag in one hand. Then a petrol tanker. Morris made a last attempt to fight back: 'Look, the truth is, I still feel disgusted by what I did then. You know, I keep waking and vomiting.'

'Don't,' she said. 'Don't. You love it, and you were beautiful.' Then in no more than a velvet whisper, she told him: 'You're so lovely when you're naked, Morri. Your body. And your face, even now, when you come. It's so epic.'

'And you, Mimi,' he answered. 'You were lovely. Your expression was lovely. So holy. With the crucifix in your hand.'

'That's settled then,' she said. 'You'll feel so much better afterwards. So much happier. Anyway, the only reason you never did it before was because your father accused you of it.'

Morris could think of nothing to answer to this. So he started up again. The car slid out onto the road. The last mile of fertile countryside unfolded, the young corn and the speckled drift of fallen cherry blossom. As he turned up the drive to Villa Caritas, he suddenly felt moved to ask: 'Apart from that, you do know what I'm planning with Antonella, don't you?'

She said: 'Of course, Morree.'

'And you don't mind?'

'She's very lonely and sad,' Massimina said wistfully.

Morris insisted: 'Listen, Mimi, I won't do anything unless I have your blessing. Anything, in all my life, I promise you that.' But already he was excited at all it seemed Massimina was going to let him do, no, to *tell* him to do.

'Keep my portrait always in your room,' the ghost whispered. 'Promise me I will always be the first.'

'Yes,' he said. 'Yes!'

'If you do that you can have sex with anybody you like. Because I love watching you. And you watching me. You know that in the end it will always be me you're doing it with.'

'Oh, always,' he promised. 'Always, always always.'

Then quite peremptorily, she said: 'Masturbate, Morri.'

'What?'

'I want you to masturbate.'

'Just like that?' he asked.

They were in the drive to Villa Caritas now, deeply rutted by the builder's truck. She laughed. 'Just like that. In fact, it's an order, Morri. Pull the car into the trees.'

Again, Morris was both shocked and excited by this new development. It was almost as if she were taking over the role that Paola had had in his life, but so much more sweetly.

Then quite suddenly she was sitting beside him. He knew she was, Mimi's ghost, even though he couldn't see her. Her perfume filled the car. She was pulling up her dress. On those same stitched and patched pants Morris kept under his pillow. He felt his hand as if guided to his zip.

She began to quote: 'My beloved put in his hand by the hole of the door, and my bowels were moved for him. I rose up to open to my beloved; and my hands dropped with myrrh, and my fingers with sweet smelling myrrh, upon the handles of the lock.'

Morris closed his eyes. At the same time, a voice said drily: '*Quod ubique, quod semper, quod ab omnibus.* . . .' Forbes was standing by the car, hand in hand with the young Ramiz, a benevolent smile on his face.

How cleverly Mimi had planned this little introduction to what Morris now accepted must inevitably happen later.

That evening he dined with Antonella at Casa Trevisan. It was a deliciously formal occasion, with the Signora's old *donna di servizio* cooking *costole di manzo* and an excellent side-plate of steamed *finocchio*. Antonella was wearing a simple black dress, but belted to bring out the extravagant hourglass of her shape. She moved gracefully against a backdrop of antique furniture, sombre houseplants. Her face had that depth of awful experience, a lesser beauty suffused and enhanced by terrible wisdom, Bobo's betrayal, her sister's unmentionable crime and fate. As if like some Greek widow, she'd lived through the whole Trojan War and worse, and now wanted only to forget.

With the maid sliding silently back and forth, they talked business: the larger and larger orders from Doorways, first interest shown by an American liquor-store chain. There would have to be some expansion of the bottling facilities, which might be difficult with interest rates back at fifteen per cent again, though Morris was willing to sell the flat in Via dei Gelsomini to raise part of the money. He'd had another excellent offer from the builder.

Then Antonella said that she herself had been thinking of selling her flat.

'Which means you'd expect me to move out of here?' Morris asked.

But she said not at all. Not at all. Casa Trevisan was big enough for both of them, wasn't it? They could econo-mise. 'Anyway there are no unhappy memories here,' she added, 'for either of us.' She dipped her eyes into a plate of cooked plums and cream.

They talked about politics. The local politicians Bobo had always relied on for cover from tax inspections were all under investigation in the wave of bribe scandals. The government was tottering, the electoral law had been revolutionised. Italy was changing. They would have to run the company in a different way now: openly, honestly, but without losing sight, Morris insisted, of this policy of employing people who needed help.

Antonella agreed a hundred per cent. She made notes on a piece of paper, discussed quotations for new plant, the possibility of grants. An architect was drawing up a design for that chapel they were to build. Morris lapped it up. When had he ever met a woman you could really discuss things with before? When had he ever felt so free, from all his anxieties, his prejudices, that constant collision of exaltation and angst that had characterised these last sad years?

Wiping her mouth, she said: 'By the way, Fendtsteig came to talk to me again today.'

Immediately every blood-vessel hardened. If the alarm didn't immediately show on his face, it was only thanks, once again, to Bobo's old guard dog. A plum stuck, unsavoured, in his gullet.

'No, he just pointed out all the contradictions in the case, all the loose ends.'

Morris almost choked into his napkin, but then managed to get out: 'Such as?'

Obviously she was determined to arrive at a point where they could talk about the thing straightforwardly and without emotion. 'He was concerned about Kwame's motive for, for killing Bobo. He was concerned about your wife's motive for covering for him. He was concerned about who made that anonymous phone call the night after his disappearance. He was concerned as to the identity of Bobo's,' she hesitated, 'woman.' She stopped, then very matter-of-factly added: 'He obviously still believes that you were involved in one way or another.'

Morris stared at her across a table whence the maid was clearing plates now. Antonella smiled rather sadly at him over an elaborately embroidered lace tablecloth above which the cruet was two tiny silver wine vats supported by a gnarled trunk of vine, cast by expert artisans for *Non-fortuna-sed-labor* himself.

'He says one disappearance and two corpses and nobody in gaol is too much for him to consider the case closed.'

Morris sighed. He decided, and told her so, that he would go and see the man tomorrow. He would go and see the man and hammer the whole thing out with him and insist that he consider it over, closed, finished, otherwise it was just too humiliating.

Later they adjourned to a straight-backed sofa and read a passage from Revelation together, closing the evening towards ten-thirty with a chaste kiss at the door. 'Your poor cheek,' she said, lifting a gentle finger to the many scars. 'You must think you were terribly unlucky running into our family, with all the awful things that have happened.'

'Not at all,' Morris replied, and his soft blue eyes must have told her: not so long as I have you.

He lay in his bed and gazed at Mimi. He liked to light the room with a candle these days. The flickering flame brought the painting alive, shifting shadows over her face, drawing out glints of colour from her eyes. When the phone rang he dealt quite quickly with a sickeningly grateful Forbes. Apparently the man had already been in touch with Stan to tell him there was no place for him at Villa Catullus. Good. Then, sitting up, propped upon the bolster and staring at her for inspiration, he once again brought all the facts together, listed them one by one, this extraordinary series of distasteful events, betrayals, blackmails, idiocies, spitefulness, lust, excellent intentions, listed them all to then toss them into the kaleidoscope of his imagination, where they might be shaken this way and that in the hope that at the end some coherent and suddenly obvious pattern might emerge which he could then memorise and take to Fendtsteig like some theory of relativity that finally explained everything.

It was an exercise that brought on a mild and not unpleasant sense of vertigo, like the night he and Mimi had lain on the beach in Ostia and looked for patterns in the stars, or when one took on some puzzle that was too difficult, and yet clearly did have a solution somewhere. And the agony of it was precisely that, that it *did* have a solution. If it didn't, he might have just let be and given up.

The idea that Bobo, having run off with his mistress, might have been responsible for Paola and Kwame's deaths brought something more than the ghost of a smile to Mimi's face.

And had the handwriting of that billet-doux ever been compared with his wife's? Could he himself count on having recognised it as Paola's writing, given that she wrote so very little?

There were circumstances in which it was not unreasonable to suppose that Paola might have made that call. If, for, example, Kwame had already told her that Morris had done it. To cover for him. Though of course he had never been able to wring from the police whether the call had been made by a man or a woman.

The hypothesis that he might have made the call himself in some somnabulistic post-homicidal trance brought on a dizziness that was almost exactly hilarity and horror reflecting each other down the interminable hall of distorting mirrors that was Morris Duckworth's mind.

An invigorating thought.

Until, far on in the early hours, it occurred to Morris to let be. He would never marshal these facts into anything like coherence. In the end this was no more of a defeat than the one almost everybody had to face when it came to understanding their lives. No more of a defeat than the one Fendtsteig would be savouring for many and many a year to come. Yes, Morris thought, yes, he would accept his mere humanity and live in the only way one could: from day to day, from hand to mouth.

'Your hand to my mouth,' he told the painting.

The candle guttered. Dying, then flickering to life again, the flame definitely stirred the fingers of a white hand on the blue velvet of her robe, lifted the corners of her lips.

'Morri,' she said. 'Morri!'

And Morris knew it was enough. He had reached a point of rest. He need do no more.

Read on for the first chapter of the new
Morris Duckworth novel

Painting Death

CHAPTER ONE

MORRIS WOULD ARRIVE LATE for the ceremony. That was appropriate for someone of his importance. It was in his honour after all. But not so late as to be disrespectful; if one disrespects those doing the honouring, one diminishes the recognition. He watched in the mirror as steady hands pushed a Tonbridge School tie tight into the still-firm skin of his strong neck. He would look smart, without being obsequious; neither formal, nor casual. These were fine lines to tread and that he could do so with ease was one of the rewards of maturity. Ease: that was the word. Morris would appear at ease with the world, at ease with himself, his scarred face, his thinning hair; at ease with his wealth, his wife, his fine family, fabulous palazzo and now, at long last, this distinction conceded *in extremis*. All's well that ends well. You're a happy man, Morris Duckworth, he told himself out loud, and he smiled a winning smile. No, a *winner's* smile; not a single niggle that nagged, not a prick of the old resentment. Thank you, Mimi, he mouthed to the mirror, admiring the brightness in blue British eyes. Thank you so much!

'*Cinque minuti*,' sang a voice from below. It might have been the dear dead girl herself!

'*Con calma!*' Morris called cheerfully. After all, they lived only a stone's throw from the centre of civic power. If he had one regret, it was that this was only Verona, *la misera provincia*; Piazza Bra, not Piazza di Spagna. But then think how dirty Rome was. How chaotic. And how grey, grim and gauche Milan. This prim little town is your destiny, Morris. Be happy.

As he left the bathroom, the flick of a Ferragamo cuff revealed a Rolex telling him it was indeed time. *Le massime autorità* would be waiting.

The maximum authorities! For Morris!

'Papà!' came the voice again. His daughter's wonderful, huskiness, so like dear Mimi of old. She was impatient. All the same, Morris couldn't resist and stepped into The Art Room for a moment of intimacy with his most recent acquisition.

The heavy old frame rested on a chair. Morris hadn't quite decided where to hang it yet. He ran a finger down its mouldings. How austere they were! The gilt had gone gloomily dark, from candle smoke, no doubt. It was a pleasure to think of sombre old interiors made somehow darker by their flickering candles. But in the painting itself the two women were walking down a bright street. It was the Holy Land, millennia ago: two bulky figures, seen from behind, in voluminous dresses. Between them, trapped by hand against hip, the woman on the right held a broad basket. It was partially covered, but the white cloth had slipped a little to reveal, to the viewer, unbeknown to the two ladies as they sauntered away, not a loaf of bread, not a heap of washing, not a pile of freshly picked grapes but, grimacing and astonished, a bearded male face: General Holofernes! His Assyrian head severed.

'Papà, for Christ's sake!'

Now there came a deeper voice, 'Morrees! You mustn't keep the mayor waiting.'

Morris frowned, why did he feel so drawn to this painting? Two women carrying a severed head. But the scene was so calm and their gait so relaxed it might as well have been the morning's shopping.

'Dad!'

In her impatience, Massimina switched to English. Morris turned abruptly on a patent-leather heel and strode to the broad staircase. As he skipped down stone steps, running a freshly washed hand along the polished curve of the marble banister, his two women presented themselves in all their finery: Antonella magnificently matronly in something softly maroon; Massimina willowy in off-white, and both generously bosomed in the best Trevisan tradition. Morris smiled first into one face, then the other, pecking powdered cheeks and catching himself mirrored in the bright windows of four hazel eyes. Only his son had inherited the grey Duckworth blue.

'Where's Mauro?' Morris asked, pulling back from his wife. Her gold crucifixes still galled, but he had learned not to criticise. He was not a control freak.

Antonella was already making for the door where the ancient Maddalena stooped with her mistress's mink at the ready. Antonella pushed her arms into sumptuous sleeves. 'The cardinal will be there,' she was saying, 'and Don Lorenzo. We're late.'

'But where's Mauro? We can't go without Mauro.'

Morris couldn't understand why his wife wasn't taking the problem more seriously. Or why the decrepit maid wasn't wearing a starched white apron over her black dress, as specifically instructed. This was an occasion for family pride.

'I don't think Mousie came home last night,' Massimina said.

'Don't *think*?' Morris stopped on the threshold. 'Home from where? Haven't you phoned him?' He was not happy with the thought that a son of his could be nicknamed Mousie.

'I'm sure he'll meet us there,' Antonella said complacently. She was standing in the courtyard now where threads of water splashed across the stony buttocks of a young Mercury apparently leaping into flight from a broad bowl of frothy travertine. All around, vines climbed the ochre stucco between green-shuttered windows while just below the roof a sundial took advantage of the crisp winter weather to alert anyone still capable of reading such things that Morris was now seriously late for the ceremony that would grant him honorary citizenship and the keys to the city of Verona.

'He went to the game.'

'What?'

'Brescia away. I called him, but his phone is off.'

'He knows when the ceremony is, *caro*.' Antonella hurried back and took her husband's arm. 'We were chatting about it yesterday.' Her manner, if only Morris had had the leisure to contemplate it, was a charming mix of anxiety and indulgence. She treated her husband as a troublesome boy, which rather let their obstreperous son off the hook. 'I'm sure we'll find him there before us. But we mustn't keep the mayor waiting. In the end, the only person who really counts today is you, Morrees.'

This was such a pleasant thought that Morris allowed himself to be pulled along, outside the great arched gate and into the designer-dressed bustle of Via Oberdan. All the same, he hadn't begged his boy two days' truancy from one of old England's most expensive schools, and paid a BA flight to boot, to have the lout abscond at this moment of his father's glory. For some reason the word 'coronation' came to mind: Morris was to be crowned King of Verona. He frowned to chase the thought away; one mustn't lose one's head.

'By the way, who won?' Antonella asked. Morris's wife had a magnanimous air; it was the mink's first outing this season.

Massimina took her father's arm on the other side. 'Alas, Brescia,' she sighed. 'Own goal in injury time.'

Comfortable between them, though it was disconcerting that his daughter was so tall, Morris marvelled that his lady-folk should be aware of such trivial things. What was injury time in the end? He had never really understood. Dad had not wanted company when he set off to Loftus Road and anyway his son would not have been seen dead with a man wearing a green and white bobble cap.

'But if he didn't come home,' he protested, 'where did he spend the night? And why wasn't I told?'

There was no time to hear an answer, for on emerging from Via Oberdan into the wide open space of one of Italy's largest squares, it was to discover that Piazza Bra was not, right now, wide open at all. They had chosen this of all mornings to erect the stalls for the *mercatino di Santa Lucia*. Damn. From the majestic Roman arena, right along the broad Liston, past Victor Emmanuel on bronze horseback and as far as the Austrian clock, palely illuminated above the arch of Porta Nuova, the whole cobbled *campo* was chock-a-block with gypsies, *extra-comunitari* and assorted exempla of Veneto pond life scrambling together prefabricated stalls for the overpriced sale of *torroni*, candy floss and other vulgar, sugar-based venoms. It was a dentist's Promised Land, which fleetingly reminded Morris that this was another area in which his son was proving an expensive investment.

Through clouds of diesel from trucks unloading trifles and baubles of every bastard variety, not to mention the construction of a merry-go-round, Palazzo Barbieri on the far side of the square, solemn seat of the Veronese *comune*, suddenly seemed impossibly distant. Morris almost panicked. What if they called the event off? What if they mistook his belated arrival for a deliberate snub? One could hardly blame the traffic, living only 300 yards away. Morris began to hurry, at first dragging his women with him, then freeing his arms to dive between a wall of *panettoni* and their leering vendor, the kind of squat, swarthy figure one associates with black markets the world over. It was a disgrace! He would say something to the mayor.

'Da-ad!' his daughter protested. 'Why do you always have to be in such a rush?' Only now did Morris realise the girl had put on four-inch heels, to cross a sea of cobbles. The original Massimina, who had been half her height, would have known better. And he had thought his first love dumb!

Antonella laughed. 'This way, Mr Nonchalant,' she said and pulled her husband to the left, out of the throng and down the small street that ran behind the arena. Here, almost immediately, the way was clear and though the change of route had added a hundred yards or so to their walk, Morris understood at once there would be no problem. Thank God he had married such a practical soul! So much more sensible than her dear departed sisters. Nevertheless, he kept up a brisk pace, past beggars and chestnut vendors, just in case something else should come between him and his overdue due. The complacency of ten minutes before now seemed a fool's paradise and Morris knew from bitter experience that there was nothing to be gained from seeking to retrieve it. It took carefree weeks and important art acquisitions to consolidate a mood as positive as that; or at least an afternoon's revelling with Samira. For a moment, then, passing on one side a café advertising hot chocolate with whipped cream and on the other the arena ticket office promising the world's largest display of Nativity scenes – from the Philippines to the Faroe Islands! – Morris found himself struggling to relate two apparently remote but peremptory thoughts:

first the memory of how he had ignominiously scuttled through these same streets thirty years ago, a wretched language teacher hurrying head down from one private lesson to another, always at the tight-fisted beck and call of people richer and stupider than himself (dear Massimina among them, it had to be said); and second, the reflection that his son was hardly likely to have taken his Tonbridge School uniform to a winter evening football game; so that even if the boy did make it to this morning's ceremony after a night slumming with thugs in foggy suburbs, he was not going to be sporting a burgundy-and-black-striped tie that matched his own. Only now, still striding along in the shadow of the Roman amphitheatre with Antonella panting to keep pace in her furs, did Morris realise how much he had been looking forward to that little touch of father–son complicity; it was the kind of quietly significant detail he liked to think a fashion-conscious Veronese public would register with a twinge of envy: style the Italians might have in abundance, but never the sober solidity of a great British educational institution. In which case, come to think of it, the ungrateful boy might just as well not turn up for the ceremony at all. Perhaps I should pull him out of Tonbridge, Morris wondered, save myself thirty grand a year, and have the boy eke out a living teaching English, as I once had to. There! Realising that the two apparently separate thoughts had after all found a very evident and purposeful link – his spoiled son needed reminding what was what – Morris suddenly felt pleased again: whatever happened this particular morning, or any other morning for that matter, he would always have his wits, his wit. Hadn't he, in the end, Morris Duckworth, got himself to Cambridge University from Shepherd's Bush Comprehensive, the first and very likely the last pupil ever to do so? Let Mauro 'Mother's Boy' Duckworth do the same!

'I asked, have you prepared a speech?' Antonella was saying. 'Morrees! *Eih, pronto?* Aren't you listening?'

They had arrived at the bottom of the grand steps. The columned facade was above them.

'Of course,' Morris said, realising as he spoke that he had left the thing at home: three sheets of A4 on the windowsill beside the loo. He had allowed himself to be distracted by Judith and Holofernes.

His wife reached up to straighten the lapels of his jacket. Very quietly, she said: 'Just be careful not to say anything stupid.'

Morris was taken aback.

'Like the time at the Rotary.'

The English husband felt a dangerous heat flood his loins. 'It will be fine,' he said abruptly.

'Only trying to help,' she explained, brushing something off his shoulder. But he knew she was laughing.

'I was drunk,' he insisted.

'I know,' she smiled.

'The punch was too strong. They should have been gaoled for poisoning.'

'We're late, Morrees,' she said calmly. 'Come on.'

Right. But now where was his daughter? Son or no son, at least the three of them could ascend the town hall steps together. Morris turned but couldn't find her. The ridiculous Verona *trenino* was passing, a fake electric steam locomotive, bright red, with an open carriage behind and piped Christmas music deafening the dumb tourists on board. 'Hark the Herald'. How anybody could have imagined introducing such an atrocious eye-and-ear sore into the centuries-long sobriety of the city's ancient piazzas was beyond Morris. Had anyone ever sung 'Hark the Herald' in Italy? 'Late in time behold Him come!' Indeed. Just as Morris fought off a fleeting memory of his carol-singing mother (he himself had solo-ed 'Once in Royal

David's' at St Bartholomew's, Acton) the train lurched forward with the clanging of a bell and Massimina emerged from behind, swaying impressively as she stepped out to cross the road, closely watched, Morris noticed, by three motorcycle louts smoking outside the wine bar at the corner. The girl was too attractive by half, too present and alive for her own good. Those heels would have to come down an inch or three. Confident nevertheless that his daughter was still a virgin, otherwise he would surely have known, Morris held out his hand as if to draw his child toward him. They would cut a fine figure entering the corridors of power side by side. Except that now an ancient gypsy woman reached up from the pavement – *Grazie, grazie* she wheedled – she must have imagined the wealthy man's outstretched arm held an offering of change. Irritated, Morris was about to shoo the crone away when he caught his wife's quick intake of breath. They were in full view of a dozen dignitaries and news-paper photographers standing under the portico at the top of the steps. Morris reached into his pocket and found the fifty-cent coin one had to keep ready for such occasions, because to open your wallet was always a mistake.

For the next fifteen minutes, it would have been hard to imagine a more gratifying occasion. On the door they were greeted by the faithful Don Lorenzo, for many years the family's spiritual adviser, who took them into the first reception room to meet Cardinal Rusconi, gorgeous in stiff scarlet. Morris kissed a puffy hand and agreed that, for all the commercial exploitation, Christmas never quite lost its magic, while Antonella spoke of the importance of sponsoring Nativity scenes in the poorer suburbs where the camels and shepherds created a much needed sense of festive spirit. Glasses of bubbly in hand, nobody seemed to have noticed how late they had arrived and Morris couldn't decide whether this was wonderful or irritating.

He might just as well have been on time, which certainly came more naturally, in which case he could have enjoyed feeling superior to the latecomers. A radio journalist wanted him to explain yet again the circumstances that had led to this honour, but under the prelate's approving if somewhat haughty gaze, and nodding to a fellow Rotarian across the room, Morris demurely told the sycophant that it would hardly be appropriate for him to sing his own praises: the mayor, he said, would no doubt put forward the *motivazione* during his presentation. Massimina, he noticed from the corner of an ever observant eye, was chatting to Beppe Bagutta, son of the man who ran the Verona Trade Fair and quite a few other things beside; decent results at art college were all very well, but a little more would be required if the girl was to make her Duckworth mark on the world. Nearer at hand, there was a pleasant buzz of mutual congratulation with the ascetic Don Lorenzo telling the corpulent cardinal how much he had appreciated his article 'A Eucharist for Our Times' – he and Antonella had studied it together, he said – and the cardinal actually deigning to ask Morris how he thought Italy might come out of the present financial crisis; a subtle way of fishing for some kind of donation perhaps. Why else would such a powerful man have bothered to turn up for a ceremony of no religious significance? Old acquaintances and business partners, gallery owners and building contractors waved their hellos but Morris decided he would be best served standing beside the ecclesiastical red, so similar, it suddenly crossed his mind now, to the Father Christmas outfit Dad had donned to hand out half-bottles of Teacher's to shop-floor friends on Christmas Eve. Was Samira here, perhaps? That was an exciting thought. He hadn't invited her, but you never knew. The girl was clearly infatuated. Or even inspectors Marangoni and Fendsteig, from the old days? That too would be oddly exciting. But the meddling policemen must have retired long ago, Morris reflected. Just as well, with all this DNA wizardry they'd recently come up with. He smiled at the cardinal who smiled back as though they had been friends for ages, and Morris was just rummaging through the clutter of his mind to see if there was some favour he could ask of the prelate before the prelate asked whatever it was he planned to ask of him, when, at the blast of a trumpet, four extravagantly be-feathered Bersaglieri raised four ceremonial flags to form an arch of honour at the door to his right: there were Europe's circle of quarrelling stars, Italy's bureaucratic tricolour, the razzmatazz of the dear old Union Jack and finally, white on red, the ladder of Cangrande della Scala, erstwhile Duke of Verona. Morris bowed his head as he stepped beneath these proud symbols into the great Sala degli Arazzi and that world of honoured tradition he had always, after his rather particular Duckworth fashion, aspired to.

So it was mildly irritating, having reached the inner sanctum, to find that the mayor hadn't bothered with a tie. 'I'm afraid we'll have to get moving,' the younger man said, hurrying between elegant chairs to give Morris his hand and then immediately withdraw it. He wore a white shirt, open at the neck, black blazer and denim jeans, so that if it weren't for the red and green mayoral sash across his chest it would have been hard to imagine why he was in such solemn surroundings at all. A delegation of Arab businessmen was expected for eleven o'clock, he explained. One couldn't be late for the Arabs. 'Our new masters, alas!'

Morris had always despised the Northern League and chided himself for having expected anything better of Verona's local hero, first separatist mayor of this exquisitely Italian town.

'We were waiting for my son,' Morris said frostily. 'I'm afraid his flight's been delayed.'

They took seats behind a polished table while a crowd of seventy or so settled in rows beneath Paolo Farinati's huge *Victory of the Veronese over Barbarossa* covering half the wall to the left, a great oil-brushed tumble of bodies, blood and heraldry with some fine fabrics and polished armour tossed in for good measure among neighing horses and silken banners. Oh to have a palazzo big enough to house such splendour, Morris thought. A whole war in your front room! But with undue haste the mayor was already jumping to his feet and plucking one of the microphones from its stand.

'*Buon giorno a tutti!*' he began, even before people had had time to take their seats. 'We are here as you know to honour a man who has been among us for many years, indeed who arrived in this town *the very season our beloved Hellas Verona won the Scudetto*. You brought good luck, Meester Dackvert!' the mayor smiled down on his guest. 'We are extremely grateful.'

This shameless crowd-pleaser of an opening, which immediately raised a shout of applause – even Antonella and Massimina clapped enthusiastically – wasn't actually true, since Morris had arrived in Verona in 1983, not '85. But the Northern League people, he remembered, were invariably Hellas fans, theatrically rough and tough, the town's would-be bad boys. Mauro surely wasn't messing with the league, Morris hoped. Even the Communists dressed better.

'Not, alas, a success we are likely to see repeated in the near future,' the mayor added with pantomime gloom, 'or not if last night's abject performance is anything to go by.'

The public sighed.

'Though the disturbances after Brescia's late goal, if I

may say so in parenthesis, and I know because I was there, were certainly *not* initiated by Hellas fans.'

'*Verissimo!*' a voice called from the back.

What on earth, Morris wondered, did all this have to do with honouring Cittadino Duckworth?

'Actually,' the young mayor laughed, 'for a while the terraces looked rather like our old painting here.' He gestured to the raised swords, rearing horses and trampled corpses in Farinati's *Victory*. 'Though I personally was unarmed of course.'

Another laugh. This was infuriating. But Morris had learned over the years to keep calm, if not exactly cool, especially when in full public view. Sitting tight, his body steaming with angry heat, he consoled himself with the reflection that he was very likely the only one in this room who had ever had the courage to raise a weapon in anger and kill a man, or woman for that matter (on the very weekend Verona had won the championship if he was not mistaken), hence the only one here who could really understand the heat, horror and wild elation experienced in Farinati's magnificent painting. What was a scuffle at a vulgar football match compared to real killing? His knowledge went deeper than theirs, Morris told himself, inches of steel deeper, though come to think of it he'd never used a knife. Reaching to pour himself a glass of water, Morris noticed his wife in the front row trying to catch his eye and shaking her head slightly. Was he doing something wrong? He hadn't opened his mouth yet. And who was the man on her right who looked so oddly familiar?

'Aside from that magnificent achievement,' the mayor paused – he had a thrusting jaw and close-set, merry eyes in pasty skin – 'Verona having been, as I shall never tire of repeating, *the last provincial team ever to be CHAMPIONS OF ITALY*' – again he waited for the obedient applause to die down – 'aside, as I said, from that alas unrepeatable *exploit*' – he pronounced the word *à la française* and turned to grin complacently at his guest – 'Meester Dackvert's first years in Verona were not entirely happy, peripherally involved as he so sadly was in the murderous tragedies that beset two of the town's finest old families, the Trevisans of Quinzano, and the Posenatos of San Felice.'

Again there was applause, but subdued this time, as many present would remember the violent deaths of three prominent citizens, unaware of course that these were precisely the occasions when Morris had been obliged to learn the lethal skills celebrated by Paolo Farinati on the magnificent canvas beside them. Sipping his glass of water, the Englishman began to wonder whether it had really been wise to accept this invitation and, glancing towards Antonella, saw that she had lowered her face, perhaps to shed a tear over her dead sisters, or even, however misguidedly, her first husband, while the man sitting to her right patted her shoulder with surprising familiarity. Suddenly Morris found himself alert. It couldn't be Stan Albertini, could it? Stan had left Verona decades back.

'There was also, as friends of the family will recall, an unfortunate incident with a German shepherd, which, er, rearranged, as they say, our English guest's rosy-cheeked physiognomy, obliging him to rely henceforth on brain rather than beauty!'

How inexcusably clumsy and insensitive these remarks were! But since Morris's old scars had at that very moment begun to sing and burn in cheeks and temples, the English guest (*guest*, after thirty years!) was grateful for any supposed embarrassment that offered cover. If there was one person who possessed the facts to bury him, if only it ever occurred to the halfwit to string them all together, it was Stan.

'But the English are a resilient race,' the mayor continued, 'as we Italians know to our cost.' Speaking without notes, he raised and lowered the microphone, swinging his shoulders from side to side with the panache of a stand-up comedian. Clearly his audience loved him, for they never failed to titter. 'In short there are many reasons for our decision to honour Meester Dackvert today.' Again he looked indulgently down on his guest as if the fifty-five-year-old multiple murderer had just been born in a stable under a sparkling comet. 'Having married the beautiful Antonella Trevisan, surely an indication of the best possible taste' – the tasteless remark raised a storm of cheers; if there was one quality Antonella did not have, Morris thought, and had never remotely claimed to have, it was beauty; unless of course you considered a sort of exemplary piety beautiful – 'Meester Dackvert single-handedly turned the family's traditional old wine company into one of the dominant economic forces in our town, offering employment to scores of Veronese and even larger numbers of African and Slav immigrants, who, it has to be said, without the precious resource of paid work, might well have become a danger to our community.'

The mayor paused, apparently unaware of anything offensive in this reflection. This time there was no applause. 'He very astutely developed the older vineyards to build a fine new luxury housing estate on the hills above Parona – Villaggio Casa Mia – offering a chance to many of our youngsters to buy their first properties. And, together with his splendid and most Veronese wife, he has been over many years a generous sponsor of the university, the arts and the church, always ready to help out when some worthy project runs into rough financial waters.'

Again the mayor paused, again there was no response

from the crowd. But now the man seemed to relish the silence, as if it was exactly what he intended. He hadn't mentioned, Morris noted, that Fratelli Trevisan SRL also made regular contributions to all political parties that polled more than five per cent in local elections, not to mention a wide range of minor and indeed major officials in the customs and tax offices. Only now, however, did it occur to Morris that what he really should have sponsored was Hellas Verona Football Club.

'But the immediate reason for our decision to extend this honour to Meester Dackvert' – suddenly the mayor's voice slowed to something pondered and solemn, as if all the preamble about championships, murder mysteries and Morris's astonishing entrepreneurial skills were the merest patter to settle the public's mood – 'is his generous and completely unsolicited response to the vicious media attack that has been launched on our town and on this administration in particular.'

There was much muttering and scraping of chairs. Nothing, as Morris well understood, was taken more seriously in Verona than the town's national and international reputation. Far more important than any concrete reality, was the business of what people thought of you.

'As you know the attempt to paint our fair city as a den of backwardness and brutal authoritarianism has been going on since the time of the Second War and the Republic of Salò. Entirely unfounded, it forms part of a squalid game of political conditioning by which our envious rivals – and I need not tell you who they are – seek to cut us off from what very little funding is available for urban development in these hard times.'

The murmurs of assent now began again.

'But if this propaganda war was bad before, it has become even more aggressive since the Northern League took over the governance of the town and brought some order to the chaos and cronyism that had been going on for far too long. It is clear that even our supposed political allies in Rome, not to mention the hopeless band of ex-Communists who occupied and abused these same public offices not so long ago, have been running a smear campaign that now extends beyond the national to the international press, culminating in the libellous article that appeared in a British newspaper a few months ago. I shall not repeat the gross accusations that were made there. They shall never sully my lips.'

At this point there was such a roar of applause that the mayor, who was checking his watch with embarrassing frequency, had to raise his arms to quieten the crowd and hurry on. 'What I intend to do instead, as sole and sufficient motivation for our conferring on Morrees Dackvert THE FREEDOM OF OUR CITY' – and here the mayor picked up from the tabletop, and quickly put down again, a parchment scroll and open, navy blue gift box containing a large silver key – 'is to read out the letter that our excellent friend wrote in reply to those accusations in the same newspaper. And I shall read it, *amici miei*,' he raised his solid jaw and grinned, 'in Eengleesh, yes, to remind our envious neighbours – their names shall never be mentioned – of the level that education has reached in this proud province.'

Morris was startled. The man was going to read his letter to the *Telegraph*. In English! When he couldn't even pronounce Duckworth properly! Morris wanted to grab the mike from his hand and read the thing himself, if read it had to be, though at this point he began to wonder whether the double-barrelled snob who had carried out his hack's hatchet job on the ancient town – the offensive article that Morris had responded to – didn't perhaps have a point after all. For at last it dawned on him that this whole ceremony had been organised, not to reward Morris

Duckworth for being a fine citizen at all, but as the merest PR for the Northern League. The separatists had a British intellectual on their side!

'Unlaiykk,' the mayor waved a scrap of newsprint, 'yor mendaayshuuus correespondent who publeeshed VERONA: CAAPEETAL OF KIIITSCH . . .'

It had all begun some months ago at Samira's place. She and Morris had made love in the usual lavish fashion on the mattress under the ochre tapestry, then, while she was preparing one of her excellent herb teas – and there was still frankincense smoking in the corner – her brother had come out of his room and started talking about wanting to do a Masters in economics in London. Tarik was a very respectful young man and showed none of the disapproval one might have feared from a jealous brother raised in a backward Moslem community, though that might have been, of course, because Morris was paying the siblings' not insignificant rent. But what was to be gained from being cynical? There was nothing bunga-bunga-ish about what went on between Morris and Samira, it was genuine affection, and of course now that he had found the girl a six-month work-experience in the local council's Heritage Department she would be more than worth the price of her two-bedroom flat in San Zeno. If nothing else she had access to the files of all paintings possessed by churches in the province.

Always ready to help, and save a friend a costly mistake, Morris had pulled his MacBook Air from his Armani attaché case and sat down at the glass table with the two young Libyans each side of him. They had browsed a few university sites, compared curriculums and requirements, and considered whether it would be wiser to apply now, before Tarik had finished at Verona, or wait till he had the Italian degree in the bag, at the expense of having to take a gap year. 'I could find something for you to do,' Morris had smiled, 'if it's a question of filling the time. I can always use a smart young man.' It seemed important to have Tarik understand that Morris's affection for Samira extended, overflowed rather, to her nearest and dearest. Tarik frowned, asking his sister's benefactor to explain again – his Italian was excellent but his English still shaky – the mysterious workings of UCAS, and as Morris clicked back and forth, enjoying his expertise these days with all things bureaucratic, he suddenly became intensely aware of their three pairs of legs side by side under the stylish glass tabletop: Samira's, to his left, wonderfully young and vulnerable as she distractedly opened and closed honey thighs in a black bathrobe; his own solid and steady in sober grey flannel, and, to his right, in tattered jeans, casually crossed at the bare brown ankles, this fine young Arab's. 'I love them both.' Morris suddenly found himself saying these words inside his head. 'I love sister and brother both!' and he felt a surge of energy and excitement such as he had not experienced these twenty years and more.

Then, intending to show Tarik where to read the economic news in the English press, Morris opened the *Telegraph*'s home page, and there it was. 'Verona: Capital of Kitsch', by Boris Anderton-Dodds. Who the hell was he? So extraordinary did it seem to open an English national newspaper and find an article on the small Italian town they lived in, that the threesome read it at once. Nicolas Sarkozy was planning to take his pregnant Carla on holiday to the town of Romeo and Juliet. It was typical of the French president's abysmal taste. Over recent years the once elegant Veneto town had seen no better way to solve its self-inflicted economic problems than to become Italy's dumb Disneyland of romantic slush and sleaze. Tourists were met at airport and railway station by pesky guides pressuring them into Love Tours of Romeo's house and Juliet's balcony where cohorts of Korean businessmen had themselves photographed with hands cupping the bare breast of a bronze nymphet before being hauled off to karaoke evenings where they learned 'O sole mio' and 'Santa Lucia', hardly Veronese tunes. The Renaissance palazzo housing Juliet's tomb – though of course no one knew whether it had really been Juliet's tomb, as no one knew whether it had really been Juliet's balcony – had become an upmarket registrar's office luring sentimental suckers from five continents to empty their wallets for overpriced ceremonies and third-rate costume jewellery. It was the globalisation of vulgarity; everywhere you looked the city was choked with cheesy cliché, the hotels advertising 'consummation' suites (and sheets!) for honeymooning couples and the mayor himself offering his services as registrar at a special price to milk the cash cow to the last drop. This was the same xenophobic Northern League mayor who pursued a racist policy against kebab outlets, denied Moslems a place to build a mosque and introduced fascist regulations that prevented people from sleeping on park benches or eating sandwiches on the steps of public monuments, and all in a town where the church pretended to be charitable but in fact kept hundreds of apartments empty (without paying any property tax) rather than rent them to poor Africans. Every year, towards Valentine's Day, lovers all over the world were invited to write a Letter to Juliet, alias the town council, with a prize for those who managed the best homage to love. A prize judged by whom? Boris Anderton-Dodds demanded. What did the city's administrators know about love? If they had any respect at all for the myth of romantic love they would return the town to its ancient dignity and remember that the quality most alien to romance was greed, the quality most akin, charity. A modern *Romeo and Juliet* would not be about the Montagues and Capulets, let alone the Sarkozys and Brunis; it would be the thwarted love between the son of a Northern League official and the chadored daughter of a dusky kebab vendor.

What pious nonsense! Morris was aghast that a reputable British newspaper, one, he would never forget, that had turned down at least three job applications from a certain Morris Arthur Duckworth thirty and more years ago, should stoop to such disgraceful misrepresentation. 'But Verona is a fantastic town!' he shouted; the thought that his UKIP father might very easily end up reading this nonsense and enjoy a chuckle at Morris's expense was immensely irritating. Then he noticed that his young friends were smiling.

'What's there to smirk about?' he demanded.

'It's true the city's racist,' Samira said.

'You bet,' Tarik agreed.

'What's that got to do with it? Just because a place is racist you can't say it's the capital of kitsch. Verona must be one of the most beautiful cities on earth. The English haven't got anything to hold a candle to it.'

'I wouldn't know,' Tarik said. 'I just think the racist accusation is the one that matters. Who cares if we call it kitsch or not?'

'*I* care!' Morris fumed. 'Everywhere's racist. You think Milan isn't racist? And Rome? You think London isn't racist? Why are they rioting? Blacks are always rioting in London. They have their good reasons. Calling a place racist is like calling a spade a spade, or telling me grass is green. But calling it *tasteless* when it's one of the most beautiful places on earth is sheer envy. It's vandalism! Imagine the number of people who'd lose their jobs if the Brits stopped coming to Verona because of a criminal article like this. Think of the museums they'd have to close. The restaurants and hotels giving work to people without papers or permits. Albanians and Pakistanis and Moroccans.'

'Come on Mo, darling,' Samira laughed and leaned a head on his shoulder. 'Don't take it so seriously.' Morris caught the wink she sent to her brother under his nose. Literally.

'How are you two discriminated against?' He demanded. 'Tell me. Is there any problem finding a kebab? No. I'd eat them myself if I wasn't a vegetarian. Do you need a bench to sleep on?'

'There is no mosque to worship in,' Samira said.

'For heaven's sake, you're in a Christian country.'

'We have trouble getting a *permesso di soggiorno*,' Tarik said, 'finding a landlord who will rent to Moslems.'

'But *I* sorted out your *permessi*! And I found you the apartment!'

Morris remembered in the past certain young immigrants who had been more grateful when he helped them.

'But if they didn't have these immigration laws, we wouldn't need . . .' Tarik stopped himself and put his face in his hands.

'I'm going to reply to this,' Morris announced importantly. 'Talk about getting away with murder!'

He opened Word and began to type. He was furious with the kids, but also aware that, at least partly, he was writing to impress them, to show them that Morris Duckworth was the kind of man who could see the wood for the trees, and get his name into print in the process. In the end, they were young; like Mauro, they needed to be taught a thing or two.

'Dear Sirs,' he typed, 'Unlike your mendacious correspondent who published "Verona: Capital of Kitsch", I actually—'

'What does mendacious mean?' Samira asked.

'Someone who lies all the time. *Mendace.*'

'Ah.'

Tarik said a few words in Arabic and they both burst out laughing.

'Now what are you sniggering about?' Morris was incensed. He liked them. Liked them both. He loved their fine young features, black eyes, and snake-smooth skin. But not if they were planning to gang up and treat him like an old fogey.

'Don't be so sensitive, Mo.'

'But what did you say?'

'Tarik said you should come to Tripoli if you want to see what beauty is.'

Morris didn't believe for one moment this was what had been said; how could Tripoli possibly surpass an Italian town in beauty and why would the remark have created so much amusement, at his expense? But he let it go. Or rather, he let the anger flow from his fingertips:

Unlike your mendacious correspondent who published 'Verona: Capital of Kitsch', I actually live in this town and have done so for almost three decades; well, I can assure your readers that Verona remains one of the finest and most elegant city centres the world over, a forward-looking and vigorous community where the rumour of Romeo and Juliet exists only as a pleasant background murmur of antique romance, its few scattered and very beautiful shrines, apocryphal or otherwise, attracting the same tourists who flock to see the London Dungeons or the execution place of Anne Boleyn; frankly amour, however clichéd, seems preferable to the bloody glamour of Anglo-Saxon vulgarity.

Pork scratchings, lager louts, race riots, football hooliganism, vomit on street corners and stinking public urinals, such are the English charms the judicious traveller is spared in the shaded piazzas and stuccoed sobriety of this Renaissance gem. No wonder romance seems credible here. Your article, the journalistic equivalent, if I may be so bold, of a contract killing (since clearly Mr Anderton-Dodds had viewed no more than a blurred photograph of his victim prior to pulling the trigger), simply aligns your newspaper with those enemies of sentiment who once brought the lives of two young lovers to tragedy. Shame on you! Shame on you too for putting at risk the jobs of those whose honest endeavours on behalf of Verona's tourist industry gives work to thousands, many of them refugees from the Third World, people who can barely believe their luck to find themselves in this Italian paradise. All power to President Sarkozy and his splendid Italian signora for choosing the perfect place to renew their love before the long, hard slog of parenthood.

Morris Arthur Duckworth
The Duckworth Foundation
Via Oberdan
Verona

Just like that! It had come out just like that: The Duckworth Foundation! Without a thought, without forewarning of any kind. This was what it meant, Morris thought, to be creative. Suddenly, from nowhere, an idea came into being. Most definitely he should have been a writer, an artist. He copied the passage and pasted it into the comment box below the offending article. Then not satisfied, because it really was such a well-written letter, he emailed it to the editors as well. Damn them. Let them see who was the better polemicist, Mr Anderton-Dodds (Boris!) or Morris Arthur Duckworth. It was years since he'd signed off with his second name; it had always worried him that people would spot the obvious acronym. But this time it felt right. If the *Telegraph* needed a man in Verona, MAD was definitely better than BAD.

'Morrees!' Samira breathed.

Entranced by the eloquence of his indignation, Morris had not registered the growing incredulity of the two young people beside him.

'I never knew you could be so romantic!'

The Englishman smiled and turned to kiss his girl on her dark lips.

'What is the Duckworth Foundation?' Tarik asked cautiously, and with new respect, Morris hoped. Speaking off the top of his head, the rich lover launched into a very promising explanation, and only four days later received a call from the town hall. The city council wished to express its gratitude.

'. . . the long, ard zlog ov paarent-hhud,' the mayor concluded with a flourish. 'Morrees Artoor Dackvert! The Dackvert Fowndayshoon!'

There was a moment's bewildered silence from a public who understood only that they were supposed to approve. Nobody seemed sure whether the reading was over or not, until, with a whooped Californian cry of 'Way to go, Morris, man!' the balding figure beside Antonella began to pound his hands in enthusiastic applause. It *was* Stan. From top to toe Morris thrilled with shivery sweat. Christ! Why? As the Italians politely clapped their ignorant ovation, while his wife and daughter, he noticed, seemed to be studying him with the rapt apprehension of one who has found a brightly coloured mould on a bidet towel, the Freeman of Verona jumped to his feet and, invited or no, snatched the microphone from the mayor's unsuspecting grasp.

'*Grazie, grazie!*'

He felt a little unsteady on his feet in front of so many people. The Tonbridge tie seemed to tighten round his neck. Undecided whether to sit or not, the mayor quite brazenly tapped on his watch. Morris was having none of it. Seize the day. There is a tide in the affairs of men. He hesitated, looking out across the well-groomed scalps of the city's applauding elite to where, in the piazza beyond, he could just glimpse the balcony from which 150 years before Garibaldi had exhorted '*Roma o morte!*' In his cheeks and above his eye, the scars that had robbed him of his youthful beauty had stepped up their song to a fierce descant. Or perhaps it was a battle cry. His face was throbbing. Once again, in the most adverse circumstances, Morris must launch himself into the fray.

'*Signore e signori.*'

The clapping abruptly stopped and a fascinated silence fell on the crowd; most of them knew Morris as a respectable and quietly obsequious businessman, almost more Italian than the Italians themselves in his understanding of what must be said and what left unsaid, what paid, whether under or over the table, and what, with grace and aplomb, evaded; a man who in twenty years had turned a second-string family vintner's into a major business concern, becoming a key figure in the local consortium of industrialists and, of course, the Rotary Club. But now, rather disconcertingly, there was a flash of fear in this sedate man's face, something wild and perhaps even dangerous had surfaced from beneath the dark scars and pale shining eyes, while his posture, oddly contracted and unsteady, betrayed the kind of hunted, animal-at-bay anxiety that would have reminded some present that this man had once stood trial for murder.

But Morris had been acquitted of course and the moment passed. He straightened up, filled his lungs and squared his shoulders. His face relaxed in a broad smile. Get a grip. Speak your best Italian. Stan was just an old friend visiting the haunts of his youth. Not the man who could put him in gaol.

'*Signori, grazie*. I had prepared, I should tell you, a long and generous speech in praise of the city of Verona, a city that has given me, to be blunt, all that I have. But I shall leave it aside. You have already heard my little letter, so movingly read by our excellent mayor. My feelings will be clear enough, even to those very few who don't know me either as a business partner or a member of the many organisations in which we are all involved. I am told that we are running late and that the mayor must meet a delegation of Arab businessmen; the last thing I would wish is to compromise a chance to bring fresh investment to our town.'

There were murmurs of approval. Seeing Antonella's relieved smile, Morris enjoyed the awareness that when it really counted he always got it dead right. And in perfect Italian.

'So I shall just say thanks to you all for coming here today. It's a great pleasure, in particular, to see a face I haven't seen for twenty years and more. Welcome back to Verona, Stan Albertini!'

Apparently there were no limits to Morris's magnanimity. Stan, of course, stood up and bowed to laughter and applause. It was the man's baldness and the absence of the old goatee, Morris realised now, that had delayed his recognition.

'But I will, if I may, take this opportunity to explain just one thing. At the end of my letter, the mayor read the signature, Morris Duckworth, the Duckworth Foundation.'

The mayor, who had sat down, reassured that his guest would be brief, now gripped the arms of his chair and half stood again. Morris motored on:

'It was precisely on reading that cowardly attack in the British press, and with a profound awareness of all that Verona means to me, that I decided I must give something back. That something, far more than any letter, is the Duckworth Foundation. Its capital will be made up, in part, of the considerable art collection I have had the good fortune to build up over the years, some eighty canvases, which, on my death I shall gratefully bequeath to the city's museums.'

As the crowd burst into applause, a door to the right opened and an elderly official hurried in, scuttling along the wall and behind the polished table to whisper in the mayor's ear.

'To celebrate,' Morris continued, determined to score all the points he could in the very brief time at his disposal, 'I have proposed a major exhibition of these paintings together with other old masters from all over the world at a grand summer show in Castelvecchio, on the theme, I am pleased to announce . . .'

Here Morris stopped a moment; for he wondered if he really had the courage to pronounce the idea that had come into his head *literally this instant*. He hesitated. This was seriously mad. What an idea! The audience waited. The mayor fidgeted. Do it? Don't do it? The truth was that however much Morris schemed and planned, it was only his moments of pure extempory genius that had ever really got him anywhere or reconciled him, for that matter, to the unhappy destiny of being his father's son – God loves those who love themselves, he thought and raised his voice – '. . . a show entitled, I was saying: *Painting Death: The Art of Assassination from Caravaggio to Damien Hirst*. An innovative show, *signori e signore*, that will put the town of Verona on the postmodern map and silence our critics for years to come. Thank you, everybody, thank you.'

Sitting down – and he had spoken for only two minutes, for Christ's sake – Morris smiled benignly into the alarmed eyes of his wife in the front row.

The mayor was on his feet.

'I'm afraid we shall have to call it a day, ladies and gentlemen. Our Arab delegation has arrived. There are important matters of trade and investment to discuss. Let me just say, because I've received a piece of news this very moment, that there is one member of the Dackvert family who hasn't been able to be with us today. Now I understand why. I have just been informed that young Mauro Dackvert, son of Morrees, and *a great fan of our beloved Hellas Verona*, was amongst those arrested, scandalously and without justification, after last night's game in Brescia. I would like to take this opportunity to assure the Dackvert family that they have all our sympathy and will receive our utmost support to ensure the rapid release of their courageous boy from unjust imprisonment. For this too is part of the same implacable campaign against our happy community.'

The young mayor turned and with genuine affection embraced the irate Englishman as he stumbled to his feet.

www.vintage-books.co.uk